Diana Saville

is the author of three previous novels, and has also written many books on gardens and their design. She worked as a literary agent in London before moving to the West of England where she lives with her husband.

From the reviews of *Capability's Eden*:

'Diana Saville was originally (and still is) a gardener and garden-writer, with an acute feeling for the natural world: predators and prey (human and animal); the glory and enchantment of growing things and the passions they engender. And she creates characters who escape from the pages and follow you around, long after the last page is turned. *Capability's Eden* is written in a poetic, almost liquid prose, full of subtleties, scattered through-out with peripheral information and stimulating asides: about Isaak Walton on fishing, the history of deer parks, the unearthly glamour of flamingos and the slow, calm, awesome voyage of the planets through "the forest of space". It is a book to be read not just once, but again and again.' *Good Book Guide*

'Diana Saville's love and knowledge of plants and the natural world informs this gentle but threatening tale, told through the eyes of the idealistic but faillible hero who strives to bring this ideal world to fruition. He fills his earthly paradise with lovely sounds and sights: the enamel glimpse of the kingfisher, the chestnut liquid eyes of the deer. His inevitable fall from grace is all the more shocking.' *Oxford Times*

'A clever novel, deeply allegorical but lightly handled and elegantly written.' *Ham & High*

Capability's Eden

DIANA SAVILLE

Flamingo
An Imprint of HarperCollins*Publishers*

Flamingo
An Imprint of HarperCollins*Publishers*
77–85 Fulham Palace Road,
Hammersmith, London w6 8jb

www.**fire**and**water**.com

Flamingo is a registered trademark of
HarperCollins*Publishers* Limited

Published by Flamingo 2000

9 8 7 6 5 4 3 2 1

First published in Great Britain by
Flamingo 1999

isbn 0 00 655186 6

Set in Postscript Bembo

Printed and bound in Great Britain by
Clays Ltd, St Ives plc

I am most grateful for the help of Ben Chester-Master who took me round his deer park; and also Ian Pasley-Tyler who answered my questions about flamingos; and Paul Haley who introduced me to Saturn. I learned valuable information too from the Wildfowl and Wetlands Trust, Slimbridge, Gloucestershire; and from the following books: *Deer Parks and Deer* by Frederick Hingston (1988), and *Capability Brown* by Thomas Hinde (1986). Any mistakes are my own. On a separate point, I have taken some liberties in summarising *Über das Marionettentheater* by Heinrich von Kleist. In its full version, it is a perfectly balanced thing, so I hope I'm forgiven. My thanks as always to Michael Sissons for his guidance; my thanks too to Philip Gwyn Jones for his support and to Mandy Kirkby for her improvements; and to my husband for his translation.

For Carole with thanks

1

A SHEEP ARRIVED on my computer yesterday morning. I was drinking a cup of coffee and, as usual after breakfast, had gone to the screen to open my post-box. As soon as I pressed the button, this cuddly round sheep appeared at the top left-hand corner. She ambled across the screen, plucked at some grass and sat down in the middle of the picture. Then she scratched her head for a moment, as if exercised about what she might do next.

I started to laugh because this is always a prelude to a message from my daughter who has a knitting company in Scotland. Each time she sends me the same sheep but varies its actions and a different programme unfolds. I find it amazing, the way she can make it do anything.

For a moment my sheep seemed to have difficulty in coming to a decision. Then her ears wiggled and she began to convey a sense of purpose. She sat up, not like a sheep but like a rabbit with her forelegs in the air. From under her armpits, she pulled out a pair of knitting needles and tied on a strand of wool from her front. She then settled down and started to knit. Till now, my little ewe had been dozy, but as soon as she started working, she got into a frenzy. She knitted faster and faster. It was now clear she was using her own fleece to make a jumper. It was so clever, the way the wool on the sheep unravelled and dwindled as the garment grew larger and larger. First, she lost the hair on her head, then the chaps on her legs, then her flanks, and finally everything went, even the last few tufts on her back. By the time she had finished her jumper, my poor little sheep was as bald as a shorn lamb. When her work was over, she stood up, bowed to me, put the needles back neatly under her armpits

I

and trotted away from the screen. Only the woolly jumper remained with a roll neck, long sleeves and the monogram of SBKC on its chest.

Then a message appeared from the Scottish Border Knitting Company to Robert Boyd, which is my name. *Dear Daddy*, it said, *I'll be coming by with Hal the day after tomorrow. We'll arrive about midday. You will let me know if you're not going to be in, won't you? Just leave a message with the office. Love and kisses, Abi.* This made me very happy as I don't often see my daughter, Abigail. She lives near Melrose and I live in Norfolk, so visits are only occasional; only, if I'm honest, when she is on the way to or from somewhere else – usually, as it happens, to or from my ex-wife who lives in Oxford. So I sent a message back, saying I was delighted and would be in as I was working at home at the moment. I signed it Oojar which is the name that Hal, my baby grandson, calls me, or, at least, we think he calls me.

Today, therefore, in preparation and as it was market day, I drove into the town to pick up some food. I bought a bunch of tomatoes that were still on the branch and some vine leaves and a pound of good local cheese with the rind on. Also six scarlet eggs from the Maran hens kept by one of the stall holders and a loaf of warm moist bread still smelling of yeast. All nice small things which is what my life consists of these days. I had a beer at the Feathers and returned to my house. I was startled to find my daughter's car in the lane outside and my daughter walking towards me.

'Abi,' I said. 'What is this? You said you were coming tomorrow.'

'There's an office crisis. I've got to go home early. I rang you this morning but couldn't get any reply. So I sent you a new message. Didn't you get it?'

'I went out.'

We hugged one another and I said never mind, it was always lovely to see her; but privately I thought it was odd she had made the detour to come now when it was possible I might not have been at home.

'Where's Hal?' I asked.

'Didn't you see him? He's asleep in the car.'

We crept over and peered through the window. He was wearing a pale blue jumper. There was a scratch on his forehead and the tip of his nose was red and also the ends of his fingers. On his cheeks, his lashes lay in two most delicate crescents. I wanted to hear him say Oojar.

'Don't disturb him,' said Abi. 'He was awake all night.'

We tiptoed away and went into the cottage. I picked up the post from the doormat. The usual assortment of bills and catalogues and an envelope of cream ribbed paper, addressed with a strong hand in blue ink, the writing sloping a little to the right, expressive of decision. It was postmarked from the Highlands, probably an estate. I recognised the nature of the letter: I don't receive so much correspondence of this kind as in the past, but enough to make it familiar, though never so frequent as to prevent each causing a fresh jolt.

'Goody,' said Abi, unpacking the shopping. 'Lovely bread, lovely cheese. Any tomatoes?'

'At the bottom of the bag. Let's have lunch outside.'

I tucked the post under my arm, and we put the food on a tray and carried it out to the terrace. The view from here in May is quite wonderful. The trees sit like galleons on a green sea and the sky soars above the long swoop of land. In the evening I can sit and watch the light change for hours.

We sat down at the wooden table. I was facing my daughter. A girl in fawn jeans and one of her own home-grown knobbly pullovers, her face neat and arched, her hair clasped back on the nape of her neck. She has changed. She is a pretty girl now, much neater and prettier than she used to be, now she is married and has a child and has started her knitting company. Four years ago I thought she was a drifter and hopeless. Now she is making something of her life. She is showing the grip that we once thought she would always lack.

We started eating and chattering. Later I said again how lovely it was to see her, but I added: 'I'm surprised though, when you couldn't be sure I'd be in.'

'I wanted to see you.'

'Are you going to see Mummy too?'

'I met Mummy in London.'

'How is she? It's a long time since I've seen her.'

'Fine. Sends her love.' My daughter paused to assess the view for a moment, then turned back. Her voice seemed to become inhibited. It came in precise little sprigs. 'As a matter of fact, it's partly because of Mummy that I've called in today. She says she's a tiny bit concerned about you.'

'How kind. Why?'

'She says that to the best of her knowledge, you haven't taken on any proper work for three years.'

'It's not true.'

'She says you do a few bits and pieces.'

'Even if it's true, so what? I'm entitled to a sabbatical.'

'Yes, but three years. You were so in demand. You were a name. Now you do nothing, she says.'

'How does she know?'

'She's heard you refuse every project you're offered.'

'I'm trying to do up this place. It takes a lot of time.'

'Oh yes?' My little Abi rolled her eyes at our immediate surroundings. At a pile of broken grey paving stones which lay as they had lain for months. At a wall which had waterfalled down. A cow had recently straddled it. I had found it licking the kitchen windowpane of the house.

'No progress that I can see,' said Abi.

'Well, I'm busy, believe it or not. I am in fact working on some plans at the moment.'

'What kind of plans?'

'A large job.' It was in fact, no bigger than the size of a room in a house, and unambitious too. A bread-and-butter assignment of the kind that only a few years ago I'd have given my office junior.

'I don't believe you,' she said.

'Are you calling me a liar?'

'A fibber.'

'A liar.'

Abi smiled in reply and raised her hand to her nose. She pulled the tip outwards. When she was little, she would always accompany a bedtime reading of Pinocchio with a graphic demonstration on my own nose.

To my great surprise, I felt a sting at this reminder of old affection. To hide it I looked out at the view.

It was a warm early summer's day. In winter I forget the intensity of the green grass and trees. In May it rises up and strikes you. Grass, trees and water, that used to be my palette, my stuff, the stuff of all landscape designers. Three years is a long time to reject doing what

4

you do best. Abi is right of course. It's unnatural, a wrench as well as a choice, this flight from the land.

I said to Abi: 'Things come to a pause sometimes.' I added: 'I still get offers. This is one probably,' and I looked down at the envelope on the ground.

'Open it,' she said.

I picked it up, pushed my finger under the slit and pulled out the letter.

'Here we are. Listen to this. Dear Mr Boyd, blah, blah, my wife and I wondered if you would visit us with a view to handling our landscape. Our intentions are somewhat ambitious and we need guidance. Could you let us know what you charge for a visit?' I looked at her. 'There you are. Standard stuff. OK? Happy?'

'Let's see it.'

I shrugged and pushed it across to her.

She read out: 'I imagine you are very busy with commissions at the moment, but would be happy to wait a little while if you are not able to fit in a visit in the near future.'

My daughter gave the letter back to me. 'Busy, eh?'

'Abi,' I said. 'This is honestly none of your business.'

'What are you going to do? Turn it down?'

'Don't go on so.'

'They may be a bit stiff but they sound nice and they do say they've seen and loved your work. Was that the bit you interpreted as blah, blah?'

'They all say that. That's how they get you going.'

'I really don't understand. That's the point. Neither Mummy nor I can understand. You sold the company. Well, all right, we could see you didn't want the nuisance of a business. But you seem to have given up entirely.'

'Not entirely. Don't nag. Remember you used to hate me nagging you.'

'Entirely. Did something happen?'

'Not at all. I just couldn't see the point any more.'

'I find it sad. You were such a big man to me. You made me ashamed because I wasn't as busy or enthusiastic as you.'

'Actually, I think I was a bit of a humble parasite really. The land does perfectly well on its own.'

5

She opened her mouth to reply but didn't. I think by now she realised there was no point in nagging. That she would only poison the atmosphere. At any rate we changed the subject and she started chattering again more freely. I do wish my ex-wife wouldn't use her as an intermediary over this. She must think that Abi will get more information out of me than she herself ever managed.

Hal didn't wake up though my daughter stayed a couple of hours. It was a pity not to hear him say Oojar. However it was quite a jolly visit, but after they had left, I felt restless. I kicked around the house for a bit but couldn't settle. I put this down to the nature of the conversation that I've recounted. Then, after a bit, I decided to go for a drive.

I backed the car out of the stone shed and turned right to go east. It takes about twenty minutes from here to reach the sea. I often come here when I can't settle. At the coast, I left the car in the park and walked through the reeds to the beach. There were a couple of fishermen on the shingle. I walked about for a time, looking out at the sea. I always like it here. It's a reminder of a landscape that doesn't need any modification. It swallows up all hills and hollows and finds its own level. I've chosen not to say anything to my ex-wife or my daughter, but a couple of years ago I took a decision about my work, or maybe, I simply lost heart as sometimes happens. Either way there'll be no more pulling of strings by me; which is sensible and I think I'm reasonably happy.

2

IT IS TRUE what my daughter said, though you wouldn't guess it
to see me now. Only a few years ago I was at the peak of a top career
as a landscape designer. It is an odd business, landscape gardening. It
comes in all shapes and sizes and is as much to do nowadays with
building a name as building a garden. We practitioners are very
varied. A few are basket-cases thrashing their egos around on other
people's land. Others, young mostly, have heaps of charm and are
known for their fancy ideas. They grab headlines with follies and
grottoes and standing phalluses of columns. We older ones are more
sober and reject the stage-set trinkets in favour of larger and more
classical schemes. Our aim is (or was, in my case) to be proper
plantsmen as well as landscape architects of substance. As I say, we
all vary, but whoever we are, what we become known for is the
individuality of our own style and that can only evolve through the
nature of our projects.

For a landscaper like myself, it is usually a slow process, building
a name, because good gardens as opposed to stage-sets take a while
to mature. Years can pass before the quality of your work shows
through. When this happens, however, a flood of commissions arrive
that take over your life. The change can come suddenly and the
effect is dramatic. One month you are a humble draughtsman who
has a way with the plough; the next you are the creator of a landscape
that a surprising number of clients want. You find you are on the
road all the time. You learn to fire people up. You hear yourself
saying things like 'My goodness, you have a fine view here,' or 'I
love this place.' Sooner or later you are a machine for making gardens.
Then, by serving the well-endowed and the famous, you develop

your own very minor status too. There is no mystery about this journey from Robert Boyd, draughtsman to Robert Boyd, landscape designer; though it can seem both odd and disruptive at the time.

Now that I've given up work and gone into retirement, I have the leisure to look back and smile at the process.

It is, I admit, early retirement. Five years ago, which is the time I am talking about, I was in my late forties. If you're going to make it, you have to have made it by then; probably by forty, most people would claim. I'd been lucky. It sounds boastful to say it but there's no point in false modesty and it's a fact – you know the good as well as the bad things about yourself – that I was working at the height of fluency and articulacy in my field. I'd also been lucky enough to build up not only a practice but an international following. I say lucky, though none of this comes easily without an immense amount of effort. When you've worked regularly in North America and South Africa, in Japan and New Zealand, as well as France, Spain and Italy, you know you have given total and dedicated commitment to your job.

My clients had been equally varied. The people I'd worked for had come from every type of background. There'd been tycoons and owners of glove factories and glass manufacturers and one gentle anxiety-prone rock star. I'd dealt with connoisseurs as well as the cash-rich-taste-poor (no shortage of those) and libertines and puritans, and Catholics and Moslems, and refugees and natives, generations of whose family had occupied the same patch for centuries. I'd worked for the young and the middle-aged and for old men who were dying of cancer. I'd striven for those who cared nothing about gardens and for others who accompanied you on every inch of the road. I'd designed plots and parks and schools and palaces. If you'd asked me, I'd have said there was little left for me to know about gardens and their owners, having hammered out problems and solutions to both.

When you're lucky like this, you never forget the sense that you're privileged. Though you know too that you pay a price for good fortune. There is always a personal cost. For instance, at some stage along this journey, to be precise about ten years back, I'd lost Louise, my wife, not because of a falling out or another man in her case or even another woman in mine, but for the simple reason, as she phrased it, that I'd never been there. 'I divorce you because you are never here,' Louise had said.

That was the only awful time, breaking up with my wife and daughter, and it had, I suppose, the predictable effect of making me work harder. Not that it seemed like ordinary work; for my interest in it was, rather, compulsive. Some projects of course were more boring than others, but each produced some small burst of enthusiasm, even when I was only required to plant trees along a stretch of road. The constraints of safety, the camber, the rhythm of the trunks, the growth of the canopy, the regular swish of sound they gave to the drivers of cars speeding by, all these were a challenge. I truly loved my job. How many people could say that with honesty? How many have the satisfaction of creating a design, of being paid to achieve it and watching it grow on. In the last twenty-five years I'd scarcely known a day's illness, no doubt because work was my pleasure. I was always strong and red-faced due to the time spent out on site; out in all weathers, my fingers like sausages in the cold, just walking and working over the land. Looking back, I think I was actually happiest walking a new piece of land. It is a bit like a new conquest. Just thinking about it, even now, makes me quite nostalgic.

The majority of the commissions were word-of-mouth jobs. The minor ones I would obviously put out to the juniors in my practice. The serious ones I'd retain for myself. One boom year we were so busy, we considered hiring a clerk of works; and even in the recession, there were a surprising number of new enquiries. Most of the letters from clients started the same way. They'd seen your work or heard about you or received a recommendation. This is the typical style. Some of course give you the old oil; the approach of others is more sober. But by and large they add up to a mixture of request and flattery.

Three years ago a letter came into my office from Cornwall: from a house called Water End. It was addressed to me personally rather than to the practice and written by a man called David Lacey. It was an interesting letter. He and his wife had seen my work and liked it. They wanted to re-work their garden and admitted that the plans for their grounds were ambitious. Almost as a postscript he added that they gardened on what was virtually an island, indeed the whole of that island: a large one, as the river at that point had diverted, rendering them accessible only by an isthmus. 'I'd explain further,' he wrote, 'but to be frank we would both be a bit embarrassed to put on paper the nature of our hopes for this place. You might even accuse us of temerity. We would be very grateful if you could visit us and give us your comments.'

The letter was unusual in several respects. I had rarely been approached in such self-deprecatory terms. Nor had I ever had the pleasure of designing a whole island. In one sense of course, all gardens are islands, but this is illusory and a contrivance rather than a reality. Here I was actually being handed the fact. The thought was very inviting. The writer seemed pleasant and islands always appeal to the eccentric and romantic. I rang him at once, stated my price for an overnight visit and we set the date for the end of the first week in May. I had still no idea of the project, but it was quite a sizeable island and the fellow sounded a decent sort and straightforward. Short of an unforeseeable disappointment, I had pretty well decided to accept.

On 8 May I went first to my office in the Cotswolds, then set off on the drive to the south. It would probably take about five hours, since the last bit is winding and slows you down. It was a cool day and cloudy with lingering fog predicted to come inland from the coast. Not ideal conditions, though in my experience these are good circumstances in which to assess a new project. A dullish light makes it easy to take exploratory photographs and the weather is fine for working, being comfortably in-between. Not that I was disposed to cavil. I was looking forward to the trip. I like Cornwall. It is a land for artists and gardeners, no matter what a friend of mine says. He likens it to the toe of a Christmas stocking because in each case the nuts always fall to the bottom.

It was nearly eleven o'clock by the time I reached the A38 and I felt hungry. I slowed down and began to grope around in the glove compartment for a packet of garibaldi biscuits to which I had recently become addicted. There were only crumbs in the wrapper but some fruit gums had rolled out of reach, so I stopped at the next parking bay. As I was ferreting in the drawer, there was a knock on the windscreen. I had just found the sweets and was intent on extracting a pastille of my favourite flavour. A boy with a girl a few yards behind him was leaning forward against the glass at the side of the car.

'Are you going to the Tamar Bridge?'

I nodded but couldn't answer. I was sucking a lime gum and spurting the juice with my tongue.

'If you are, you couldn't give us a lift, could you?'

I assessed what portion I could see of the couple. A hairy pair certainly, of the greensward tribe, both of them dressed in earth colours, the girl wearing a long brown skirt. However they looked harmless and neither was actually dirty. And even the boy's Scottish accent was quiet rather than strident. He was not a lad who had come fists flying out of the Gorbals.

'OK. Hop in,' I offered, though no sucker for hitchhikers.

'That's great,' said the boy. 'By the way, my name's Danny and she's Suki.'

'Daniel what?'

'Oh, you know. Just Danny.'

It was irksome, the casualness of this era of no surnames. The girl followed him into the back of the car leaving me alone like a chauffeur in front. They perched themselves on opposite ends of the seat, looking about them with curiosity like a pair of young Masai I had once transported years ago in Kenya.

I started the car and pulled out on the main road again. There was little traffic and I decided to while away the time with my passengers. Random exchanges between the young and the middle-aged are often quite funny and illuminating; though I was sure that I knew not only their type but also its limitations. Herbivores certainly, folk singers rather than ravers and probably at some sort of college though God knows what they were doing away from their institutions of learning at this time of the year.

'What do you do?' I raised my voice to be heard at the back.

'We're kind of students.'

'What students?'

'I'm at university. Suki – she's sixteen – she's at a tec.'

'What do you do there?'

'We're both studying psychology.'

I suppressed a sigh. All the young seem to study nowadays is psychology. Half of the western world spends its days earning its living by grooming the other half. We're all in the service industry or simply suppliers.

'It's mid-term, isn't it? Funny time of year, I'd have thought, for you both to be out on the road.'

'We thought we'd take a few days off,' said Suki.

I caught a glimpse of her face in the mirror. She was pretty, quite pretty enough to be feckless, with long, dyed fair hair and dark roots.

'I pay my taxes so that you can study psychology,' I said, 'and you take a few days off. What do you think about that?'

'We've been to Oxfordshire for a really important reason.'

'Oh yes? What's that?'

'Oxfordshire is full of crap. We've been on a road demo. A protest. You know.'

'A demo, eh? I used to do roads. You know.' I was beginning to regret my willingness to take them on.

'You did road demos?' said Suki incredulously.

'No, no. I mean I have landscaped roads. I'm a landscape designer.'

There was a moment's silence from the back seat.

'Fuck it,' said Daniel. 'I mean sorry and all that but we're taking a ride with the enemy.'

'I've landscaped fairly few roads, as it happens,' I said emolliently. 'And let's not disagree about roads unless you want to consider getting out. I'm sure we can both agree that if roads have to be made – and they do, I'm afraid – it's better that they are turned into an asset that blends into the landscape rather than an eyesore that stands out. So you see in some ways we're on the same side really. But for the most part I do other things. I do –,' I hesitated over and then suppressed the word 'estate', knowing it would be liable to misinterpretation '– I do big gardens mostly. My job is to make things nicer, more beautiful.'

'You can't. It's arrogant, isn't it, to think you can make things nicer.'

'We think the landscape should be left as it is,' confirmed the girl.

I shook my head, exasperated by the confidence and ignorance always on show from the young. 'Evangelical conservationists like you always discount the natural side of the picture. Leave nature to herself and you get nothing but nettles and docks and thistles. The thugs just inherit the earth. If you actually knew about these things, you'd know that the reversion to natural scrub takes place with a dynamism that would shock people like you who spend all your time just nurturing your fantasies. Believe me, I know.'

There are better contexts in which to say one's little piece than cooped up in a car. Inevitably it was followed by a huffy silence, but it had to be said and in some ways I was quite glad to have shut them up. I didn't mind giving them a lift, yet it was a long way and if they were going to argue, there was nothing for it but to make them get out. No point in wasting energy on the gormless young. I turned on the knob of the radio. A stream of classical music tinkled out, a little Lehar, not my choice actually but nice and easy, nothing so challenging that it couldn't be interrupted by ads.

Instead it was interrupted by Suki.

'Are you going very far?' She spoke politely like a subdued child. Her voice was almost inaudible.

I rather regretted having snubbed my young passengers. Of course it was right they should have their ideals.

'To Cornwall.'

'Polluted,' said Daniel. 'Bunged up with crap. If your lot had done their bit with demos years ago, it wouldn't be like this now.'

Privately I agreed with him, though his lack of deference still had the power to irritate.

'Which part of Cornwall?' asked Suki.

I told her vaguely that it was in the south, near a river.

'You going to do a garden?'

'Probably. I'm going to look at one anyway. On a sort of island.'

'An island,' repeated Suki in awe.

'Like that mount at the foot,' asked Daniel.

'St Michael's Mount? God, no. I wouldn't have thought like that.'

My enthusiasm came back, just thinking about it again. I would have been happy to expand a little more on my subject, but a pair of luddites in the back make you cautious, quite apart from the usual rule of protecting the privacy of clients.

As a result, my obvious reluctance to talk in more than monosyllables caused the supply of questions to dry up and in this way we passed the remaining hour of our journey together in silence. I wondered about the job ahead and the clients. The youths dozed, dreaming perhaps of shared triumphs of the road. We had reached a modus vivendi, accepting each other's difference. Nearing the Tamar Bridge, I stopped at a petrol station to buy a sandwich and let the hikers out.

'Thanks for the lift,' offered Danny 'though if you take our advice you'll leave well alone.'

'You'll learn,' I said, 'but good luck.'

With some resignation and amusement, I watched the pair trudge off. Loopy hairy environmentalists with no surnames, but not bad. In many ways, in fact, they were like the eighteenth-century idealists who thought that nature was always tending to the ideal and only failed to reach it because of accidents and obstacles. This is a belief that those who work the land never embrace. It is droll that friendship of the earth should express itself in such opposite ways.

Relieved to have shed my passengers, and vowing as usual never to pick up hikers again, I drove through the toll gates of the Tamar Bridge. I am always happy to be bound for the coast. There's the holiday lift, of course, but in my case it feels like going home. I really love the marshes and the sea. I am a water child, born at the edge of the land, under the water sign of Cancer the crab. It marks you with a love for the places where the rivers and the sea mingle. I opened the window of the car to pull in the smell. Nearer the coast, a brackish scent would enter in a gush of salt wind and wet air, a smell that I relish even though I know that after a time it always becomes enervating.

I wondered again about the nature of the place ahead. It is always an error to indulge in too high a level of expectation. One should never allow the owners' ambitions to nourish one's own. Owners so often convey the wrong image. They write letters that arouse your ambition which reality makes quite absurd. I could easily have been wrong, for example, in imagining it to be an island that excluded the world. It was more likely to have a rim of beach huts or holiday shacks. Or it could be a mud flat that, like the keel of a boat, suffered from fouling. Worse still, the wind and salinity might prevent anything but a limited range from growing at all. I could be making my way eagerly towards a place that amounted to a seaboard disaster. It would have been wiser to have questioned David Lacey more closely on the telephone, but I had felt like a trip out to these parts.

Perhaps the temerity for which the man had blamed himself in his letter was the hope of raising life at all from a dump which had proved to be a horticultural grave.

The fog that had been predicted closed down in patches nearer the coast. I drove more slowly, but in any case the nature of the roads reduced progress. I was off the main route now and running south on a lane which kept forking in a little maze of mist-filled turnings. They were bounded by herringboned stone walls topped with hedges. The land at this point was running gently downwards like a liquid force to melt into the sea. It was noiseless and sheltered here and on both sides there were stands of huge old trees. From the car only their trunks were visible, but they were so thickly planted that, if seen from the air, their canopies would link up and resemble a mound of soft green sponges. This density of the overgrowth made it clear that at least my concern about wind would not be realised. Then the lane which was still dipping turned at right angles. Before me suddenly lay a mosaic of river and trees. A sweet old seaweed smell rolled up and filled the lungs.

I stopped to consult the map they had sent me. It confirmed that I was nearly on top of the place. I looked at the view, started the engine again, took the left fork which turned south for a quarter of a mile, then crossed the cattle grid which had been marked on the instructions. I was now crossing the isthmus with the river on either side. The mist had lifted. Further down, far down the river vale, I could see the grey rock-like hulks of ships that were rusted.

I stopped the car and got out. A wind sigh moved steadily up the mouth of the tree-lined funnel. In its wake, I heard a soft lap of water. Gulls screamed overhead. From a distance, in a higher key and shyer, there was a pretty cry like the call of an oyster-catcher though it was too far from the coast. I stood looking about me. At such times your job requires you to be emotionally responsive but cold enough to gather information to absorb the place. The first meeting with it is always important. Better to greet the site before its people. It does not, cannot conceal itself; whilst the latter are often confusing.

I remained still for a few minutes then drove the remaining three hundred yards to Water End. Victorian shrubs, spent of their spring flowers, reared over the track. They were of noble size. It was clear that the earth was a rich and fertile growing medium. The house, glimpsed through the tunnel of foliage, grew larger. Older than the shrubs, eighteenth-century probably with some later additions, a sprawl of stabling and servants' quarters behind it. Built of grey stone, the colour of herons, a proper house for a river world. I stopped the car and got out, breathing in the wet smell. The ground was soft and spongy with the spillage of old leaves.

Holding my briefcase, like a visiting accountant, I began walking towards the gravelled area that swirled before the house. The path skirted a lawn that had recently been mown into stripes. Everything was still and quiet apart from repetitive human movement that was taking place on the other side of the garden. An unusually tall, strong boy was digging in a border, quite a giant with a woolly cap pulled down low over his head. The lad was facing away from me. He didn't appear to have heard the car or was too engrossed to turn round. Then, the door of the house opened and a man came down the steps, making signs of welcome.

'I see you have a good young digger,' I said, indicating the boy.

'You mean Trevor? Quite a character.'

We shook hands, assessing one another, both of us judging the degree of cooperation we would be likely to meet. It is essential to get on with a client. This is an important part of the job, as important as getting on with his land.

'You found your way here? Not lost at any stage, I hope.' David Lacey blinked hard, screwing his face up a little.

'Not at all. Thanks to your map.'

'Any first impressions?' asked Lacey. 'Or don't you have any until you start on a job?'

'It is a wonderful setting. It has the promise of great capabilities.'

Lacey looked amused and surprised, though his face didn't demonstrate recognition. 'Is that what you say?'

'Only privately and as a joke. And not always. By no means. But I've just thought, driving along this last bit, that you're very lucky.'

'We are,' agreed Lacey. 'You'll see. Come inside. Virginia – my wife – has got some tea. Afterwards we'll take you around.'

He hadn't picked up my reference and there was no need to explain the comment about great capabilities, but it was how my hero, Mr Lancelot Brown, was given his nickname. He would ride round a site and assess its promise. It has great capabilities, our finest landscape architect would say. I think of him often. I see him trotting about in his dark green coat, with his bright eyes and long nose. In some ways the nature of his job has changed little. I ride after him as we all do, we landscape designers, and watch him with admiration.

3

OVER THE YEARS I have found it usual for meetings of this kind
to follow a ritual. It is quite enjoyable tracing its pattern. At the start,
an exchange of social platitudes, then the search for and exclamation
about people and projects in common, and only then can the last
stage, the purpose, be broached. It isn't abnormal for this to open
with some anxiety.

When I was a student, my tutor had told me: 'Remember that
you are paid to want what they want. But often the punters don't
know what it is that they want because they cannot imagine. They
therefore have to rely on imitation. They say: I want something like
this and they indicate a famous garden. It's completely inappropriate
of course, but that's not a fact you can ever tell them. They have
come to you in search of a dream which, believe me, they're not
paying you to puncture. You have to steer them to somewhere
between the dream and reality. This closing of the gap requires a
considerable imposition. Your job handle may be a landscape designer
but you are dealing here with people, not plants. Don't underestimate
the degree of manipulation that will be required.'

Conscious as always of this, I followed Lacey through the cool
tiled hall of the house and into a drawing-room. I don't have much
interest in interiors but in the days when I was married, my wife
Louise would always require me to dissect their ingredients. As a
result I grew into the habit of noticing my surroundings. The room
I had entered had two large shuttered windows with seats on one
of which was a pair of sleeping Havana cats. It was well-furnished
with deep gold walls, whilst the curtains and some chairs were
covered in peony red, a shade which Louise, with her sharp suburban

eye, had once declared to be the English countrywoman's favourite colour. In the centre a tray had been placed on a small mahogany table. It bore three cups, a teapot and a big fruit cake with some promising home-made bulges and deep cracks. It looked very appetising. I was hungry, having eaten only two tuna sandwiches and the packet of fruit gums, a half of which I had shared with my hikers.

'Food but no wife,' said Lacey, blinking again. 'I must find the wife.' He left the room.

I reconciled myself to the fact that the cake would be momentarily deferred. To divert my attention I went to one of the windows and looked out. The boy in the garden had been joined by a similar lad. Same height, same barrel chest and woolly cap. There seemed to be a lot of gesticulation going on. Some kind of dispute in progress? They broke apart at the appearance of two borzois who were chasing one another round the lawn, twins also, it seemed, but forming a comical contrast to the boys with their quickness and grace. The lads dived after the dogs. For a few moments the four gangled about in loops and circles like a Russian cameo. A voice from behind interrupted, so I couldn't see how it ended.

'I'm sorry,' a woman was saying. 'I had to answer the phone.'

I turned round and saw Virginia Lacey coming towards me with an outstretched hand, her cheeks bunched into smiles.

'It doesn't matter at all. I had plenty to watch from the window. What handsome dogs.'

'They're not ours,' said Mrs Lacey, 'and they shouldn't be out. They chase the cats. They belong to Trevor and Gavin who won't leave them tied up at home. They think the world of them.'

'Virginia,' said her husband. 'Shall I pour out the tea? It will stew. Mr Boyd must be starving.'

'I'll do it,' said Mrs Lacey. 'Just hang on a minute.'

She went to the window, pushed up the bottom half and leant out before calling across the lawn. 'Gavin, how come the dogs got off the leash?'

There was the sound of hobnail boots on gravel.

'Sorry now, Mrs Lacey. Trev told me it went and broke. We'll put them in the van for the last hour.'

She nodded, closed the window and returned to the centre of the room. 'Where was I? Tea.' She bent to the table. Her smile had returned.

I tried to place her accent. She spoke with a lilt. It was charming, American certainly, but very soft, long Anglicised, though originally Southern, perhaps from one of the more civilised states. Her manner was elegant. She had dark eyes and hair that bushed out. Only her hair was wild. It was obviously the kind that was uncontrollable.

I accepted her large slice of cake.

'Just a little bit for me?' asked Lacey. 'As this occasion is something of an event.'

'No, darling. You know what the doctor said. I've brought these for you instead.' She took the lid off what looked like a biscuit barrel.

I guessed that the man was probably about sixty, quite a bit older than his wife, and not a member of the baby-boomer generation. He looked well enough but must have recently run into a little trouble. It was obvious that the couple were referring to a new infirmity.

Lacey held the biscuit up to the light. 'So thin it's transparent,' he complained.

'Diets take some getting used to,' I said. 'All those withdrawal symptoms.'

'He's not exactly on a diet,' said his wife. 'He's been told he's got to cut down on fat, that's all.'

'There's a national obsession with food and health these days,' said Lacey. 'In my opinion it's to do with too much peacetime. No enemy on the horizon and you start examining your navel.'

'So reactionary in all his views,' exclaimed his wife.

I grinned and accepted a second equally generous slice of cake. I said: 'I'm not sure I'd agree with your theory. The most peaceful and least health-conscious place I've ever been in – certainly the biggest consumer of puddings and buns – was a nunnery, actually. Plenty of self-assessment there too, you might say.'

'What, may I ask, were you doing in a nunnery?'

'Not in it, exactly. I laid out their garden. A big one. The nuns were delightful people to work for, though somewhat distracting. To relieve the silence imposed by their order, everyone used to escape it by talking to me. I made very slow progress.'

'How funny.' Virginia Lacey leant forward, her face gushing in response. 'How appropriate too. English gardens began in monasteries, didn't they?'

'You're right. I felt I was returning to origins.'

She glanced at her husband and smiled. 'What we're proposing to do here is based on origins, as it happens, but I'll go into that later.'

This was a classic case of the ritual I have already referred to. We were still at the first stage; there was a long way to go till the last when the purpose was stated.

She asked: 'More tea?'

'Thank you, Mrs Lacey.' I passed over the cup.

'Virginia, do, if you don't mind.'

I nodded but this kind of suggestion prevents you from addressing someone by any name at all. I am always cautious with new clients and never grow pally in the initial stages. It's usually better to preserve all formalities until the commission is on.

'What style was it in?'

'The nunnery garden? Plain. Formal. Geometric. Box-edged beds for vegetables and esoteric herbs. Lots of weeding required.'

'I'm surprised they had the money.'

'Some orders are well-endowed.'

I didn't add that because I had wanted to do it, I had agreed to a greatly reduced fee. This was unusual because like most people who are paid for performance, I am inevitably motivated by the size of the fee. (With a business to run, I have to be.) In contrast, it was curiosity that drove me on this one; and besides, the reward for a previous job had been handsome, a garden for a chap who'd made his pile from selling oil tanks to China. In this case one commission had balanced the other. This is good when it happens because it means you can vary your clients and the nature of the jobs. It is one of the benefits of growing older and established. You can afford to be choosy. This way it is an open question whether they pick you or you them, which is just how it should be. The outcome of a good, equal and independent relationship is a better design.

Virginia Lacey was leaning towards me. She had put down her cup. She was asking: 'Do you know why we approached you? You, that is, as opposed to anybody else?'

She looked as if she was keen to have an answer to what seemed a silly question.

'I can't possibly guess. But commissions are often the result of word-of-mouth recommendations.'

'I'm sure, but not as it happens in our case.'

I sighed. It would be hard to answer without sounding pompous. 'Then, perhaps because I'm a known and available name, in a limited circle of people anyway. I try not to get too known actually. I mean, I don't write books and I don't do interviews, since I prefer to keep a low profile. But, over time, you do of course become a bit of an institution. It's not very helpful. It's important to keep fresh.'

'That's why we wrote to you. Because we do think you're fresh. We've looked at several of your gardens. Bentons Abbey and –'

'That was an early one,' I said, disowning a job I've always been ashamed of; though you can never admit to this. I sometimes wish I could rake the earth over my earlier work. When you deal with plants, it can be terrible to see your mistakes live on and grow larger.

'– and Leapham –'

'That one's a bit later,' I said, meaning better.

'– and you did the one near Bruges, didn't you, and then there was your big Japanese garden that I've seen photographed. Every single one's different. We like that a lot. Some of the other landscapers seem to spend all their time just imposing their own ubiquitous formula. Their brand name. Then they get copied by others, don't they? I see it like badge engineering. We don't want ours to look like any other. We've something rather different in mind.' She paused as though embarrassed by herself. 'Or do all your clients say that?'

'Of course they do,' said Lacey, frowning. 'There is nothing new under the sun.'

I was quite touched by the warmth of her assessment and it never upsets anyone to hear their rivals intelligently discounted. I said: 'If we're happy, on both sides that is, to go ahead, then you can be absolutely sure that I'll treat this place as an individual. I would anyway – you were kind enough to remark on that – but this one is special. After all, it's almost an island.'

'Yes. Exactly.'

Silence. It is sometimes the case that a client needs prodding into a start. This man was self-conscious, maybe shy. His wife was neither

– she had all the horse-power – yet I still had no idea of the nature of their project.

I looked intently at her to encourage. I didn't want to spend the whole afternoon stuck in a gully. 'Can you give me some idea what you've got in mind?'

'If you don't want more tea,' said Lacey, 'perhaps we should go and take a look around? We think it's better if you see it first. You can then see if the idea works in context.'

So we went outside and stood for a moment beside the porch. There was no mist left now and the clouds were parting. The rays of late afternoon sun poked through gaps, warming the tops of the trees, their trunks remaining in shadow. A thick scent came from an unseen lilac but, beyond it and stronger, that old river smell, half-fish, half-vegetable. No sign of the boys or their dogs. David Lacey stepped forward and halted at the top of the steps.

'Don't let's hang around,' said his wife. 'I've got to get back in time to pay Gavin.'

Lacey looked at the stone staircase in front of us before making the descent. 'Take care as you go down the steps. The bottom tread is narrower. One isn't troubled by this going up. You always notice a first step. But it's the last going down and by then you are careless.'

We crossed the lawn, went through a doorway in the wall at the side and into a yard with a shed and some chickens and ornamental crested ducks. They waddled over, the larger ones grotesque rather than fancy, bearing wads of white roll-mops on top of their heads.

'Playthings,' said Mrs Lacey. 'The pretty things of life. Ridiculous, isn't it? That small things are so important.'

'They are important. No point in ticking yourself off for that. Unless you're a Puritan which you can't be if you've called me in.'

'She's a Cavalier,' said Lacey. 'I'm the Puritan.'

We went out of the yard, northwards, and down a gravelled path which soon unravelled into a mud track. A wood of deciduous trees lay ahead. A copse is always a joy for a landscape designer. He can glade it. Drive it into rides. Shape it to patterns like clay. But as we entered, I saw that someone had already played with the wood. It was neglected but full of tall tree rhododendrons, their boughs straining sideways and upwards in search of the light. Many of them were still heavily in blossom – mauve and white and ruby, a few spotted or blotched. It was a marvellous surprise to see this gathering of unknown foreigners, spilling their petals from the wet monsoon mountain zones of Asia. Through their trunks I caught glimpses of water as the Laceys led me to a large pool of black liquid. A bough of white bells stretched over, reflected in its still depths.

Mrs Lacey looked down at the reflection, then up at the trees. 'This was all planted over a hundred years ago by a man called Maurice Hudson. His diary came with the deeds. He lived here at Water End alone with his mother. Secretly and silently building this foreign world. I'll show you his diary. I know some of it off by heart. *Monday 4 March 1874. Mother poorly. Humphrey and I started to put in the first batch of larches. They will act as nurses to the new rhododendrons.* His last entry was for 8 October 1877. *All six of the workmen were needed to lift the banana tree in preparation for the winter. It would probably survive but be a little reduced.* He took a photograph. All the workmen in jackets and flat caps, lifting the root ball of a thirty-foot banana.'

'And then it all finished,' said Lacey. 'Pretty abruptly.'

'What happened?'

'He died. It was very sudden. The diary just ended. All those entries for "Mother poorly", but he was the one who dropped dead and she lived on till the 1920s.'

'The garden was left unfinished?'

'They planted some nice trees on the other side. We're going over there so you'll see.'

So we walked on and out of the foreignness of the wood and into the light. The track had become bumpy and led upwards until it reached a plateau of open grassland with some trees which were scrubby and copsy.

We were in an impressive position here. It was the highest point of the land. From the top I could see the river, long and metallic, looping around us, making its passage to the Gulf Stream, its final meeting-place where the two tides become one. In the wood you had looked inwards. Here you looked out to the open river that would join the warm sea, where it would meet an ocean that touched different parts of the world. There is always this thing about a river, that it is a road in motion that melts into other roads. This is the romance of the river world, that it is open-ended, a travelling space.

I said: 'This island is special. Can we get down to the river? Is it accessible?'

'It's where we'll be taking you next,' said Virginia Lacey.

The water swept high up the bank of the river. At the edge was a small wooden boat house and a landing stage. Looking down on it, I could see the ground was hollowed in parts with subsidence. I walked to the stage and stared into the depths of the liquid. We were nowhere near the coast here, quite far inland, but I would still have to check on any mingling of fresh and saline water which represented the exchange of the river and the sea, the breathing out and the inhalation. Sometimes the sea blows far upland. As always there would be a number of indications. Marine crabs or shrimps sometimes migrated. I bent down and put my hand in the water. Green befurred fronds arched and rippled beneath the surface in synchronised movements. To the north, up river and below the opposite bank, a heron was standing and stabbing near the edge, the supple broom-handle of its neck bent over. Thick, plush trees grew all around on the upper bank where the land rose steeply. There were no visible neighbours apart from a distant glimpse, far along, at the top of the opposite bank, of the side of a white cottage.

'If you can row, which David can't, it would be fun for you to go round the edge of the island in a boat,' said Virginia Lacey. 'But perhaps this isn't the right moment. And I've got to get back to pay Gavin. In fact I ought to start getting back right now.'

'What do you think?' asked Lacey. 'I know this first look is a bit hurried, but it's just a guide and you'll have plenty of time to yourself tomorrow.'

'It's pretty wonderful,' I said. This was genuine, I was very taken. 'But before we go any further, I need to know what you've got in mind.'

Lacey screwed up his eyes. He seemed to be having difficulty in finding the right words.

'I'll tell him.' His wife looked impatient with the faffing around. 'It's quite simple. What we're after is Eden.'

This was not a declaration I had expected. I was puzzled. What to say? She had chucked at me an absolute that was both vague and obvious, yet it had been offered as self-explanatory, which it certainly wasn't. The fact is all private owners expect their patches to be Eden by which they mean abundant and fertile paradises. Why did the Laceys imagine they desired a landscape that was different?

Even so, I was required to make an answer, and one which would not disappoint them. I said, stumbling a little: 'Of course I understand that you are reaching for perfection. The genius of the place and so forth. Don't worry. I'll bring that out and discuss it fully with you not only at the beginning but at every stage. I keep the closest possible supervision of my team. You know that. I understand you intend a paradise.'

'No. No. You don't quite follow,' said Mrs Lacey. 'We're not proposing anything so woolly as paradise. We are suggesting something extremely specific. Literally Eden. As in the Eden described in Genesis. With four rivers. As in the old paintings. With animals and birds.' She spoke with great confidence and emphasis.

'Involving the whole island?'

'Yes.'

'Not just a symbolic part? The quartered garden on a cross of water, a Persian paradise concept?'

'The whole island, divided into four parts. Not a miniature gesture.'

I frowned. Impositions of this kind are always false. In addition there was a touch of the show garden about her proposal which was unattractive. It is always terribly difficult to make these grow out of the land.

'You look as if you want to tell us we are quite ridiculous,' said David Lacey. 'I did warn you. I did mention our temerity.'

'I know it sounds a bit fundamentalist,' added Virginia. 'That was why we didn't want to tell you till you got here. We were convinced that unless you got the real feel of the place, you wouldn't hesitate to write us off. I hope that's not what you're doing. Is it? You're not, are you? Don't you think it's possible?'

She stared at me with intensity. I looked back, wondering exactly what to tell them. It is always difficult when a client is both precise in his or her requirements as well as exceptionally ambitious. In fact, it causes no end of problems. In this case, for example, I would have to eliminate the entire real world. I still said nothing but realised that in these circumstances the basic law would be required. *You have to steer them to somewhere between the dream and reality.*

Mrs Lacey was making big dark eyes at me. She seemed amused by my reaction. She was smiling. I noticed her teeth were prominent. She said: 'It's a big project, we realise. But then it's for a big date. In our small private way, we did think it would be a nice way to mark the millennium.' It was lightly said, and I guessed she realised an English professional was best played this way.

'Consider this,' she said. 'We need your help. Will you do it?'

I was still uncertain. Normally I could recognise immediately what I would or wouldn't accept, but here the matter was more complicated. Without the whiff of a doubt the site was wonderful, but I was uneasy about the premise and I knew also it would bring atypical problems.

'Give me another day's exploration,' I said.

'My husband said you said it had capabilities,' she said slyly.

'That was a joke,' I protested. 'I'll explain it one day.'

I realised in making this promise, something within me must have accepted her proposal. Virginia Lacey was a practised persuader.

4

WE WALKED THE circuit over the fields together, past some fine old trees though they were spoilt by scrubbier neighbours, and back through the lines of overgrown hedges towards the paths surrounding the house. The place had different moods and was full of potential, though mishandled and neglected. Landscape like this is the most rewarding to turn around, but I was still uncertain because I was not being offered as free a hand as I might require. Yet the mood of my hosts had lightened as though I had already accepted. Virginia Lacey in particular was chattering away, dispensing offers. They'd introduce me to Gavin and Trevor when we got back. It was a shame for me to go to a hotel. It would be no trouble for me to spend the night at the house. This afternoon had been such a hurried excursion, whereas spending a night always gave you an extra feel for a place. She warned me she was simply brimful with ideas, all of which she simply knew I would try and shoot down.

She was so happy and excited, just like a child, yet I also knew that the excitement would evaporate and that some of my sobriety would rub off on her. Already I was feeling doubtful about the degree of expectation and the problems that lay ahead. Surely they didn't expect me to divert the river? It would, I knew, be illegal, for a start. The only hope was to trace the inflow and egress from the lake in the woodland.

'Where does the water come from for the pool?' I asked.

'There's a spring at the top which never dries out,' said Lacey. 'We'll give you a map.'

'There are springs all over the place,' added his wife. 'I promise, the water isn't a problem. You'll see.'

We followed the gravel path past the house and returned to the yard where we had started out. The colony of fowls pressed round our feet, pecking expectantly and pushing out their feathers. She went to the bin and scooped out a bowl of mixed grain which she scattered in a thin veil over the ground.

'I love them,' she said. 'They're so frivolous.'

I noticed the expression on Lacey's face as he watched her and wondered how long they had been married. It was evident that he was still captivated by his wife.

A couple of sparrows and finches flew down to try their luck but Lacey waved them away.

'Don't,' she said. 'That's so unfair. Why shouldn't they?'

'She's hopeless,' he exclaimed. 'Always rooting for the underdog.'

'Don't you agree with me?' She turned to me. 'Left to himself my husband would only look after the ones we'd paid for.'

I gave what Louise used to call my portly chortle, a device for avoidance, and decided it would be better to decline their offer to spend the night. Instead I would stick with my plan to go to the local hotel. Making smalltalk at this stage could be tiring. It would be simpler to be left on my own.

The door that led into the yard suddenly slammed shut. The two lads who had been chasing the dogs on my arrival, had now entered the square and were standing, one a few feet behind the other. Both were gulping mugs of tea. They stood rooted and obedient, like a pair of trees lined up.

'Here's your money, boys,' said Mrs Lacey, emerging from the shed with a fistful of notes.

'Do you want us again on Friday?' asked the one in the vanguard. He pocketed the money.

'Yes, Gavin.' She stepped sideways so she had a view of his brother. 'You did that bed very well.' She nodded vigorously and smiled. Then she turned back to me. 'I want you to meet Gavin and Trevor. Boys, this is Mr Boyd. He's the man we've told you about. We're hoping to persuade him to create the garden for the island. If so, you'll be working for him.'

'Pleased to meet you,' said Gavin, pulling off his woollen cap. He put down his mug, turned to his brother and conveyed the information by means of the deft and intricate use of his hands. Only now did it become evident to me that the other boy was a deaf-mute. At the same time I realised that it was an impossible and insensitive moment to clear up a misunderstanding on the part of Mrs Lacey. On a project of this nature, unlike some designers, I always prefer to use my own teams of trained professional workmen and gardeners. With anything ambitious, I am not in the habit of inheriting and pressing into service those of my clients. With some foreboding I watched the interchange of signs between the two brothers. It was discomfiting to see the misunderstanding demonstrated, and the smile it was given on the face of the wordless boy.

Gavin the talker turned back to me. 'That's great. We're really looking forward to it.' He jammed his cap back on his head, picked up the mug and began to shift position to signal departure. 'Trev left the lobsters in a bucket in the kitchen, by the way.'

'Lovely. Fresh lobsters tonight,' said Mrs Lacey to me. 'You've got to stay.'

I opened my mouth and shut it, intent on the problem. In silence the three of us watched the two boys lope off, their height and size making their shoulders roll to either side.

'They're a terrific pair,' she said. 'Trevor – he's the deaf-mute – used to help as a lifeguard at weekends, then they moved too far inland.'

Something in her words, a reminder, an echo, struck me, but all I could think of was the warning I must deliver. I waited till I was sure Gavin was out of hearing. When I registered the sound of their van starting up, I said: 'I couldn't mention this before – not in front of them – but there's a misunderstanding. I can't use your gardeners. This is a big job. If I take it on, I'd prefer to employ only members of my trained team. I'm very sorry indeed if this upsets your expectations.'

Mrs Lacey stared at me aghast. 'They're looking forward to it, Trevor especially. If I'd known this before, it would have been different.'

'I can't. I'm terribly sorry. It must seem harsh, I know, but I have to judge things by professional standards. *I'm* judged by professional standards. The workers have to be first class.'

Earlier I had started to think of her as Virginia. Now I noticed that increasingly she was becoming Mrs Lacey again.

She pulled the edges of her jacket together. A rainbow of feeling crossed her face. 'I see them as the wild ones. Like these.' She indicated the finches and sparrows which were still fluttering and pecking away in the gaps between the expensive feet of the ornamental poultry. 'It seems to me that's what Eden is. A place for the wild ones. A celebration of diversity. Has it really got to be done on the boring old professional lines? Can't it be different this time? Can't the doing be part of the ethos?'

'Virginia,' said Lacey, restraining. 'You are always so charmingly ingenuous. He's the expert, you know. Experts aren't just being boring if they tackle their work in the proper way, as you very well realise.'

He cast a colonising glance at me to show that, as two professional males, we had formed ranks, but I think he realised that I wasn't listening. The reason was that, simultaneously, almost too late, I had traced the reminder that I had heard when she spoke of Trevor being a lifeguard. Many years ago, as a young designer, I had worked on a strange and maverick job for a few months in Iran. One weekend I had taken a trip up from Isfahan to the northern edge. That Sunday morning I had been riding a pony along the shore of the Caspian Sea, when I had seen a huge deaf-mute, who was employed as a lifeguard, rescue a child who had been swept out of his depth. I had watched this magnificent specimen of a big bronzed surfer walk out of the water with the rag doll in his arms. The Persian boy had revived. You forget these incidents, then years later find you can work them as cogs.

I looked at Mrs Lacey. 'How long have the boys worked for you?'
'A year.'
'Can they do this five days a week?'
'I can't be sure. I'll check. But I think so.'
'Do they, does Gavin listen to instructions?'
'Yes.'
'Is he? – are they? – hard workers?'
'Yes.'
'Are they meticulous?'
'As much as I am.'
'Do they know one plant from another?'
'Not exactly.'

I was dismayed.

'You see?' said Lacey to his wife. 'You see the problems?'

'But Perry does.'

'Who's Perry?'

'She's young and strong and knows her stuff.'

'Do you employ her?'

'Not yet but I could. Part-time.'

'You may not like it, but I've got to put it this way. What we have here at the moment is two untrained oxen – one of whom, let's not beat around the bush, has problems with words – and an occasional girl' – with a funny name, I thought, but didn't say it – 'to plough a big furrow.' I added: 'What does that sound like to you? Surely a bit haphazard?'

'No. Full of potential.'

I smiled. 'You are an optimist, aren't you?'

'Because I know it can work.'

I too was tempted to think that on this day, 8 May, it might work because I was tempted to try. Tomorrow would confirm it.

I still refused to spend the night, though I wanted to stay and have dinner with them. Not because of the lobsters (which Virginia wasn't squeamish about boiling to death, or, as she claimed, chilling them in the freezer and then heating them to a 'peaceful and heavenly nirvana': either case, in my view, severely reducing their appeal). I was keener to stay because it is crucial to get a feel for your clients. You are catapulted into this situation, and a lack of understanding will grow into a rock which will sooner or later destroy the contract. I didn't think they'd be any problem, but there are degrees of knowing people and when someone's foreign, they're so charming and different that it's not uncommon to be fooled by this rapport.

Virginia was certainly captivating. She was spontaneous and fresh and relaxed. Before dinner, she sat on the sofa in the drawing-room dressed in a pair of navy trousers and a high-necked cotton top and hooped earrings. The chocolate cats pushed at her ankles. She opened her arms and said to the pair of sleek Havanas: 'Come, climb, my little monkeys, up into the branches of the tree.' Lacey and I watched them jump and swarm over her lap while the male who was called

Ciggy teased off her earring. It was, I suppose, a demonstration, yet not at all actressy. That was how she was, affectionate and foreign and natural.

That evening, as we deconstructed the lobsters, I learnt she had come from Virginia. 'All girls like me were christened Virginia.' It explained the photos I had seen in the hall. One, an old sepia print of Richmond at the end of last century, still gas-lit and with unpaved streets. Next to it was a family group, with belles and beaux admiring a pony. Another showed a good brick house with pillars and a pediment. At the centre of this heritage group was a black mammy with a turban and big skirts and great dignity. There were newer photographs too, but only one of Virginia: as a child with a lapful of chickens. A girl with a country upbringing, was the way she described herself, though she said she had never fully subscribed to the family cult of the horse. Instead she had trained as a lawyer, married an English doctor and come to live in Britain. It explained the cadence of her accent. A softness of speech: the lilt, not the twang. Only, sometimes, the kink of her foreignness came through.

I thought it unlikely that the man she had married at this stage was Lacey. Theirs was a second match, surely. There were moments that evening when she was talking and he was watching as though she was still a strange and wonderful novelty. Lacey spoke little about himself. Virginia was the talker and he was often silent. Then, when he spoke, he tended to make comments about his wife: that she used the word train-station because that was a match for the bus-station; or that for breakfast she still sometimes had cinnamon toast. It was doubtless a second marriage, probably fairly recent and certainly happy. They still paid a lot of attention to one another.

At one point I turned the conversation to him. All he said was that he had retired from the pharmaceutical industry, then he deflected the conversation back to his wife. His habit of blinking persisted, not a blink in the normal sense, a flick of the lids, but brief hard squeezes of the eyes. He was dressed in a country check shirt and his grey hair hung over the back of the collar, a little too long for a man of his age and type. Yet it wasn't the uniform of defiance, nor an attempt to pose as a younger man. Perhaps it had more to do with his wife. A woman like that, acquired in later life, provokes a change of style, a show of flair, a tiny bohemian denial of dullness.

In a sense none of this mattered. It was simply important that we pleased and trusted and understood one another well enough to embark on a big contract. I found both of them likeable and when I left later that evening, we were all happy. We arranged that I would return the following morning when I would visit the island alone, to assess its prospects. I warned them of problems, and that their plans might have to be modified. We also agreed that I would use my own contractors whenever necessary.

That night I stayed at the local hotel. It wasn't much more than an inn, a pleasant and old-fashioned place with settles downstairs and rods and a glass case of pike on the wall and branches of hawthorn in vases. About to climb into bed, I had the idea of opening the cabinet to the side. There it was, the Bible. I sat on the edge of the mattress and leafed through the prelims in search for the right place in Genesis. What I met was what most of us meet on these occasions: it is terribly familiar yet also strange, for one comes to it after a gap of three-quarters of a lifetime. Not since school, in my case, when there were prayers every morning, then again every evening in my school house, then up to four times on Sunday. For me the Bible is lodged in my childhood and, like that, has been left behind. How odd to read it again in this context, in a little hotel near the coast. *And the Lord God planted a garden eastward in Eden; and there he put the man he had formed. And out of the ground made the Lord God to grow every tree that is pleasant to the sight, and good for food; the tree of life also in the midst of the garden, and the tree of knowledge of good and evil. And a river went out of Eden to water the garden; and from thence it was parted and became into four heads.* I had not expected to meet this again or thought to take its words and its meanings out of Genesis and look at them as a map or a stratagem.

The following day I returned to carry out my own reconnaissance of the capabilities of the island. It took me an hour to retrace yesterday afternoon's route and two hours to walk round the edge of the land. At the end of this time, there was at least some satisfaction: they were right in one respect that water would not be a problem. It was a fact that springs arose all around, not only by the woodland pool which was on the north-facing side of the island, but also, which was more important, on the other sides. Channels were not imposs-ible, striking out to north, south, east and west. This was positive. Yet all the while I was finding practical solutions, the theoretical side of the project returned to nag like a recurrent itch. The problem was this: to create an Eden of a garden, literally as they required, would be in one way and if it were subtly and skilfully handled, a triumphant climax to any career. Yet in another way it was obvious that it could be no more than a glib pastiche. How could you try to evoke something in which no one believed? An Eden in an ungodly, perhaps even a nihilistic age, was surely something of a misconstruction.

Reflecting on this, I sat on a rock at lunchtime on the crest of the site and munched a sandwich. I turned the problem this way and that. You have to face facts. Nothing is worse in the countryside than inflated pretensions. Nothing uglier than a fake intended to reflect a whole philosophical outlook. The last thing I wanted to do was a faithful reconstruction.

I lay back on the short tufted grass and stared at the sky, where birds were wheeling and screaming. How easy it always is to make patterns on the ground and how difficult to give the illusion of nature and freedom. Yet that is precisely the illusion that one's artifice must attain. This is the object of all pastoral myth. Freedom and harmony in happy conjunction and every beast of the field and every fowl of the air, every tree that is pleasant to the sight and good for food, a tree of life in the midst of the garden and let us disregard for the moment, if one can, that pesky tree of knowledge that caused so much trouble. What exactly would I feel comfortable to do? After all, I'd been asked to be the creator.

When I left, I was cautious but told the Laceys that I would work on the proposal.

5

ON THE DRIVE back to Gloucestershire I decided to go and see my ex-wife. I rang Louise from a motorway station. As always I was brisk when I spoke to her because I found this easier, perhaps because it isn't misleading.

'I would be very grateful for your help on a job. Are you going to be in if I come by?'

'Why?'

'I'll explain over lunch. I'll take you out.'

'You owe me a dinner, not a bite in a pub. But you needn't bother, or not now. I've got some food in the house. We might as well finish it up.'

Louise lived in Oxford where she worked as a computer consultant. She had been very successful and her abilities had paid handsomely. She now had the leisure to do a part-time degree as a mature student in art history. When we had first separated, she stayed in our original house with our daughter. It was only when Abi left home that Louise had bent her mind to the modern female vogue for extending herself. Her new home was in Osney, a tall thin segment of a brick terrace overlooking the Oxford Canal on which barges ploughed to and fro. She had no need of the money, but she let the top floors to two post-graduate students. Their rent was real but their presence phantom. Scientists both, one Japanese, they were rarely there. She therefore lived virtually on her own; happily it seemed, which was a mystery since it was my absence that had been a provocation to divorce.

Louise was alone now when she answered the door. She looked pleased to see me. Maybe, despite appearances, she was indeed lonely. Maybe she missed me. Now that neither rights nor responsibilities, nor envy or competitiveness for that matter, lay there to be thrashed out between us, it was possible for companionship to flower in that spot which had been occupied solely by intolerance.

I bent forward and kissed her cheek. Her hair was shaped in a new way, short and swept back as though windblown. She was fairer too than last time, I noticed. Altogether more blonde and stylish, dressed in what she had once called Siamese cat colours, cream and mocha brown.

'Have you come straight from a job?' she asked.

'A new garden to see.'

'Oh God. Glossy magazines open all over the table and them saying I want one just like that, if you please?'

'Something like that, I'm afraid.'

'Who are they?'

'A Mr and Mrs Lacey. David and Virginia Lacey of a place called Water End, to be precise.' For some reason I withheld the fact that it was an island.

'Nice?'

'Very nice.'

'Are we pally yet? Have we reached the call-me-Gina stage?'

'Still very much yours sincerely as far as I'm concerned.'

She sighed and stood back. 'This all makes me quite nostalgic for old times.' She put a hand on my arm and looked me up and down. 'Very nostalgic actually. How handsome you are now. Getting older suits you. Too bad I can't still introduce you as my husband.'

'Come on, Lou. None of that bracing flirtatiousness.'

'Sorry. I'm just trying to stop you getting re-married.' She spoke with unforced flippancy but it occurred to me that it might be true. It was certainly one of her veiled enquiries. She always made some reference to marriage on our first meeting after a long interval to check out my status. It was not without reason. I recognised the same syndrome in myself. Whoever was the first to re-marry would give the other a jolt. Maybe it was the old competitiveness. Or just the umbilical cord between exes who could live neither together nor, with complete satisfaction, apart.

I followed her into the kitchen which, like the rest of the house, was full of objects we had once bought together. I sometimes thought I was as much married to the furniture as to my former wife. Here I was, sitting at my ex-table on my ex-chair about to eat with my ex-knife and fork. At least all the curtains and white goods were new.

'How's the thesis?' I asked, as she pushed a pile of papers to the side of the table. I knew she was at this stage doing a study of the nude.

'I'm taking it very seriously at the moment.'

'I know that. You're nothing if not thorough.'

She put a plate in the centre of the table with some pitta bread and fans of tomatoes interlaced with wafers of cheese.

'Don't worry. I've got some nice, solid, filling soup to start with.' She opened the cupboard and indicated the tins. 'Pumpkin, or stilton and broccoli, or lentil?'

'Lentil, I think.'

'An old favourite if I remember.'

'Same old things as always, Lou.'

I watched her run the butterfly opener round the edge of the tin and decant half the broth into a saucepan. It provoked in me a sudden and sharp sense of *déjà vu*. I was momentarily silenced by yet another detail which reminded me how much would forever stay the same despite a changed context. In search of diversion, I looked at the pile of papers and books she had pushed to the side of the table. Uppermost seemed to be a list of titles which were presumably required reading.

'There,' she said, bringing over a bowl of soup, brim-full, which she placed before me on the mat. 'Lentil *and* vegetable. Truly your very favourite.'

In some ways I feel she is like a sister to me. It is quite hard to remember having sex with her. Yet when we first met, we couldn't get enough of one another. She was so pretty and clever then, and with a high hormone-rating. I started up again. 'You said you were taking work seriously.'

'Very seriously is what I said. What I mean is that I'm going to life classes too.'

'You're painting the nude?'

'You sound surprised. Just because I can add up doesn't mean I can't be creative and paint the human body as well.'

'Not at all. I'm not surprised and I approve.'

She made a gloomy face. 'It's terribly difficult. Frankly, the tutor laughs at what I do. But I don't want to be just a middle-aged bluestocking or one of those fussy fastidious types in silk scarves. For better or worse you've had an influence on me. I want to study something artistic by doing its practical side too.'

'Are you painting men or women?'

'Only women so far. Mostly sagging and fat.'

'The older and fatter the better I'd have thought.'

'That's the artistic theory, yet if you look at most of the famous old master nudes, apart from Rubens of course, they tended to be very elegant with high self-supporting breasts like apples.'

'*Où sont les seins d'antans?*'

'Gone away. Every one.'

We smiled to have stumbled across our old capacity for sharing a joke. I paused to allow myself time to spoon up some of the soup. 'Do you know how Eve was depicted?'

She stopped buttering her pitta, in order to think. 'Well, obviously she varied from one century to another. Different male painters, different conventions. Pre-or post-Fall. Why?'

'An idle enquiry. I'll tell you the background in a moment.'

'By some she was shown as wilful and sensual and dominant. And in contrast, by others –'

'Who?'

'Hugo Van der Goes for one, a medieval Flemish painter. She looks pitiful. Like everyone's mother. Like me as I was. Flat-footed, exhausted, a servant. Very undesirable. It's the serpent who steals the show.'

'Can I see?'

'Why?' she asked again.

I emptied and pushed aside the soup bowl. 'I've been asked to do a version of Eden.'

She raised her eyebrows. 'Oh God. How yukky. Not your sort of stuff, is it? Is this the place you've just visited?'

'It is.'

'Not only glossy magazines all over the table but also the Bible?'

I smiled at but did not reply to this new form of jibe which I read as a sign of jealousy.

'A rather demanding version of the me-too factor, isn't it?' she asked.

'It could be.'

'Presumably money no object?'

'Who knows yet. But within reason, I would think probably not.'

'Can't you just do them a lovely place?'

'Et in Arcadia ego?'

'Why not?'

'They're rather more exacting. I'm afraid Arcadia alone won't do. They want a more literal interpretation. Water and animals and birds.'

'Not Adam and Eve?'

'Fortunately they've not been mentioned. I think we keep them under wraps.'

'Something to be thankful for, I suppose.'

'However I did wonder about a non-representational lump of stone which we could call "Forefathers".'

She laughed. 'You always called them pretentious.'

'I still do.'

She leaned over to the pyramid of papers and extracted one of the books. She started leafing through the pages.

'There.' She passed me a picture of a painting. 'That's what Van der Goes thought they looked like in the fifteenth century.'

I examined the painting. It showed two Gothic-looking young people aged about eighteen, both undernourished, too thin to be erotic. Adam on the left, shielding his parts with one hand whilst the other reached up in readiness for the apple. Eve in the middle with a prominent stomach, a fleur-de-lys iris hiding her pubic hair and an apple in both hands. Then to the right and beside them, clasping the tree of knowledge, the serpent, half-human and half-animal, half-weasel and half-reptile, with webbed feet and a sweet beseeching face.

'Captured at the moment before the Fall,' said Louise. 'I think it's quite wonderful. Terribly poignant.'

'It is wonderful,' I agreed. We stared at the image in silence together.

'But honestly, you only have to see this to realise that Eden without people rather misses the point. It's a garden without a story.'

'You don't need "a story" as you put it. These owners want something very beautiful which has been lost. Something with which they can mark the year two thousand. What I really came to ask is whether you know a painting of the garden itself rather than the people.'

She looked at me vacantly for a moment then screwed up her face. 'I'm not sure. I can't think.' She rose and fetched a dish of early cherries and pears which had been sitting on top of the fridge. 'It's not really my area, you see. I'm looking at people rather than things.'

'Do try, Louise.' I helped myself to a fistful of cherries and gestured towards the dish. 'Eat. Fuel for thinking.'

She ignored me. She rubbed the back of her neck slowly. 'There's one by Cranach which shows the animals as well as the humans.'

'What animals?'

'It's famous. Deer, a lion, a boar, a stork, I think, and others. I'm sure you would recognise it.'

'But nothing of the garden?'

'Some bushes and the tree of apples of course. Not much else.'

'You can't think of another?'

She stood up. 'Wait. I think there is.'

I watched her walk out of the room. I looked at the cherries and took another bunch. Left to my own devices, I got up and wandered round the room and read the backs of postcards which were propped up by a jug. The sound of scuffles reached me from the bedroom above. She must use it for work. That struck me as sad. My old Louise without a husband and only books and a computer for comfort in bed. The scuffles went on. Poor Louise. I had put her in search mode and being all or nothing, she would continue until she had nailed her goal. I went to the window and looked out at her long, thin back garden. It was perfectly kept and lovingly composed. The garden I had failed to give her. 'Why do you spend all your time embellishing other people's lives,' she had cried at the end, 'and neglecting our own.' I felt a rush of old guilt and a new appreciation. She was very good to help me and show no trace of bitterness now.

I heard the soft tread of her feet down the carpeted stairs. She returned to the kitchen.

'I'm very grateful,' I said stiffly. 'It's so good of you to take this trouble. I hope you don't think I presume.'

She looked surprised. 'Presume,' she exclaimed. 'What a funny word. Presume indeed. Forget it. I enjoy this,' she added simply. 'Perhaps because I miss it. Or is it because I'm no longer involved? Look.'

She placed an open book on the table.

'Oh, Christ,' I said. 'That's astonishing. But that's exactly what it's like.'

The landscape was almost an exact representation of what I had observed yesterday on the island. The metallic river meandering in the distance. The blue wooded slopes. The huge trees, leafy and domed. A grassed clearing, golden in sunlight. A little stream in the foreground. The natural ingredients were all there.

'"Adam and Eve in the Garden of Eden" by Jan Breughel the Elder,' she said triumphantly. 'I knew there was something.'

Every beast of the field and every fowl of the air. Brown monkeys and red parakeets, tigers and lions and a leopard rolling in play on his back. There were peacocks and swans and patterned guinea pigs and stags and horses and roses and vines and ripe fruit. And in the distance, reduced to the status of background, the two tiny human figures, naked and forked, her hand stretched up in readiness to pluck. The possession of all this curious and wondrous abundance was held in suspense.

'Such a loss,' my ex-wife said. 'Don't you feel that as you look at this? How they fucked it up. Such a loss.'

'But this is perfect,' I said. 'Exactly what I need. You couldn't lend it to me could you?'

'It seems a bit ambitious to copy. You can't stick in this bevy of birds and animals. Dog didn't eat dog then. They do now.'

'Forget the animals. It's the scenery that's the same. It's extraordinary. As for the rest, it might give me ideas.'

'Take it. I don't need it for the moment.'

I shut the book and stood up.

'You're not going are you?' she said.

'I've got to get back.'

'But you've only just arrived.'

'I've a meeting at four.'

'Did you only come and see me for help?'

'It's nice to keep in touch. Isn't it?'

'But you haven't asked about Abi, or me, even. Not really anything about me.'

I hesitated then blurted the first thing that came into my mind. 'How are the lodgers?' I asked helplessly.

'For God's sake, Robert.'

'I'm so sorry. You know what it's like when I'm in a rush. I spoke to Abi last week, by the way. She said she's getting on fine. Has she said anything different to you?'

'No. She said that.'

'Well then.'

She looked away. 'You know, if you hadn't spent all your time on other people we'd never have separated.'

'Louise, please, not that again.'

She took me to the door. I thanked her profusely for the meal and her help and swore to be in touch very shortly again. I promised dinner.

'Dinner,' she repeated.

She closed the door behind me. I climbed into the car. She always made me feel guilty. I tried not to think of her leaning against the wall, and going back into the kitchen and clearing up and looking at the pictures and thinking of loss and closing the books and taking them back to the bedroom as companions.

Two minutes later I passed Mr Naramoto, her lodger, at the end of the street. He would be letting himself into her house and going up to his room to meditate before going out again.

6

THERE WERE THREE urgent business phone calls waiting for me when I got back to the office and two personal. One from Alice Kerr, a friend in her late thirties and also divorced. She was sweet and serious, if not very sparky, though in my experience that is better than women of high voltage who are tricky and more liable to fuse. The second call was from my mother, who would go on and on, so I judged it must wait. I could put the phone down on her for five minutes and she'd still be there talking. I did however ring Alice and we arranged at whose place and what time we'd meet up for the weekend.

I also completed the main calls, the first two to clients and the third to a subcontractor who was advising the delay in the delivery of hardware to a site. I then assessed the state of my desk and called in the chief designer who headed my team of six. All of them worked on separate jobs and each had his or her own specialities. Some were good with old ladies and their gardens, others were at their best with country landowners, and one had found a niche invigorating municipal parking lots. You might draw a parallel between us and vets, for example, who practise on small and big animals.

Tim Rowland had been waiting for me and appeared as soon as he was summoned. He was my henchman and I looked on him as almost a son. Dear Tim was charming and affable and precisely spoken. Quite a favourite with the wives of bankers and the types who have a fancy for urns. He came in and stood expectantly before me, then sat down. He was wearing an indigo shirt and grey cotton trousers, both shabby, though the first thing you noticed was his fresh complexion which gave him the air of a choirboy. As always he was smiling. I had never seen him lose his temper despite the constant provocations of a business that dealt in people and perishables. I liked him immensely and hoped that this member of the new generation would take over the business if I were ever forced to retire. In my experience it is always difficult to keep these younger ones. As soon as you train them to a working standard, they are tempted to go off and hunt for themselves. It is part of growing up and something that I found hard to argue against, since in an earlier life I had passed through this same stage myself.

I surveyed Tim now, before speaking.

'Any problems?' I asked.

'Where do I start?'

'Where it hurts most.'

'People-problems, as always.'

For the next ten minutes Tim ran through the usual list of obstacles which accumulated every week: late payments, approvals withheld after they had been granted, growers failing to deliver the right plants, defective builders, a series of mishaps that had to be turned round. In my early days this was the kind of trouble that had given me sleepless and sweaty nights. Now I just took it for granted. It had become such an everyday aspect of running this business that I no longer minded. Indeed it was part of the challenge and I was quite pleased to have proved myself a businessman as well as an artist. Today, however, was different and I felt restless and critical.

I looked at Tim, trying to evaluate the younger man's reactions to a proposal before it was broached.

'How would you feel about taking over one of my projects?' I asked. 'Something else has come up.'

'What is it?'

'The new thing or the old?'

'Whatever it is that you want me to do.'

'What I'd like to suggest is that you finish the Japanese garden at the Institute in France. It's halfway through and largely a question of policing, but it does mean regular attendance.'

Tim's shiny face fell inwards a fraction. His smile dimmed though did not entirely disappear. 'Rowena's about to have the baby. I'd hoped to be able to stay in England for the next couple of months.'

He leant forward, unable to stop himself moving the jar of pencils on the desk a fraction to the left, a tiny gesture of distress, the nearest he would ever come to protest, though he could be firm if required when it came to clients. It was only conflict in the office or at home that he did not like. I knew this and thought: poor old Tim, it'll have to be one or the other. I shook my head with regret. 'I wouldn't raise this with you if I didn't have to. I know you're in a difficult position, and wouldn't have asked if I could see a way round it. But I can't ask one of the others. They're not —' I stopped to search for an adjective which would praise present company without damning the absent '— well, between ourselves, not quite authoritative enough yet for the nature of the job.'

Tim hesitated, straddling the pull of his personal and professional life.

'If I could manage trips to and fro without actually being on tap,' he ventured ineffectually. He looked away, still smiling although stricken. I guessed he was recalling the sleepless nights caused by their first child, and anticipating more as well as a row with his wife. He was trying not to sigh. He was already juggling too many contracts.

'You'll have to stay there some of the time, I'm afraid,' I said.

'Must I? I see.'

There was a pause.

'You *are* in your early thirties, you know,' I said as gently as possible. 'The age of professional commitment, isn't it?'

It was not intended to be uttered in rebuke, but it was difficult to put as a neutral fact, and hung there indigestibly in the air between us. I had to let it, so that its suggestive force would prevail.

'Yes,' said my junior. 'Of course.'

'So I have your firm agreement?'

'Yes.'

'No going back even if a fuse blows at home tonight?'

'No. No.'

'Right. Thanks. I needed your agreement in principle. I'll confirm within a week about putting it into practice.'

'What's come up to cause this?' asked Tim curiously.

'A funny old project,' I replied. 'I'll tell you if it goes ahead.'

I yawned, suddenly tired, for I had risen very early that morning and had been preoccupied all day and now felt as I did sometimes that, however worthy the subject for my attentions, it had demanded too much and caused a surfeit. One needed to blow it away and to relax. I got up and looked out of the window, then back at my room. At the cream-painted walls with their progress charts, at the blown-up photographs of projects, before and after, at the cork board with its testifying letters of gratitude from clients, at the wall of medals awarded, at the door which was propped open to the small boardroom used for our more important meetings, at all this striving paraphernalia of a successful professional life that had been started and maintained by continual acts of will.

'I saw the sea today,' I said. 'I saw it yesterday too. It was grey then. It was blue today when the sun came out. It looked wonderful.'

'Bully for you,' said Tim.

'Sorry. Not fair is it?'

I thought that I couldn't wait to get back.

A new challenge gives such a shot to your adrenalin that I expected to spend half the night awake, especially since I'd gone to bed early. I slept well, however, and felt refreshed the following morning. I pulled on my old navy dressing gown and went downstairs in bare feet. My home was the kind of Crucially Traded place where you could pad around noiselessly all over the floor. After the divorce, I'd bought the house from a young bachelor and, most conveniently – this had been one of its attractions – it had been fully furnished by the boy's parents for their only son. He must have been half my age so, when I, a rogue male too, acquired it, this confirmed my feeling of having failed to move on. Even so, it was an ideal cottage, set on its own apart from neighbours across the lane, weekenders from London, the wife a Frenchwoman who was always irate. Inside, the boy's mother had made a good job of the house. Professionally wallpapered, rush-matted throughout, given a duet of new bathrooms, no expense spared but excess avoided, it suited the few necessities of my present way of life, not least because it provided a high degree of comfort without requiring any fresh input of my own. Even the garden didn't need gardening. It consisted of paddock and that was being cropped this year by a gentle grey mare on loan.

This pony was visible from the kitchen window as I ate my usual half-grapefruit followed by two slices of fawn toast and marmalade. It is funny how doggedly one pursues the same food for breakfast through all the vicissitudes of a grown-up life.

In the distance the mare was dipping her head over the paddock rail as she tried to reach a tuft of grass on the other side. As her head swung backwards and forwards, framed in the window, she formed a moving picture out of different materials, her head marble in the stained glass. It was a reminder of something, an artistic problem, that had nagged me on the journey back. It is the problems in projects that make you obsessive. The difficulty here was how to bring the animals into the garden at Water End, to paint them into the picture. Animals and plants don't mix, the one feeding off the other. You could of course cordon them off. Yet corrals are unsightly, fit only for farms. Did this mare in the frame suggest a possible answer? Might I carve openings like windows out of the hedges? Clair-voyées through which the birds and the beasts would be glimpsed? Would it work, this old-fashioned contrivance for framing a view?

Often the old notions are better than anything we can come up with nowadays. This one embodied the ancient and satisfying balance between opposites. The grey mare in a green frame. A flock of white sheep browsing past. The void in the solid would for an instant, catch life. Movement and stasis, lightness and weight. People are frightened of abstractions. They see only the horse in the window, but if they actually knew, the abstractions, the principles, are working away there.

Once a central idea like this comes, the others follow. How to explain? It's as if a blockage has been removed that releases a torrent. Still wearing my dressing gown, I went to my desk, took out some paper and started to make sketches and jottings of which half at least would soon be erased. It is inevitable, this huge wastage of effort on a project. One reason is that the problems are different every time, so the solutions too are never the same. This maddens you but is also oddly addictive. It makes you pummel away to find the answers, though the search is full of traps and false alleys. Some answers elude you. Others are deceptive, only appearing to be right. They look beautiful but they fail you; they are merely artistic solutions which are faulty on practical grounds. This is the nub of the difficulty about my kind of job which grows out of the soil. Ideas in abstract are useless; they must be tied to the sun, rain and earth. A landscape architect is not only a theoretician but a practical man and whenever he comes up with an answer, he must ask: will it work? And not just now, either, but forever, and in summer and winter?

It's so difficult, this business of being tied to the constraints of physical laws. Sometimes I think that the new designers are taught nothing about this at all. Last week I found myself telling our latest recruit that we wouldn't have seasons at all in our part of the world, if our planet weren't tilted at an angle of twenty-three degrees in its orbit round the sun.

'Crikey,' said Isobel, looking at me blankly.

'What do you think of that?'

'I don't know,' she said. 'It's quite interesting but does it really make any difference to what I'm doing?'

Anyway, I think the point I am trying to get over is that this process is really hard work, as hard as trying to shift a ton of concrete. Though it's also a joy when the plan starts to form. When you see its geometry and know you are ploughing the land into a map. When you feel you are worthy of the old landscape designers like my hero, Capability Brown. I have thought often that you couldn't move one single tree of his schemes without destroying the elegance of the scene. All these centuries later, that's truly amazing.

It was not until late in the evening that I finished. Not a finish exactly, for in most ways it was no more than a beginning, yet on these occasions I knew also that I had caught the tail of it too. In the months to come, I would walk the land endlessly, revising its clumps of trees and hedges, assessing which to take out and which to change. But today at least I had made a proper start. Later this week I'd cost it and make the presentation to my clients. After some ritual hesitation about money, a go-ahead would be certain to follow. I was very chuffed with my plans.

7

OVER THE NEXT few weeks I grew familiar with the journey down to the river world. It was a long trip, but it filled me with enthusiasm. Besides, I never find driving a bore because I notice the trees, always, by the roadside, in the same way as an engineer responds to the camber. I had worked out a route for the last few miles that was meandering but beautiful, dipping unnecessarily south onto the coast road so that I could see the sea, before travelling north again up river to cross the isthmus that led to the island.

I also became more familiar and at ease with my clients. I discovered that, although this Eden-in-the-making was an island, the Laceys were no isolationists. Rather, they seemed a popular and sociable and generous couple. In some ways their life reminded me of that of the expats I had known when working abroad. The weather was good at the beginning of this first summer and the Laceys played tennis and swam and held the odd bridge party on the verandah, drinking mint tea, and soon after, magnums of wine with their friends. Virginia had the gift of enjoying herself and of drawing others in, and she was obviously keen to include me as well. 'Don't work at it the whole time,' she urged me. 'We like to think you're becoming a bit of a friend too.'

Out of caution and habit, on the first three Fridays I went home but the fourth weekend she induced me to stay on, and this time the division between work and leisure was effectively severed. On the Saturday she gave a lunch party to introduce me like a trophy to some of her friends. They held it alfresco on the main lawn. It was green and plush after recent rain, and, as Virginia said, the backdrop was particularly pretty, with the borders in full June flow.

There were masses of blue geraniums, dark roses and some clumps of homelier candytuft too. Near the house stood two trestle tables, both with a linen cloth. One had the glasses and bottles, the other a good choice of new-fangled summer food which consisted of foreign bread, foreign vegetables, foreign cheeses and a selection of foreign cold meats too. Only the cold duck was English, as Trevor had wrung the neck of three Khaki Campbells and plucked them earlier that week.

The guests stood about on the lawn forming little archipelagos, as people usually do when assembled outside. There were only a few whom I recognised on sight. I had assumed beforehand that they would be mostly retired – old has-beens and the never-wozzers and the walking wounded, mixed in with the farmers or artists or gentle-landed who are the staples of provincial country life. In this I was only partially right, for the majority of these guests were obviously a much more motley crowd. Their midsummer clothing, like uniforms, flagged different age-groups and varied ways of life. Some were dressed for safari, whilst others wore Panama hats or looked like youthful lumberjacks. Several brought children including an eight-year-old girl with her parasol and a little boy who was going on to a fancy-dress party and decked out as a ladybird. The baby of the family sat on the grass and made friends with two of another guest's dogs. It also made friends with Virginia though she said it had only two words which were 'hot' and 'hello'. They sat and talked for five minutes, just saying 'hot' and 'hello' which isn't a bad summary of any party.

David Lacey was more detached than his wife. He didn't mingle but spent more of his time behind the white-linened table, passing glasses, dewy with condensation, from the barman to the guests. Virginia circulated, semi-attaching herself but never quite joining. I watched her move round. She was wearing a light-hearted bright pink blouse, her movements were vivid and sympathetically quick. I noticed the way the sun splintered around her curly hair, and the impulsive laughter, the responsive creasing of her face. I saw the way she colonised. Clusters of people stood about on the lawn, mingling and dissolving, but tightening into a knot around her. Now and then she put her hand on men and women's arms and leant forward. She seemed to touch them a lot. At one point I saw her go over to the border, snap off the head of a lily and lift its trumpet to her nose, then with a smile pass it to the man who was with her.

She didn't allow me to watch at the edge but brought people in irregular relays to meet me. I found myself talking to a woman with dark tragic looks and a gold tooth, then a man with his trousers tied up with string who was a potter, next a tax lawyer, James Barclay, who had a yacht at the coast, and, last, a noisier couple. The woman was stout and rumbustious, the husband pallid and thin. The wife who was grey-haired and called Penny, shouted a lot. She was very ebullient, the kind who would spill the beans. I wondered whether she had given her husband an ulcer. He was rubbing the heartburn area in a feeling way. In contrast to him, she was eating, popping vegetable fritters in quick succession into her mouth.

'So you are the creator,' she said to me, between morsels.

'How do you mean?'

'Virginia tells me that they have asked you to make Eden.'

I tried to curb this extravagance by doing a typically English job of evaporation. 'I rather wish she wouldn't put it quite like that. One tries one's best to make a nice thing of what one does, that's all.'

'Virginia is a great one for making silk purses,' said Penny. 'Just look at what she's done, for example, with David in the past couple of years.'

'Penny,' said her husband, Colin. He spoke in a rebuking way.

'Nothing wrong with that. I didn't say anything against it, did I? I have a lot of admiration for my neighbour.'

'So have I. For both of them,' I agreed. 'But what exactly did you mean?'

'Only that he was known to be quite a recluse. He and his sister. All that changed when Virginia came on the scene a few years ago.'

'Oh,' I said. 'I didn't know he had a sister in this part of the world. Is she here too?'

'I shouldn't think so,' said Penny looking round. 'No. Imo's never here. But she lives in that cottage on the top of the hill just over the river.'

'I've often thought,' said Simon the potter who had drifted back, 'that omissions at a party are every bit as interesting as those present.'

'She was widowed a few years ago,' said Penny. 'It seems very sad. Appalling luck really because it was so early. She has every excuse to be a recluse. But David had none. However, as I say, Virginia changed all that.'

'It's all go now,' said Colin. 'One takes one's hat off to Virginia. One gets the feeling she's making up for lost time.'

'All the same,' said his wife, 'we do wonder if she hasn't gone over the top with this project. You're being asked to fulfil a tall order, aren't you? Not that we don't envy it. We're all pop-eyed to see what you'll do.'

'It is terribly ambitious,' agreed the potter. 'Virginia says they'll give a large fireworks party in celebration when it's done.'

'Oh,' I said. I was surprised to find how delighted I was. 'I didn't know that.'

'It deserves it. The creation of Utopia.'

'I don't know about Utopia exactly,' said Colin. 'Dystopia more like it. Eden was doomed if you look at it objectively.'

'Oh, he's always such an awful old misery,' exclaimed his wife.

'Utopia or Dystopia, whichever you like, but it does come with an awful lot of baggage.'

'It seems to me it's a fable for the class system,' said James Barclay who had also joined us. 'Him on the ground, Sir up above, and them in the middle. The one trips them up, the other kicks them out. It's always the middle classes who get it in the neck.'

It was the kind of comment which is only uttered to strangers at a party but I joined in with the laughter. 'If you concentrate on the water, grass and trees, I promise you the people don't matter.'

'The woman matters all right,' said the potter. 'She may have played second fiddle to Adam in your case, but the earlier gardens of delight were always ruled by a female.'

'Like who?'

'That was a bit rash of me. I always go blank when I'm asked to elaborate. It's why I work with my hands.'

'Oh Simon,' exclaimed Penny. 'He's awfully sweet, isn't he?' she said, looking at me.

'Oh dear,' said the potter. 'If I'm going to be called sweet, I'll have to have a try. Well, I know that Hera, for example, ruled the Garden of the Hesperides. That, too, come to think of it, was guarded by a serpent. The serpent figure is actually a very old god.'

'Phallic, no doubt,' said James Barclay.

'Very obviously.'

'Absolutely no phallic symbols for this place,' said Lacey who, more relaxed now, had emerged from behind the table and come up with a bottle of wine. 'No obelisks. No totem poles. No serpents. No nothing. Anyone need their glass filling?'

Penny and James Barclay extended their arms. Lacey poured the wine, raising the bottle too high so splashing a little of the stream over the sides. The potter watched, withholding his goblet of lime juice in his large craftsman's hand.

'There was a very early belief,' said Penny, too noisily because it was her fourth glass, 'that menstruation starts when a female gets bitten by a snake.'

Another woman might have taken up this interesting titbit of sisterhood information and carried it further, but here it fell into male silence. The rest of us felt embarrassed and excluded, with nothing to say. A long, nonplussed pause ensued.

'Well, I suppose it doesn't take a genius to work out why,' said James Barclay eventually.

'No,' I agreed.

Nor could anyone else think of a follow-up they might add. We were suddenly subdued and stood sipping our drinks together, not really wanting to muse over our human inheritance. We were merely aquaintances, not brothers.

'Well, all I can say,' said Barclay, raising his glass to me 'and I really mean it, is the best of luck. Here's to a successful conclusion. When do you think it'll all be done?'

'The basics by the end of the year, I hope. Mind you, you always need to come back for the next few years and there are unpredictable elements so you may have to come back later still to check things are going as planned.'

'It seems rather speedy to me. I suppose you do everything by machines and computers these days.'

'The day of the human digger isn't past.'

'Presumably you've got a bank of ready professionals,' grunted Simon who produced pot after pot alone.

'Only three at the moment, and two of them are over there.' I indicated Trevor and Gavin who were huddled on the edge of the lawn awaiting their summons to dismantle the tables.

'Golly,' said Penny. 'Their usual handymen. Not exactly professionals, are they? Are you economising, David, you stony old skinflint, or what?'

'It's what Virginia wants.'

'They're very good,' I said, a bit annoyed. I felt suddenly protective about my committed and hard-working brood, even though they had been foisted on me. 'I couldn't have picked a better trio if I'd tried.'

'If they're willing diggers and nice to work with,' said Barclay, who was nothing if not an opportunist, 'I could do with them myself. You might make a garden for me when you've finished.'

'Maybe,' I said.

'Do you do gardens for anyone who asks?' enquired the potter. 'No, no,' he said to Barclay, who appeared somewhat affronted by being called anyone. 'I don't mean it that way. I mean,' and he looked back at me, 'I mean, in principle. Would you, for example, make a garden for someone you didn't like?'

'Do you refuse to sell pots to people you don't like?'

'That's different. It's a commodity, I'm afraid. I can't fool myself over that. But a garden's not the same. It's an extension of the receiver just as much as the maker.'

'Look,' I said, unwilling to get into an inventory of the clients I had refused because they were impossible to get on with, 'I am required to do a job. I do it.'

'Why not?' agreed Barclay. 'My God, you should see some of my clients. Do you think I like them?'

'Yours is a fiscal, not an artistic service,' said Colin fastidiously.

'Don't kid yourself,' replied Barclay. 'When it comes to gardens, we're talking investment and property. But that's beside the point. If a man is well paid and likes his job, and that job is useful and helpful, what else does he need for motivation?'

'My point is this,' persisted Simon. 'What if you felt they didn't actually deserve it? What if you'd been asked to make an Eden by someone else, by rotters?'

'You expect me to pass judgement?'

'We all do,' said Barclay.

'According to Jung,' I said, 'an appreciation of art or nature is one of the five or six things a man needs for a happy life. Who am I to deny the means of happiness?'

'What are the other things?' asked Lacey, who had not gone away but remained listening, with the bottle in hand.

'Oh, I'll tell you another time,' I offered.

'What is he going to tell you another time? What is he going to tell us in instalments?' asked Virginia who had just arrived. She looked flushed, her face plumped up. She fanned herself with her hand. 'I've drunk too much, I think,' she said. 'All I can now say is hot and hello like that baby.'

'You mustn't interrupt,' said Simon. 'He's about to tell us something important.'

'Mercy me. What's that?'

'The ingredients of a happy life.'

'Oh my,' she said. 'We all know that.'

'What is it?'

'The secret is to enjoy yourself. If you don't enjoy yourself, you might as well be dead, mightn't you? It's so simple, this first rule of life.'

'It's not actually what Jung said,' I replied. 'But I think you might be right. The rest is all flummery, isn't it.'

Later that afternoon I had to leave the party and drive home. I thought again of what Virginia had so confidently said. It grew dark on the last stage of the journey. In the dusk I turned on the car radio. There was a snatch of Roxy Music but as I was no longer young enough I didn't care to hear it out. On another station I caught one of Strauss's Last Songs. The stream of sweet, sublime, melancholy notes suffused the car. Before the music took over, I decided again that Virginia's judgement was right. For any civilised person, enjoying yourself was the first rule of life and you could dispense with the subtleties. Even Eden was often and rightly considered to be a state of mind.

8

THE FOLLOWING WEEK, as I watched my team of young workers, I was surprised to realise that I hadn't overpraised them at the party in the cause of their defence. Odds and ends some might call them, but all three were not only great enthusiasts but were proving very able. It was a bonus also that they were more compatible than expected. No one was jarring or silly or competitive and, when they worked, I found their silence soothing and, during breaks, their chatter fun.

It was clear from the start that both boys were in awe of Perry. Partly because of this but also in deference to her training, this last recruit was allowed to assume the role of boss. She was strong and bouncy, a generous-faced blonde in her mid-twenties with big thighs and hands which had pianist's thumbs, which is to say proper thumpers. She also had a tattoo at the top of her right arm, which peeped out of the shoulder edge of her sleeveless blouse. This remained undiscovered for a week until the weather warmed up, at which point she stripped off her jumper. For a while the two boys could look at little else.

'What's that?' asked Gavin. 'Is it the head of a snake?'

'Not a snake.'

'What is it then?'

'A lizard.'

'A wee lizard?'

'Not so wee. It's a lizard with a tail.'

'It's only the head Trev and me can see.'

'It's got a tail which is very long.'

There was a silence during which Gavin boggled. 'How long is its tail?'

'It goes down and down.'

Another silence. 'How far down?'

'Oh, very far down. Down and down and down and down.' Perry rolled her eyes.

'Down to –'

'Now, Gavin,' I said, though I too would have been quite interested to hear the answer, 'I think that's more than enough.'

Between these bursts of what amounted to office teasing, the three of them worked quietly and with great dedication. Right from the beginning, I had made the decision to involve them fully in all plans. I didn't want them to be just the labouring type who come in, pull up the weeds and go home. I wanted instead to treat them exactly as I would my usual team of core workers. This involved showing them the goal as well as the means to achieve it. They therefore had to be introduced to maps and sketches with detail as well as overall pattern. It was difficult and time-consuming but I knew it would be worth it. Only the highest expectations would enable me to extract the best from my trio. I had genuine confidence and no doubts about working them hard and for long hours.

I had decided to complete all the serious construction this summer, so now, like a battle commander, I was deploying my forces on all fronts, marking and staking and lopping and scooping in pursuit of the great aim. Trevor and Gavin, insured and decked out in safety harness and helmets, had been despatched to cut back the great hedges whilst Perry was helping me organise the excavation of the four-fold trenches along which the little rivers would run. For this purpose, three farm tractors led by a Caterpillar earth-moving machine had been hired. In the capable hands of Mr Arthur Trelleck, a man with a beer belly of noble size, it was likely the job would be completed in the course of a couple of weeks.

Its route, staked out by the two boys in advance, had been carefully planned to follow the contours of the land rather than man's imposed geometry. Trundling forward, the dragon ploughed its motorways of sinuous swathes. Forwards and downwards it went, sometimes with little excursions to the sides, pushing and smoothing the soil like butter, leaving in its wake wide banks of excavated soil which trickled in droplets into the troughs.

It was a most odd time, this, surrealist in intention, so prosaic in the doing: this river that went out of Eden to water the garden, from where it was parted and became four heads. Here, in the moody world of nature made by man, there were four long muddy craters that were only slowly filling up with water. Here, there were banks – great, intractable earth mounds – that would have to be iced with top soil. It was truly an act of faith to visualise their future. To imagine the running of the sweet clear water, the clothing of the sides with meadowsweet and irises and early-flowering petasites, the reflection of the trees dipping the tips of their branches into the liquid, with the kingfisher, a stranger, shy and turquoise, at the edge. As always a landscape gets turned into a garden by the mutual nourishment of the vision and the reality. It is true that I have travelled this process countless times, yet it never fails to stir me, for it is an inexhaustible source of imagination, this turning of the embryo into the dream of the client, into someone else's obsession that for a time must become mine.

The agreed original plan had been that the channels of water should divide the land into quarters that faced roughly north, south, east and west. This was being achieved with only a little adjustment. Every weekday, Mr Trelleck crammed his powerful body, with its stomach slung between its legs, into the cabin of the yellow Caterpillar and divided the universe according to instructions, down the north, east and west. But the route to the south was different, for it was here, in a natural declivity, that a pond on a large scale had been planned. Here that the channel would swell into a lake before being constricted into a runnel again that would lead it eventually to the river and from there to the ocean.

This area for the pool differed from the depression cradling the pond in the rhododendron wood on the north side of the island. That was black and intense with a vaulted ceiling of trees. This, its opposite, was a sun bowl. Here, it was hot and open to the sky. Gloriously secluded and peaceful, it was hemmed beyond with a belt of native trees. If flooded with water, it could be exploited to give fine reflections. It wanted only a little temple to make it one of Capability Brown's most charming prospects. Yet it was not quite a garden temple that I had in mind. Or, if it was, then I thought it would have to be a menagerie temple.

I left Mr Trelleck manoeuvring his machine round and round instead of up and down, and went in search of Virginia. I found her up at the house, on the wooden verandah, translating a court case from French into English, which was one of the legal specialisms she still practised. She was wearing a sun dress with straps, as green as grass, and sitting on the rocking chair. She had once explained that her rocking chair never failed to remind her of her Virginian childhood. When her mother and aunts and grandmother would rock to a rhythm in the wooden chairs and weave stories for each other on the tiled verandah, blue with morning glories.

She was rocking a little now, her head bent down, the dark hair bushing forward. Her arms were smooth and brown, her legs bare, flip-flops on her feet, one of which had fallen off. She looked up as I walked towards her and smiled and laid her pen on her lap beside Ciggy the cat, but continued rocking to the beat of her childhood world.

'How are the earthworks?' she asked.

'Very earthy at this stage but progressing.'

'It must be awfully hot for Arthur Trelleck.'

'He's taking a break. But it *is* hot where he's working. It's what I came to see you about.'

She looked enquiring. 'Is he getting sunstroke? Is that it? I love the heat. I still can't stick the English winter.'

'It's nothing to do with that. It's something that's come up. We've got to decide now. It'll affect what he's doing.'

She stopped rocking.

'He's started to dig out the pond, as you know. We were going to make it really deep for the diving-ducks. But I wonder now whether we couldn't have another as well that's much shallower.'

She pushed her mouth forward. I read this as the beginning of a protest.

'You know how warm it is there,' I repeated.

She nodded.

'And sheltered too.'

'Yes?'

'It encourages me to make a suggestion.'

'Yes?'

'I think you could keep flamingos.'

'What?'

'I am proposing flamingos.'

She stood up. The cat slid to the ground. The white-painted chair, suddenly vacated, rocked backwards and forwards on its own account with some violence. She threw out her left hand towards me in pleasure. 'Flamingos,' she said joyfully. She was laughing. 'How amazing. That was one thing I didn't think of.'

I noticed as always how white and prominent her teeth were. They gave her a French look, Creole perhaps, more Southern and wilder than Virginian. It was in these little ways, leaked rather than overt, she always seemed foreign.

'That would be too wonderful.' She added disbelievingly: 'Would they live here? I mean thrive?'

'Any could live here given measures of protection, Caribbean even. But Chilean flamingos would be best. You're almost frost-free and they are on the borderline of hardiness. But you ought to have the facility at least to have covered quarters for them, with heat lamps too. If only as a backstop in a hard damp winter. Were the pool to ice over, they could damage their legs. And in wet weather, their feathers can grow algae.'

'So it's possible?'

'Anything's possible, you see. You have given me a project where anything's possible.'

'Flamingos,' she said again with her lilt. 'Too wonderful.'

I felt quite excited myself. I had not gone to see her impulsively but had been mulling this over since early in the morning. Used to the process of powerful visualisation, I had seen the curved teardrop of the pool, the shallow rushed banks, grassy slopes, the emerald belt of trees and the warm melon pink of the stooping long-necked birds. It answered perfectly the blend of exotic and natural that we sought.

'You have to feed them, you know. And there are many necessities. They have to be set into a netted enclosure to protect them. And they're pretty expensive. And they live a long time. It's an obligation for you.'

'How expensive?'

I gave her a rough idea of the price.

She nodded slowly, pushing her mouth forward.

'How long do they live?'

'For ever.'

'Don't be silly,' she said. She was so happy it sounded more like a caress than dismissal.

'They are almost the longest lived of all birds.'

'I agree we would have to be obliged.'

'And then of course there's the correct daily feeding.'

After the initial rush, I had become noticeably more hesitant. I wondered whether I shouldn't discuss the matter with Lacey. Having launched the idea, I didn't want it to be shallowly embraced by the one, only to be rejected in depth by the other.

'Where is your husband?' I asked. 'Do you want to talk it over with him?'

'He's in London for a couple of days. He has a little sorting out to do.'

'I think we should wait for him to come back.'

'I thought you said Arthur's in the middle of it.'

'I could divert him. He can Caterpillar his way to somewhere else until you decide.'

'I have decided,' she said with some imperiousness.

This was somewhat disconcerting. In my experience, it is essential to get agreement from both employers, especially man and wife, unless a matter is trivial which this wasn't.

'It can wait a bit, can't it?' I offered. 'Why not wait? Isn't that better?'

'That's not what you said at the beginning. You said we've got to decide now. It'll affect what we're doing.'

I reminded myself that she had a legal brain, trained to remember the comments of a witness and return them to where they were of most use.

'Don't worry,' she said. 'It's a fantastic idea. He'll love it. It doesn't matter what extras it involves. Let's go ahead.'

Still I hesitated.

'*Das muss ein Mann mir sagen, eh'ich es glaube.* Is that it?'

I speak German not inadequately but was so startled that I was too slow to react and understand what she was saying.

'What?' I said, knowing from the tone of her voice that I was being mocked, not sure how.

'It's from Kleist, an old German writer. It means it's got to be a man who says something for it to be believed. Really, Robert. How exasperating of you. I am quite surprised. Do you want my agreement in writing?'

I felt wrong-footed and embarrassed enough to laugh. 'No. I'll go and tell Arthur.'

Walking back across the lawn, I tried to shrug this off. I thought that it should be an advantage that she was so decisive and that it was her business, after all, to deal with her absent husband and that in this case it was justified and might be again in future. Yet the niggle remained that I should have had the confidence to stick to my guns. I knew from personal experience how often inequity, even on a tiny stupid scale, was the Achilles heel in a marriage. I recalled how easily, for example, Louise used to become inflamed by minute losses of control, by not being involved in what she perceived should be joint decisions about areas of interest to both. 'You might have asked me,' was the least she would say. More frequent and haughty, to be uttered with a constrained posture, was: 'Is my opinion of no interest?' Sometimes, the bad times, it had provoked a river of rage: 'You just fucking well go and do things without consultation. I'm warning you, I'm going to cancel the agreement.' At which point we would have the mother of rows. Or later I would learn to walk out and leave her rowing at full pelt with herself.

Nor, if I were being honest with myself, was this only one-sided. I remembered that I too had not been immune from this syndrome myself. At the time I would have put this down to the weakness of a flaky marriage in which little fissures could crack into rifts. Yet I had learnt from my dealings with clients that such behaviour was too commonplace, too typical to be dismissed as over-reactions that were peculiar to our situation. How often I'd been told by a wife or a husband: 'I must ask the boss.' Though when the boss was asked, admittedly he or she usually said yes, no doubt because of the supplication. It is something, I suppose, to do with self-esteem and territoriality which goes deep: and it is for all these reasons that I have evolved my rule of thumb to secure agreement always from both my clients. A rule that I had effectively breached today.

Mulling this over, I made my way over the fields towards Arthur Trelleck. It was perfectly possible, of course, that my niggle was about nothing. Lacey would say: 'Flamingos. That's a wonderful idea. What I've always wanted.' Though that wasn't the point of course. They were extremely expensive and he might have wanted them even more if he'd been consulted.

Instead, the probability was high that he'd start frowning and blinking and grow stingy and careful. He'd fret about things like their quarters for winter and their daily ration of food. He'd say they were too costly, too much of a commitment and a liability. He'd even say, perhaps, that two light-headed Cavaliers had ganged up against the Puritan whose job it was to foot the bill.

It was hot as I walked over the fields and thinking about what I should or shouldn't have done made me feel even hotter. I stopped at one of the little trickling springs and cupped the crystalline water to my mouth for a long drink. The grass was flowering and drying beige and mauve in the sun. It was still and quiet, without the slightest ghost of a wind. The birds had fallen into their mid-day silence and, beyond, unseen, the noise of the Caterpillar and its retinue of tractors had ceased. Arthur Trelleck and his drivers must have stopped for their liquid lunch. Around him, the three men from the tractors would have formed a small gathering. Together in the heat they would be sharing their snooze, their stomachs pushing their white vests up, their belly buttons slowly rising and falling.

Far ahead, I could see little colour spots in the distance. The borzois tethered in the shade under a sweet chestnut tree and beside them Perry and the two boys eating sandwiches for lunch, which was their standard fare. Eating was clearly a mindless exercise for the brothers turned up with the same food every day. In three weeks there had not been a single change to the four big white rounds of sliced cheese and sweet pickle. Today wouldn't be any different. 'Don't you ever get bored?' Perry had asked yesterday as she ate a range of delicacies which included Waldorf salad. Apparently not. Either that or it was all that their grandmother, with whom they lived, was willing to prepare. Virginia had told me she was not some apple-faced old lady with a cottage-loaf style of hair. She was a dyed blonde with green eye-shadow and simply furious that her daughter had bolted, leaving her with the pair of sons.

Perry must have sensed this and in recent days had seemed to be taking over the role of their absent mother. Today her maternal instincts had expanded to include not only the boys but their borzois. She had appeared this morning with a pair of children's hats to protect the heads of the dogs from the strong sun. They were already decked out in her adornments when I arrived at the foot of my workmen's lunchtime tree. Beneath the brims, the dark almond-shaped eyes of the animals slid upwards. Their muzzles hung open and their tongues lolled sideways.

'Don't they look sweet?' exclaimed Perry.

'They're just suffering in silence if you ask me,' I said.

'I've written a poem,' said Gavin. 'Do you want to hear it?' He put down his sandwich and took from his pocket a piece of paper. Without a trace of self-consciousness he recited a verse of doggerel. Perry and I clapped appreciatively when he came to an end.

It occurred to me that, in all their strangeness, the brothers had evolved a partnership that resembled a marriage. It was a see-saw of compensations. All the words that eluded the big, handsome deaf-mute boy were gathered in and valued by Gavin instead. One of his jobs in life was to recycle words: back to his brother and out again to the world.

As I listened to the boy in the mid-day heat, with the borzois panting in sun-hats beside him, I stopped worrying about the Laceys and thought that I had done some peculiar jobs in the past, but nothing quite as idiosyncratic yet charming as this, the one where I found myself now, this oddity that was inducing me to break all my rules.

9

TWO DAYS LATER, there was a predictable hiccup when David
Lacey returned from London.

It was the evening and I was sitting on the deck of the boathouse
where I had now made myself at home. It was very simply but
comfortably furnished. It had a single bed with red check blankets,
a table and three wooden chairs, which was an oddly large number.
It reminded me of Thoreau at Walden with his one chair for solitude,
two for company and three for society, the latter scarcely to be
expected here. There was also a fridge in the corner and a three-
ringed cooker; and a loo and a shower unit in a cupboard. Water
and electricity had been connected here two years ago, presumably
at some expense. Virginia had told me that they intended the place
to be used as a holiday cottage at some time in the future, though
there was still much room for improvement.

I was spending on average about three nights a week here and the
rest of the time in Gloucestershire. The nights at the boathouse were
far more enjoyable. I would fall asleep, listening to the water slipping
and slapping against the banks. I felt so much a part of this liquid
world that, at the point of sleep, I seemed like a swimmer about to
dive into the river. In the early morning I would wake sometimes;
perhaps because the water had broken into a different tidal rhythm,
or if a small boat or a family of swans had splashed by, or, once,
hearing what I thought was a heron stabbing again and again at a
fish. Then the incident, whatever it was, would drift over, and I
would dip back again into my sleepy sub-aqueous world until the
day began.

This Thursday evening – it was just after seven o'clock – I was seated on the wooden deck, resting with my legs stretched out. It had been a physically very strenuous day. All the days were now. I wondered whether I didn't deserve a little restful recreation and was considering whether to buy a fly-fishing rod. There was a stream some miles to the north of here that was paradise for an angler: an idyll of water, trees, sunlight and shade. I had not in fact fished for years, not since I was a ten-year-old child, at my happiest messing around with maggots and flies. I still had a box of the latter at home: all the little bright feathery hooks, each of the flies bearing a different and special name. I thought I would dig them out of my attic and bring them back on my return. My interest had also been encouraged by finding a reprint of *The Compleat Angler or The Contemplative Man's Recreation* by Izaak Walton in a second-hand bookshop in Truro.

I got up to fetch this from the bedside, then went to the fridge and pulled out a can of lager. When I returned with the book and a glass to the decktop, I found that David Lacey had arrived in my absence and was waiting ill-at-ease.

I was not in the least surprised. You know when you have mis-played your hand and a reaction is inevitable. It is bound to come so the only question is when. It was not a good sign that my client had felt unable to wait until tomorrow.

'How nice to see you,' I said. 'I gathered from Virginia you were away. Can I offer you a lager? It's all I've got in the fridge.' I felt in a moderately ambiguous position. I was in their boathouse for which they were charging a peppercorn rent. And here I was role-playing host, and about, I just knew it, to be carpeted.

'I don't think I'll have a drink,' Lacey said. He stood there, showing a degree of indecisiveness, which was odd in someone who must have been in the grip of a decision to have walked almost a quarter of a mile across a couple of fields shortly after his return from London. But then, like many uncertain people, it was possible he could veer between stubbornness and wobble.

'You don't mind if I go ahead?' I asked, starting to drink from my glass. I gestured to the chair on the deck beside me, but the man remained standing and so compelled me to stay upright too. My back was aching and I longed to sit down again and relax.

'Have you just got back?' I asked, since he seemed to have difficulty knowing how to begin.

'About an hour ago.'

There was a silence.

'What can I do for you?' I asked in some desperation.

'It's about the flamingos.'

I nodded. 'Is there a problem?' I was irritated with myself for not having rehearsed quite how to handle this. I couldn't (nor would I be justified if I did so) make any rejoinder which could possibly put the responsibility on Virginia.

'It seems a rather expensive ambitious addition. But it's not that. I've got to know about these things. You went ahead in my absence.'

'It's entirely my fault,' I said. 'As you know, I did ask your wife, of course. She was unequivocally enthusiastic.' I did not add that she quoted Kleist at me which, in cold blood, did not seem quite as persuasive as it did at the time.

'She can get easily carried away.'

'I'm so sorry. The trouble was it had to be decided there and then. But I should have waited for you. It won't happen again.' I knew there was nothing for it but to go belly up on the ground in self-abasement. 'We can cancel the whole idea if you like.'

'What? Put the earth back into the crater? A costly operation.' Lacey gave a wry little twist. He had clearly been very miffed.

'Not expensive but would it be possible to look at the issue thoroughly before we take action?'

'Well,' he said. 'I suppose there's no harm in talking it over.'

'Let me explain,' I said. 'Let's go through it together and then you can decide. We'll do whatever you want.'

Desperate to draw my guest out from under the shadow of an insult, I fetched him a glass and put a can beside it, even though he had refused a drink earlier, and the two of us sat down side by side on the deck. I ran through the costs and the keeper's basic requirements. As I spoke I thought of all the to-ings and fro-ings that Capability Brown must have had with his clients. The parallels never changed through the ages. The landscape architect who was a master of the universe was also a servant to his master. There was bound to be a clash between the egos, between the one who spends the other's money and the other whose fortune is being spent.

I finished by saying: 'If I can recap, you've asked me to make a special, very special type of garden. To achieve this the composition

68

must have many dimensions, some of them exotic, some on a large scale. I'm not sure that a few ornamental ducks will do for the birds. In a place like this one needs a critical mass of a particular kind of beauty. And flamingos are the answer. I'll explain why in a moment. I promise, they'll be very beautiful indeed.'

As I said this, I knew I was starting to cast the line for the fish. The feather was on the hook, the fly on the water amongst the swirling currents. I knew how much I wanted to land the fish. I needed Lacey without reservation on my side.

'Look,' I said. I leant forward, twisting the glass in my hand. Below and beyond us, the river was swollen. It was running fast. Ribbons of reeds underwater were streaming flat on their backs.

'Look,' I repeated. 'The pastoral idyll hasn't changed in thousands of years. It isn't a modern idyll. It's ancient. It's always had trees, sunlight and shade, water and animals, though the forms of these things have been different in different ages. Now, you can have the modern version, with smart ducks and amazing sheep and so on, sure. OK. Fine. But I thought from what you said at the beginning you were after a much more poetic reality.'

I was keeping my eyes off Lacey, on the grounds that a man who must undergo a U-turn prefers not to be watched.

'My own feeling,' I continued, aiming for an easy conversational tone 'is that the interpretation of the animals is extremely important, and tricky in this case. It's a question of balancing costs and practicalities against the conveyance of different artistic moods. The supreme art of the possible if you like. Let me show you the map again and see what you think.'

I rose and went inside to fetch the copy of the overall plan. When I returned, Lacey was standing at the edge of the deck with his back towards me. He was looking up-river with his head lifted, his too-long hair touching the back of his collar. He seemed to be staring at the end of the white stone cottage just visible among the trees at some distance on the opposite mainland bank of the river. I had worked out that this was where his unsociable sister, Imogen, must live. I was concerned that he had been distracted.

'Here. Can you come and look?'

He turned round and came over.

'Here,' I said. 'Here's the north quarter of the island where the rhododendrons are. This is the part where we agreed we'd develop the shrubs and herbaceous flowers. Then, next, is the east, which is the quarter which contains the house. This is the south with its bird pool for wildfowl. Here is the spot I'd earmarked for the flamingos. And here' – I was pointing with the ruler – 'here is the western quarter. Right? Now, you thought of sheep here. This is where I'd like to suggest a little deer park. A fallow deer park.' I was moving on fast now, under my own power, not anticipating any obstruction. 'It'll have to have fencing and cattle grids but they won't show, especially if we put in a JCB to form a ha-ha. We can also cut windows in the surrounding hedges from which we can glimpse the deer. I promise you it'll be wonderful, like glimpsing gazelles.'

'Deer,' exclaimed David Lacey. 'Deer, is it? I come over about the birds. Now it's deer as well. Isn't this getting out of hand? We'd agreed on some pretty ornamental sheep for Virginia, hadn't we?' He was making upward thrusting movements with his chin like a man challenged.

I grimaced. 'I don't want it to look like a smallholding. Can I explain? Eden is about a state of grace which is lost. The wilder the creatures, the nearer one gets to conveying that the paradise has been re-found.'

I sensed a hesitancy had entered the man beside me. I needed to edge him into a willingness to be toppled.

'You don't need a lot of land for deer,' I urged. 'The minimum is five acres, though you have the space to give up much more. And you have the trees so I could make them a park. A park would be best. I'm not suggesting farming them. You'll just run into a load of nonsense from Brussels. Simply run them wild. They'll be classed as game.'

'What are you costing me?'

'Less than a conservatory. Less than a fancy wooden garage. They cost little to feed. In winter, give them hay and silage. A fallow doe might be £150 or £200. A buck £700. Start with a handful and they'll soon double.'

I leaned forward. I was suddenly desperate to persuade my client, and ached to convey the glory of wholeness and unity I had sought in private. How to find words that were adequate to support the pictures? Over the last couple of months I had strained my way towards them. To marry the genius of an idea with the genius of a place was sometimes elusive. For weeks, often, there would be this rift, this gap which seemed unbridgeable. Then suddenly the last piece of the puzzle would fall into place. It was intoxicating this moment, when it came, the sense of rightness. I had it now. It filled me with urgency and satisfaction.

'Over the years,' I said, 'I've learned to be strict with myself, to be ruthless with the materials. Sometimes, the simplest of statements are the most suggestive and evocative. It is a question, always, always, of finding the right subjects, the right ingredients, the right expression, blended as I've said out of the art of the possible. Texture, colour, volume, movement. You were in search of a golden age. Don't you see? How everything comes together? The golden pink of the flamingos in the southern quarter, the golden russet of the fallow deer to the west. Against the green of the grass and the trees. Think of the shapes, can you? The birds tall and very static, but the deer fleeting.'

The force of the picture in my head was an inebriation. In essence I was asking for a vision to be exchanged and shared. In practice I knew I was asking for money for its realisation. The endless battle between the artist and the patron which the artist must win.

'Perhaps,' I said, 'perhaps I haven't been clear.' I had a moment's doubt though I knew I was, had been, must surely have been both clear and cogent.

Then I thought, instinctively, that my faltering might not be a mistake. Sometimes when I had retreated before a man, a client, this show of submission had worked to advantage.

'What do you think?'

I waited with tension. It was still in the balance.

My client turned away. He seemed to look up again at the white cottage on the hillside. He hesitated and turned back.

'It's more than we agreed,' he said.

'These things evolve. The best things aren't always predictable.' I stood up. 'However, if you prefer, if Virginia prefers, we'll stick with the blueprint.'

'No good asking Virginia. She'll always agree. It's simple for her.'

The implication being, I thought, that it was difficult for him, but the concept of difficulty didn't make sense unless it was financial. In this case I would just have to give up as there was no answer. The commonsense of normal business practice was unalterable. It was not in the interest of the mad artist to succeed and bankrupt his patron. All the same, I was slightly puzzled.

'Well,' I said. 'There it is. Never mind.'

Lacey didn't seem to be listening. He gave the impression of someone having a struggle with himself.

I went to look at the water. I had made a pitch for my vision but it was now receding. I wondered whether I might take the boat out for a row, as a consolation. Then I was jolted by Lacey saying from behind me: 'OK. We'll do it. Let's go ahead.'

I was so affected that I did something which I thought afterwards was quite out of character. I went to my client and shook him by the hand. Despite normal business trade practice, I have always disliked and avoided shaking people by the hand. It is never a spontaneous gesture for me. Perhaps this is because my father and grandfather had been barristers and traditional barristers were bad at shaking hands because in the old days it was claimed that money might pass between their palms, so it was discouraged. Yet now, I found myself repeating, 'That really is very nice. I'm very happy. That's so nice,' and shaking and shaking the man's hand.

When I finally detached myself, we were both quite flushed and excited.

'Come on. Do have a drink,' I said. I was overjoyed. I felt that for the first time I had made a proper bond with the more reluctant of my two clients.

10

AFTER LACEY HAD left me to go back to the house, I went to pour out another glass of lager and returned to the deck. For the second time I also picked up the copy of *The Compleat Angler* which I noticed was dedicated to 'Mark from Grandad Bertie' in a wavery script. Settling back into my comfortable position again, I tried to concentrate on the conversation between the angler who was called Piscator and his companions. They too were sportsmen: a hunter, Venator, and Auceps, the falconer. It was clear that Walton had better things to do than tax himself about names.

It is an extraordinary book, full of vivid if debatable facts. It tells you that gloves made from the fur of the otter are the best fortification against the wet weather; and that the pigeon flies further for his breakfast than any other kind of bird, a fact that I would have been prepared to dispute with the author, as indeed the editor already had, claiming the record for the heron instead. It is good as a vigorous and amusing companion, and on any other evening I would have wanted to be told more about the Contemplative Man's Recreation. Yet now I felt restless even though only an hour ago I had been tired. Presumably it was due to the aftermath of the agreement with my client which had pumped me with energy.

I put the book down and stared out at the river and wondered whether to take a stroll along the bank. Then I decided it would be nicer instead to go for a row. So I put the book back on the shelf, and walked to the side of the deck and down the wooden stairs to look under the house where the dinghy was kept. I stepped over the dry ground and scanned the boat to check that it was in good order. It was probably some time since it had been used. It was clean and varnished and the oars clipped neatly to its sides. In stages I pulled it out to the bank, tied it to the post and slid it with a gentle splash into the water. I clambered inside. It rocked uneasily under the weight but stabilised as soon as I sat down after releasing the rope.

It had been some thirty years since I had rowed and it took a while before the rhythm of the oars fell into place. When it came, I recognised it as an old familiar, as you do with past habits. That easy transition when the blade no longer scatters the surface into uncoordinated chunks. When the water suddenly coalesces and offers resistance to the stroke of the oar. I had forgotten too how pleasant it was to be at the level of the water. To have a floater's view along its surface, to feel it ripple around. From this angle the banks reared hugely on either side. At their base the tree roots were mossy and slimy as if in some tropical forest. They dipped below the level of the river. A little more erosion, and one day at their leisure, they would drift languorously in.

Down river in the distance were the rusted hulks of the ships I had noticed on first arrival. They had not shifted, would never go to sea again. Perhaps they would always stay there like the relics of an old civilisation, slowly rot into the water and be dredged up by some busybody of an archaeologist in a couple of hundred years time. I wondered whether to row down to them but they were a mile away, which seemed too far for a first outing. I then considered rowing round the island but that was like going home rather than taking the fresh air of a proper excursion.

I thought I had better make my mind up pretty quickly about my destination as the boat was drifting in a slow circle, mirroring this indecision. I therefore resolved that, after I had practised rowing up river a little, I would make my way to the opposite bank which was less than a hundred yards distant.

It was still early evening but sunlight had long since been replaced by shade. It was shining golden down river where the land began to flatten out; but here where the valley cut deep, the sun soon disappeared. A river bird was repeating its harsh grating melancholy call. I couldn't name it, but recognised its guttural and throaty sound. The smell of the water was full and thick in my nostrils. It was part-animal, this scent, part-vegetable. Like being in a cavern of mushrooms. Everything around was deep green and blue. In this floater's world, you soon stopped noticing the sky. It was the depths that drew you in. They were dark and silky and tempted you further.

It was great fun, this rediscovery of childhood, but it was also surprising how quickly my arms grew tired. I pulled the oars in for a moment and rested, rocking quietly in the water, then put on a final spurt and reached the opposite bank. I lassoed the loop of the rope over the post there and stood up, uncertain whether to stay here for a bit or follow the path up the slope. It seemed more tempting to climb and view the island from the opposite side. The ascent would be steep but it would probably only take twenty minutes to the top and rather less down. In an hour I would be back at the boathouse, cooking a fresh trout which Gavin had brought me, then eating my dinner and turning the pages of old Izaak Walton, learning that you could use mulberries as bait for carp.

I started the climb. The hillside path was very winding, but this at least meant it was less steep than expected. Every few minutes I paused to look back at the island. As an architect, I wanted to view the pattern my land made, from a distance and, ideally, from above. As I climbed higher, it was less easy to see between the trees, but there were also some clearings which acted as windows and, as far as one could judge, I thought I was getting my design right. It looked beautiful, in fact, and very peaceful, shaded at the foot and lit at the top. Only the crest of the tree canopy was in sunlight. It seemed golden, almost autumnal this evening, though we had not passed beyond the middle of August.

Up to this point I had paid little attention to where the path led, having spent most of the walk looking back, so I was surprised now to reach practically the top. There was no more forest. The trees stopped abruptly. Now it was open and also in sun which mirrored what I had noticed on the opposite bank. In front of me lay a hedge, which was a boundary to some pasture beyond. The grass was scrawny and looked overgrazed. A group of sheep including this year's lambs glared out. The lambs ran to the udders and knocked them with their snouts for consolation. There were one or two bleats, and then, as I stepped forwards, a racket started up in the hedge. Leaning over to find the source, I caught sight of a frantic white wool rump. It was obvious that a full-grown ewe was jammed in the netting. Her efforts to free herself had served only to lock her in further.

I climbed over the fence netting at a point where the hedge was sparse and went over to help her. But it was hard to get a grip on this woolly bolster as she was greasy with lanolin and bucking as vigorously as a horse. There was no option. I would have to fetch the farmer who could cut the wire and let her out.

Wiping my palms on my trousers, I made for the other side of the field where I could see part of a building. But since only the roof and two upper windows were visible the field must slope down to the cottage in a hollow. I realised that, given its position, this must be the house of David Lacey's sister. The prospect of starting a conversation with her held little appeal. I had been given the feeling that she was a tiresome, intense sort of woman. Still, this was no more than a straightforward transaction.

The cottage was small and white-painted, not especially clean, with a row of marmalade sunflowers at its edge and a couple of apple trees in the garden. Their branches were low with ripened fruit and a stock lamb had broken in and was eating one of the windfalls on the ground. It was a big apple and the beast was having to yawn it in, like a snake eating a huge frog by unhinging its jaws. It was preoccupied with this and untroubled by me.

The back door of the cottage was open but I stepped in to knock on it all the same and gave a muted shout. The room was untidy, on the edge of chaotic. There seemed an accumulation of papers on every surface. They gave the impression of not having been sifted; some of the envelopes had not even been opened. I shouted again, more loudly this time. In response, a baritone dog began to bark in the distance. A second dog, much closer and higher-pitched, joined in. I decided to go round to the other side. There was another door to the house here, of stable-type design. The top half was open. Peering in, I was impressed by a large telescope mounted on a stand and tilted at an upwards angle. It was a proper machine, expensive and worthy of serious respect, certainly beyond the grasp of the usual amateur.

As I stood there in admiration, a woman with a terrier and a collie arrived. The collie was sand-coloured and had one blue eye. Distracted by this deformity, I could look at nothing else for a few seconds.

'Yes?' she said discouragingly.

I explained the problem. There was no doubt she was Lacey's sister. The resemblance was apparent, though she was quite a bit younger and not unattractive in a bony, tense kind of way. She had brown eyes and dark hair and a fringe and could once have been smart. She was not one of those tiresome ones as I had previously decided, but had an air of defiance. As I talked, she was using her gaze as a challenge, staring me out.

'Where's the ewe?' she asked.

'The other side of the field.'

'I'll get some wire netting and a pair of cutters. Come to the kitchen. I won't be a moment.'

She left and returned a few minutes later with a portion of netting which would be needed to mend the hole in the fence. She then walked over to the kitchen surface and, from the pile of papers produced the tool.

'Not a place for everything and everything in its place,' she muttered.

'I'm not surprised, if you manage all this by yourself,' I said, and was immediately annoyed because it revealed I knew who she was or at least that she was on her own. This would no longer be an impersonal visit.

'You seem to know who I am.'

I said reluctantly: 'I think you must be David Lacey's sister.'

'And you are the landscape designer, aren't you?'

'Right.' I wondered how she had recognised me.

We started to walk across the fields. The collie, who had managed to herd out the apple-eating lamb, ran wolfishly ahead. The terrier was bobbing like a little tug at her heels. After a silence, and to make conversation I said: 'That was a fine telescope you have.'

'Are you interested in these things?'

'As a boy, yes. I've forgotten all of it now, it's so many years since I've looked at the skies, and never through an instrument with the power of yours.'

'It's rather special. My husband was involved in astronomy and I've kept it up.'

By now we had reached the brow of the hill.

'There she is,' I said, pointing diagonally across to the left. The white buttocks of the ewe were still visible in the hedge, but they were no longer so busy. Sheep give up easily and she had grown dispirited with her efforts and resigned to her plight. But as we drew near her, she was frightened and provoked into struggling once more.

'These damned sheep,' said Lacey's sister, 'They're a lot of trouble but I like them.'

We stood quietly for a moment, assessing the ewe.

'If you can soothe her,' I said, 'I'll cut the wire.'

She started stroking the wool shoulder as though it belonged to a cat. The ewe shuddered and jerked. Her back feet had worn grooves in the ground. I squeezed the jaws of the wire-cutters together. The wire snapped. The ewe felt the sudden release of the grip. We had both anticipated she would spring forward and were grappling to push her backwards, our heads close together, hands criss-crossing like crabs in the effort.

The collie leaped over the hedge to the other side, blocking the ewe's passage. Faced with the devil of the milk-blue eye, the sheep retreated into our hands and ran off. We straightened up. Both of us were panting. I felt the ache from earlier in the evening re-lodge in my back. It didn't seem likely I'd be in a fit shape to row home.

'Christ,' I said. 'I've got to row back.'

Lacey's sister was bent over the fence, hooking the wire ends of her netting to patch up the hole. She looked up. She seemed anxious, even solicitous. At any rate, all former defiance was gone, though she still had this discomfiting habit of staring me out.

'Let me give you a drink or something. It was good of you to fetch me. I'm grateful.'

'Thanks but I've got to get back. It's getting late, I'll be rowing in the dark.'

'Can't I give you a drink another time? Feel free to call in. I really am grateful.'

I made lots of supportive nodding movements but didn't say yes. She was nicer than expected but, given her position, I felt the great male terror of getting involved. I wondered how to wriggle out of such an open-ended invitation.

'If you like, you could come by one evening and I'll show you the telescope. It's interesting.'

'Well,' I said, surprised but also quite taken. 'But I wouldn't want to put you to any trouble.'

'Have you ever seen Saturn?' she asked.

'Saturn?' I repeated. 'Can you really see it? Can you see the rings?'

'Oh yes. You can see the rings. It's very beautiful. Why don't you come by,' she paused, 'well, why not next week? The long-term forecast is clear. Drop in on Tuesday, or if it's cloudy I'll expect you Wednesday instead. Come about half-past eight. Is that all right?'

Captivated by now, I nodded and thanked her and walked off.

It was a quarter of an hour later and twilight when I stepped into the boat. It eased gently away from the bank. Upriver I could see three firefly lamps at intervals from some night fishermen. There was no suggestion from the shape of the figures whether they were merely old geezers or three contemplative men having a little recreation feeding ripe mulberries to the carp. Perhaps it was that stage of the evening when the one is transformed into the other.

I rowed quietly across the darkening surface of the water until I reached the boathouse.

11

FEELING SOMEWHAT GUILTY that I had not thanked my ex-wife for her help, I asked her out to dinner on Friday on my weekly journey home. Abi, my daughter, was also there, so I took them both which was unusual. It was normal for me to see either one or the other. It worked better that way. Three, I think, is the wrong number. It is the nuclear family which does not allow for a split. When the pack has been shuffled, it can so easily end up with two against one, rather than the original unit of three.

The restaurant was local and noisy and the choice of my daughter. A brasserie formerly, it had long since converted to Greek, with summer tables set out on the apron in the open air. We sat down outside and agreed on roast peppers and haloumi cheese as a starter, to be followed by rice with kebabs. Oxford was full of tourists and as we had chosen to eat alfresco, it was an idle diversion to watch them drift by. Most were city people with bare legs and traveller's baggage and temporary lives. They were restless and young. Australians with backpacks, a group of Japanese over half of whom wore specs, a pretty white girl kissing a black girl's neck. In a global world, how few seemed to want to drop any permanent anchor, even in gender. They were permanently in transit, on the edge, enjoying falling over.

I looked at my daughter and saw she could fit into this crowd with her strappy black tee-shirt and jeans the colour of maize. I thought she seemed sleepy and there was a spot under her fringe and she was running her nail-bitten fingers through the strands of her hair in an absent-minded kind of way. Had she been someone else's daughter, I would have said she looked as though she had been overdosing on sex. How displacing it was to find youth, especially one's children, taking over the areas that my generation had discovered and perfected. I recalled that my parents' generation, the original flappers, had often made a similar complaint about ours.

'Everybody is young now,' I said to Louise.

'We were young too. When I was sixteen, I used to wear a yellow tee-shirt which said "*Je m'appelle Brigitte. J'habite St Tropez. J'adore les copains, la grande vitesse*" – and a few other things I can't remember. Didn't I ever tell you?'

'Why Brigitte?' said Abi. 'Who's Brigitte?'

'Bardot,' Louise and I said together. We were both shocked.

'Oh her,' said Abi, losing interest.

I thought of all the past, all the popular culture, the art-house movies that Lou and I must have in common, even stuff that belonged to the era before we had married.

'What do you most associate with Jeanne Moreau?' I asked in sudden curiosity.

'What a weird question.'

'Go on. Just answer.'

'Umm,' said Louise, quite intrigued. Then she said: 'I think of her in *Les Amants* getting into a 2CV with her lover.'

She looked triumphant to have found an answer. I thought to myself, recalling the bedroom scene, that this was not the feature for which the film was best remembered.

'Right. And what do you remember from *A Bout de Souffle*?'

'Is that another film?' asked Abi.

'*A Bout de Souffle*? Belmondo running his thumb over his lip,' said Louise reflectively.

'Nothing else?'

'Jean Seberg clambering over Belmondo in her striped sweater and saying in her thin little American accent: "*Tu me dis que tu ne pouvais pas te passer de moi, mais je trouve que tu le peux très bien.*" I've never forgotten that.'

'There. You see how we're all filled with this popular culture. I find it extraordinary the way it becomes part of us,' I exclaimed. 'Shared toys.'

'Dad's always like this when he's in Oxford. I mean reminiscent,' said Abi.

'It's partly because I have to live in a bubble when I'm working. I'm living in a bubble now. I forget everything but the present. I forget the outside world. I like to join up when I come out.'

'The bubble factor,' said Louise. 'How's it going, your bubble?'

'Quite demanding. How's yours?'

'Getting better. I'm getting more accomplished.'

'She's really good,' said Abi. 'She showed me her latest painting. Don't underestimate my mother.'

'Tell me,' said Louise. 'How far have you got?'

I told her about the earthworks and Arthur Trelleck and how the boathouse got damp. I didn't say anything about the deer or the flamingos or the river-fishing. I kept quiet about Saturn which I knew she would love. I steered her away from anything glamorous or elegant or enviable or even different. I didn't want to hear the sarcastic profile return to her voice.

'As you know, these things are never romantic,' I said, 'and this one is harder graft than most.'

'Then it's not much of a bubble, is it?' said Abi.

I grimaced. 'It is, you know. Because I'm having to give them something that's different from all this.' I gestured to the people walking past. 'They're paying me to erase this kind of world.'

'Normal life in the normal world,' said Louise. 'Exactly the kind of life you like, Abi. That's what they're paying him to erase.'

'Is my life so horrible?' said Abi. She laughed. 'I think it's really nice.'

'Just how would you describe your kind of life?' I poured out the wine whilst she was thinking, then began to tuck into my starter. She was not a vivid girl, although we had hoped otherwise or we would not have called her Abigail, but I was genuinely interested to hear how she would describe it.

'Well. Lots of friends. Going to the movies. The job on the magazine.'

'Very suitably vague,' said Louise. 'And too many omissions. I'd be more specific. A new boyfriend every couple of months, it seems to me. Not all of them gainfully employed either. Emotional crises in the night. Going to work with bags under the eyes. Eating salad leaves instead of a proper meal.'

She sneezed suddenly. She was prone to hay fever, I recalled.

'You all right?' I said. I noticed her watering eyes.

'Fine.' She blew her nose. 'Anyway, that's my definition of our daughter's life.'

'Is your life any better?' said Abi. She turned her head aggressively towards her mother.

'Abi,' warned Louise.

I noticed their faces give and receive information. They were suddenly clannish and exclusive. Unexpectedly I could bump into this kind of rock. I wondered what was going on in Louise's life that I was not allowed to be privy to. Nothing too wonderful if it involved bags under the eyes. If the development was medium bad as opposed to significantly bad, I didn't think I really wanted to know.

It was always difficult parachuting like this into their lives. I wasn't indifferent, yet it looked synthetic if I offered sympathy about subjects I knew nothing about and would drop in ten minutes. Was it possible the fallow period was over and she had become involved with another, perhaps troublesome, man? Maybe she was no longer alone in her bed with only her books for company. I wondered who he was, but decided it would be wiser to change the subject.

'Anyway,' I said, 'I wasn't passing judgement on anybody's way of life. All I was saying was that I'm paid to give people order, stability and permanence. Materials that seem to be, generally speaking, in short supply in this age. And that's what makes it a bubble. See?'

'Oh, Robert dear,' said Louise. 'You of all people should know.' And I heard then what I always hated to hear. The old sarcasm behind the door.

'Yes, well,' I said. 'It's true that as a bad example, I'm probably the best person to bring order and permanence and stability into other people's lives. I know how difficult it is, don't I?'

The waitress, a jolie laide, perhaps an out-of-work actress, stylish enough anyway to suggest another life, arrived bearing three platefuls of kebabs. Louise handed these round. She spooned out the rice. She was Mother.

We ate for a few minutes in silence, twirling the skewers like toffee apples in order to get a grip and a bite. It was quite useful to have food that needed such concentration. From the neighbouring tables we caught scraps of different conversations.

'. . . is that a compliment or an insult?'

'. . . He was only appointed to the job because he's so bloody amazing at raising funds.'

'. . . in the civil service, of course, where looks are not a bar to promotion.'

It was nine o'clock. The fishermen would have settled down at the river. Some of them might stay all weekend. The thought of them took me away and gave comfort and roused a smile.

'Why are you smiling?' asked Abi.

'He's escaped to his bubble,' answered my ex-wife.

'When you were young,' I said to Abi, 'I did hope that when you grew up you'd want to join me in the business.'

'Of making bubbles?' She looked surprised.

'She might have,' said Louise. 'Had things turned out otherwise.'

'I wouldn't have wanted to,' said Abi. 'I want my freedom. A job I can leave tomorrow if I really want.'

Louise sighed. 'So she can go backpacking round the world. She's into risk, don't you realise?'

'You won't always want to do that,' I said. 'One day you'll grow up.'

'I'm grown up now.'

How old was she? I gave her birthday presents always but could not remember her age without working it out carefully. This wasn't a question that could be easily asked. Was she twenty-three or -two or -four? All I could remember was that she was born one year after I had gone independent.

'It doesn't matter how old you think you are,' I said. 'Age is about taking on commitments.'

'I'm not very good at things like that. Commitments mean just plodding along to fulfil them.'

'When you're really grown up, you'll realise that plodding along is all that anyone ever does,' said Louise.

'Oh,' I exclaimed. 'The plodders shall inherit the earth. With notably few exceptions, they always have.'

'I'm not like that.' Abi leant back on her wooden chair and stretched.

'Remember this. One has to be very beautiful or very clever or very lucky to be any different.'

She wrinkled her nose. 'I didn't turn up this evening to be lectured.'

'Sorry,' I said. 'I didn't really mean that.'

'Nor, might I add,' said Louise who had just emerged from a sneezing fit, 'is it very morale-boosting to tell your only daughter that she's not very beautiful or very clever.'

'Or even lucky,' said Abi.

'I didn't mean that either. I just meant – Oh, forget it.'

I pushed aside the plate. I felt terribly tired. Sensing a jolt, I looked up and then moved the leg of the chair out of the way of a red-faced diner who was pushing past. What I meant was – Oh, forget it. It was knickerbocker glory time. Daddy taking the family out.

'Shall we have pudding? Or do you just want coffee instead?'

Later that evening, I walked with my ex-wife and daughter back through the terraced streets of Osney to the house where I knew Abi would be staying the weekend.

'Back to the earthworks on Tuesday,' I said as I kissed them in turn on the cheek.

'Go on,' said Louise. 'Who are you trying to fool? It's all you ever wanted.'

I felt a rush of sympathy and, with it, denial. The evening had been imperfect as I could have predicted because it always was, and I wanted to put it right. I often felt a rush of fondness like this on the point of departure. Or was it, rather, relief that it was over and a sense of release?

'Not true. It's been good to see you. A nice family evening. We must do this more often.'

I wished them goodnight again and walked quickly away. I was aware that the two would be entering the house, more united than at the start of the evening. It must always be so when the three of us met. It was true too that their togetherness would make me its butt. They would be gobbling away at me; little pieces of me would be bitten off. My deficiencies as a husband and father would be most thoroughly explored.

As I drove home through the night, I thought it was sad that our marriage hadn't lasted. We might have hoped otherwise and should have tried harder. Instead we gave up. Abi must have been in her mid-teens when we finally parted. After this, there had been a period of two years when I had seen little of either. At least now I was regularly in touch. And if one evening was not perfect, the next evening six months later or so could put it right. Improvement depends by definition on there being another time.

More cheerful, I looked forward with pleasure to the inactivity of the weekend ahead. Apart from Saturday morning which was the only time one particular client was available for a meeting, I decided against doing any work. All I planned for tomorrow was supper with Alice as usual. I would spend the night there and maybe the first part of Sunday.

We both knew it was only sex and companionship and that the limits of the latter could not be tested too far. But this was no more than we agreed that we wanted. For both of us it was convenient and that was enough.

12

BACK ON THE job, I spent Tuesday on the new stages of the earthworks. The pool for the flamingos was gently scooped out and then teased into a natural shape by Mr Trelleck who had an artistry that his body belied. No more than forty-five centimetres deep, we made it for birds that spend their lives in estuaries or at the river's edge. Then the flexible Caterpillar drove east to its next task which was the making of the ha-ha at the edge of the deer park.

All day the machines went backwards and forwards, churning the earth into meaningful shapes. Like everything, nothing was as easy as it seemed. Curves and cambers and depths had to be weighed from all angles. Measurements, whether millimetres or hectares, were also most important. A landscape architect lives in a world where exactitude applies. It would be nice but false to think that you can rely solely on your eyes. The eye makes adjustments to the laws which are already there. Its art is to make it seem as though there are no laws at all.

I was so engrossed in directing my little operations that I almost forgot about the evening's appointment. Only once when I happened to look up at the bright lunchtime sky, did I remember that Saturn was waiting. I went and switched on the radio in my car to hear the weather forecast. It confirmed that the fine clear weather would last out the night, with mist developing only in the early morning and fog at the coast.

I wished the evening's visit weren't a social occasion. How much simpler if Lacey's sister were absent. I could just jog along to the end of the pier, put a penny in the slot and tilt the telescope in roughly the right direction. If I knew where that was. It might be a bit hit and miss. I might have to roam around, but surely the planet was recognisable when you came across it.

At the weekend I had read up what Galileo had to say about it. 'Saturn has an oblong appearance and is somewhat like an olive.' But then Galileo, whose weak telescope lacked the power to see it sharply, had got it wrong four hundred years ago. It seems he was mystified by its rings. It was left to his follower, a Dutchman called Huygens, to see the true nature of the pattern.

Now, as I looked at the toy Caterpillar on its toy mission, the absurdity of all this struck me. Here I was, the professional creator, making these patterns in the earth on an infinitesimal fragment of our planet and being paid good money to make them. Yet in the firmament above me, not actually visible now, there were all these beautiful ghosts – Mars, Jupiter, Mercury, Saturn – all making a mockery of my efforts. They made me no more than a hen scratching on the surface. Even my goal was illusory. I watched the roof of the yellow Caterpillar rise and fall above the top of the ha-ha it was ploughing. It was funny, even. Could anything be made to look sillier than a human being with pretensions?

Then I remembered that often on a big project I had sloughs and desponds of thought that ate the heart out of my work. I forgot these until the next time when they came around again. The trouble was that the doing of it was so hard. The materials so very raw. It took so long for the creation to be justified, longer than in any other art. Years and years, twenty, fifty of them, a century. Delayed results on this scale require a huge stretch of faith. How long had it taken before it became evident that Capability Brown had changed so much of the surface of his country? Yet unassuming, cheerful, asthmatic old Brown had gone about his business confidently. He hadn't been put off by Saturn. He hadn't been put off by anyone or anything. At Blenheim, he'd taken one look at Vanbrugh's bridge over the Glyme and flooded it up to the waist. Incredible audacity.

Feeling rather more buoyant, as I always did when I thought of Brown, I carried on. Why not just pretend I was working in another century? A bubble within a bubble was one answer.

At half past four the men stopped their tractors and pushed off home. Half-past eight to half-past four, the manual worker's normal day. Home for tea at five, for the usual fry-up. Their tractors were always left exactly where they had reached at the point the clock struck. Never neatly assembled in the corner. Half an hour later, the boys and Perry went. From now on, it was the custom for me to be left on my own.

I wandered around and checked that the areas were ready for the fencing to go up. In the distance I could see Virginia walking across. I hadn't seen her to talk to alone since the altercation with her husband. Five days had elapsed. Long enough for it not to be necessary to mention it now. She picked her way over the uneven, displaced soil and stood beside me on the bank above the ha-ha. I explained to her that it would be sown with grass. 'The fencing starts going up tomorrow,' I added.

'Good.' (She could put a swing into even a single word.) 'Good. The sooner the better.'

'They're going as fast as they can.'

There was a pause. Glancing at her, I saw she was changing tack.

She spoke hesitantly. 'I just wanted to say, I was glad you sorted it out with David. Maybe you were right. Maybe I should have waited. Not gone charging ahead.'

I wondered what had passed between them. 'Never mind. It's all settled now and there aren't any other big new decisions to come. Now it's just a matter of getting it done.'

'I didn't say anything at the beginning, because it didn't seem important. Or rather, it seemed important not to say anything. But the whole thing was my idea.'

'The idea of the garden?'

'Yes.'

I was surprised. 'But it was your husband who wrote to me. You seemed very much in it together.' And he out in front, I thought but did not say.

'Yes, well, I guess the letter was really mine. I'm an enthusiast. I carried him with me.'

'I see.'

'I just thought you should know now.'

'I'm glad you told me.'

'Don't get the wrong idea. He's keen now. You were terribly persuasive the other night. It was really good what you said.'

I frowned. I didn't like the implication that somehow Lacey was being manipulated by the pair of us. That, as a twosome, we would know how to manage him like a puppet from now on.

'It wasn't a question of being persuasive,' I said. 'I feel strongly about the worth of what I do.'

'I know you do. That's why I'm so enthusiastic.' Her face broke into one of her smiles. It was dazzling. Her dark eyes glowed with warmth and appreciation. 'I have complete faith in you. And we both think it will be wonderful.'

'It will.' I spoke with fresh conviction. I might have had self-doubts at lunchtime, but whenever my confidence is challenged it always returns.

'Anyway, what I really came to say was, if you're just going to be in the boat-house tonight, why don't you come over and have a meal with us. We'll celebrate.'

'That's a great idea but,' I paused, having to think quickly, 'it's a real pity, tonight's not a good night.' Unprepared, I couldn't immediately come up with an explanation, yet without it, I knew I would sound churlish.

'No?' she said, slightly discomfited.

'I'd love to, but the unfortunate thing is I've got to work on a proposal.'

I would have liked to say I was going out, but could not think of a plausible destination. The last thing I wanted was to lie. And why lie? What was wrong with the truth? It was perfectly acceptable, wasn't it? Why not just say I was popping over to see Imogen? Why not? It was ridiculous not to, yet strobes of warning flashed through my mind. Something cautioned me that in the matter of their relations, sides must have been taken up years ago, and that I might be deemed to be in contact with the wrong side. Somehow, I just knew, I would be judged to have gone out of bounds.

'I'd love to another night,' I said, trying to make progress. 'Do you think we could all have supper together later in the week?'

'Not this week. Next week of course.'

She had laughed again, but I knew that the spontaneity of celebrating the togetherness of our threesome was gone. We'd all have dinner together next week just to go over the plans.

After she had left, I walked back to the boat-house, thinking what a pity it was to miss an important chance. I could have kicked myself for not being open. But then, what excuse could I have offered? I just ran into Imogen and she said drop by, take a look at my favourite planet? The whole thing was absolutely bizarre. Or was it? If it had been a man who had given me access to his telescope, it would have been perfectly acceptable. Virginia was no ordinary woman. She was not prosaic, not in hock to a mundane world. She would have understood and been enthusiastic. The sole source of the trouble was the context of the offer. Fuck it, I thought. I rather wished now I weren't going. If I'd had easy access to a telephone, which I didn't of course at the boat-house, I would have been tempted to phone and put her off. This wasn't possible. Nor, for obvious reasons, could I ring her from the Laceys' house.

I thought that I had put himself in a foolish and unnecessary situation and hoped with some fervour that neither of my clients would find out that I had in effect lied. And that neither would catch sight of me rowing across the river tonight. 'The unfortunate thing is I've got to work on a proposal.' How stupid. How stupid not to stick to facts. Facts were at least neutral. You liked them or didn't like them. Lies in contrast were never acceptable. Yet the honest truth, and paradox, was that I had lied in order to please.

No doubt the root of this trouble lay in the ambiguity of my position. It was a sour thought. I like to fancy myself as a complete independent, never a lackey. And in a way this is true. Yet, in being on the pay roll, I am also a hired hand. Necessary and knowledgeable; even – and, whatever the advantage, this had often made me uncomfortable – a name to be courted, but also in some ways no more, no less than a domestic servant. The world I am hired to enter is my clients' world; a world I enter on their terms. And these terms of employment carry restrictions. The ceiling and walls of this world might be made of glass, but they are still there. And in this particular case, I had inadvertently broken a glass wall, and lied about it in order to please them.

Though intensely irritated with myself for having jumped into a hole of my own making, the thought also struck me that this was not a mistake old Brown would have made. I couldn't help smiling. Wasn't it Walpole who had implied he was free of the usual deference? No glass walls or ceiling for him. 'The moment a fashionable artist, singer or actor is insolent, his success is sure,' Walpole had written. 'The first peer that experiences it, laughs to conceal his being angry, the next flatters him for fear of being treated familiarly, and ten more bear it because it is so like Brown.'

So like Brown. Oh well. I would clear the air about this one another time. Meanwhile, there was no good reason not to enjoy myself.

At the boat-house, I put a bottle of wine in the fridge and went to take a shower. A toad had climbed into the room and was crouching at the bottom of the tray. Quite often this summer they had crawled in, presumably in search of the cool and the dark. This one was very beautiful with onyx and gold eyes. I carried it out and put it down at the foot of some reeds. It fumbled its way slowly in, beside a pair of damselflies engaged in their weightless coupling.

At a few minutes past eight I set out. I wrapped the bottle of wine in my jumper for protection and put it in the bottom of the boat, then began the row across the river. It seemed more routine this time. The rhythm came quickly though my thigh and arm muscles still ached a little from the previous week's effort. I thought it unlikely that I could be seen by either of my employers – after all, they were on the other side from the boat-house. If so, I no longer greatly cared.

I tied the boat to the same place as before by the bank and, clasping the bottle, walked up the hill. It was an obstacle course, all right. Over the fence and across the field, eddies of sheep skittering away to leave me a path. As I neared the cottage, I could see that the telescope had been mounted full of purpose outside. It was tilted, I thought, towards the south-east. The sun had already set. The horizon was a thin duck-egg blue, transparent. Layers of thickened darkness were pushing it down. The eternal slow-motion vertiginous spinning was showing itself in colour as it did every night and one never noticed. Your job is to leave your mark on the ground.

I walked up to the open door, bottle in hand. Imogen was visible at the back of the kitchen. She hadn't heard me arrive. I realised that officially I didn't know her name because she had not introduced herself. Nor did I have any idea of her surname.

'Imogen,' I said hesitantly.

She turned round. She looked pleased, or rather relieved. 'I thought you might have forgotten.'

I went in and put the bottle straight onto the table, not wanting to make an occasion out of it.

'Thanks. Thanks a lot.'

I stood watching her. 'How's the ewe?' I asked, for want of anything else occurring.

'She's fine. No ill effects. What about you?'

'The only ache comes from unaccustomed rowing, I think.'

'Better that than going the long way round by car.'

'Much better. Anyway, there aren't many places left where you can go as the crow flies. Or swims, as in this case.' I paused. 'Which way do you choose when you visit your brother?'

She was busy tossing a bowl of basic salad, which is to say green, not the lurid assortment that is deemed smart. 'Oh. Well. He tends to come here. When he gets the chance, that is.'

'By boat?' I forgot Virginia had said he didn't row.

'No, actually. He's not a swimmer, so that's a deterrent. He prefers to make the trip round by car, though it's not often.'

She put the bowl of salad on top of two dinner plates and set these on a tray. She added some cold meat which looked like lamb, appropriately enough, and some roughly-cut chunks of bread.

'There. I thought we'd have a bite to eat outside. See the sky come out. Do you want to carry the tray?'

I picked it up and carried it out to the wood table on the paving outside. Then, as she appeared to have overlooked my bottle of wine, went back into the kitchen.

'Do you have a corkscrew and glasses?'

She pointed to a drawer and took a pair of glasses off the dresser.

The place looked as chaotic as the last time I had come, but it was a good sign that she hadn't tidied it up. Nor herself, for that matter. She was wearing an old white shirt and fawn jeans. I had been on the brink of saying at any opportune moment that I hoped she hadn't gone to any trouble, but it was very evidently superfluous.

'Okay?' she asked. 'Got everything you need?'

We sat down. I pulled the cork and poured us each a glass of wine. We began to eat. It was a very obvious question but I asked her if it was her own lamb. It was certainly tender.

'No point in keeping them if you don't eat them,' she said matter-of-factly. 'And they don't have names, so it's not as if I feel like a cannibal.' She took a mouthful. 'Anyway, I can't afford not to eat them.'

This was blunter than I had expected or really wanted. 'How long have you had them?'

'If you include the time at the house, six years.'

'What house?'

She looked up surprised. 'Water End.'

'Water End? I didn't know you lived there.' I put down the fork.

'They didn't mention it?'

'No. Nothing like that.'

'Well. There you are.' She spoke flatly.

'You lived there before you came here?'

'After my husband died. Or didn't you know about that either?' She stared at me, dominating with those brown eyes.

I flushed slightly. 'I think it was mentioned.'

'It was mentioned.' She echoed my cautious neutrality exactly.

'I'm sorry. I knew nothing about your living in the house. I hope I haven't blundered.'

'Don't worry. And I certainly didn't invite you here to talk about myself.'

'Perhaps I might make fewer blunders if I were better informed.'

She looked away as though this might be a worthy point to consider. Then seemed to reject it as she passed me the bowl of salad, telling me to help myself. She now drew a deep breath, indicating she had decided to launch into an explanation.

'Just for the record, after my husband died, David suggested I leave London and come to live at Water End, which he'd bought a few years before. Then various events happened. Virginia came on the scene. I moved here. That's all.'

So she had been moved on. That went some way to explaining the prickly relations. I leant forward and topped up her glass of wine. I cast around for a question to ask which would not cause further disturbance.

'And you run this farm by yourself?'

She nodded. 'In spring it's exhausting. It's okay now. The ram will go in soon, probably in a few weeks. Busier for him than for me.'

'Where does the telescope fit in?'

She turned her head sideways to look at the instrument, which gave me a chance to examine her profile. She had a spiky face, but intelligent, with a slightly more prominent chin than is usually considered feminine. I placed her in her mid-forties. Superficially a very different type from her sister-in-law with her easy, hospitable southern charm. Yet this was a contrast merely in style. Both women gave the impression of being dominant and resourceful types. It occurred to me that such a situation was fraught with the potential for a clash.

'My husband was a radio astronomer.'

'The telescope was his?'

'He left me a legacy of the stars.'

This was nice. I smiled. 'A good legacy.'

'He used to say it was the original spectator sport.'

I laughed, though she had said it quite seriously.

'Just look,' she said.

We were sitting in a triangle of light thrown through the open kitchen door, but she was drawing my attention to the darkness that was gathering weight beyond us. The sky was indigo. It was amazingly clear.

'August is a good time,' she said. 'Masses of meteors. The Northern Cross. And then Saturn. The most beautiful, beautiful thing in the world.'

'It's not in the world.'

'Once you've seen it, you'll know that it is.'

'Where is it?'

'Out there.' She pointed. 'In the south-south-east.'

I took out my spectacles. 'My sight isn't very good.'

'You're not looking in the right place. And it's pointless. Even with binoculars you can only see its shape faintly. We'll use the telescope in a minute. There's no hurry.'

'I can't wait.'

'There's no hurry,' she said again. 'It takes nearly thirty years to orbit the sun. It is terribly slow moving. Almost static in Aquarius now.'

I stood up and adjusted my spectacles to stare at the sky.

'Where's the Great Bear?' I asked, seeking the familiarity of a childhood landmark which could lead me by the hand.

'Behind you. Very low on the horizon. Hold on, I'll put out the lights.'

Imogen rose, went back to the kitchen and switched off the lamp. She returned and stood by my side. We were now in full darkness. It was a warm night yet I could feel the extra breath of her heat.

'Let's start from what you already know. Follow the line of my finger. Up from the Great Bear to Ursa Minor and Draco. It's a long straggling figure, very faint. See?'

'What is Draco?'

'He figures in several legends. A sea monster in one. In another, the serpent or dragon who guarded the Garden of the Hesperides with its golden apples.'

As she spoke, I recalled Simon the potter saying that this had been one of the mythical gardens ruled by a woman, by Hera, and guarded by a serpent. It gave one the impression that the old world was more of a continuum than the modern cosmos that replaced it.

'Are you watching me? Now come up. Still in a straight line. Okay?' Imogen looked at me to check I was able to follow. 'No. *there*.' She took my arm and pointed it in the right direction.

'Now *that* is the Northern Cross. Cygnus the swan flying across the sky and, nearby, steel-blue Vega.'

'Steel-blue? Yes. I see.'

She let go of me. 'The stars are different colours. They're like, oh, like sequins. If I showed you a photo of them, truly you'd see what they're like. Blue, lilac, pink, lemon, cream. All against the indigo.'

I stared at her in astonishment, then dropped my arm which was aching.

'Nothing is static,' she said with a fervent emphasis. 'I promise you, we live in a forest of stars and nothing is static. They grow and decline.'

'Like all matter.'

'Like all matter. And some grow fat by gobbling others.'

'Like us.'

'Very like us. Now, are you ready to see Saturn?'

'I am.'

'I didn't show you it first because you needed a context in which to see it. Can you bring over the chair to the telescope?'

I pulled out the chair on which I'd been sitting, noticing that neither of us had finished our wine, and placed it beside the instrument. She sat down and moved the tube slightly, appearing to make some adjustments.

I looked upwards again. It was an almost tropical summer night. Fine, soft and clear, dark blue through the leafy stems of the apple tree. Star-aware now, I saw clusters caught in the tops of its branches. A few were grazing the limb of the moon. I was beginning to see the forest, and trace the mass and clearings of its pattern. It struck me again that, with my way of life, I always looked down or out to the horizon. Never upwards. Never at the context. Never at the larger forest.

Imogen stood up to make way for me. 'There. Sorry I was a bit slow. The atmosphere is unsteady. Air currents can be so turbulent that sometimes the image seems to jump around.'

I sat down, took off my spectacles and put my right eye to the viewer. The search was confusing. 'I can't see it,' I said despairing. 'Wait,' she said. She came back, checked and made a second adjustment. I tried again. This time the picture was waiting. This most beautiful thing in the world. The milky celestial sphere swimming across the sky with its girdle of moon rings. I could not, for a moment, quite believe it. How clear it was, how solid, how shockingly real. I could have stretched out an arm and plucked it like an apple from the end of the telescope.

'It's so very beautiful,' I said. It was the kind of sight you devour. You cannot stop looking at it.

'See how its rings are tilted only slightly towards us. Next year they will be edge on. A few years more and they will flatten out to our view.'

'My God, it's jumping.'

'Those are the air currents I mentioned.'

I took my eye away from the lens. The intensity of the vision was tiring, but like an after-image it remained on the iris. I rubbed my eyes.

'That's enough for one evening,' said Imogen. 'But at this time, this year, it's visible all night. Sometimes, if I can't sleep, I get up and look at him floating in the sky.'

I stood up and stretched. 'Imogen, I am very grateful to you for showing me. I can't say I expected anything quite like this.'

'It's not imaginable, is it? But now you've seen it, wasn't I right?'

'About what?'

'About it being in the world. Your world now.'

'You were right. A bit too right, actually. It makes me think all I am is a groundsman.'

'Oh no.' She puckered her sharp features together to show sympathy. 'Don't say that. You're wrong to say that.'

'Just a manner of speaking. An exaggeration anyway.' I moved away a fraction to break the moment.

'This was very kind of you,' I said more formally. 'To pass on your legacy, as it were.'

'I don't usually.'

'Don't you show your brother?'

'No longer. Not for ages.'

'No?'

'His wife isn't very interested in this kind of thing,' she said dismissively.

'I would have thought she was.'

'How would you know?'

I shook my head and frowned in the dark. This was not the kind of talk one wanted. 'I don't. Really I don't.'

From the other side of the house, the deep-voiced collie gave a series of abrupt barks. There was the sound of a chain rattling.

'Rabbits probably,' said Imogen.

It seemed an opportune interruption to me. 'Well,' I said, 'I don't know what the time is but I suppose I ought to be getting back. It won't be too easy to climb down in the dark.'

'Don't you have a torch?'

'No. I forgot. Pretty stupid. I got the wine but no, not the torch.' My voice tailed off as I didn't want to draw attention to my offering again. Nor, I realised, did I want to invite the loan of her torch.

'Hang on.'

'No need,' I called out as she moved away, knowing she would now lend me hers.

The triangle of light flooded back as she returned to the kitchen and pressed the switch.

I stood in silence. I felt a little impractical and foolish at having forgotten my torch. Nor did I want to make a return visit so soon to hand hers back.

She came back again and handed me a large heavy flashlight. 'My lambing torch. Bring it back some time.'

'Really. There's no need.' I began to back off.

'Don't be silly. You could fall.'

As this was true, I stopped protesting, thanked her, nodded, repeated my thanks for the evening's demonstration, then left.

The warmth held in the earth from a full day's sun released itself and rose against my legs in the darkness as I walked back across the fields. There were thuds and rustlings as the sheep heaved themselves up and out of the way, some panicky, others, more mature, sighing heavily at this interruption to their cudding. A few sheep faces caught in the lamplight looked the colour of bone. I clambered down the hillside, nearly tripping once, and grateful therefore for the guidance of the light. Stepping cautiously now, I reached the bottom and climbed into the boat. There was a startled screech from a bird and a plop nearby as some small animal dived into the water.

As I rowed across, I thought that the apparent self-sufficiency of Imogen was akin to actively-managed loneliness. 'My lambing torch.' Awake and all alone with her sheep. Awake and sleepless, looking at Saturn. It made me aware of the difference between us. I know that I am genuinely self-sufficient; and, because of this, I wasn't easily deceived by its look-alike and recognised the contrast, that underneath she was genuinely lonely. I realised too that it was this that I was wary of. Loneliness has needs which can be triggered very easily. I didn't intend to trip them. I would indeed return the torch as soon as possible, but in daylight this time. It was a pity. It was also ungracious. She had shown me the most beautiful thing in the world, that once seen could never be forgotten. I knew I would need to see it again. Luminous Saturn in Aquarius on his slow calm voyage towards Pisces.

I stopped rowing for a moment, let the boat drift silently on the water and looked up at the sky forest of stars, named after divinities, expanding and contracting and gobbling each other up. I noticed the dark hulks of the tree forests on the slopes of the banks to either side. They were a reminder of the trees I would plant this winter. Constellations of trees, quincunxes of willow oaks and belts of pine, rowans with fat Chinese berries, red stars, ground forests reflecting sky forests. I allowed the boat to float on for a few moments, savouring the water pleasure, then continued to row to my own bank. I made a decision that I would mention this visit to Imogen when I had dinner with my clients, just casually and in passing. Better to control this minor information than just let it ride.

13

THERE ARE RESOLUTIONS that one makes in private which simply cannot be enacted. It is not a question of lack of will but lack of opportunity. I had decided to mention my meeting with Imogen to the Laceys over dinner the following week but their conversation concerned only the plans. During the meal they discussed exclusively the map of events for the rest of the year. In this context, to come out with the fact that, by the way, I'd met Imogen would have seemed peculiar and disruptive. I decided to wait. A better opportunity was bound to occur.

The weather had broken and it was raining heavily. The pools and rills had filled up. The narrow rivers which had been diverted and dug were rattling away in their courses. All liquid areas were now in working order, though, after the rain had stopped, they would have to be checked for leaks. Then, assuming there were no problems, the sequence of autumn arrivals would be the flamingos, followed by the deer, and finally in the late autumn, after leaf-fall, the main planting of the trees.

As we ate I ran through the arrangements of this sequence with my clients. We were sitting in the kitchen with its faded terracotta-orange walls, matt and slightly cracked like the paint on a Neapolitan villa. We had thick watercress soup to start with and then a salad with big pink prawns and baby squid and last a puree of peaches and mangos. No butter, no cream, no cheese, no biscuits, no fat. I thought wistfully of Imogen's freezer of homely, home-reared lamb chops. We talked about Gavin and Trevor and Trelleck, then ignored all the people and talked only of the plans. There were no problems and, at the end of it all, I was also relieved to have finally persuaded

Virginia against any representation of a tree of knowledge. I reiterated my favourite theory that gardens reinvent themselves from one generation to the next, let alone after a hundred thousand years, and have to put on a different uniform.

'I urge you to forget it,' I told her. 'This will only work if it's understated. Don't press the illusion. This place will be lovely enough to tell its own story.'

Lacey, whose natural inclination was, as I now knew well, to say no to everything, supported me.

'Let's say it's every tree and no tree,' I continued. 'Let's say it's that old mulberry, or the grove of Sorbus sargentiana that will go in this November, or the sweet chestnut, or even that ash that's near the flamingo pool. It's an idea that works best without a single representative.'

'I've no doubt he's right,' Lacey said for the second time to Virginia. He leant forward, blinking.

She was still doubtful, glum even.

'The greatest mistake is to try and crystallise things.' I spoke slowly, to press the words in. 'Shall I tell you what always has the most haunting effect? It's things you see and don't see. Things beyond your grasp.'

This struck home. They both nodded. It is always satisfying to reach a sympathetic agreement with people who trust you. You have helped them understand.

'Let's celebrate,' said Virginia.

'I know,' said Lacey. 'I've got just the thing for a celebration.' He rose and walked out of the room. He was not an inelegant man, slim and tall, though from the rear I noticed, as always, the hair that hung over his collar. I wished he would cut it.

'What's he up to?' asked Virginia smiling.

'He must have a secret.'

'Then he's managed to keep it from me.'

In Lacey's absence and at the word secret, I wondered for a moment about mentioning his sister, but Virginia carried on talking. She was asking me about Perry, whose name I had now found out was Maureen Perry.

'Good, isn't she?'

'She's good. Knows her stuff.'

'Her father's a farmer. I'm not sure he can read or write but he's brilliant. See him at market and you'll know why. He buys cattle without movement or sound. No one sees how he does it but at the end of the bidding he's acquired them. Quite a gift. We used to see this with the farmers back home when I was little. My grandmother –'

She broke off as Lacey came back into the room.

'Look at this.' He held out a bottle to us under the lamp over the kitchen table. 'Port. See? 1942. It was in the cellar. It was left over from my father's belongings.'

'Mercy me,' said Virginia whose Southern accent had deepened during her reminiscences. 'That old bottle of wine. You clever thing. I'd forgotten you had it.'

'It's a bit black under this light,' said Lacey. 'Isn't it? Too black?'

We all looked at it with mingled awe and suspicion. There was a dark sediment of grit at the bottom of the bottle.

'My God. Is it going to kill us? What do you think?' asked Lacey.

'Best way to go,' said Virginia.

The cork had been sealed with wax. Lacey got a skewer and chipped it off. The translucent white crumbs scattered all over the table, all over the plates on which we had eaten the fatless pudding to which we were doomed by his diet. Lacey drew the cork gingerly. The wartime stopper glided out unbroken. We exchanged glances of admiration for the human spirit and the way grapes had continued to be pressed and good corks had been well made and put in bottles whilst the convoys and wolf-packs pulped each other to death in the Atlantic. Now, fifty years later, in peacetime, and planning that most peaceful of constructions, a garden, that is in itself a mark of a stable society, we were about to drink this leftover wine of war.

'Funny, isn't it?' said Lacey. 'What a time warp.'

'It's a time capsule,' I said, 'dug up half a century later.'

'I wasn't born then,' said Virginia. 'How strange to think it's older than I am. Maybe better preserved too, I guess.'

She watched Lacey pour an inch of the wine into his glass, swill it up and down a little and sniff it. He passed it round. We all inhaled.

'Why didn't your father ever get around to drinking it?' asked Virginia.

'When you've got a cellar, you don't just work your way through it like a fridge,' he protested.

'Why haven't you drunk it before?' I asked.

'I haven't had anything to celebrate.'

'Oh David. What about me?' Virginia put a hand out to him.

He took it and held it. His face smoothed. 'You. Yes. You, always.'

'Let's drink to Virginia,' I suggested. I was suddenly very touched by the little demonstration. Yet the warmth and brightness also brought its shadow to me. I felt momentarily very unmarried and missed it.

Virginia took her hand away and put it to her glass.

We each sipped gingerly, then more boldly.

'Despite the grit, not bad, is it?' said Lacey.

'Not as sweet as it usually is. Better for that.'

Virginia leant forwards. 'I'll put this in my diary. You know I'm keeping a diary of this year a bit like the one I showed you?'

'I remember. "Mother poorly. I planted six rhododendrons. Mother poorly. The boys lifted the banana trees. Mother poorly."'

She giggled. 'Poor mother. Yes. But my diary's not like that.'

'What's your diary say?'

'Things like . . .' She sat back, thinking. Her dark hair was drawn up into a bushy cobby pony-tail, youthful but not inappropriate. 'Well, this for example. "One of those perfect golden summer days. The kind of day when everyone's face looks golden. Sat on verandah with Ciggy on lap working on the translation. Robert came, suggested flamingos for lower pool. Imagine. Flamingos."'

'David very poorly,' said Lacey quietly.

She turned her head and laughed, put out her hand again.

'Not in my diary. It's censored.'

'Not much of a diary,' I said.

'It is. Tonight I'll write. Let's see. "He says all hedges have been trimmed. Ha-ha sown with grass. Rivers flowing. Opened 1942 bottle of port to celebrate our goose being turned into swan."'

'Tell him what you wrote the first time he came,' said Lacey.

'Shall I?'

'Yes,' I said.

She pushed forward her mouth, remembering. She closed her lids. The light removed the rich shadows in their hoods. '"The landscape architect turned up. The Name we want. Cautious but darling. So English. We told him about scheme. Thinks I'm a nutter."' She opened her eyes suddenly and looked at me. 'You did, didn't you. Some kind of fundamentalist Bible-belt nutter.'

'Never,' I protested. 'Very forceful is what I would have said.'

'That begs the question.'

'What she wants, she gets,' said Lacey.

'I know.' I remembered the power with which she had dismissed my hesitation after I had proposed the flamingos. The look of amused disdain as she had quoted me the line from Kleist. I wished I had found out more about this writer.

'You thought I was a nutter,' she was reiterating. 'And probably a bit vulgar too.'

'No, never,' I said again.

'Yes. You English of your age group,' she exclaimed. 'So correct. So contained. We Americans know you have taste but, Lord, such suffocating containment. To think I've spent all my adult life among you.'

'How so?'

'My first husband was also English, a cardiologist. I came here over twenty years ago. Just think. More than twenty years of cold winters and white skins. No warmth and not enough black faces.'

'She gets like this sometimes,' said Lacey.

'When she's drenched in 1942 port,' said Virginia.

'When she's gin-sodden and drenched in 1942 port. I tell her to cheer up and go to Brixton.'

'No flamingos there,' I said. I shifted heavily in my chair. I noticed that a third of the bottle of port had been drunk. Not much by Lacey, not much by me, but the old rich wartime taste was still coating the inside of my mouth. I had begun to feel sleepy. I felt close to them too.

We were clannish together that evening. Quite a trio, and I therefore found no opportunity to mention Imogen, the outsider. It was a bit sad really. Us together and she alone whilst we cracked open her father's 1942 bottle of wine. Still, I've had to accept the paradox over the years that whilst other people's relationships are no business of mine, those of my clients most definitely are, because I have to adopt them.

14

A MONTH OR so passed. I was terribly busy at this stage and my life returned to something of its former pattern. Time on the island became patchy and fragmented. I spent many hours instead going up and down motorways and on a trip, once, to Paris where Tim, who had handled the project in my absence, needed approval for the last stages of the Japanese garden. The day of my visit was unseasonably warm. The sun hit the stone walls of the courtyards, and the heat piled up in the enclosure. We stood in a furnace. I thought with longing of the dankness of my island; of its everglades of hanging trees; of the fish dimpling the surface of the water. I swore that never again would I do one of these rigorous Japanese exercises in gravel. Not now that I had made my escape to Eden, as even I was now beginning to call it.

Yet it was not until the late autumn that my life stabilised and I managed to return. It was at the end of October, near the time when I knew the flamingos would arrive. Such out-of-the-ordinary experiences are fragile and unforgettable. How to describe it? Buying unusual and exquisite birds isn't like picking your average guinea pig from a pet shop. It is a moment of privilege and responsibility. You are in love and you feel humble and a little unworthy of this object of awe. You fear that this delicate and wayward beauty will leave you. That it might be spirited away. In the early days of possession, before you have built confidence and trust, you are nervous of the dangers. It is alive, it breathes, moves, flies, and is therefore mortal, so you want to put it in a glass cage. There is safety in embalmment.

I know all this because I have been through these feelings often before. Sometimes with swans when I have brought nestfuls of soft birds in boxes to my clients, their long necks melting in a flat S on themselves. You open the box and like a lily, like a snake, the necks swell and rise out of the box and the beaks quest forwards till, in a cumbrous bustle of feathers, the swans stand up and with the gait of a man who has lost proper use of his legs, lurch into the water; and you hold your breath until they have joined up with their own element. And only then, when you are sure they are happy, can you breathe again.

Often, as I say, I have known this with swans. Only once or twice with flamingos. And it is different with flamingos because you feel the awe and protectiveness and the need to embalm to an even greater degree. Unlike swans, they are passive yet slightly nervous birds. And they have such long, such vulnerable and delicate legs. They remind me of nineteenth-century women. Dowagers perhaps. Fin-de-siècle pearl pink mounds on frail legs. Think how it must be to spend your life, and it is a long life, sixty or more years long, bending down and balancing on exquisite stilts, picking your high-heeled way through the shallows.

We had made all the preparations with infinite care. In the shadow of the trees, the boys had built a stone shelter to house them when the water froze, lest the ice make a cage for their brittle ankles. There were lamps in the roof to warm the mould from their feathers in the dankness of winter. Outside, the depth of the water in the pool had been judged to be not too much, not too little, a foot or two, lest it should rise above their knees (though these are in reality their ankles). We measured their habitat to the fastidious demands of their legs. They will swim in the wild but, in captivity, adapt to the cosseting. They grow fussy and sensitive and hate to immerse their thighs.

The six pink breeding pairs arrived in the early afternoon, long enough before nightfall to discover and adjust to a strange world. The van rolled over the grass to the stopping point. Ron the keeper got out and we carried the boxes from which the birds would unfold and stretch. The two big boys came forward and helped. Handle with care, do not break, fragile. Twelve tall creatures with rosy and scarlet coverts and bills like an upturned shovel. They were mute and invisible. We spoke quietly or whispered, in awe of the moment of unveiling.

I was extremely nervous: of myself, of my clients, of the birds. However sure you are of your judgement, you never know, or not in an absolute way. You act out your assumptions but are they always infallible? I could so easily have made a crude mistake. At that first release, that first bewildered stirring of legs and feathers, my failure or achievement would become apparent. I knew I had taken a risk and forced it through.

Just consider. This setting which was that of the English country-side was reticent, the scale small, the light soft. Even in Cornwall, where the light levels are high, they cannot match the brassy clarities of Southern skies where Southern birds live. Had I miscalculated? Was this, this bowl where we stood, too muted a reception room for my exotics? For a moment I feared it could make them seem decadent. In my business you dread the false note more than anything.

It was autumn, as I said. It was a still day. The trees were turning scarlet and gold. The sun slanted across the water. The two big boys who had helped us carry the boxes were standing with woolly hats pulled down over their foreheads. It made their browless faces look dumb. Virginia and David Lacey stood together but apart from us, at a judgemental distance. I could tell they were also nervous. For them it was an expensive moment.

We unhinged the slats on the crates which we had balanced beside the water. Ron the keeper had unflappable hands. He was slow and deliberate in all his movements. Above, a few gulls screamed as always, big white bullies and ruthless exploiters. How different from our hothouse exotics. What would they make of these new arrivals? The darkness of the cabin had quietened the travellers. They would have thought it was night. As we gently removed their doors, we would bring them a sudden daytime without any dawn. I knew that the key was to draw them out quickly so that the first thing they saw was each other. These birds feel secure in a colony. They can even be fooled into breeding by mirrors.

There was a stirring of pink feathers from straw. The hook of a black and pink bill emerged and withdrew. Then one of the group gave a chuckle. The duck-like chuckle drew music from the others. The rumour of the colony touched one after another on the shoulder. Almost at once this nesting corps de ballet rose, uncooped themselves and minced forward, drawn to each other and the water. They began to mingle, pressing their feathers against each neighbour. They dipped their toes and slender ankles in the liquid. Their legs made parallels of vertical lines up from the pool. The water, blue until now with sky, turned pink from their feathered reflections. On their oval backs, the low sun gilded their pink to orange and gave it a flash of coral.

Maybe it was the sun shining, perhaps the red and gold of the trees, or even simply the unselfconscious movements of birds accommodating themselves to freedom, but I knew at that moment that it had worked. They had joined up with a wider nature and had found a way to belong. A creative idea is nothing until you can see it in all its working parts. With this single step the garden had evolved.

I don't think I was the only one to recognise it. The others lacked the tools to explain or understand it, but I could tell that they were happy and excited yet relaxed. The false note always creates tension. The true note brings ease. The amateur doesn't comprehend or know why. But from this point I knew there would be no further obstacles to pressing forward. Like all bold steps, mine had carried risks but also greater rewards. Caution leads nowhere, yet with boldness you might plummet but can also jump.

We lingered by the pool a little longer, watching the birds dipping their heads in the water, scooping and dredging for food with their upturned bills.

'They're fine,' said Ron the keeper. 'Can we unload the rations?'

We sent the boys to help him lift the flamingo food into the airtight containers. A carotene mix which would help maintain the birds' colour. Then we walked slowly back to the house in the wake of his van. Already a new idea was forming in my mind. I thought I would test it later when I returned home across the fields at the end of the afternoon. For the moment I put it out of my mind.

As Lacey was walking the keeper up from the barn to the house, I stood with Virginia in the kitchen. She had poured out a jugful of iced mint tea and was fetching four bottles of beer as an alternative.

'What will your diary record?' I asked, quietly because Lacey and the keeper had arrived on the verandah.

'I'll write simply: "It has worked."'

'How very English and restrained of you.' I was slightly disappointed by this lack of enthusiasm.

'Honestly there's no better summary,' she replied.

She had started to lever the top off one of the bottles of beer, but now she stopped and looked at me directly. Her expression was both sober and challenging. 'I was right, too, wasn't I, to agree? Give me a tiny bit of credit, three per cent, say, for that.'

I realised then what I had failed to consider. That a degree of harmony between my clients had been at stake. She had been nervous, not only about the expense and its justification, as I had assumed, but because the subject had been the cause of a dispute between herself and her husband. This always leaves a residue. It is a fact that however successfully a dispute seems to have been laid to rest, one can never tell whether it is truly resolved or simply dormant, only to reignite. This was why she would write in her diary: 'It has worked'. Nothing about the unearthly glamour of the birds or the coppery gold beauty of the scene, but simply 'it has worked'. I said to myself: i.e. Lacey no longer poorly. Perhaps deep down I had known this which explained the excessive degree of my unease earlier in the day.

'You *were* right,' I said. 'I owe you thanks for your support.'

'You didn't believe my support was enough at the time.'

'I didn't, did I? As you told me in no uncertain way, it was a case of *Das muss ein Mann* etc.'

'*Das muss ein Mann mir sagen, eh'ich es glaube.* The word of a woman's not good enough. I see now my taunt must have cut pretty deep for you to remember it so precisely.'

'It stung a bit at the time.' I didn't add that I had been entirely justified in hesitating and that she had no reason to crow over me now that it had worked out. 'No one I've ever known has quoted Kleist at me, let alone in a ticking-off. I've never even read him.'

'The German students did him at school,' she admitted. 'I didn't, I only did French. But I was a feminist. One of the rebels. Picking up tags from all over the place and recycling them into banners.' She grinned as she put the glasses and bottles one by one on the tray. 'There you go,' she said as she asked me to carry the drinks outside to the verandah. Foreigners always pick up the worst English phrases. However long they've been here, they find it difficult to judge tone.

The two men were standing together, still talking, Lacey thinner and taller, the keeper sturdily built but middle-aged also. His sleeves were rolled up to his elbows, showing forearms which were muscular enough to master swans. He looked red.

Lacey said to me: 'Ron is telling the story of how he came to be a keeper of flamingos. It's in his blood. Carry on, Ron.'

Eagerly, the keeper picked up a bottle of beer and a glass from the tray. 'Hot work,' he explained, after he had drained half in a few gulps. He brushed the foam from his upper lip against the back of his hand.

'My uncle was a seaman,' he said, in his slow steady voice. 'When he was young his ship's captain was given orders to bring back from the Antarctic a group of King Penguins.'

'Why?'

'For a zoo.' He paused. 'Now, the funny thing is that my uncle was a whaler and the ship he was on was a whaling ship in the Southern seas.'

'A whaling ship,' I exclaimed.

He nodded. 'I know. You can't explain it, can you? Here they were killing whales in the Antarctic and being asked to conserve the birds.'

We looked at him incredulously.

'When was this?' I asked.

'I'm not sure. Late forties, I think.' He stopped to consider.

'There was a tremendous drive for a long time to save King Penguins which had begun to die out. In the nineteenth century, penguins were slaughtered in their millions. They're magnificent swimmers but flightless of course. We preyed on them. We killed them for their oil, their meat and their skins. For the same reason that we preyed on the whales.'

'And the seals,' said Virginia.

'The seals, too, I suppose, but that's regulated.'

'What happened to your uncle?'

'Like I said, they took on the penguins. They're very smart birds, good looking, nearly three feet tall, white front, steel grey back, face and head black with patches of bright orange on the sides of the head and the throat. As I said, terribly smart, as though they're wearing black tie. Well, it was my uncle who was given the job of being their keeper. Every day on the journey back he would feed fish to the penguins. They got very fond of him. He got very fond of them back. He got very fond of one in particular. A real perky character.'

'This is like a fable,' said Virginia.

'What happened to them? Or is that the end?' I asked.

'That's not the end,' said Ron. 'I suppose it is like a fable. Several years later, one holiday, my uncle went to the zoo where he knew they'd been taken. He walked to the penguin cage. His penguins were there. They were nicely kept. Nice simulated blocks of ice. Nice fish. Everything a penguin could want for a happy life. He stood pressed up against the cage with a gathering of other spectators. He was quite pleased and proud to have brought them safely to this peaceful existence.'

'No easy thing, I imagine,' I said. 'On a whaling ship, the nurture of precious cargo must be the last thing on everyone's mind.'

'No easy thing. But you listen to this. I've never forgotten it because when I was a boy he used to tell me and I would make him tell me this story over and over again, especially this last bit.'

We too were utterly transfixed, as he was when a child. He drank again from his glass, holding it out for a refill, commanding our attention.

'As my uncle was standing there, a penguin, who had begun to stare at him, detached himself from the little colony and began his rolling waddle towards him. As he got closer, my Uncle Bobby realised that this was his very special penguin. There was no doubt. The marking on his face was slightly different. As the penguin got nearer, it peered closely at him and then as fast as it could it rushed up. It had recognised him. It remembered him. There was no mistaking its delight. There was quite a passionate reunion and the others came up and joined in. And this happened when he visited again.'

'What an extraordinary story.'

'What happened to your uncle?' I asked.

Ron turned towards Virginia. 'Here is your fable,' he said. 'He couldn't bring himself to go on being a whaler. He became a keeper in the zoo.'

'But whaling was stopped anyway, except for Norway and Japan.'

'That wasn't till years later and it got worse before it got better,' I said.

'Yes,' said Ron. 'This was before the ban. But you see from all this why I became a keeper of birds. Every Christmas I would say to my Uncle Bobby, tell me the story. And my uncle would tell me the story.'

As I walked back over the fields at the end of the afternoon I thought of the story. Of this Ancient Mariner and the child saying 'tell me the story'. It's been said that the tasks and interests we are introduced to when young are imprinted on us forever.

I stood by the pool of flamingos. I thought of the contradictory ways of man and animals. The killing fields and the sanctuaries. How strange to think of the sanctuary of the whaling ship ploughing through the red seas of its killing grounds. I heard my flamingos chuckle. Then one gave a trumpeting sound. They said they were happy and safe here, several showing that sign of rest and contentment which is signalled by standing on one leg. I thought that later we would bring the other ducks and geese over to the neighbouring pool. All the fowls of the air. All the fowls of the water.

This was the bird quarter of the island. My original plan had been to have one quarter for the birds, one for the animals, one for the house which was the human quarter, and one for the flowers. This, then, was my first quarter. The kingdom of the birds.

15

I WAS NOW hoping for a long clear run at my work. I was in hock to a schedule and seasonal deadlines are always tight. As the evenings close in and the periods of open weather give way to rain and wind, you start to fret about the attainment of your goal. In November, for example, the deer were due to arrive and some installations needed to be made in advance in their park. I was not, I admit, like a builder under threat of penalty clauses if he failed to finish on time. But illusory penalties can still be created by the preoccupied mind.

The reason I state this is to excuse the fact that I might appear a bit selfish about what happened next. It must be to do with the bubble factor that Louise already mentioned. Once you've withdrawn to a bubble, it's hard to break out. It's only now that I know that the more abstracted you get, the more dehumanised you also become. So, when Virginia told me on Wednesday that my office had called with bad news about my mother and that I was to ring the hospital without delay, my first reaction was ten per cent irritation as well as ninety per cent dismay.

I asked Virginia if I could borrow the phone. She waited beside me in the hall as I pressed in the numbers. I thought that an English person would have melted away. The hospital told me that my mother had collapsed; they advised me that I should come at once. They added that she had asked for my wife. I said that I wasn't married. It seemed a funny sort of a conversation to be holding in the hall. She thinks you are, said the ward sister, and she's asked for your wife. I put the phone down and thought this over.

'It seems she's asked for my wife,' I said to Virginia.

'Your wife? I thought you told me you were divorced.'

'I am. She thinks my ex is still my wife.'

'You can't expect much in the way of short-term memory. You've got to go, and so has your ex-wife.'

I wished I'd established how ill she was and what had actually happened. I was reluctant to say this to Virginia, but three years ago my mother had gone through a period of false alarms. I rang Louise at her office and explained the position.

'She's asked to see you. She thinks you're still my wife.'

I waited for an explosion. Perhaps: 'It's a bit much to have your family on my back when we're not even married.' Or something more general about liabilities not being acceptable when they can't be bartered with assets. Louise is a truthful person and can be blunt in a crisis. She has never, not once, given me a mouthful of false pieties.

Instead, now, there was silence. After a moment she spoke.

'She didn't even like me.'

'Perhaps it's to make amends.'

There was another silence.

'I'm terribly sorry, Louise. It's awful even to ask you.'

'Is she dying?' she said.

'I didn't ask.'

Could one ask? I should have. Instead I had reacted like a bewildered child, failing to ascertain and get an adult's grip on fact. Yet didn't it seem a tactless way of evaluating the importance of a claim? Ill, dying, dead, gone? For the first time, these gradations seemed an inexorable probability. The alarms of the past had been deemed false only by hindsight. Death has everything to play for in the future.

'Louise. Please come with me,' I said.

There was a pause. 'Very well.'

She promised to make arrangements and we agreed that I would pick her up soon after two. It would take all afternoon to drive cross-country to Norfolk.

Virginia made some sandwiches and a flask of coffee so that I need not stop for lunch. She pushed my apologies to one side. She said I wasn't to worry about the arrangements for the garden, nor about hurrying back. She urged me to feel free to be away as long as was necessary. She was in every detail understanding, a self-effacing model client, in fact a friend. She took my hand and held it. I thought that there was the quality of refreshment about her. In all my dealings with her I had been given evidence of the strength of character that had sustained and, perhaps, renewed her husband.

Louise was already waiting for me when I arrived. She looked less sleek than in our meetings of late. She was wearing a wine-red jumper and trousers, both of which were rumpled. She had the squashiness of middle age which I found comfortable. She had never been soft or squashy when young.

I said how grateful I was she had come.

'It must be something to do with my self-image,' she said.

Louise has always maintained that we do things solely for our convenience or satisfaction, that virtue is merely a cover. I suspect she uses this theory to serve as part of her armour.

I drove into the city of Oxford, past Magdalen College, and out on the Banbury Road. The town is tree-filled and its suburban pavements were adrift with leaves. Term must have just begun and girls with long hair were pedalling in little flocks on their bicycles. In a few years time they would metamorphose themselves into bankers and chemists and lawyers. Those who became creatives in advertising would get up at eleven o'clock. The boisterous medics would soon be sobered by disillusion. Every single one would absorb the manners of their trade. In the end everyone becomes their job. I know because I have.

Louise had started to doze in the seat beside me. She looked tired, even in profile. There was a diagonal line of fatigue running down from the inner corner of her right eye. I sighed and wondered why my mother had wanted to see her. It was true that neither had liked one another. They had certainly shared nothing in common. I recalled the first meeting between my mother and the girl I was going to marry. It was the kind of occasion when one would prefer to be absent. Just put the two women in the ring and let them fight it out with their undertones and innuendoes. As the missing link, I would later be given a detailed and lively account by both sides. In the event, I half-enjoyed being a spectator. The occasion was funny as well as surreal. Afterwards I agreed with Louise that it should be known as the battle of the bosom.

My mother was a dominant woman, not least on account of her formidable bust. Every few years she would have it fitted out at

Rigby and Peller, the corsetier which holds a royal warrant. She would sail home freshly upholstered, like the figurehead on a ship's prow. It was in 1971 that I took Louise back to Holt, to the family house. Louise had burned her bra. She was flopping all over her chest. Beneath her skinny-rib sweater, because she was nervous perhaps, her nipples were pointing out. I mumbled some introduction and wished I could look the other way. Had I only realised beforehand, I would have suggested that Louise should truss herself up. The trouble was, knowing my mother could be a bit of a duchess, she had decided to be defiant, not to let herself be intimidated. It may sound peculiar, but I honestly think it likely that the females were using their breasts as weapons. Both women were tall, and at that time, before age stooped my mother, they were equal in height. Their bosoms therefore looked each other in the eye. They summed up not only the clash of generations, but of culture and also of nature. Neither bosom would concede an inch. I have often wondered whether it was this that doomed any chance of friendship. If Louise had only been willing to please rather than challenge. For my part I also remember thinking how odd that I, the man in the middle, should have suckled so intimately at both such contrasting breasts. But then, according to Louise, men are at their least discriminating when it comes to boobs.

The truth was Louise had not been Good Enough for my mother. No one had: not my father, not Louise, not my sister, only me, and then I cannot say I had done better in her rating than break even.

Thinking of my sister made me wonder whether she would also have received a summons. The hospital had not mentioned her, nor had I thought to ask. I would have to ring her this evening. Jenny was married to a French economist in Strasbourg. She was a few years older than I. From plain beginnings she had become a very polished and trilingual piece. High-ticket clothes, a short bob with a fringe and an armour-plated urban exterior designed, I think, to defend the fact that as a girl she had not been Good Enough for my mother. To challenge the fact that, in contrast, I had. Jenny and I might have bickered a bit in youth, but had got on well enough on the occasions when we'd met in the last decade. Her husband was a dull old dog, the type that is easy to underestimate: desiccated, tight-lipped on anything but the trends of European money and, in his own sphere, immensely powerful. He enabled Jenny, who had trained as an interpreter, to rattle around, workless, as a hostess in their mini-château. He had enabled Jenny to become Good Enough for my mother. The result was that, in the last ten years, my sister had probably grown closer to my mother than I. Maternal favours had been reversed. In any case I had sensed that the heat had been taken off me, which was a considerable relief. It is always onerous to be the family flag-bearer.

Looking back, I think I probably connived at my slippage. A dominant mother has a distorting effect on a son's life. He either knuckles under or tries to leap the fence and escape. It wasn't conscious but I suspect I aimed for the latter. Objectively I think it's the better route, better in the sense of avoiding filial deformation, that is. You could argue that the reason behind both my work and my marriage is my mother. I married a competitive type who is also suburban, qualities in an in-law which were likely to act as a wedge. I also married a profession which loosened home ties and took me away, all over the world. A profession, moreover, which is dedicated to the pursuit of the ideal. An ideal, a goal, which one looks to find not in people but in nature.

As I sat in the car it came to me that my marriage and my profession had been poised to collide and, behind this collision, half caught in the shadows, was the blameless, because innocent, figure of my mother. Trace anything back and you confront its inevitability. Run the same sequence forward and you see only a choice of free will forks on the road. That each will reinforce your last decision is scarcely apparent to any of us at the time.

It is always a mistake to skid off into introspection, but it tends to be hard to avoid on gloomy journeys to the past like this.

'Louise,' I said with some urgency, 'please talk to me.'

There was a stir in the seat beside me. 'What do you want me to talk about?'

'Anything.'

'Anything? Just the sound of a familiar voice will do?'

'Tell me about your painting or your lodger or, yes, anything.'

'My painting has improved and one of my lodgers has left. Mr Naramoto has returned to Japan to work on his digest. I rather miss his meditation vibes.'

'What are you painting?'

'A portrait.'

'A nude?'

'Not a nude.'

'Head and shoulders then. Of whom?'

She hesitated. 'Someone I know.'

Her hesitation was enough to help me realise precisely what she meant. 'No one I know.'

'No.'

'Who is he?'

'He is thirteen years younger than me.'

'Quite a gap,' I said neutrally. One holds one's primitive reactions at arm's length, yet youth with its energy and power and challenge is always a threat. 'Who is it?'

'It is, as you put it, a mathematician, a professor to give him his full title.'

'What's he like?'

'Sweet, all over the place, always on the edge of a nervous breakdown that he'll never actually have, and in need of a mother, having lost a wife to a colleague. What else would he be like?'

Somewhere along this list of ingredients, the threat of his youth had begun to recede.

'How long has it been going on?' I asked.

'A few months.'

'Why didn't you tell me last time we met?'

'I'd only just met him. In any case, why should I? You never tell me about your Alice. I don't know whether she's still around or not.'

'I don't know myself.'

She clicked her tongue against her teeth. It was clear she thought this a prevarication. It wasn't. In the last couple of months, Alice had started to complain that I was never around. What was the point of a relationship? She'd even left me a note to that effect. Women have such a passion for declaration. I feared I would soon be given an ultimatum, and who could blame her? It must have been a month since we'd last met. During this time I felt she had entered a vacuum. She was shouting more loudly but growing more distant, and smaller. The words which were hurled were becoming harder to hear. Soon a wind would come which would blow her away.

We stopped talking. I had hoped for prattle, not for anything that made me think. Outside the car, it was a grey tossing autumn day. Driving east, we were cutting into the wind. We made a stop for tea, then carried on. By now we had reached the flat blackness of the Fenlands. When I get to this strange lost landscape, I start to be pulled into the orbit of home. It is like the crossing of the water to another land and other time. The fens are no longer swamp or marsh: they have been resurrected. But they are crossed by few roads and some of their older peasants, hunched and pale like field mushrooms, still look inbred and medieval. But however ancient they seem, the land looks yet older. In winter you can even imagine the glacier pushing across in the Ice Age; spewing chalk and Jurassic material out of its way and towards the edge of London. As I cross this land which I crossed so often coming back from school and university, the familiarity of the place names fills me with boyhood; with that mix of nostalgia and exile with which we must all see our past.

But this wasn't a journey that was going to end in home. The house with its flint walls and red crow-stepped gables was now empty. My booming-voiced mother in one of her hairy winter skirts was no longer there. She was lying instead in the concrete hospital. Ill, dying, dead, gone? On the last false alarm from my mother, she had been returned by the hospital to a nurse at home a few hours before I managed to arrive. Perhaps this would happen today. One's father dies but widows are tough and one's mother endures for ever. I couldn't imagine her at any stage just fading away. My father had become three-quarters of the person he was, then a half, then a tenth before he had died. But my mother would still be ruffing and clubbing at bridge in her nineties.

She wasn't the kind of woman for whom you buy old ladies' flowers. If you didn't know it, there actually are dwarf roses with names like Sweet Dreams and Gentle Touch and Queen Mother that have been designated to reach the core of this market. Healing names that would have made my mother shudder. Nonetheless, when we struggled through the crowds on the ring road and found a place in the car park, I bought three bunches of miniature rose buds from a stall in front of the hospital. I hoped she wouldn't turn her nose up at these.

As we entered the main door I said to Louise: 'How I really hate, hate, hate hospitals.'

'I know,' my ex-wife said. Then added very quietly: 'That's why I've come.'

I turned back to her startled. She had inconvenienced and distressed herself because she cared more greatly for my comfort than her own. Support like this is a gesture of love of a kind at least. I put my hand up to touch her cheek then let it fall. People were pushing us on from behind but for a brief instant we exchanged a look in which the best of a shared past was gathered.

It was just after six o'clock. Carrying my shameful peach-pink bunches of flowers, I walked to the reception desk and spoke to a woman with grey shoulder-length hair. As she checked for the whereabouts of my mother, I reminded myself how some people love the constant crisis and bustle. These warm, bright creatures don't want to stand on the sidelines of illness and death. They relish the politics of drugs and bedpans and lino. Then the woman smoothed the grey hair back from her forehead and directed us to the staircase and up to another desk on the first floor. Only in stages do you penetrate the underworld. On the stairway we passed a Chinese nurse with cherry-red lipstick and hands like subtle butterflies. The sight of a pretty thing in a ghastly place cheers you up, though what on earth was this porcelain treasure doing here? Still, I suppose there's no philosophical reason why beautiful people shouldn't give you enemas and take your pulse. It's just that good looks usually earn them a ticket to another life.

At the desk the receptionist apologised for eating a chocolate bar. She explained that she hadn't had any time for lunch. I gave her our name, this time as man and wife. It's Mr and Mrs Robert Boyd, I said. She looked grave and said that my sister was already here. She pointed along the corridor and told us to go through the doors marked 110–120 and a nurse would be waiting for us at the other end.

The passages through which we'd walked had been growing narrower. As the space closed down on me, so did a feeling of dread as though one would end up locked in a cupboard. One would be face to face with a body in a box. At the end of the corridor a nurse and a doctor had emerged. They were talking. He was young enough to be my son. I thought: our daughter Abi won't marry a doctor. I thought: she is wasting her life. I said: 'We are Mr and Mrs Boyd.' The words fell stiffly out of my head and into an empty space. My wife cleared her throat behind me. I was married to my wife. We had never divorced. We had come together to see the body in the box. This is what married people do together. 'We've come to see my mother. I understand my sister is already here.' A man comes through a door. He says: 'I can't find Barry.' The nurse points to the door through which he has come. The scene reverses itself. He leaves. She turns back to me. One hand is across her breast. It doesn't look like a pretty butterfly. I know what's happened by looking at her hands. They let the hands of her senior, the hands of the doctor, do the speaking. 'I'm so sorry. Your mother has died. It happened a quarter of an hour ago. Do you want to come in? Your sister is here with her.'

Still holding my bunches of salmon-pink roses, I enter the pale green room. Sweet Dreams, Gentle Touch, Queen Mother, with their bogus healing presence. My sister gets up. She is very pale. My mother stays in bed. She's lying on her back. There are white tubes like twigs on a winter tree all around. They were in her, but have now been detached. I put my arms round my sister. I feel her shake but she doesn't cry. 'You remember Louise?' I say. I am saying this to the wrong person. I was going to say this to my mother. I was going to ask: is there something you want to say to Louise? I was going to tell her that we'll have you out of here in no time at all. Here are some flowers. Sweet Dreams, Gentle Touch, and this rose, the Queen Mother, you know, is well into her nineties. I say nothing. The words have nowhere to go. They look back at me like a reproach. Behind me I sense the hands of the nurse flutter. The doctor is saying something about a haemorrhage. My mother looks pale like candlewax. There can't be any blood left inside her. They had prepared to operate but couldn't save her. The walls which had narrowed are now closed. Here is the end of the corridor. It is the body in the box.

16

WE WERE ALL, I think, in a state of shock for the first twenty-four hours. We had travelled a long way and were numbed by our journeys and numbed on arrival. We didn't go back to the house that first night but spent it in a city hotel. I think neither Jenny nor I could face the home. My ex-wife and I took separate rooms. A rearrangement seemed to have taken place. I was no longer married but instead had two sisters.

The following morning I took Louise to the station and kissed her goodbye. She hadn't wanted to stay. I felt guilty because the light of day had stripped illusion away. She was no longer my wife, nor even my sister, her position displaced by my real sister. A funeral sorts out the pecking order. It's no job for in-laws who are exes to pick over the family photos or sell the empty clothes or open their palms to the will. These aren't exactly mechanical jobs and people who don't have the same memories don't belong.

Jenny and I drove to Holt and spent the morning cleaning up the family home. We said to each other how dreadful it was but that really our mother was lucky. It was a good, quick death with much less suffering than most. Wouldn't we prefer to go the same way too? I then carried on scrubbing whilst my sister made the ritual telephone calls. A man with a professionally subdued voice came and sat in the drawing room. We talked prices and woods and linings, and arranged a service in the local church. Our mother hadn't chosen any hymns, but there is a reliable safety-net. *To Be a Pilgrim*. *Onward Christian Soldiers*. *When I Am Laid in Earth*. Those old totems of optimistic will-power and fatalistic despair that rub shoulders at most funerals. Jenny was good at all this, on arrangements and delegation.

It must be the hostess in her coming out. A funeral demands a level of organisational skill which is similar to the most elaborate of parties. I rang Louise to check she was back and thank her again. She said she would prefer not to attend the service. Abi was also keen to be excused her grandmother on the grounds that her cousins in Strasbourg wouldn't be there.

In the early evening just before dusk, I walked out of the house and into the back garden. I could hear the voice of my mother calling for her dogs, for Jake and Mop, the remaining two from a pack of lurchers. She was shouting in monosyllabic barks. Then a bark at my father. More monosyllables. 'Tom, you must do this at once.' My father's faint protests. 'There are too many *musts* in this house.' The noises of twenty years ago when I had laid out the garden for my mother and father. The sapling cherry trees they had wanted were now mature. The reddened leaves of 'Shirotae' and 'Shimidsu-zakura' hung over the courtyard, as red as the horizontal lines of bricks that alternated with the patterns of flint on the walls. Norfolk patterns. I was fond of Holt with its open skies blown in from the coast. I had loved the house, our family home: it was safe, predictable, a nursery base. You plant larches as nurses to shelter young trees. The house was sturdy like larches watching over its two young charges. The thought of selling it was abhorrent. I wondered whether I could afford to buy Jenny out and keep it on. In reality this would amount to hoarding, it would be so little used. Can one keep anything for the sake of the past?

Looking up I could see Jenny perched on a window seat in our mother's bedroom. She glanced out, I waved and she waved back. She was thin and serious, like my father, beaky in outline against the light. I remembered it was my father who had especially loved the garden. In retirement he had proved himself to be a peony man. The garden was full of these sumptuous plants. I owe everything to my father who had brought me to work with the land.

When I said he was a barrister, this wasn't the complete truth. He was uncomfortable as a lawyer, poised to bump around the legal ladder. But instead of bunkering into a solicitor's office, he accepted a job as a company secretary. From here his business connections brought him the part-ownership of a local quarry. 'Come with me,' he had said to me one summer's day. 'I want to show you something.'

I was eight, at home on holiday. I had climbed up on the running board and into his car, a fug, as always, of the mingled smells of petrol and leather. We drove to the quarry, a place from which I was mostly excluded, not only on account of the danger, but rather because I would come back covered in dust. 'Look,' he said, pointing out of the window to the hills of flints that pooled over the ground. 'Now wait and see,' said my father and drove me straight from there to a garden five miles away.

I have never been back but I've never forgotten the house or rather its garden. The owners had built a high wall around it with my father's flints. An enclosed garden, a *hortus conclusus* that had risen from the ground. How proud my father was that it had been grown from his quarry. The walls were covered with tiled ridges, intricate arrangements of stone on stone, flint on flint. A cloistered refuge that had been teased from his land. I have never chosen to go back to that garden but I shared his pride that what he had quarried would last so far into the future. I've said I can trace my profession back to my mother. I know now I owe it more directly to my father. I repeat, we're all imprinted by the tasks we encounter in youth.

Perhaps it seems strange to think of your father when it's your mother who's died, but when the last parent goes, the ghosts link hands and become one. Everything is inaccessible now. They leave some kind of a building inside you, yet part of your childhood fades when both your mother and father have gone. There is only a husk with patches of gone-ness inside. You don't want to pack up the empty clothes or burn the papers or sell the house. They are all there is to stand as witnesses of the past.

There was a knock on the window. My sister was making signs and beckoning me in. As I walked back into the house, I noticed that the door had a crack. A corner of paper was also peeling away from the wall. The old don't bother to get things repaired. Renewal isn't part of an old person's life. The house ages in step with them and they are sensible not to watch it with a critical eye.

My sister was kneeling on the bedroom floor. She was surrounded by piles of hairy skirts and woollen jumpers. A mink cape was heaped like a nest of sleeping mice in the corner. Who would wear it? Some bag lady, some old tramp? Would we one day see a man with boots and a staff, stinking of tripe and shuffling along the road in our mother's mink cape?

'This is awful,' I said.

My sister was crying. 'It's not the clothes that upset me. It's seeing her handwriting.' She passed me a bridge diary. 'You're such an arsehole,' she said.

I opened the diary, bewildered. It was five years old. Most weeks held three bridge sessions, permutations of people with a core of the same partners. The only other reference was to Robert. Robert called. Then, sometimes, just Robert, or Robert advised. I couldn't tie up the name or the dates with myself.

'Who's this Robert?' I thought my sister must be wrong in referring to me. 'Did she have a financial adviser?'

'You stupid arsehole, it's you all right,' sobbed my sister. 'She adored you so much.'

'It can't be me. It's not true. Why should she keep on referring to me? It became you that she wanted.'

'I was only a *pis aller*. You were a boy. You had a tassel between your legs. She never stopped adoring you.'

I couldn't believe it. I went on leafing through the diary. Robert rang. Then Robert is coming this weekend. Robert, Robert. Robert in Paris. Then Robert rang from California. California being underlined. No mention of Jenny. It wasn't the sight of my mother's handwriting that had upset her. It was the terrible absence of herself, invisible in our mother's life.

'You were always her favourite,' said my sister, wiping her eyes.

'It's not true.' I didn't want it to be true.

'It is true. You just don't want it to be true because you've always found love a burden. You can't face having to be equal to it. It creates demands.'

'Please don't go on, Jenny. We're upset.'

I was afraid that sooner or later she'd say something particular. Something so precise and so cutting that I'd have to accept it as evidence. I was afraid she'd say that I hadn't even managed to reach my mother before she died. That I'd failed her by a quarter of an hour. Soon she would tell me why my marriage collapsed. Accusations start in one context and end in another.

'Don't, Jenny. Don't imagine things. It's all over. We mustn't quarrel.'

She looked up with a jagged face. Then it eased and the ugliness went over. 'No.' She put out her hand. 'We shan't. I'm sorry.'

We sat huddled in reconciliation on the floor, one more pile among the existing piles of clothes. Some time, after probate, we would have to face dividing the furniture up. The walnut desk, the paintings and engravings, the lamps, the few books, and what about the lightbulbs? Turn and turn about. Your go. Now it's mine. Your turn again. An hour ago I'd wanted to sell nothing, even keep the house. Now I didn't want any of it. Not now that I'd been shown up as unequal to love. I must heap the stuff over Jenny to even out the inequalities. Desks and bracelets and pictures would block out the cold. Soon her armour would be secure again. She'd be efficient and confident and practical.

Not that these things are more than bits of sticking-plaster. This kind of inheritance is only a second coming. The first legacy, the real one, is parcelled out at birth. A sunny nature or gloom. A strong heart or the diabetes that lies in wait until you're fifty. Being a girl or a boy, in our case. The scientists say we are only starting to know what we inherit. They are pulling us back to our first ancestors, to the Eve of our beginnings. They say it is mitochondrial Eve who has handed down to us her bacteria which has given all our bits and pieces, our neurons and beads of life on a string. It is a great puzzle. Where have we come from and where are we going with linked hands?

'Do you want to have this?' asks my sister.

She passes me a photo of us on the beach. I am three, my sister is six. My hair is an infant's blond, hers has begun to darken. We have spades and a bucket, even though we walk on pebbles, not sand. My sister holds me by the hand. She is looking down at me and smiling. I say I don't need her protection. I am a man. I am sticking out my chest.

'I'd like it but not if you want it,' I reply to my sister.

'It's OK. There's another print here.'

'That's nice. We can both have it then.'

'Do you remember?' asks my sister.

17

JENNY STAYED ON for a fortnight whilst I commuted between the office and Holt. The funeral took place. My sister wanted to go out in a boat and scatter the ashes on the sea. In the end we didn't. It was stormy, and we also thought it might be illegal. Socially unacceptable, anyway, since the remains of your own dead are everyone else's pollutant. So we took them back to the garden and put them under a buddleja which likes calcium, though probably not all at once. I hoped they wouldn't kill it off. But ritual is ritual, and you can't treat your mother's ashes like bonemeal, spooning them out every year at the rate of 75gm per square metre.

I raked the ashes in, so that they wouldn't blow around in the wind. The pair of us stood in silence. Nearby 'Shimidsu-zakura' had shed its leaves with perfect appropriateness. To the Japanese, the transient blossom of the flowering cherry symbolises the brief span of human life. When the ashes are in the ground, the process of renewal is supposed to start. We might not have been too sure in the case of the buddleja, but it's true that such symbols do manipulate a bereavement. Life had now started to close over the loss and over the things that had been said or nearly said.

I left Holt for the island an hour after dawn on the Tuesday. It was a fortnight since I had first arrived. Inland from the coast, there had been an air frost. It was still very cold but the light was clear and a pared morning moon was in the south-eastern quarter of the sky. It looked fresh and new, much cleaner than it does at night when its reflected radiance is smudged by shadows. It reminded me of the vision of Saturn. The thought was a tiny revival. I needed to return to my bubble which I had forgotten in this two-week immersion.

As I drove back, crossing the Fenlands again, I realised with sadness that I had left the past for the last time. It would be necessary to return to sort out the furniture or sell the house, but it was clear that these too had died. My visits would be no more than part of a numb aftermath. Perhaps it was this that made the island to which I drove seem like a haven. In my mind it had turned into the paradise I was trying to create. This doesn't usually happen. You make a pleasure garden for others, not for yourself. It's normal for your creations to be pegged down by the limitations of work, enjoyable but frustrating and never an escape.

The long landlocked journey took all day and the sun was low in the sky by the time I arrived. I rolled over the isthmus with a sense of liberation and of coming home. I didn't go back to the main house but ran the car to the end of the track and then walked to the kingdom of the birds. When they saw me, they chortled but didn't seem scared. They stayed in the shallows and those that had stirred returned to resting at peace on one leg. For a while I sat silently by the lake. There was only the murmur of feathers and the trickle of water as they lifted their bills from the pool. The sun dipped and dusk began to gather and thicken. In the twilight the flamingos gradually turned into silhouettes. Long traceries of legs and necks, interposed by a blurry sleeping softness. Mesmerised by their patterns, I could have drifted to sleep myself but the air was growing chill and soaking the turf with dew.

Eventually I rose and walked over the grass and back through the field to the boathouse. It was dark and damp and cold, but I was tired and, more than anything, it felt like home, a base to which you return however short on comfort. Inconveniently short, I was about to realise. As I was heating up the remains of the steak and kidney casserole that Jenny and I had shared the previous night in Holt, the electricity fused. Swearing furiously the way you do when your appetite is robbed of expectation, I lit a candle to investigate the trip switch, but the flame wasn't strong enough. I now remembered Imogen's lambing torch. Its very existence was a reproach. I should have returned it weeks before, but for the interruptions. Walking carefully and balancing the candle, I tried to find it now. It was an impossible search. It was difficult to see in this flickering of shadows and, if I moved too fast, the candle nearly blew out. Meanwhile its wax was diminishing into a little puddle. Soon the wick would burn out and this was my only candle. I sat down on the bed to think. The torch wasn't on any of the surfaces. Could I have put it down on the floor? As I lowered the candle, I realised I had probably left it in the boat. I went to check and found it on its side in the stern. When I brought it back to the house, the torch confirmed that the fault wasn't confined to a trip switch.

There were now three options. 1. Feel evil and go straight to bed without food. 2. Go to the main house and heat up the casserole, in which case one would be fed and one would feel less evil, but this meant talking about the funeral with my clients, which held no appeal. 3. Chuck the casserole, walk over the bloody field to the car and go out on my own to dinner. I had had enough of the car, but number 3 seemed the only possibility.

I took the torch and walked down the steps of the boathouse. As I did so, I heard a rustling, then a splash as though a stone had been thrown, then the sound of my name being called. It must be Virginia. I flashed the light back and forth along the track but nothing was apparent. There was another call. Now I was away from the building, it was easy to determine the acoustics with more accuracy. I realised it must come from the opposite bank, a fact which was simultaneously confirmed. There was a firefly swoop as the beam of a small lamp shone across the water.

'You've got my big torch,' said Imogen with justifiable truculence.

I stared into the darkness with dismay. I recognised that she must have seen me walking around with it and come down here to command me to return it.

'I do have your torch,' I said lamely. 'I'm so sorry. I've been going to return it but I've been away.'

'I can't hear you.'

It wasn't surprising. Where she had shouted, I had whispered. I wished she would keep her voice down.

'I've got your torch,' I repeated. 'The lights have fused. Would you mind if I returned it to you tomorrow?'

'I can't hear. Can you bring it across now?'

I suspected she could hear perfectly well, but perhaps she had an immediate and genuine use for the lamp. I was tired and hungry and had driven over three hundred miles. Still, it was impossible to refuse.

In the matter of torches she was more sinned against than sinning. It then occurred to me I could kill two birds with one stone. Return the torch and have a meal. I asked her to wait whilst I went back into the house. Five minutes later I was in the boat with my travelling casserole as well as the torch. Nothing so revives a man as the restoration of the dinner of which he has been robbed. There was a bargain here to be struck. No casserole, no torch.

I arrived at the opposite bank, got out and tied up the boat whilst Imogen waited on the side. It is odd but you don't have to see or hear a woman to read body language. She emits a force with the reach of ectoplasm. I had sailed into a fog of huffiness which would require some negotiating around.

'Look, Imogen,' I said and apologised, reiterating what I had explained on the bank. I'd been away, endless interruptions, the lights had fused etc. Her saying, 'May I please have my torch.' Me: no casserole, no torch, but putting it as nicely as possible, so it went: 'In the circumstances may I please heat up my casserole and share it with you as an apology.'

Still engulfed in her fog, we walked in silence up the wooded path of the hillside. She was brushing off all attempts at small talk. I wondered whether I would be doomed to eat the meal in a continuing atmosphere of chastisement. Better for me to have stayed in the kingdom of the birds, lulled to sleep below the wings of the flamingos.

The little terrier ran barking to the gate as we arrived at her cottage, jumping backwards and forwards on stiff legs as if clockwork. The kitchen was littered with papers as before and a bottle of sheep-wormer stood next to the coffee. Still, the room was warm and she had turned on the oven. She had also stopped walking in a manner to convey offence. I too had given up wondering whether to stay or go. She gave me a few potatoes to scrub. She laid the table. We were eased into some sort of companionship by shared jobs. I stopped thinking out conversations to enact. She was too intelligent and complex to be humiliated with topics. I remembered the cruelty of sharing her father's wartime bottle of port in her absence. There was more to remain silent about than to say. In any case I was half-knackered.

Over the meal she asked where I had been away.

'I drove back from Norfolk today.'

'You must be terribly tired.'

I agreed and took another forkful of food. The potatoes were fluffy, the casserole rich and hot.

'It's good,' said Imogen. 'Did you make this?'

'My sister. I've been away on family business.' I had resolved to say nothing of my mother's death. To talk of my death would be to share the death of her husband. There is an assumption that loss unites strangers – we are all in the same boat – but this easy familiarity leads to embarrassment. We open each other's privacies and tomorrow find we can't wait to close them again.

'Family business usually means trouble in my experience,' said Imogen.

'Not trouble exactly.'

'It does in my case.' She did her business of trying to stare me out.

'How?'

'Don't pretend you haven't noticed relations are a bit strained.'

'It's not my business to notice.'

'As you said last time, your job is to keep your eyes on the ground.'

'Precisely.'

I finished eating and pushed the plate to the side. I was so tired that the lift given by the food was already passing.

'I'm tired, Imogen. I can't talk straight. Perhaps I'd better go.' But I remained inert, just sitting.

There was a dry fluttering at the window. It was agitated and insistent. It wouldn't give up. The terrier which had been curled in its basket jumped up at the trigger of the sound. Imogen rose too and went over to it.

'It's a peacock butterfly. I hate to see them trying to get out now.'

'It'll die if you let it out.'

The terrier was trying to snap at this papery mouthful. He was sent back to his basket. The butterfly stopped throwing its feelers and legs against the pane. It too succumbed to tiredness. It folded its wings together and slept. I was watching all this in a daze.

Imogen stood with her back to the window. She was wearing a dark woollen jumper. Its roll-neck reached right up to her chin. She said: 'When I was little and got overtired at the end of the day, I sometimes found it difficult to get to sleep. My mother would come up to me in bed and sprinkle magic dust on me. If that doesn't sound too fey.'

'Not fey at all. What did it do?'

'It would send me to sleep.'

'Did it always work?'

'Always.'

'There's no magic dust when one grows up.'

'You learn to make your own. For me it's the meteor showers this month. The slow bright Taurids in November. I let them fall onto my eyelids. I imagine them falling like dust.'

She drew her fingers down in the air as though parting a curtain of grass, a shower of meteors.

I watched her demonstrating her own world. 'I must go, Imogen.' But I remained, fascinated, and she remained, leaning with her back pressed against the window. Then she said very quietly: 'Have you told David or Virginia that you've been here?'

'No.'

'Or that you've met me?'

'I've not had a chance to mention it.' Then taking equal care to sound careless I asked: 'Have you?'

'No.'

There was a silence during which the shift of collusion took root. I should have got up to go before the shift took place. I stayed sitting. Part of me hypnotised by the meteors showering on my eyelids. By the papery wings of a butterfly giving up trying to break out. And then, the other thing. There had been so much withering in these last days. The laying to rest in the earth. The dropping of leaves on 'Shimidsu-zakura'. Imogen's loneliness was mine too, though she couldn't know it. Her back was against the window, her arms which had been folded over her breasts were unfolded. I could only see her in bits, not as a whole person. Her unfolded arms, a long neck turning, the roll-collar reaching up to her throat, her breasts beneath the wool of her jumper. All these parts were open to me, the shadow between her legs was open.

Do they know that you know me?

No.

Then who's to know?

'Don't, Imogen.'

133

'Don't what?'

Don't what? I bent my head, trying to grow cold thoughts, but a woman wanting you drives them out. And then the butterfly started its tapping again. I remembered the fluttering of the nurse's hands. I got up and went to the woman against the window because only the living can push away death. I knelt down and she didn't resist me. She stroked me and held my head still in her hands. She drew me towards her. Her stomach was warm and soft. The beat of life, her heartbeat, throbbed in her stomach. I felt it pulsing and stretching the skin of her trousers. I opened the fastening and plunged my face into her flesh. Only the living drive away death. She parted her legs and sucked me into her thick, sweet, carnal smell, the smell of sex that drives away death. At the foot of the pane the butterfly slept. Outside it was dark. I was a swimmer in her sub-aqueous world.

In the night I slept against her, holding her in my arms. It was cold but our touching parts flushed each other with warmth. I woke and drew the fringe back from her forehead and felt the point where it grew in a widow's peak. It was hard to see anything. Only her eyes were dark shadows and below, where the sheet was rolled down, her nipples were visible, flat and black on the dusky breasts. I said: 'You've got to realise there's only this one night. You know that.' It was an ugliness that I was afraid she might not understand. I feared that for her last night's casualness had been replaced by intensities. Later she came at me like a torpedo again. She was starving, she wanted me all the time. She opened herself outwards but was concentrating inwards on her own satisfaction. In the dawn when I woke, she was standing at the window looking out. As I saw her, the cool thoughts came back that the night had kept out.

I decided to leave while she was still in bed. I kissed her and stroked her. I didn't want to hurt her.

I said: 'You know, this hasn't happened.'

She turned over and lay with a sulkiness on her front. 'I know perfectly well what you're afraid of. That I'll blab. That I'll tell them. That I'll tarnish your currency.'

I recognised she was one of those unlucky people who find the raw spot to pierce with unerring accuracy.

'It's not that.'

'What is it then? Eh?'

'I've got a job to do. It's important. I'm staying here only for that.'

'You mean she's playing out her Watteauesque fantasies in which it suits you to connive.'

'It's not like that.' I was shocked at myself for failing to realise the sourness of envy. 'It's not like that at all. You know that.'

'Do I?'

'You do.'

She rolled over, her breasts falling emptily to her sides.

'Are you sure you're all right?' I asked.

'I'm fine.'

'Are you glad?'

'Are you?'

'If you are, I am,' I said gently.

'Then, why not, I am too.'

'Then I'll leave.'

'Don't forget the casserole dish.'

We had seemed to be making progress but this wasn't the cheery wave that one might expect. She'd left a pause between each of her words. Droplets of irony had been exquisitely measured out. Women can be so moody that you never know which way the wind will blow. Did she want me to think that I'd used her? Was that what she wanted? I wished she would understand my position without side, or edge or rancour.

I said: 'Before I go, can't I bring you a coffee or tea in bed? Won't you let me do that?'

I was still hoping but she shook her head. I went downstairs and let Binkie, the terrier, out. The dish was where she'd left it, still encrusted, on the surface beside an envelope addressed to Mrs I. Roscoe. It was the first time I had seen her surname.

I thought as I left with my dish that this lack of organisation should be confined to youth, that familiarity was what one wanted, that a stranger's body could bring oblivion but with a stranger inside it, where was the comfort? Poor Mrs Imogen Roscoe must be lying in bed and thinking much the same.

What could I expect? The impossible? I had hoped for a capsule: one of those tender and passionate encounters without any sequel. What a hope. They never exist, these answers to idealism and cynicism combined. Without dwelling on the matter, I knew I had made a mistake, yet it had carried its own inevitability at the time.

Rowing the boat across the early-morning water dispelled these thoughts. Otherwise I might have reminded myself of the same conclusion I had drawn a fortnight ago, driving across the country to my mother. *Trace anything back and you confront its inevitability. Run the same sequence forward and you see only a choice of free-will forks in the road.*

Statistically, the majority of these forks may not matter, but you can't tell at the time. *The truth is that at the time you've no idea where you're going.*

18

A PERFECT WORLD is an orderly one, isn't it? Take any system and you'll find that its beauty rests in its orderliness. Even a humble man-made organisation like the financial market, say, is defined as orderly when it is good, and disorderly when it goes bad. And what is religion but the belief in divine order? What is old Eden if not the dramatisation of perfect order? What is the natural world but one of marvellous order: perfect cycles of growth and decay, perfect marriages of predator and prey.

Perhaps as a landscape architect, I'm more committed than most to the creation of an orderly world. Mad, isn't it, bearing in mind how bad it must be for one's character. You risk ending up as the sort of person who has obsessional distortions, a grim fate to volunteer for. But once you are trained, you are bound like a homing pigeon to follow your programme and I can't help subscribing to this notion of an orderly and perfect world. The trouble comes when you apply it to your own private world. When that is disrupted, as mine had so recently been, it makes you slightly abnormal. The result was that all I could think of was returning to the orchestration of my harmonious world. More than ever, I needed to shut out the real one which persisted in breaking in.

That morning after my night spent with Imogen, I set off to find Virginia to announce my return as well as tell her about the fault in the electricity. On the way I visited the kingdom of the birds. It was a mist-grey morning but how beautiful they looked. Unlike yesterday evening, they clustered forwards, expecting their food. I thought when the weather was warmer, I would erect some lanterns by the pool so that we could see them at night. There's a famous painting by Sargent: 'Carnation, Lily, Lily, Rose', an absolute masterpiece, an evocation of childhood showing two girls in a garden holding paper lamps that are round and golden like pumpkins. They light up their faces and the folds of their dresses and the flowers in the twilight. The smell of spice from the blooms is warmed by their glow. I could put these lanterns like pumpkins by the side of the pool.

Across the field Virginia was walking towards me. She was wearing a thick woollen check jacket and trousers bleached of their colour. Her hair was blowing. She would have made even an anorak look nice, and not like an anorak.

'I was on my way to see you,' I said.

She asked me how the funeral went. She was making a clucking face, puffing up her cheeks.

'Well, you know. These things are always awful.'

'My father used to refuse to go to all funerals.'

'How very enviable if you can get away with it.'

'He used to say that after a certain age, all you do is see people off.'

'Didn't friends object?' I asked.

'Friends accept one's funny ways. Anyway, a bargain of mutual non-attendance was struck.'

'Family are different from friends.'

'Once his mother had died, and his wife, my mother of course, and his brother too, my father didn't make any distinction. Cousins, in-laws etc were given short shrift.'

I didn't want to talk about funerals. This was the reason I had not gone to see her last night. I wanted instead to explain the fault in the electricity. I asked if she could possibly phone.

'Why on earth didn't you come over last night? How could you cope in the dark?' she exclaimed.

I said something about not wanting to bother her.

'I heard voices actually,' she said, looking at me. 'About seven o'clock, was it? You know how they carry on a quiet winter night. I thought it must be you. I guessed you'd come back.'

There is never any time to think on these occasions. You go into gear. You give the truth but only emit sufficient to act as an inoculation.

'It was your sister-in-law actually, shouting across the river. That's who you would have heard. It surprised me. Months ago I rescued what turned out to be a sheep of hers. She'd loaned me her torch and I'd completely forgotten to return it. Entirely my fault. I suppose she'd seen my torchlight in the distance. Anyway she asked me to return it.'

'You mean she deprived you of your only light?' said Virginia incredulously. Then she said, 'Really. For God's sake,' and looked all dry expectation.

This was awful. It demanded some chivalrous line.

'No. I've some candles and a torch of my own. It was my fault entirely. It was remiss of me to forget.'

'Why didn't you mention you'd met her before?'

'I forgot, I'm afraid. Just like her torch. I'm so busy I forget these things.'

She accepted that. Then asked: 'What do you think of her?'

'Nice enough. OK, isn't she?'

There was a covered door to the woman in the bed last night, the woman I'd left in bed this morning. I'm sorry, Imogen, forgive me. This is how it is.

'She's very difficult,' said Virginia slowly.

'Her husband died, didn't he?'

'Eight years ago.'

'How?'

'He fell outta the sky.'

She said this in her southern accent. I thought I must have misheard.

'What? He did what?'

'A plane crash. On an internal flight in Russia. Pretty dreadful.'

It was impossible to speak for a moment. *Can I at least bring you a coffee or a tea in bed*, I had inadequately said this morning.

'I had no idea,' I said now. 'How terrible for her.'

'David told me they were separated at the time. She was always hard to live with.'

'I see.'

'I've known three people who've been killed in air crashes.'

I knew she would meander into reminiscence. I felt a compulsion to return the talk to Imogen. I asked what her husband had done. I knew of course. I wanted to check.

'A radio astronomer. She still uses his home stuff to look at the sky.'

He fell outta the sky. I reminded myself there wasn't a jigsaw here, no pattern in the way pieces fitted together. It was just the way Virginia had put it.

'Well,' I said, 'that's very sad.'

It wasn't the most comfortable of chats, with me straining to compartmentalise in the background and wondering whether to say that we had both looked at the sky together. But I seemed to be one step behind in this conversation, and then there's always the risk that if you divulge anything too late, its earlier concealment will become apparent. In the end I decided to tap the ball in another direction and for a few minutes we exchanged views on the merits and demerits of various airlines.

'When I fly home,' said Virginia, 'I always use Delta. They have a very good safety record.'

I agreed and on that note of agreement, we walked to the stone hut to fill the bucket with food for the flamingos. As usual the two boldest and most handsome birds which my client had christened Casino and Las Vegas, were the first to chuckle and come forward. We watched the colony cluster round the pellets, rummaging and trawling their catch by using their bills like upturned shovels. We decided that in the next few days we would bring in the other ducks and geese to inhabit this kingdom of the birds. The Carolinas with painted heads and drooping crests. The Mandarins with their little chestnut sails and nodding courtship rituals. The blue and red-billed Bahama Pintails and Rosybills and blond red-crested Pochards. Fecund and tame Nénés, the Hawaiian geese which had been saved from extinction.

Then we stood in silence and looked beyond the flamingos to the lie of the landscape which Mr Trelleck had pushed into folds and pillows. Just water, grass and trees, forming shapes and soft undulations. The perimeter belt of trees to the rear (hiding the protective fence), a middle distance of water, and lush rolls of turf curling around. The peace of my eighteenth-century template. Even on frenzied days, when the light and shade scuds within you, as it did now when I thought of Imogen, such a landscape has the power to impart calm. A hazy sun sent light through the mist and shone on the changing levels of my landscape, a Capability Brown landscape really, our orderly kingdom, our orderly world. The land looked as it should, timeless. On a human scale certainly, but big enough to be indifferent to us human beings who come and go and err and blunder.

Virginia went back to the house to sort out my electricity, I hoped. I didn't go with her. I had a lesson to give the boys. I found them mending some fences, the borzois beside them. The dogs, their deep chests prominent in their sitting posture, looked up as I approached and shuffled their tails on the ground. In between chasing the cats, they were always obedient and sweet-natured, like their owners, I think. The boys put down their nails and hammers and wire-cutters and waited like a pair of clockwork toys to be wound up. Their docility always made me smile. I put the two spades I had brought into their hands. They were very capable so long as they were shown everything, but I had to give an exact and detailed demonstration. They were real workmen, which is to say excellent stooges. They would put nothing in on their own initiative, that I had left out – which is an advantage of course. It is not a fashionable thought but workmen with bright ideas can create havoc. I told them they were going to start planting trees this morning.

'Here is the tree,' I said in Ladybird 'John and Jill' style. I indicated a sapling sugar maple I was holding. A large North American, very vigorous, with fine autumn colour.

'We've planted trees,' said Gavin, speaking of course for both.

'Those were container trees, these are bare-rooted. Let's run through the basics to be absolutely sure.'

We went to the area which had been previously staked out. The trees would be grouped and arranged as fastidiously as flowers in a herbaceous border. I should add that I had abandoned my ambition to teach them about my larger plan. I'd learnt that strategies just zoomed past them. They were happier faced with the simple task of putting a plant in a hole. We were all happier in fact.

'Dig, Gavin,' I commanded. 'Two spades' depth.'

Gavin made a sign to his brother. 'Trev will do the digging,' he said.

'Right. Dig, Trevor. Churn the bottom spit around just as you did before.'

Gavin sent forth a flow of gesticulation.

'Add the compost. Add fertiliser. Mix together. Put stake in middle of hole.'

Gavin demonstrated with his hands. Six months ago I'd protested it wouldn't be possible to work with these boys, it would be much too disruptive a method. But from the beginning I'd always enjoyed it. It was leisurely and moments like this defused nervous tension, slowed me down. There was a peaceful rhythm to the tasks. A pulse in the giving and receiving of instructions, from the voice to the hands to the eyes to the body which bent and stretched in response. It was orderly. In the golden age of the pastoral world, you wouldn't snatch and grab as we do, but take your time.

'Spread out the roots in the hole and crumble the soil and compost around them. Fill in, and heel it firm.'

Trevor eased the tree into the hole, steadied it and bent to crumb the soil through his fastidious fingers. The demonstration planting was almost complete.

'What have I forgotten?' I asked.

Gavin looked empty and shared his blankness with his brother. Trevor responded with triumph. The pulse of the message rippled back. *The tree needed tying to the stake.*

I decided not to ask any more questions. Questions were a bit of a mistake. I had enjoyed being slowed up enough.

'Good,' I said but explained that from now on and for all new plantings in this area, they would need to add a tree guard.

'Rabbits?' asked Gavin.

'Deer,' I replied smugly. 'Deer.'

I'd cheered up. The activities of this morning had been a help in putting my tangle with Imogen aside. I looked forward to tomorrow. We'd be going to choose the deer for the kingdom of the animals. My little world would be combed into orderliness once more. A perfect world is an orderly one.

19

IT WAS OUR own new deer park that would be the kingdom of the animals. In the last few months I had worked hard in preparation. It was in the western quarter of the island, next door to the kingdom of the birds from which it was divided by one of the newly dug streams. Separated too of course by fencing which we had erected beside the surrounding tree belt.

Over the weeks a pattern had emerged as the trees which were felled disclosed the shape made by those which remained. Such patterns almost never occur by chance. You choose them and it is often a difficult process. I had walked repeatedly over the land to be sure. I had looked at it as a botanist and a timber manager and an artist. Landscaping is always a trial of strength between the architect and the land. Even now, after years of practice, I still find it hard sometimes to cull trees though one knows it has got to be done. You weed out the weak and the scrappy and the wrongly positioned. You leave in the strong, the best of the big men in their prime. Freed of dependants, they stretch out their limbs, knowing they stand among equals. This way you make a park out of scrubland. You force the park to emerge. And the older it looks the better, because it needs to fit into a history.

There are two great ages in which the deer park has thrived, both utterly different. The first was the medieval period when there were over two thousand. Imagine them then with the wild boar and deer slipping through thin trunks, and the green knights with grey hounds and grim bows in their hands, and the sound of the horn and the horses' hooves. This is the age of the hunters and the hunted with its kinship between love and death, so awful, so beautiful.

The second heyday was the opposite of the first. It was the age of reason and beauty, my favourite, so you can guess I'm talking about Capability's world. The eighteenth century is the golden age of the pastoral myth. Such a lush, green time when deer were prized and kept in fabulous parks of Arcadian beauty; and it was now more the old fox's turn to be hard hunted instead.

In between these two pinnacles of flourishing existence, the pendulum swung against the parks and there were times when they nearly died out. Once, thanks to the savage and killjoy Puritans; the second time in our own century which has been dominated by war and then, subsequently, by the industrialisation of our land. How could anything as fragile and lovely and perishable as a deer park survive? Utopian landscapes require external stability. Only now are we starting to create these wonderful places again.

Perhaps I seemed crazy at first to urge the idea on my clients, but it wasn't just the egotism of the mad artist. It was also because deer parks are fragments of paradise which belong to a tradition. I want to do my bit to ensure that they never die out. It may sound pompous to say this, but a landscape architect has his responsibilities just as anyone has whose work requires taking account of the past as well as the future.

I had made as many arrangements in advance as I could. My plan was for the Laceys to come with me to the park from which they would buy the deer. We had agreed to start at nine o'clock. The park was less than a hundred miles away, so we'd be there and back in daylight. Shortly before time, I knocked at the front door and waited. I could hear shouting, then silence, then Virginia calling, but no reply. She opened the door and looked out. She was wearing a large fox hat. Being foreign meant she wasn't obliged to kit herself out in the wax and mud of the English countryside.

'It's only me coming today,' she said.

'No David?'

She paused. 'He doesn't really want to. I wish he would.'

'Shall I ask him?'

'No.'

'Is he all right?'

She gave a short nod.

I hesitated. I was worried. I wanted to ask what was up, why was there shouting, but if she didn't want to tell me, then there was nothing to ask. We got into the car, drove slowly under the big tunnel of rhododendrons, over the link to the mainland and up through the shelter of the lanes. To either side the trees were leafless. The green sponges of their first appearance were gone. There were just trunks and brown arms around us, moving narrowly in the wind.

'I dreamed of you last night,' said Virginia suddenly.

'Me?'

'I dreamed you were in France. You went into a café. You told the garçon, you wanted a cup of coffee. He asked: Do you want two cups?'

'Was your dream in French or English?'

'French.'

'How clever. So what did he really say?'

'He said: *Deux cafés?*'

'*Monsieur désire deux cafés?*'

'Yes, though I don't think he was as old-fashioned as that. Then you said: *Une tasse simple. Je suis seul.* And he replied: *Ah, pauvre monsieur. Il est seul.*'

'Oh dear.'

'*Il est seul.* Just like that. I think I dreamed it because of, oh well, your mother dying.'

'Because of my ex-mother and my ex-wife, that's what you really mean, isn't it?' I glanced at her and caught the tail-end of a minute grimace. She obviously felt there had been want of tact in recounting her dream. 'Well, I suppose that does make one pretty *seul.*'

'Sorry,' she said. 'It's not a dream to lift the spirits, is it, though it seemed rather nice at the time with that heart-warmer of a waiter. Perhaps I shouldn't have told you. I'm a bit down today. It's so grey, isn't it, in winter here? How I long for the sun. I think I'll move to France.'

I was affronted. 'I'm making this wonderful place and you're talking about moving.'

'Sorry. I didn't mean it. It was a manner of speaking.'

'I love the seasonal changes. I like the rhythms. I don't understand this fashionable new illness of SAD.'

'Seasonal Affective Disorder?'

'Is that what it is?'

She looked out of the window. 'Seems to me David's got a touch of it this morning.'

'I'm sorry to hear that.'

'That's why I'm gloomy too. I tried to buck him up. I told him my dream about you.'

'Didn't it make him laugh?'

'Quite the reverse. He said – oh, forget it. One can go round and round with these things forever. Come on. Let's have a terrific day. I was really looking forward to this.'

It was the first time I had seen Virginia's guard slide.

'You *are* looking forward to this,' I corrected. 'Live in the present.'

'Right. I *am* looking forward to seeing this park.'

And to divert her, as we drove, I told her about the origins of such parks which go back even further than I've said. They lie in the Persian *pairidaeza*, and I told her in the words of Xenophon, the Greek general and historian who took it upon himself to tell us.

Once upon a time, I said – Xenophon is more precise, actually in 407 BC – Lysander visited the palace of Cyrus the Younger in Sardis. The Persian Cyrus who was very grand and covered in jewels, showed him his garden. 'Here is my park,' said Cyrus, or some such phrase. 'It is my pairidaeza,' and he spoke this word which comes from pairi which means 'around' and daeza, a wall.

'What was it like?' asked Virginia.

'All we know from Xenophon is that it looked like an enclosed and formal park. Cyrus was very proud of it for he'd measured and planted part of it by himself. Anyway, it must have been special and influential for we think that Xenophon's description inspired Virgil to build a similar grove of trees, a paradisus, around his temple. This was how the word paradisus came into our language. From the Persian park.'

'So it's the true paradise garden that we're going to see today.'

'It is in a way, I suppose. The original pairidaeza, the Persian park.'

'How wonderful that these things go back so far.'

I looked at her and smiled because dear Virginia, who I was sorry to see so low this morning, had given the right response. She'd said what I feel always. It is a comfort when things go back so far. It stops you from feeling *seul*.

Of course the pairidaeza we were seeing today didn't go back quite as far, though it was one of the oldest and purest deer parks in England. Not many of them are left, just a scattered and glorious few at the tiny top of the pyramid whose base, as I explained, has long since been eroded.

I rattled away about this to my client as we roared up the motorway and she seemed happy enough to be entertained by listening. I also told her about the deer. The little roe and the muntjac which is the oldest deer in the world, and the sika, a stocky chap which came to us only a century and a half ago. But then I told her about the one we would choose this morning: my favourite, the most graceful, the fallow, the traditional creature of the park. So docile and pretty and sweet-natured, I exclaimed, that the Persians are thought to have clothed it in collars and leashes; so precious that the Phoenicians brought it to southern Europe and the Romans from there to the North.

By now, we were at the end of the journey and were driving along the twisting road that wound through a valley. We turned into a tree-hung lane that ran round the park. As we emerged from the blindness of a wood, I felt my passenger lean forwards.

'There they are,' said Virginia suddenly. 'Stop the car.'

'What's the point,' I protested. 'You'll be seeing them properly in a couple of minutes when we go in.'

'Do stop the car. This is how we should see them. Wild things like shadows at a distance.'

And I stopped the car because she was right. We got out and looked through the palings at the faintly glimpsed beasts in the mist-filled distance. How beautiful they were through the trees, some indolently lolling on the grass, some lifting their antlers to the branches, a few of the furthest dipping their muzzles delicately into the silver water of a pool.

'I've never forgotten what you once told me,' said Virginia quietly. 'It's things you see and don't see which have the most haunting effect. Things that you think you've half-imagined. Do you remember?'

I looked at the golden and dappled creatures among the trees. Did they exist or were they an image idealised, an illustration in some Persian manuscript? Enchanting survivors from old ways of life when there was leisure and time and a sense of beauty: turning their graceful heads, tossing the boughs of their antlers, lifting their necks like unicorns out of a myth. Paradise animals for our own pairidaeza. How strange it seemed in our ugly and urban, short-termist age. How important that we should do this, do whatever we could for the sake of maintaining our old pastoral beauty.

'Let's go in,' I said. We got back into the car and drove past the lodge at the entrance and through some old gap-toothed limes in the avenue and up to the foot of a grey and ramshackle house.

I looked around me as I rang the bell and waited. The building, two-winged like an E without the central prong, was mossy and damp with small windows. A certain amount of romantic decay was in evidence which is to say a certain amount of unfortunate falling down.

'There's no one in,' said Virginia who was still sometimes guilty of a foreigner's impatience.

'They're expecting us. They must be in.' But I rang again and then knocked after allowing an interval for politeness. There was the sound of shuffling steps. An old man opened the door, very formally dressed, in a waistcoat even. I'd been told he was getting on by the agent, but had not expected a man of eighty. Of an age when socks are a struggle to get into and a waistcoat exacting to button.

'Mr Curwen?' I enquired. His name, I knew, was Percy.

We shook hands and apologised inappropriately, the way one does to disarm, me for knocking so loudly, he for the fact that the bell didn't work. I introduced Virginia whom he assumed at once to be my wife. He bowed a little when he shook her hand. It was a fine display of the manners of a period that has long vanished, when contact between people was maintained with a whaleboned courtesy. I saw that Virginia was enchanted.

'No,' she said. 'I'm not actually his wife.'

'She is my client,' I explained, to dispel any ambiguity, but knowing that this was a modern bridge too far.

Behind him, a woman was approaching us down the darkened hall. As she entered the only slice of light, that thrown by the open door, I saw she was not much younger, her head bent deep into her chest. I wished Mrs Curwen a good morning. She made a rheumy but not ungentlewomanly noise.

'Miss Curwen,' he corrected. 'May is my sister.' He turned to her. 'Mr and Mrs Boyd have come about the deer.' He slurred his words a little.

I feared he may have had a stroke. Soon, I thought, this brother and sister will die and take their gentle formalities with them. A new vernacular is sweeping them away with a shiny new broom, replacing their simple and natural dignities because it finds them stuffy and remote.

'If you go round to the back of the house, you will find the keeper in the yard,' said Percy Curwen. He added that only a year ago, he would have come with me but was too tottery now to do the walking. 'But when you return, we must complete the transaction over a drink in the house.'

At this point, he called me 'Sir'. I realised now what I had failed to anticipate: that there was a ritual flavour to this kind of purchase. The waistcoat, the drink – a sherry most probably – the Sir: here was something of a Japanese tea ceremony. All the ingredients of a world on the brink of being dismantled by the glib and the quick.

'What happens to all this when they go?' whispered Virginia as we walked together down the steps.

'God knows. One hopes he has descendants, or at least nephews and nieces who care. If not, who knows? Pop stars? German software manufacturers. The men from the ministry? My God, who knows?'

At the back of the house, the keeper was energetically loading bales of hay onto a tractor. A young man with curly hair and deer eyes set widely apart in his face, he introduced himself as Connor. He looked at me shyly and listened to what I had to say while two black and white cats, this year's litter, were chasing each other round the yard. In the distance there was the sound of a belching groan. It was deep and repeated, or was it the reverberation?

'The last of the rut,' said the deerherd in his Irish voice.

'What?' asked Virginia.

I was surprised. I thought the season of mating was over.

'They rut from October to the middle of November,' said Connor. 'The big boys choose old trees in the park for their rutting stands. They stay there and groan and belch. Like this.' He gave a demonstration, as good as the one we had heard. 'It drives you mad the way it goes on and on and on all the time. The does come and are taken.' He hesitated. 'Would you not like to come and walk with me to the park?'

'Oh yes,' said Virginia. 'It's time I saw some real life. Believe me, I'm enthusiastic but ignorant and have been stuffed the whole way on this trip' – and she turned and glanced at me with one of her gorgeous toothy smiles – 'with all sorts of fancy antiquarian theories. It's time that someone rammed my face into real life. A buck getting the old heave-ho sounds just right.'

Poor young Connor didn't know quite what to make of this speech, so he turned round in embarrassment, climbed onto the tractor and we fell in behind him as he led us out of the yard.

We followed him over a field, and then through a big metal gate which had been freshly painted and welded. A ditch and palings separated the field from the park. Every so often he would stop the tractor to allow us to keep in touch. A slight sun had come out and had sculpted the land into patterns of floating light. I noticed the springy nature of the closely cropped turf. It was as soft and as plush as a mattress. The grazing of sheep had refined the coarseness of the grass.

Before us the scene was quite lovely. We were walking over the lip of a shallow bowl, into the eighteenth century, the land slightly falling then rising beyond and in wings to either side. There was a mix of space and bosky shelter, of glades and open pasture. Old autumn and new winter soaked it in colour. That red and the green, so close in tone which heightens their contrast. The green of the grass and the rust of the trees and the slopes where the bracken was copper. What a scene. The trees were in full and resplendent maturity. Oaks and a few beeches planted two hundred, more, I think, two hundred and fifty years ago, stood widely spaced but clumped into choirs with a few noble and random outriders beside them.

Connor stopped the tractor and waited for us to reach him. He pointed at one of the trees. Here the grass was shaved bare and the soil pushed into a hollow. We stared at it like two trackers. 'There's your rutting stand. The buck scrapes at the ground with his forefeet and antlers. He stands there and calls. The does gather. The young boys, the sorels and prickets, watch what their fathers and uncles get up to.'

'Where is the chap who was groaning?'

'He didn't get lucky. Must have gone away and given up hope.'

'Where are the others?'

'Can't you see? Look behind the trees and in the bracken.'

I looked. I was blind. I am an amateur.

Connor put his fingers in his mouth and sent out the most colossal of whistles. In response there was a stirring as if a frieze were coming to life. The red bracken began to disintegrate into moving shapes of chestnut and fawn. Fern fronds fanned out into antlers. They came stepping towards him with their straight backs and long giraffe necks. A few big bucks with their heads of forked lightning, swaggering prickets, elegant does with their racing ankles and, there amongst them, a little jostled, their small legs working the hardest, this year's fawns, so poised, so pretty with their innocent faces.

Connor got off the tractor and started to unload the hay, snagging the twine and rolling the soft stuff over the ground.

'We start feeding them now, just in case it's a hard winter.'

I gestured to Virginia to stand back, expecting them all to be wary, but they were springing forward, making hungry noises as they ran. They ignored us. They pulled at the hay, sifting and spreading it over the ground.

'Our herd's quite tame,' said Connor. 'Not like the park where my friend works. They're really wary there, wild boys.'

'Why the difference?'

'They don't need to feed them, do they? The stocking rate's lower and the land's richer than ours. Full of acorns and beech mast which keep them in good condition.' He had lost his shyness. He stood there, slightly bow-legged, in his muddy coat and black boots, his nose as pink as a chaffinch, his brown eyes set widely apart. 'I'd like to work there when the old man here goes. Maybe he's a stickler, but we get on just grand. He loves his stock. I don't want a new bloke coming in with his fancy ways when I know best what's right.'

'Who'll take over when he goes?'

He rolled his eyes. 'The nephew from London.'

Here it was, the old battleground between the big city and the big countryside, between the owner and the one who does.

'More likely he'll leave you alone,' I said.

A droplet hung from the end of Connor's nose. He sniffed it back with disparagement. It had started to shower. He pulled an astrakhan hat out of his pocket and jammed it over his brow like a Cossack.

Good keepers are the same the world over. Young and fit and strong and in the pink – mountain boys. They love their stock. They have high standards. They give total commitment. They get up at night. They walk miles. They know every tuft of the ground, every face in the herd, the look of the eye.

'See that big fellow?' said Connor, nodding towards the buck at the back. 'He'll have to go.'

They love their stock but are unsentimental.

'He's getting old. See his drooping Adam's apple. See his head bent down. He'll have to go.'

'How do you do it?'

'We get in the best marksman. A shot through the head. Instant. Like that.' He slapped his hand hard on his thigh. 'Not through the heart like some buggers. The deer takes longer to die. The shooter can make a blunder.' He challenged me with his eye. He repeated, 'Instant. That's what you want.'

'I didn't realise we'd have to think about culling,' said Virginia. 'Oh God. Why can't we just buy nice young ones, and they'll get a bit older, then a bit older still, then they'll die and we won't have to cull?'

'Looks like your wife's just wanting a few pets,' said Connor. 'Not too worried about standards, is she, or supplies.'

'She's my client, not my wife,' I said again, more for her benefit than his, though part of me rather liked these references to my status. It was quite nice to be upgraded from my position as the landscape architect.

'It's different for me,' said Connor, ignoring my comment.

I could see what he was thinking. What the professional always thinks when he's faced with a pair of dilettante amateurs. That it's all very well for the likes of us, but that he was a keeper, a man with a proper job to do. A manager, a man answerable to posterity for the quality of his herd. He could ruin the lot if he didn't worry about everything. He had to be alert to the balance between the size of the herd and the extent of the land, to the ratio of bucks to prickets and prickets to does and fawns to does, to their condition and colour and the shape of the antlers. A good herd has a good deerherd. A poor herd has a keeper who is always asleep.

'I know,' said Virginia. 'It's different for you. Not so easy. You can't just play at being a shepherdess, can you?'

We all three stared at the object of his problems. The herd was busy munching, their flanks moving in and out, the few bucks greedy as lions, the fawns cuddling close to the round-bodied maternal does. The range of colour was wider and richer than at first sight, their pelt thicker and softer in the dark dappled camouflage shades of winter. But there were also a few who were lighter. And, then, in the distance, where a group were crowding behind palings, I noticed a small newcomer, pushed into obscurity by some other companion does. Only her white head was visible, the colour of polished ivory.

'What's that one?' I asked.

Connor followed my eye. 'The one over there?'

'Behind the palings.'

'White?'

'Her head's pale, certainly. She's fully white, you say?'

'Absolutely white.'

'I didn't know you had white.'

'We don't. We don't encourage it. Some parks do. We don't. She's a surprise. We think she's a throwback. Ours are mainly common or menil, fawn and white, see? The colour comes from the sires.'

'You want to get rid of her?' I asked.

Connor looked startled. He sucked in his teeth, re-arranged the hat further down his head. He must have thought I was asking if she would be culled. 'Don't want to breed from her, that's for sure.'

'But she's beautiful.'

'She's a grand girl but she's not right for the herd.'

'She's a unicorn,' exclaimed Virginia.

Faced with the unreasonableness of women, Connor looked at me for help.

'Will you sell her?' I asked.

There was a pause filled with the sound of the falling rain, the whispering of the strands of hay and the grinding and rolling of their mouths. Steam rose from their bodies.

'Do you want her?'

'Why not?'

'Right,' said Connor. 'She's got a good conformation,' he added, moving into selling mode.

We walked towards the enclosure where a group of pretty young does were clustered. I was eager for this lovely thing to be revealed in the open, but the others were still crowding around. I wanted her desperately, but I was keeping this hidden in the interests of not being upped on the price. What he was discarding was our find. So unexpected and what a trophy.

'Can't we see her properly,' I said coolly, like any prospective buyer. I hoped Virginia would shut up.

'You will in a moment,' promised Connor.

'How old is she?'

'Of an age to suit you,' he said in pure horse-dealer style.

'Which is what?'

'Coming up for eighteen months.'

'Why is that best?'

'Because she hasn't been taken. At this time, the rutting season, we keep the young does separate from the bucks. The old man told me to choose you some nice girls from this lot. Too young for us to let carry fawns. Next year we can send you a few prickets and also a buck if it's quick breeding you're wanting so you can have your very own wee fawns the following June.'

'Look,' said Virginia.

By now, the herd was beginning to mill around more loosely. The cluster of maidens had stopped jostling. They backed and trotted off, the black switch of their short tails flickering. Naked and virginal, the little white doe was now entirely revealed. She was tossing her head, her slender tall neck tilted upwards, her jaws moving from side to side.

'Pretty one, isn't she,' said Connor.

'The Landgrave of Hesse-Darmstadt,' I said, forgetting my resolve not to do any talking up, 'had his deer parks stocked with white stags. The last few were sent to the Elector of Saxony as a present. After the French Revolution, the stags took part in a carnival procession in Dresden, drawing a carriage bearing the figure of the huntress, Diana.'

'Fancy that now,' said Connor. He looked at her with new interest but some perplexity. He'd get it muddled when he recounted it in the pub tonight.

Beside me Virginia had more sense than I and kept quiet.

This animal was really enchanting. Wild but civilised by her whiteness. I could see her amongst the green, lovelier than any Watteau fantasy. White amongst green is a magnet to the eye. It is an absence of colour like starlight. I am a landscape architect. I suppose I feel I have to justify my response to her. It sounds so foolish to say what I really think now. It embarrasses me. But I think I knew then that a creature like this utterly steals your heart away.

20

WE WERE IN high spirits for most of the journey home. The day had turned out even better than we had expected. Virginia was in raptures about the park and the deer. I was equally happy. I'd gone for a purpose which had been fulfilled, and you're never prepared in these circumstances for extra discoveries. A white doe, we repeated to one another.

'You know what was the nice final touch?' I said to Virginia.

'What?'

'It sounds corny but having a drink with that old brother and sister in the room full of heads and antlers.'

'A bit morbid, that.'

'Not morbid. They weren't trophies but friends which made the room friendly.'

Virginia said: 'The Curwens were darlings but sort of sad. There was something so sad about their situation.'

'You know what I thought?'

'What?'

'They are the old world. You are the new. Confident, energetic, with a future. It was funny to see you both together.'

'They made me feel vulgar.'

She fell silent. She stroked the fur of the hat lying in her lap. Then a moment later, she broached something that made me surprised. 'You know what I felt?'

'What?'

'Looking at that old brother and sister. It reminded me that Imogen and David would have grown old together if I hadn't come along.'

'Unmarried brothers and sisters often shack up together.' It was the blandest thing I could come up with. I wished she would let me forget the woman. I had forgotten her completely all day.

'It wouldn't have been good for David.'

'Why not?'

'Because.'

'That's not much of an answer.'

'She's so possessive.'

'Is she?'

'She's very possessive. He's very responsible. Being so much older, he looked after her when she was little. I think she manipulates his sense of responsibility.'

'How?'

'When she was newly widowed, he invited her to stay with him for a month. He thought it would be good for her. She would be in a state of shock. What happened was that she gave up her job and stayed on.'

'But I thought he worked in London.'

'He did. His business was there but he would come back every week-end. I can't deny it suited him. He was divorced and his sister filled the gap. She'd do the cooking, the washing, keep the place dry and warm. In return she was kept. But for Imo it was the easy option. It lasted for two years. For both their sakes, he should have got her out.'

'Then you happened?'

'I met him again.' She hesitated. 'I'd known him years before, through my first husband who was a heart specialist, as you know. The medical world is divided into two sorts, you see. Those who work face-to-face with the patients and the others, the scientists. They're no good with people, so they work on their contents and deposits. But the two groups often know one another, I guess because the patients and their deposits overlap.'

'Surely they co-operate rather than just know one another. I'd have thought the interests of the two groups coincide.'

'Usually. But when there are two groups, occasionally, there's a conflict.'

'How?'

She took her time. 'Oh, I don't know, this and that.'

The length of her pause made me wonder if a conflict of interest had arisen between her first husband and Lacey.

'You said your first husband was a cardiologist.'

'Yes.'

'And David was a chemist, he told me.'

'Not exactly. He was a director in a pharmaceutical company.'

'That's how they knew one another?'

'Originally, yes,' said Virginia who was showing signs of impatience. 'Look, how did we get onto this subject? We were talking about Imogen.'

I was as keen to avoid talking about Imogen, as Virginia about the work of her husbands.

'I've forgotten what you were saying about her,' I said with the utmost vagueness.

'I was saying that when I came on the scene, Imogen had to move out.'

'Ah.' I was getting muddled by bits of the jigsaw and whether it was Virginia or Imogen who had filled me in.

'You know that David bought her the house and the land.'

'You mean the cottage she lives in now?'

'Yes.'

'I didn't know.'

'It was incredibly generous.'

'It was. But you must have been relieved in a way.'

'Why relieved?'

'I don't know. Because it relieves you of any feeling of guilt, I suppose.' This was risky ground with a client. This was going much too far.

'Why should I feel guilty?'

'No reason at all.'

'It wasn't my fault she had to get out.'

'No. Of course not.'

'These things happen. Anyway it was all for the good. Imogen would have dragged David down. I saved him. I've given him a life.'

I made no reply. I couldn't find a tactful way of telling my client to shut up. To remind her that this was none of my business. If I remained silent maybe that would suppress her. I wondered why she was talking about Imogen and her husband. Perhaps it was because we were nearing home and she was being drawn into its orbit again.

He had been a stone in her mind at the beginning of the day. She had made an effort to push it away, had managed to escape into diversion, but now it had found a way to roll back again.

Perhaps — which was worse — like all women, she had a sense of emotional charge in the air. Perhaps she guessed that something happened the other night between Imogen and me. Women are so cunning the way they probe so innocuously. They set a trap with intimacies of their own, in the hope these will yield a similar reciprocity. They send out their questions like off-target arrows and then make a single deadly dive for your vitals. We men are hopeless at this. We are all novices.

Beside me, Virginia had stopped stroking the fur on her lap. She was immobile, thinking. She gave a sigh. For a second I wondered whether I should tell her what had happened. If she were not setting a trap, there would be no trap to fall into. But the course of action was too high risk. It was true I had a respect for Virginia and had grown very fond of her, and I had been given some reason to think she felt the same about me. But instead of making things easier, this made them more difficult. It had drawn the bonds of our social, as opposed to professional, contract more tightly, which would make my entanglement with her sister-in-law yet more untrustworthy, unscrupulous even. I was furious with myself. It had been an 'accident', a classic one-night-stand, but as a grown-up how could I claim it had happened when the balance of my mind was disturbed? I was furious that I had given an outsider the power to jolt the harmony of the world I was creating. My worlds are all about otherworlds: they're all about order. This is the reason that people employ me.

I realised that it was impossible ever to tell her. The critical moment receded. It was replaced by a welcome objectivity. The event was too close for me to judge it. It would not be repeated. Soon it would seem not to have happened. In the meanwhile it might be a good thing for me to leave. My presence could be a provocation. Better for me to go away. Remove any emotional field. Absence would make me impersonal. When I came back, I'd be only the landscape architect again, neutered and neutralised, a man with a job to do well.

'Virginia,' I said. 'I've been thinking. It's not easy to work the land in bad weather. And it'll soon be a bit wintry for me to spend a night in the boathouse.'

'I know. I had meant to ask you if you wanted to move into our house.'

She sounded doubtful: all ifs and buts and would haves. Lacey must be an obstacle.

'That's very kind. But there are jobs I've got to do elsewhere this winter. I think the best plan is for me to see the deer in, later this week. Then I'll come back next year very early in the spring.'

'I'll miss you,' she said. 'We've all got used to having you around.'

'If I'm away and you can't get hold of me, Tim Rowland in my office will always help.'

'I didn't mean that. I'm not talking official. You know you've become a proper friend.'

'I hope so.'

'I'm not my normal self today, a bit down this morning, but honestly it's been a wonderful day.'

At this point we were crossing the link from the mainland to the house. I asked her: 'Do you remember the party you gave here in the summer? When you said the secret of a happy life is to enjoy yourself?'

'I remember. I believe that.'

'I think you're right.'

'You started to give me Jung's list for a happy life. You said he said one needed an appreciation of art or nature. You never did tell us the other things.'

'They're very obvious.'

'Of course. All obvious things are true.'

'Good health. Good marriage.'

She was quiet. She then said: 'Do you agree?'

I think she was making a reference to the omission in my case. The *seul*ness of this morning.

'Not necessarily. I think that more of one can make up for the lack of another.'

She didn't reply.

I stopped the car outside the house. Virginia got out. Lacey must have been watching. He came down the steps.

'Look at my hat. It's drenched,' she said.

'Did it go well?' he asked me. 'I'm sorry I couldn't come with you. I expect Virginia told you, I was called away on business.'

I didn't look at Virginia. 'Yes,' I said. 'I too am very sorry you couldn't come. There's not long to wait, though. I've arranged with the deerherd to bring the deer here by the end of the week.'

And we left it at that. Whatever had happened must have blown over.

In the next few days, I forgot all the ambivalence created by these cross-currents. This was partly because there was plenty to do – a mass of finishing touches – but also because I was full of anticipation. All this while the park had been waiting to be filled with life. Its trees might look majestic but it was only a new park and its fresh paint would show until its surface was ruffled. The animals needed to move in and make it their home.

On Thursday Connor drove the deer over. They didn't arrive at the same time of day as the flamingos had reached us. It was mid-afternoon, nearly dusk when the small lorry turned up. Deer settle in well in the evening. They are crepuscular creatures though it is true they are also active at the beginning of the day. In the fading light we watched the lorry crawl over the ground, taking care at each of the bumps and corners. Low down in the van, through one of the ventilation slats I was reassured to glimpse the beautiful face of my little white doe. I remembered that fallows take their travel easily. They don't stand up, preferring to lie down on the soft straw floor.

Lacey and I beckoned Connor onwards over the track to the park. The lorry crept forward, in through the gates and onto the field. When it was well away from the fences, Connor did a circle like a taxiing aircraft and finally halted with the rear aimed at the centre of the park. He got out, and motioned me into the van, and told Virginia and Lacey to stay out of sight at the side. He explained that his job was to stand at the back of the lorry and entice the deer outwards, whilst mine was to push them gently towards him from inside the vehicle. I climbed in at the front whilst he unlocked the rear to let down the ramp. The deer looked up startled. They were all snuggled together, their delicate knees bent forwards, their toes pointing backwards. In the gloom, my white pet was shining. She struggled upright. There was a scraping of winkle-picker hooves on the floor. I made gentle whooshing signs with my hands in the hope of blowing them outside. The first of the hinds put her nose into the clear fresh air. Connor thrust his hand in his pocket. 'They love apple,' he said. 'Giving them an apple is a grand thing to do.' He bit the fruit into roughly four chunks. I watched him hold one on the flat of his hand. A nose grazed his palm, took the paring of russet with great delicacy into her mouth. I was so close I could see the long fur of her eyelashes cast down. The others came in search of their portions. One by one they began to stagger down the ramp.

Before us the trees were already black in the evening and the air had the keenness of eastern cold. A new moon was in the sky. Two songbirds in the trees shared shrieks of alarm and flew off. For a moment the cluster of deer stayed near us, perhaps adjusting to the stability of dry land after the rocking of their vehicle. Then as a herd they turned and trotted off into the indigo blackness of the trees. Long after the others, the white one was visible, threading her way like a plume of smoke through the trunks.

I could tell from my clients' faces that like me they were completely entranced. They weren't at all nervous. Even I wasn't nervous. This occasion didn't resemble in any way the release of the flamingos. It wasn't an experiment, it wasn't uncertain. It was, I think, rather, a most glorious fulfilment. Moments like this are pure happiness. They cast their spell. They transcend everything one knows. I am not at all religious, not in the orthodox nor the tree-hugger sense, but that evening I defy anyone not to have seen Pan and his dryads and naiads moving among those trees. I shall always remember this moment of transition when the field of trees, the essence of stillness, turned into a deer park full of movement. I shall never forget the necklace of deer running helter-skelter through the glades, running for joy like gazelles without the leopard or the cheetah, safe from night-hunters, even from poachers. The white one reappearing with her long neck like a moonbeam though the moon was too thin that night to throw any light.

We all watched in silence. Keepers supposedly, but really the audience to a dance, an inauguration. 'I have never seen anything like it,' said Lacey, and I was truly glad that he was the one who said this rather than Virginia, because, I, too, now felt I had been given an obligation to bring relief to his dark side.

'They're grand little things,' said Connor. 'Which man on earth would not love to have them?'

We stayed there for a few minutes longer, just to make sure there were no immediate problems, then, seeing Connor grow restless and knowing he had a long drive, we returned him to the house, offered him a meal which he refused and went over his instructions again. When he left, he reminded me it was always a grand idea to have an apple or a turnip to hand in one's pocket.

Afterwards, I shared a meal with the Laceys that evening in celebration. The three of us were so happy and moved and excited, we even toasted the garden with our glasses of wine.

At the end of the evening, I made a detour on my way back to the boathouse. First, to the kingdom of the birds to see the flamingos and the ducks in the pool beside them. I was afraid my torchlight would distress them, so turned it off and accustomed my eyes to the darkness. At first I could only locate them by their watery noises. Then their shapes became visible, the flamingos suspended like islands in the sky, the ducks twirling mounds in the water. I wished them goodnight and then left them to make my way out to the neighbouring kingdom, our deer park. Opening the gates, I realised I knew every inch of the land, every hollow, every rise, the trees that had been taken away and the trees that remained growing. The maiden fallows were not visible. They had melted away, less substantial than shadows, but there was a noise of bodies, of animals breathing. It was cold and the warm puffs of their breath would be steaming into the ice of the air. Tomorrow I would have to leave their singing and dancing. I wished I hadn't made a commitment to going away.

21

IN MY ABSENCE from home, a few Christmas cards had accumulated on the mat at the cottage. There were rarely many. Most of the professional ones – paintings by old masters or photographs of the owner's home – came to the office. There was an ostentatiously large one from Strasbourg which must mean Jenny, and a local one in Alice's hand and another small envelope which I recognised as Louise. All, I knew, would be environmentally anxious, made from the soft wood pulp of sustainable forests and for each card a new tree would have been planted. I opened my ex-wife's first. Greetings from Louise were not exactly convincing. She had once remarked that the people to whom one sent Christmas cards represented only the sediment in one's life. After this it became harder to exchange salutations. Her card showed a cat and a robin, the one about to lunch off the other. Inside was a note that it was my turn this year: since I wouldn't be going to spend Christmas Day with my mother, how about me giving them a lunch instead?

I took the cards and some bills and went into the kitchen. The noise of Christmas made arriving back in the real world even more of a cultural shock. I made a coffee and opened Jenny's which promised a prezzie would come under separate cover (typically drink and a tie had alternated over the years). Last of all came Alice which in a funny way carried the most baggage, though all it said was 'Love, Alice', with no reproach despite her earlier protestations. She must have decided to make allowances for the death of my mother. She had that combination of qualities that makes one feel guilty. She was forgiving and kind and dependable and thorough and nice-looking but so boring. This degree of boringness I would forget in her absence. I would be reminded only when I met her again. Mildly boring pople make you feel bored. She did not belong to this category. I'm afraid she belonged to the fundamentally boring, who have the effect of making you boring as well. Alice and I were no good for each other, but I thought again, in the same way I had so often argued, that for the sake of sex and a limited companionship, we would salvage some of the Christmas holiday that Louise would not occupy.

The thought of Louise and Abi coming for Christmas Day was actually very cheering. After Alice, I knew that a little asperity would come as a relief. I wondered whether to take them out to a meal, but hotel and restaurant Christmasses must be so awful, with elderly strangers in paper hats. I decided I'd give them a traditional dinner at home but one with a difference. I'd dispense with the turkey and pudding and give them a ham baked with black-eyed peas instead. It was a dish that Virginia had told me everyone in the South cooks on New Year's Day. 'It brings you luck,' was how she'd explained it. I'd put up some holly and ivy and, after the ham, I'd give them an almond and lemon flan and we'd open our presents. It would be an alternative as well as a conventional Christmas. I'd make it the kind of occasion when no one could look backwards and say 'do you remember the Christmas when . . . ?', reminding us of the time when we were truly a family and all lived together. I hate that false moment when you see people trying to reassemble lives they have fragmented.

The following morning I went into Cheltenham and looked for some gifts. It was strange not to be treating my mother who'd always been easy. Every year I would keep her going with a fresh batch of Floris. For Alice, I bought a Victorian brooch with opals, remembering too late that opals mean tears and that Christmas might well end with more than just these. For Abi, I was going to get some earrings but was inhibited by my daughter's stud in her nose; so I bought her a jade ring instead and hoped it would fit on her finger. For Jenny, I went to a bookshop and bought a work on medieval gardens. Jenny was always easy. Anything for her demi-château held appeal.

Louise was a problem. She was always more difficult, but I decided to stay put in the bookshop rather than return to the jeweller's. If she had a man in her life, then the task of adornment had passed over to him. I looked for a few appropriate titles. Louise was awkward, even in this area. I wished I knew somewhat less about her tastes. She disliked most of the obvious fiction bestsellers. No Latin Americans ('too many words'), no professorial novels ('clever dicks'), no Aga sagas ('let her cook on a primus stove' – a bit rich since she had installed one of the dark green cookers herself). What the hell would she like? If I went for an art book, she'd be bound to have it already. What about a silicon valley thriller – a high-tech adventure? Not when I'd given our daughter the personal and romantic gift of a ring.

I drifted on into the back of the shop: the second-hand section, the graveyard for books that had started out life in the front. The choice here was greater but this wasn't a success. It was simply distracting because it was so random. For myself, I found the monthly sky guide and Norton's *Star Atlas*. Then as I was leaving, I saw the works of Heinrich von Kleist in a single volume. I remembered the tone of Virginia's voice saying '*Das muss ein Mann mir sagen, eh'ich es glaube.*' It was an irresistible challenge. Unfortunately, the text of this book was in German which was a bit of a deterrent, but it was only two pounds so I looked through the contents and turned to the stories. I tested some bits to see if the text was beyond me. My German's quite passable, better than in my schooldays. I visit there often because the Germans are good breeders of grasses and plants. They have high standards. They weren't eugenicists by chance.

I tested at random, a bit here and a bit there. A paragraph from *Die Marquise von O*, the film of which I had greatly enjoyed, and then one at the end of *Über das Marionettentheater (About the Puppet Theatre)* which seemed a nice title. Here, the words *Baum der Erkenntnis* attracted my eye. This meant 'the tree of knowledge'. I started to read. *Would we have to eat again from the tree of knowledge . . .?* I added the book to my personal pile. I usually mend the clock if I am home at Christmas (one year it will work), but this year between Alice and Louise and the stupor of holidays, I resolved to translate *Über das Marionettentheater* instead.

It was snowing when I emerged from the shop. Grey town flakes in a town sky. Even the white doves fluttering over the roofs looked grey. It had been predicted to move in from the south-west that morning. Had it been snowing on the flamingos and the deer? I thought of the crystals sparkling on my white doe's straight back. Her fur would look creamy under its icing of soft diamonds.

I returned to the antique jeweller's shop. I bought Louise the pair of earrings I had rejected for my daughter. They were garnets and would go well with her short freshly blonded hair. A less generous part of me even hoped they would eclipse any present that her new fellow gave her. I thought too that I would promise her some of my portion of the legacy that would come from my mother. Not money, to be honest, but perhaps a few bits of furniture she had often admired. I hoped she wouldn't reject them on the grounds that they reminded her of my mother.

Ham with black-eyed peas is an easy dish to cook. You put them in a casserole dish and let them simmer gently forever, so I wasn't concerned they might spoil when my ex-wife and daughter turned up late on Christmas morning.

'I'm sorry,' Louise said, as she arrived. 'We overslept. There's been a bit of excitement.' She sniffed. 'What a nice appetising aroma.'

'It's a special dish. It brings you luck. What's this excitement?'

I hung up her long black wool coat and Abi added her own which was a tan poacher's jacket. She was wearing tight herringbone pants and a red kerchief over her head. Like her mother, she looked slightly on edge. I noticed that the stud in her nose was gone, though the edges of the hole had yet to join up. This was more shocking than when it went in. Here was a change of policy, rather than of mere style.

'Has something happened?' I asked, looking to the side of her nostril. Was it possible she wanted to apply for a more serious job?

'Lots,' said Louise.

'Lots and lots and lots and lots,' confirmed Abi.

'What?'

'Not now. Let's eat. We'll go into this later.'

'Stop looking at my nose,' said Abi with some dignity.

It has never been any good nagging Louise. It only makes her tight-lipped and curmudgeonly. She has to spill her confessions in her own time. So we went to the table which I had laid to be festive.

I had found a white tablecloth and placed some sections of holly in the centre. I'd also added a dozen crackers in the hope of inducing a party atmosphere, though when there are only a few of you, there is rather an anti-climax when the bangs are over. One does wonder whether previous ages made the same connection we do between noise and enjoyment.

'My goodness,' said Louise. 'You really are trying. And such a lovely roasting smell.' She leaned over the casserole with curiosity. 'Can I take the lid off?' She lifted the cover and peered inside. 'Beans. Gracious. It must be Christmas.' She put the lid back and sat down with a thump.

'Not beans. Ham and black-eyed peas. It's a New Year Southern custom. It brings you luck,' I repeated. 'It's not out of a tin.'

'Actually, if I can interfere, I'd suggest putting the ham on a plate.'

All three of us anxiously crowded together to transfer the ham. One man and two women lifting a joint. I think I wasn't the only one who was trying quite hard. I took up the knife and fork and started to carve slices as thin as a handkerchief. It sounds Pooterish but, like most men, I take pride in my carving. Whilst Abi was waiting, I saw her pick up a cracker and look for the tag of 'recycled paper', in the same way that some people peer under a plate for Chelsea or Meissen.

'I haven't asked you how the funeral went,' said Louise.

'I hope, Dad, you didn't mind I wasn't there either. Honestly I couldn't face it.'

'Don't worry.' I thought of Virginia's father who never went to funerals. 'There were very few there. Jenny and I were the youngest.'

'Jenny looked nicer than I remembered.'

'She is nicer too. More openly vulnerable.'

'You used not to find vulnerability appealing.'

There was no edge to her voice but this kind of remark between exes is never neutral. I concentrated on fanning the slices of ham on the plates. A ladle of beans went at the side.

'Jenny and I will meet up again to sort out the furniture.'

'You'll sell the house?'

'I'm not sure. I'm not sure what she wants. If we do, I thought you might like some of my portion of the furniture.'

'Oh Robert. That's terribly generous but it's not fair on you.'

Anxiety flickered over her face which was puzzling. She was always scrupulous to a degree. Could this be the reason?

'Why not? You deserve it.' I leaned forward to pass her a jug of Cumberland sauce. It was runnier than expected.

Louise abandoned the spoon and poured it. She also helped herself to a large yellow bowl of salad: leaves and olives and tomatoes and avocado. 'This is the most remedial Christmas lunch I can remember.'

'I thought you'd like it.'

'I do.'

Abi was staring down at her plate. She looked pale.

'Help yourself, Abi.'

'I'm terribly sorry, but I don't think I can eat this.'

I tried to remember if she had an allergy. 'Have I got something wrong?'

'It's not that. I've got a stomach-ache.'

We both looked at her. Nothing else matters at Christmas except eating.

'Leave the peas,' I encouraged.

She rose. She seemed wobbly. 'Can I go somewhere and lie down?'

'I'll take her,' said Louise. 'Can she lie down on your bed?'

I nodded. 'Does she want aspirin?' We were already talking of her in the third person as though she were disabled.

'No,' said Abi. 'I've got some pills in my bag.'

The two women went out, Abi bent double. The treads creaked as they climbed slowly upstairs. I looked at the cooling pile of peas. They had lost all appeal. Appetite and its disappearance is infectious. Abi wasn't, couldn't be, on hard drugs, could she? Was there some connection with the removal of the stud from her nose? Was she off drugs, which was inducing a form of cold turkey? If this was the case, why had Louise said nothing? Behind me, the door opened and she came back into the room. I stood up, relieved she was so composed and efficient.

'Is she all right?'

'It's nothing. She's got the curse.'

'Oh.' I sat down again. This sounded so normal, my appetite began to return. It was their business. Men of my generation got to know everything there was to be known about the vagina, but nothing of what lay to its east, west and north. Nowadays boys

169

over-identify with girls' bodies. That is part of today's trouble. No wonder they are androgynous.

'She said she's never had period pain in the past,' said Louise. 'Personally, I think this is psychosomatic.'

'Why?'

'She's worried. She's lost her job. She didn't want to tell you.'

I had a mouthful. I waited to swallow. 'Poor little Abi. How did she lose her job?'

'I don't think she was up to it. It's very competitive.'

'What's she going to do?'

'She's going to the Hebrides.'

'What the hell is she going to do there?'

'Knit.'

'Knit! Knit what?'

'Hats, gloves, scarves. Don't say anything. I know. Everything you'll say I've already said. There's been an almighty row.'

'Can't I talk to her?'

'No. It won't make any difference. Besides, there's another thing that I don't think is unconnected.'

'What other thing?' I hadn't got over the Hebrides hump. Already there was another behind it.

'I wasn't going to tell you immediately. I wanted to wait till we'd finished eating.'

'What is it?' Again, I put down my fork.

'I'm going to move in with the man I told you about.'

This was even more unexpected. A skidding feeling within. I remembered what had struck me most forcibly at the time. 'The one who's thirteen years younger than yourself?'

She moved her hand in dismissal. 'The mathematician. Jonathan's a professor.'

'Louise.'

She wasn't looking at me. 'I'm thinking of marrying him.'

I could say nothing. Never before had she declared she was think-ing of re-marriage. 'You must love him?' I was skidding and floun-dering.

'He needs me. He is periodically inadequate. He needs me.'

'Jesus Christ. What kind of reason is that?'

'Every reason.' She was now staring at me, accusing and speaking very fast. 'When I came with you on the day your mother was dying, I came because I cared about you. I thought you needed me. If you'd carried on needing me I'd have stayed. But I realised you didn't need me. You only needed me as long as you were susceptible. Once you had a dead body, you didn't need me.'

'For Christ's sake, what the fuck could I do?' Starting to shout which was like going through the divorce again. 'I did need you. But you were busy and wouldn't want to go through the practicalities of sorting things out with Jenny and me.'

'You didn't ask me. You let me go. Sacked me.'

'Sacking! Louise, don't sweat up a part. If you want to marry him, then do, but don't blame it on me.' One says things one wishes one hasn't heard. I didn't want to push her into the arms of this nerd. Once we had lived in a cottage. She baked bread at the beginning. She had a computer in the corner. We made plans. We had a baby. I fired clients up with baroque schemes. She did computer graphics for me. Now she would re-programme her computer for a man thirteen years younger than me.

I said: 'I can understand you wanting to re-live your youth.'

'You don't see, do you? What do you expect me to do? What am I waiting for? Look at me. What do you see? Aphrodite? Look at me unemotionally. Aren't I lucky to get a younger man who needs me? My mother always told me to get a younger man so that he looks after you when you're old.'

'That sounds like your mother.'

'Mothers are often right. They speak with the knowledge of hindsight.'

'In this case she was wrong. Or was only right in the days when there were jobs and marriages for life.'

She ignored that. 'And you? What are you waiting for? Something better than Alice? Or have you lost Alice already? Let her go, as they say? Sacked her too?'

I said sullenly: 'She's coming to stay tomorrow.'

'Well, there you are. You're all right too. There's someone for everyone. Isn't that wonderful?'

'I have not asked Alice to move in with me.'

'Maybe you should. Though if you did, let me warn you, it's odds-on she would move out. You are the kind of man women leave. Your work is a ruling passion. Ruling passions rule other things, other people out. You want women only if it's convenient to you. You always have done. I accepted that but couldn't live with it in the end. Most women need to be needed a bit.'

I put my head in my hands. It was empty, tired, weightless, soft. The hardness was gone. My hands went through it. 'I want you to be happy, Louise. Forget everything we've said. All that matters is that you're happy.' My head was trustworthy. It was going through the right exercise. I did want my wife to be happy even though she was committing a bigamy. If one has not found a good successor, one's first wife is always one's wife.

'I haven't handled telling you very well,' said Louise. 'I wasn't prepared. I always thought you'd be the first to re-marry.'

'So it's not undecided then. You are definitely going to marry him.'

'Nothing is definite till it happens.'

'Better for me that I should think it is.'

She stood up and came round to me. She stroked my face. Her fingers as soft as bedclothes.

I was drifting. 'Why is Abi dropping out and going to the Hebrides?'

'She doesn't want to get another proper job. She doesn't want to compete any more.'

'She's never had any grip.'

'You've got grip. I've got grip. Hasn't it ever occurred to you that our grip has scared her gripless. It's made her give up trying?'

'Does she like your professor?'

'She's met him. He's kind to her. Used to perennial students. But I daresay she doesn't like change in the family home any more than the rest of us.'

'Do you think she'll be all right?' I added. 'Don't stop doing that.' Louise had stopped stroking her fingers across my cheek. She started again.

'Will you be OK?' she asked.

'Will you?'

'Such solicitude. A bit after the event, isn't it?'

I said: 'You are another man's problem now. And don't say I made sure you were never mine.'

She sat down beside me, bent forwards. Our foreheads touched and rested together in mutual support. No one knows you better than an ex-wife or husband with whom you have shared years of your worst frailties.

'I have a present for you,' I said. 'Wear them today, won't you?' I did not mean this to sound dramatic.

'What are they?'

'Earrings.'

'What kind?'

'Garnets. Go with your hair.'

'Dear Robert. I've got a present for you too.'

'What?'

'Binoculars.'

We were children. We loved one another. Imminent loss releases emotion. It is a shrine to the past. It is love without responsibility.

Alice came. We exchanged presents. She gave me a nice pair of tartan pyjamas with a matching dressing gown. It was very wifely. She brought a brace of pheasants for dinner. I was glad to junk the uneaten remains of the ham and peas. Maybe there is a natural delay in the luck it brings. Over a year it is bound to be doled out slowly. We made love which was nice and comfortable with her sturdy supportive legs braced around me. I looked down at her kind broad face. Her mouth opened and shut. She never opened it wide when she reached orgasm. She kept it half-closed even when she sneezed. A little bud of an atishoo would emerge. My great-grandmother used to say she could never open her mouth larger than a small 'o'. When Alice grew old, perhaps she would tell her descendants the same. Was it possible they'd be my descendants too? 'What are you waiting for?' Louise had taunted. Tomorrow I might ask Alice to move in with me, or the day after, or the day after that.

The following morning I began on my annual effort to mend the clock. I had learnt that in Alice's company, it was best to keep busy and active. It was a small black marble clock with an austere pediment and had been made in Paris. This year like every year I would glue the bit within, which had fallen off. Normally it worked for two days; then broke again. This was a pity as it had a melodious chime.

'Listen,' I said to Alice, as I pushed the large gold hand towards the hour. It rang with the pureness and clarity of old glass.

'How pretty,' she said. 'Was it your mother's?'

'It's always been mine. Or, at least, I got it when we were first married.' I thought of my promise to give Louise some of the furniture left me by my mother. Professor Jonathan's bottom would rest on it whilst he worked out his calculations. One tells oneself that these are only little things, petty etc., but my God they have the power to irritate. I turned my mind back to the present.

'You see, Alice, this little cog in the clock keeps breaking. What can we do?'

'Take it to a mender's.'

It is amazing how the same words are given colour by their speaker. Louise would have made this sound dry and funny, with me the ponderous idiot. Here it was an example of the literal-mindedness of Alice.

'It has become something of a challenge.'

'I see. You need some more powerful glue. I'll get some tomorrow.'

It was dull and cosy, our heads nesting together, looking at the clock; our clock, now that we'd mend it with an extra-strength glue which she'd bring in with the shopping. Tomorrow I'd ask her to move in for ever: or for the day after.

I put the clock aside to wait till the glue saved it. Alice went to run a bath. A fresh scent of lime and geranium steamed out. I wondered whether to go out for a walk, but the sky was leaden and sleet had begun to fall. It looked like a day for staying inside, so I picked up the collected works, the *Sämtliche Werke* of Heinrich von Kleist. I started reading the introduction. It was slow progress, but I found I could absorb enough for the life of the subject to take shape. What I learnt I found fascinating. It was an account of a man born at the end of the Age of Reason and Enlightenment, at the end of Capability's age. Yet growing up into its antithesis: a world on the brink of revolutionary change, the Romantic Age, when reason no longer prevailed and chaos was more of a friend than an enemy.

Poor, doomed Heinrich von Kleist, 1777–1811: only thirty-four when he died. Army officer ('lost years' he called them), student of mathematics, physics and philosophy, dramatist and writer and man of ideas. What a conflicting life. Here was a man of reason who loathed the idea of being tossed around by chance like a toy or a puppet. Here, in contrast, was the sort of Romantic who believed in Rousseau's idea of man as the noble savage. Here too was the ultimate Romantic who talked of death and dying, who thought that the most sublime thing we can do with our lives is to die sublimely. I was reading with difficulty at this point because a single sentence seemed to cover half a page, but already it was becoming apparent to me that this man who lived by his ideas would also be fated to die by them. In such a case, death could only be an act of will. The question was, which form would it take? What happened was that Kleist fell in love with a married woman with terminal cancer. She sought a pledge from him to do whatever she asked him to. He agreed. She asked him to kill her. In 1811 on the shore of the Wannsee, he lifted his gun and shot her; then he shot himself. Sex and death. Poor Kleist, only thirty-four years old, master of destiny, toy of chance.

After I had finished the Introduction, I put the book down for a moment. The young man was unbalanced, of course, a pessimist – though we are all fated, alas, to live and die by the ideas of our own age. But in the light of what I'd just read, I was by no means sure I particularly wanted to go on to read *Über das Marionettentheater*: or *About the Puppet Theatre*. Regardless of its relevance to paradisaical virtue and the tree of knowledge, this might not match up to one's notion of best holiday reading. However, the prospect of a day spent doing nothing with Alice spurred me to continue. And on the page before me, there was also quite a tribute by Hugo von Hoffmansthal, the great Austrian poet and dramatist:

No Englishman, Frenchman or Italian, indeed no one since the Myths of Plato has produced such a deft and charming piece of philosophy, glowing with intelligence as Heinrich von Kleist's essay on the marionettes.

Such an endorsement, for a man who had scant literary success in his lifetime.

Encouraged, I leafed through the flimsy pages of the book in search of the essay. Here it is. This is the nub of what I found. Most is only a summary but the rest I've translated as it stands. I've worked on it hard because von Hoffmansthal was right: it is a most wonderful little piece. It is a world of puppets and animals and us and of lost grace and how to regain it. *About the Puppet Theatre*. It's clung to me, and had an effect on my life.

22

THE STORY OF *Über das Marionettentheater* is set two hundred years ago at the turn of another century. To be precise, the time is a winter evening in 1801. The place, a public garden in a town called M. Two men meet. One is the storyteller (not named, but I'll call him just A., in the style of the old convention); the other, Herr C., the principal dancer at the opera. What they talk about is the marionette theatre which has been set up in the marketplace for the people's entertainment.

Herr C. says something surprising: that a dancer who wants to develop his talent could learn a lot from the grace of these puppets. He explains that each movement of the puppet has a hidden centre of gravity which is no less than the path of the soul of the dancer. To find it their operator must transpose himself into the marionette's centre. In other words he can only do this by dancing. His job is not like turning the handle of a barrel organ. It's not mindless. Instead, the movements of the fingers of the puppet-master relate to the movement of the dolls attached to them in an artistic fashion, rather like numbers to their logarithms or the asymptote to the hyperbola.

Till now I had followed the sense quite happily, but the last reference was puzzling. What was the asymptote? Or even the hyperbola, for that matter? At this point the door opened and Alice appeared after her bath. I thought better of asking her and just carried on.

Herr C. was in the middle of saying that if an engineer could make him a marionette according to his specifications, he would perform a dance with it which neither he nor any other skilled dancer of his time would be capable of performing. The storyteller asks him what he has in mind.

'"Nothing," replies Herr C., "that cannot already be found here: balance, agility, lightness – but all of a higher order; and especially a natural arrangement of the centres of gravity."

"And the advantage that this doll would have over living dancers?"

"The advantage? . . . namely that it is never affected. For affectation appears, as you know, whenever the soul is situated at any point other than the centre of gravity of the movement."' He says this lack of affectation is a wonderful quality which one looks for in vain in the majority of dancers, and he backs up his statement by rubbishing several of his contemporary rivals. He gives examples of the way they strain, are affected, not natural. '"Such failings," he adds, "are unavoidable since we have eaten of the tree of knowledge. But paradise is under lock and key and the cherub is behind us; we have to journey through this world and see if there's a back way in somewhere."'

The storyteller has to laugh. Isn't it obvious, he thinks, that a mind cannot go wrong, if there's no mind there to start with? But he's stumbling behind Herr C. who is taking his argument to the next stage.

These puppets, says Herr C., have the extra advantage that they're weightless. They know nothing of the sluggishness of matter, that factor that is the greatest enemy of dance; the power that lifts them up is greater than the power that chains them to the ground. In fact, it's quite impossible, he says, for a human being even to approach the puppet.

By now he gives the effect of becoming a tiny bit heated. He descends to rudeness. He accuses his friend of being too ill-read to discuss any period of human development let alone the concluding one.

A. rises to the challenge. He makes a pretty good rejoinder. He says with great dignity that he's well aware what chaos has been caused by consciousness to the natural grace of humankind.

And he cites as an example a boy he had known who was wonderfully charming. He was about fifteen years old then, with just the first traces of vanity prompted by women. It happened that they had recently seen together a well known statue in Paris of a youth pulling a splinter from his foot. Afterwards, the boy, placing his foot on a stool in order to dry it, glanced in the mirror, and was reminded of the pose of the statue. He said as much to A. who, though struck by the same thought and remarking his grace, joshed him and said he was seeing ghosts. The boy repeated the movement in demonstration. But its grace was lost. He repeated it four times, ten times. It was gone. The effect was comical. Bereft of all natural elegance. Ruined by self-consciousness and affectation.

From that day on, the boy was changed. One charm after another fled from him. He had lost the free play of his gestures.

Herr C. who has been listening in silence, nods gently. He now tells the concluding story that makes everything that has preceded it – the debate, the shared experiences – wonderfully clear. He gives an account of his visit to Russia to Herr von G., a Lithuanian nobleman whose sons at that time were top class fencers. One morning the elder offers him a rapier. They fight. Herr C. wins. The boy admits he has met his master. But everything in the world has its master and he is about to introduce Herr C. to his. With that, the sons take him by the hand and lead him to a bear which their father is rearing on the estate. From now on I'll leave the storytelling to Herr C.

'"The bear was standing on its back legs when I approached him in amazement. He was leaning against a post, to which he was tied with his right paw ready for action and looked me in the eye: that was his fighting stance. I didn't know if I was dreaming or not as I looked at such an opponent, but 'Go on! Attack,' Herr von G. said. 'Try to land one on him!' I fell upon him with my rapier, having recovered a little from my astonishment; the bear moved his paw fractionally and parried the blow. I tried to deceive him with feints; the bear did not move. I fell on him again suddenly, with great agility; I would unfailingly have hit a human chest; the bear moved his paw fractionally and parried the blow. Now I was in the position of the young Herr von G. The seriousness of the bear caused me to lose composure, blows and feints alternated, sweat poured from me: in vain! It was not simply that the bear, like the best fencer in the world, was parrying all my blows; feints (which he would not encounter from any natural foe) did not deceive him in the least. Eye to eye, as if he could read into my soul, he stood there, his paw ready to fight, and if my blows were not meant seriously, he didn't stir.

"Do you believe this story?"

"Absolutely!" I cried, applauding with pleasure. "I'd believe it from a complete stranger, it's so probable: all the more so from you!"

"Well, dear friend," Herr C. said, "you are, then, in possession of everything that is necessary to understand me. We see that to the extent that deliberation becomes dimmer and weaker in the natural world, grace always emerges the more brilliantly and dominantly. Yet just as the intersection of two lines on one side of a point after passing through infinity suddenly appears again on the other side, or the image of a concave mirror, after it has travelled through infinity, suddenly emerges in front of us: so can grace be found again when knowledge has passed, as it were, through an eternity; so that it appears at its purest in both those human forms which have either no consciousness at all or an infinite consciousness; that is, in a marionette or in a god."

"So," I said, a little baffled, "would we have to eat again from the tree of knowledge to revert to a state of innocence?"

"Indeed," he replied, "that is the last chapter of the history of the world."'

23

THAT CHRISTMAS I didn't ask Alice to move in with me though we got on quite well. We spent three days together. We mended the clock, we went for brisk walks in the sleet on the hills, we had a beer in the local with friends, but much of the time my mind was elsewhere, thinking of Kleist's real and imaginary world.

When I had finished the *Marionettentheater*, I had closed the book. I had no wish to carry on reading. Anything else might have robbed the piece of its truth and enchantment and perfection. How could Kleist, a literary failure to himself in his lifetime, ever have foreseen he would share his insights to men two hundred years later, not only of his own nationality but to foreigners with another tongue? Yet the truth lasts. The perennial myth about innocence and grace never dies because it is true. It is the force behind the pastoral idyll. We live it out in even the simplest ways, in our homes in the cities as well as the wilderness.

When Jenny and I were very young, our parents gave us a guinea pig, some rabbits, and a series of cats and dogs. We also had a tortoise – Peter the Rock – who left us one day, going south I imagine, in the southerly manner of tortoises. On her tenth birthday, my pony club sister, whose nose was always to be found in books like *My Friend Flicka*, was granted the next stage which was a shaggy palomino. Our parents like most parents believed that animals had a civilising effect on the young. If asked whether they thought that wild creatures tamed humans, they would have laughed and denied it. But in a way it was these beliefs they enacted. Why? It is a puzzler. You'd expect the opposite when night after night animals savage each other to death on the television. Yet we find beauty in this cruelty. We

181

are all romantics now, seeking nobility in savagery. Kleist speaks as simply and as truly to us now, as much, maybe more than he did in his time. How we ache to return through the keyhole to that wildness and innocence which is more distant and irreversible than ever. How we yearn to pull up the long road we have travelled of clones, bombs, and Freuds. We try instead to travel another way back with the help of the pastoral idyll.

All that Christmas and into the New Year, I longed to return to the island. This real yet imaginary world seemed to have taken on a new importance for me. Now more than ever it wasn't only a job. At the office, I was inundated with other works. We were at that stage in the economic cycle when everyone wanted their garden redone. Most of the jobs I pushed over to other designers. I took on a couple of extra staff. In a normal winter I would have been happy to escape to the warmth of work in Sydney, or Greece even. This year I knew I would travel only with the greatest reluctance. For myself I therefore tendered for only two of the more ambitious projects. One in Brittany, another island, which I visited on a rain-soaked day by means of a local sardine boat. The other in Portugal, which was the garden of a friend of a friend, because I thought it would be nice to work in the style of their glorious Moorish tiles. But when my tenders were accepted, my heart wasn't in them. They were nice jobs and the people were charming, but they seemed to be soulless assignments. Mere tinkering with the ground when the woods of my island were full of running deer and the pools with flamingos and Saturn was making his journey to Pisces. I agreed only because I dared not run too much down, which was no way to manage a business. I agreed only because I could still give the broad balance of my time to Eden's island.

It was absurd how often I thought of it. To be honest, not about Abi or Louise or Alice, but the island. My mind was exercised with worries. When it rained heavily, I was concerned about flooding. When it froze once for three days in a row, I even rang to enquire after my flamingos. In neither case was there cause to fret, but I decided that I would return earlier than intended. If the weather was open, I would be back in the middle of February. Meanwhile it was snowing. At the end of January, a thaw provoked more flooding on top of the first. I read news of rivers breaking their banks. Virginia was in Louisiana and I did not dare ring Lacey with whom I had less easy relations, only to receive fresh reassurance that the banks were steep, which I knew, the boathouse secure, the deer safe and the pool had not risen above the knees of the flamingos. I decided that to stop being such a fusspot, I would propose putting a cordon sanitaire around the garden, symbolic of course. I would use an idea borrowed from old churches whose outside walls were studded with carved incubi and medieval beasties. Such figures were thought to keep evil spirits outside the church, barring their entry to the sanctuary of the interior. On my return I'd ask Simon the potter as he did a little stone carving. We could have one in each of the four quarters of the garden, carved on a stone pillar as a look-out guard.

I think I was a little crazy, giving the place these transcendental and spiritual values. I think it was the germ of Kleist that infected me.

I rang Louise the night before I set out for Cornwall to see what had happened. I knew she was due to move in with the professor once she had negotiated the complete letting of her house. After the first breathless-making shock, the need to cling, I was now resigned to the inevitable. It was surprising she had remained so long on her own. It was important she was happy.

'What's your new address?' I asked her.

'We've changed plans. He's coming here.'

This was somewhat discomfiting. I had got used to the house over the years. I was reminded of the usual sensation I had when I visited, of being married to the furniture as well as my wife. Now they would all acquire a new owner, or whatever post-feminists negotiate nowadays.

'You can still come and see me here,' Louise said. 'For God's sake, don't feel inhibited.'

I agreed that would be nice and that inhibitions didn't come into it, which of course they always do. I had intended to broach the arrangements for her portion of my mother's furniture but her entitlement seemed somehow to have slithered unseen into limbo.

After a further exchange about Abi who had assured Louise she was terribly happy and wanted to knit in the wind and the snow for the rest of her life, I came off the phone, though not before Louise had urged me to do something about Alice. It semed only the endeavours of my ex-wife would ever get me near the altar again. Her degree of effort indicated that she was going away for good. I sat for a moment after I had finished speaking to her, realising that not only all the old commitments were severed, but contact as well. My mother, Louise, Abi, had all now floated away. Nothing remained except Alice who evaporated for me in every absence.

The following day was astonishing. One of those brilliant, spring bursts with the sweet air of early summer. It gave me a wonderful drive south. Along the impassable lanes, the hedgerow bottoms were filled with primroses and heliotrope. Purple and white dog violets had started. The pleasure and diversion of an interest in nature is inexhaustible, because it feeds you with so much detail and that detail is always on the move. I had worked up a huge appetite for the fresh season here. Everything had been new to me so far. Summer, autumn, winter. Only spring remained unknown, the beginning or rather the resurgence. It was time to start on the third quarter of the island, or what Virginia referred to as the kingdom of the flowers.

Running along the last section of the drive, through the black tunnel of the tree rhododendrons, many now spilling open into huge gorgeous funnels, I was happy to be reaching home. I was no longer worried in the slightest about Imogen. That nagging threat was now behind me, out of sight. I was coming to a place of harmony, order and beauty which would grow even better according to its own rhythm. It is one of the joys of being a landscape architect that you watch over the prospects, nursing and adding and improving. Your work has a built-in future.

I got out of the car, stretched and sniffed at the languorous river air. It was not quite dusk but the windows of the house were lit up. Through one of the panes I could see Virginia's profile silhouetted above the desk in her study. I stood for a moment and watched. Her face was caught in a halo of light. She was wearing a wintry-coloured jumper and had clasped her hair with a silver plate at the nape. The pair of cats were curled up on a cushion on top of her desk. Without looking, she was stroking their flanks in an absent-minded circular wave, following the pile of their fur. It was smooth and gentle and rhythmic, as though moving in time with their purrs. I had been going to knock at the door, but bent instead to pick up a few beads of gravel to chuck at the glass. As I raised my hand to aim for the throw, I heard a sound at the top of the steps. Distracted, I turned round to look. It was Lacey. I felt an idiot, like some foolish troubadour. My hand fell back, letting the gravel dribble as unobtrusively as I could to the ground. I had the feeling he might have been watching me for more than a moment.

'How very good to see you,' I said. 'I've just caught a glimpse of your wife through the window and was going to attract her attention, but if she's working perhaps I shouldn't interrupt her.'

'She is working but I'm sure she'd like to know that you're back.'

I followed him into the house and through the black- and white-tiled Victorian hall. Past the photos of the black mammy with a turban and voluminous skirts; past Virginia, age ten, with stick legs and a ribbon in her hair, nursing a lapful of chickens; past an oil painting of a red-nosed squire in a Puritan hat and collar whom Lacey had claimed as an ancestor. Nothing had changed. There was still a trail of damp down the corner of the wall and still a long vertical crack in one of the panels of the drawing room door. There was the usual stack of shoes at the foot of the newly carpeted stairs. It was thoroughly nice to be back amongst the familiar, despite the feeling of unease that Lacey always induced, due to his own stiffness in dealing with himself.

'Robert's back. Can we come in?' asked Lacey, opening the study door.

Virginia looked up. 'Oh Robert,' she exclaimed. 'It's wonderful to see you. Are you well?'

I thought again how fortunate Lacey was to be able to ride pillion on her easy manner.

'Very well. Have you recovered from your trip back home?'

'Just about. Seeing relations is so exhausting. All that exclaiming. Such a relief to be back to a routine.'

'How is everyone here?'

'You didn't trust us, did you? Ringing up like that to see if we were looking after your flora and fauna.'

'Did you feed them?'

'Of course we fed them.'

'Gave them their lick?'

'Yes.'

She ran through the news whilst Lacey was despatched to get

drinks. I asked for a glass of milk and an apple. She halted her flow about Gavin and Trevor and Perry and the land and the animals.

'I don't approve. Milk maketh mucous,' she said in the mock-bossy doctor's manner she used so often with Lacey.

'Milk maketh man.'

We smiled happily at one another. I thought again how nice it was to be back, but that there were some compensations for not having a wife.

'I cooked your ham and black-eyed peas on Christmas Day,' I said.

She hooted. 'That's the wrong day. It's wasting your luck on the year that's past. There may be none left over for this year.'

'Perhaps that's true. It certainly hasn't been terribly lucky so far.'

'It'll come now you're back.'

'Promise?'

'I promise.' She smiled. 'What else have you got up to since you've been away.'

I told her about the *Marionettentheater* and gave a brief summary.

'How amazing,' she said. 'I must read it myself.'

She paused as Lacey returned with some wine, some apples and a glass of milk. She handed me my order with a shudder, then raised an eyebrow when I crammed my pockets with the apples.

'Don't forget that giving them an apple is a grand thing to do,' I said mimicking Connor's accent.

'I tell you the boys have stuffed them full of apples.'

'Is there nothing you've not done in my absence? I can see you're easing me out.'

'Nothing. The boys have even named the little white deer.'

I frowned. 'What?'

'Evie.'

'They can't.'

'They have. There it is. I knew you'd groan. I like it 'cause I'm vulgar. I've been dying to find an Eve.'

'I should never have gone away.'

'Perhaps not,' agreed Lacey. 'Everything comes back into our possession again, doesn't it?' He blinked at me.

★   ★   ★

186

Half an hour later, before the light had gone, I walked back across the field to the flamingos. For a while I shared a chuckle with Casino and Las Vegas, then walked on to the deer park. I could see dappled shadows amongst the trunks. I gave one of Connor's colossal whistles. The shadows took shapes as they came running and gambolling forward, but neat and beautiful in all their movements. It was truly as Kleist had described. Without consciousness of self, they had perfect balance and agility and lightness, whilst we embody the sluggishness of matter. I bit chunks off the apples and felt their noses nuzzle my palm. I was close enough to see the dark slashes of the vents beside the eyes which give their expression such sadness. My white pet pushed her long serious face forwards. She had a high Gothic forehead like the Eve of Renaissance paintings. 'Evie?' I tried. 'Eva.' Perhaps it wasn't too bad. I noticed Evie had got her pretty mouth and feet and ankles muddy. The spring sunshine would have tempted her to step into the pool for a long drink of water. I favoured her with two chunks of apples. In the days to come I would woo her with turnips and swedes and potatoes and carrots. There must be some things her owners had forgotten in my absence.

The next day I went to see Simon the potter. He had a shop that sold shiny mugs and containers mainly to the passing tourists, and more serious clay pots of all manner of shapes and sizes. Some had such tiny openings you could not have inserted a crow's quill, whilst others were large enough for a hunchback to dwell in. These pots tumbled in decorative piles all over the floor. Urns and swelling olive jars and Ali Baba pots and amphorae. The ground looked like an Arabian or Roman archeologist's dig.

In the rear of the shop, there was always a good cooking smell that came from the studio. If you got close enough to Simon after a day's baking, he would smell much the same. It was the scent of earth roasting in a nice hot oven. I suppose he was like me in that he was a groundsman, though one on a jeweller's scale, taking small bits of earth and making them gems. He was certainly a good crafts-man, but in this life it's not quality that's valued but quantity. I deal in large tracts of earth which are an investment, so I am well paid. Simon deals in fragments and gets paid nothing. He sometimes grumbles about this. He once said that he was the only person he knew for whom dirt poor had a literal meaning and that he had made a dazzling career out of this.

I found him at the back of the workshop. He was potting, his big hands caressing the wet slopes of a whirling jar. It was always a fascination to watch, the stuff of old TV interludes from one's childhood.

'I may have a job for you, Simon.'

'What?'

'Carving four beasts on four separate pieces of stone.'

'Makes a change, I must say, from another pot. How big?'

'Quite little.'

'Small, eh? That is my downfall.'

'The size of figures on the corbel table of a church.'

'Tiny.'

'I'll show you.'

I waited till he had finished the pot, then held up my sketches and explained their purpose. He looked at them thoughtfully.

'You say these are figures to represent the evil spirits teeming outside that cannot enter the garden.'

'Yes.'

I had drawn a sheila-na-gig monster, a fertility symbol, for the eastern quarter; a bird-dragon for the southern kingdom of the birds; a gargoyle head for the western portion; and for the last quarter, a thistle head with an inflorescence of swords.

'No serpent,' said Simon.

'No.'

'You must have a serpent, a phallic symbol. The snake bridges the gap between the age of reptiles and our age. The ancient gardens had serpents, especially the one yours is meant to represent.'

I remembered at the party last summer where I had met him for the first time, he had said the serpent was a very old god that had guarded the Garden of the Hesperides.

We agreed to exchange the bird-dragon for a serpent.

'How much will you charge?' I asked.

'One thousand pounds each. Four thousand the lot.'

'Come off it, Simon. That's not your style.'

'How much will they pay?'

'Not a lot. Virginia is keen but it's going to be hard to get this past Lacey.' I reminded him that at the party last summer, Lacey had said no totems, and no phallic symbols for that matter.

Simon looked glum. 'How about two hundred and fifty pounds each?'

Poor Simon. He wanted the job.

Three days later, it was agreed. In a month, these guardians would be up. It only occurred to me later that I had now been given two of the elements I had never wanted: an Eve and a serpent. The intervention of others can often lumber one with an embarrassment.

24

IMOGEN CAME TO me. This was a few weeks later and, although a visit had seemed impossible as she lacked a boat, in a way it wasn't unexpected. Is this because one's mind carries an ever-present image of what it apprehends and must therefore prepare for?

It happened about half-past ten at night. I was sitting reading about the tales of the deer-stealers in Gilbert White's *The History of Selborne*. Over their ale, he wrote, they used to recount the exploits of their youth, *such as watching the pregnant hind to her lair and, when the calf was dropped, paring its feet with a penknife to the quick to prevent its escape, till it was large and fat enough to be killed; the shooting of one of their neighbours with a bullet in a turnip field by moonshine, mistaking him for a deer; and the losing a dog in the following extraordinary manner —*

At this point, there was a series of small splashing sounds followed by a bump. There were always river noises at night, often quite loud because they were amplified in the hollow between the two banks. I therefore thought nothing of the interruption and returned to the extraordinary tale of the dog: *Some fellows suspecting that a calf new-fallen was deposited in a certain spot of thick fern, went with a lurcher to surprise it when the parent-hind rushed out of the break, and, taking a vast spring with all her feet close together, pitched upon the neck of the dog, and broke it short in two.*

Outside, the splashes and bumps had halted. I could hear feet drumming lightly, but without haste, up the wooden steps. It was perplexing as I didn't think it was either of my clients. At this time of night, it could only be a call of alarm and there was no hint of panic. I put the book down and opened the door. When I saw Imogen in the darkness, I was startled. We eyed each other for a moment. She was wearing dark trousers and a black parka, her face expressive of nervous tension. A vein on her forehead protruded.

'Can I come in? You don't look very welcoming?'

I shifted aside. 'I'm sorry, Imogen. It's just that it's so late. I was about to go to bed.'

She entered. She noticed the telescope I had recently bought by the table. 'Oh, so you're taking your own peeks at the sky now, are you?' There was a touch of resentment here.

'Thanks to you. I was grateful for your introduction.'

I offered her a coffee. As I was filling the kettle I asked, 'How did you get across the river? I didn't know you had your own boat.'

'Then you didn't notice your boat was gone?'

I shook my head. I was feeling most uneasy.

'When Virginia was away, David came over and brought me here to show me round. To save him a return trip, I said I'd row the boat back.'

'I don't understand. I'd have noticed if it had been tied up on the opposite bank.'

'It was, but further up. Beyond the bend. I thought it would be safer there.'

I thought this was a lie. I didn't doubt her intention had been to hide it there. The kettle was boiling. I poured the water onto the coffee and handed her the mug.

I said: 'What can I do for you, Imogen?'

'You don't seem pleased to see me?'

'If there's something I can do to help?' I let my voice falter in the hope of squeezing a practical purpose out. I hoped it would be mend my lamp, or fix my gate; some finite objective task. No chance of this, or was there? I suddenly cheered up.

'Aren't you in the middle of lambing? Is this it?'

'Not until late March, actually. I always avoid early lambing. It's much too arduous.'

I slumped. 'Look, it's a funny time for a visit. What's up?'

She shrugged. 'Nothing. I came to return the boat.'

This seemed reasonable and even a relief, but, even so, I looked at her, amazed. 'At this time of night?'

'I know,' she said, 'I know. But you haven't been here. And I've just got back this evening and seen your light. And I had to come at a time when you were in so could row me back.' She shrugged again, looking sideways.

I took a mouthful of coffee. I could think of nothing to say. It was all perfectly logical yet I was sure there was some other reason. Until this emerged, one could only tread water, but it was late and she was not the right person for smalltalk. Mentioning the sheep had proved to be a cul-de-sac. As for the heavens, I could think of nothing to ask about planets or stars.

She stood there swaying a little, then said: 'I like what you're doing here, by the way.'

'In this boathouse?' I asked, bemused.

'In the garden, of course. When David showed me round, I thought it beautiful. I was terribly impressed. The birds, the deer – so much prettier than my poor little work-horses of sheep which end up on the table – I mean, they don't get a chance to be decorative, do they? I thought it was lovely. I've come to say so.'

A mixture of praise and envy is almost impossible to handle. It's churlish not to show gratitude, yet you know that the praise is poisoned. Both sides fake the exchange. On the other hand, I was also genuinely sorry for her, though the situation was partly of her own making. She could have left, shoved off, got a proper job rather than frigging around with some sheep and some part-time adult teaching, rather than continuously facing the huge discrepancy between her brother's way of life and her own, which had been funded originally by him. She had chosen to remain, in a position to diligently feed the grievance. To envy the possession of a better class of ungulates. It occurred to me to be very, very careful with her. There are a lot of loose wires with this kind of circuitry that can spark the explosion. Wounded vanity is dynamite.

'That's very generous of you to speak well of it. I'm very glad you like what we've done here. It's hard work, as I said before, but I think it's been worthwhile. It's nice to hear that confirmed.'

We had creaked along so far. Now I got stuck. There was a new silence which Imogen didn't fill.

'I've been reading this evening about deer-stealers in the eighteenth century,' I said conversationally. I sat down on the arm of a chair to show that this was only a temporary perch. Imogen remained standing. She didn't look too interested in deer thieves. 'Returning the boat isn't the only reason why I've come this evening.'

'No?' I said gingerly.

'I don't want this stuff.' She put her mug down and came towards me. The edges of the room were taken up with basic items of furniture, so it took only a few steps to cross the space in the middle. She was standing close to me. One strains instinctively backwards in this situation, but, braced on the arm, there was nowhere to go without toppling into the lap of the chair.

It seemed utterly improbable but the only conclusion I could now reach was that she had come for a fuck. Why else would she come so late in the evening? When you have been to bed with someone and that night had undoubtedly a certain intense sensuality because of the circumstances – the recollection is there like a template. I kept pushing away the unwanted memory of her parted legs. Her nipples black as moles against the skin that night in winter.

'Steady on, Imo,' I said in my most jovial, detumescent of manners.

It was years since I had been in this sort of situation. When I was young, very occasionally, with some powerful predatory type of girl, American or Australian probably, asserting a claim to her rights, castrating certainly.

Imogen was giving the dark fixed-eye look. Thirty years ago, I remembered turning up at midnight at a girl's flat with much the same intention, and manner, no doubt. She had deflected me onto mending her typewriter. No amount of libido can survive this kind of transition.

I looked round for something for her to mend. I wished I had the dear trusty clock I repaired every Christmas. How faithful it seemed in a crisis. I sighed. There were no props to hand. It was obvious I was alone in tackling the issue.

'Stop goggling round the room,' said Imogen. 'It makes you look comical. What do you think I'm trying to do? Eat you? I haven't come for sex – if that's what you're worried about. Is it? Are you?'

'No, of course not. I didn't think that.' I was old again, sitting on the arm of my chair. The cobwebs of age returned. I got up. Put the spectacles on that I had taken off. 'Just tell me what you've come about. I'm very tired.' I must row her across, I thought. I urged her to move, so that I could start rowing, remove this monolithic block of irritation.

'I didn't just come to tell you the place is beautiful. I've come with a tiny piece of friendly warning. You've taken it over. You're dominating it. Let me remind you it's not your own. My brother's paying for it yet I look over it and see not my brother's hand but yours.'

A bullet of fury made me stand up, I think to regain majesty. We were on top of one another, chests brazening it out, a foot apart. It was ridiculous really.

'You are not my client.'

'I speak for him.'

'There are two of them. I have two clients.'

'Well, I don't speak for the second client, obviously, who I gather is entranced by your work. But it's his land, isn't it?'

'I don't think we should discuss this, Imogen. I take my instructions from Mr and Mrs Lacey.' I must be a lawyer, an old-fashioned don, I thought, formal and precise. All I sounded instead was a red-faced buffer. 'If Mr and Mrs Lacey have any complaints, I discuss this with them.' I wanted to ask: Has Lacey complained? Has he grumbled? – but this was enfeebling.

I remembered his strange comment when I had first returned and said I should never have gone away. *Perhaps not – everything comes back into our possession again.* Had he said this to her? Or had she said this to him? Or had nothing been said? One has to deal in realities, not the scurrying shapes in people's minds. But so often it's the shapes which drive a situation. I thought again of my need to be careful with her, with both brother and sister.

'Please don't let's argue,' I said. 'What are we talking about? I promise you I'm not taking it over. I'm sure David couldn't think so. Nor could you. I'm, as it were, their servant.'

'Hers or his?'

'I have no idea what you mean. What on earth do you imagine? In a professional relationship, a product is commissioned which you're required to supply to the highest standard.'

We stared at one another. Or I stared with a chance this time to beat her in the staring-out game, whilst she watched with great care, switching her gaze ostentatiously from my left eye to my right eye and back again.

'Oh well,' she said, stepping back. 'We're getting nowhere, are we? It was a friendly piece of advice. Do you feel like taking me back?'

I stretched the corners of my mouth and went to fetch my jacket from the hook. Neither of us spoke. We walked down the wooden steps, Imogen ahead, and over the muddy grass to the boat. The oars were laid, forming a V like a pair of salad tongs.

'I'll row, shall I?' she asked, though it wasn't really a question. 'Save you doing two journeys.'

We got in. The boat spasmed twice as we climbed in. She put the lamp on the stern and took up the oars. I thought: madame likes this strangeness with herself in command. She has come to probe and disturb. She has not come as a friend. I thought she was loathsome but I needed to crawl and pacify as long as there was any point. It was politic. Had she told her brother we'd had sex together? It was impossible to ask. It would weaken the status and independence of my position. On balance I thought she probably had. It would explain much. Her probing about Virginia as though she queried that something was going on. His comment on my statement that I should never have gone away: *Perhaps not – everything comes back into our possession again.* Christ, what a mess-up on my part.

The lamp shone like a single candle flame on the water, tipping the crests of the waves with its golden light. It was the strangest journey I have ever made. Outwardly lyrical, inwardly charged with destructive friction. She was rowing with the vigour of a Boadicea, to demonstrate power over her passenger. I was worried. Inadvertently for the second time I had given her cause for enmity. With normal people, emotions are transitory. They are displaced by daily chores. With her, one could sense a fixity of feeling and purpose.

'You are a good strong rower,' I said, crawling. A politician. 'A far better rower than I.'

She made no comment. I wished she would fall into the water. I decided to cut the flattery. Expediency which fails to pay off leaves one feeling doubly dirty.

That night I realised I would have to sort this out. All night it had made an enormous noise in my head. The next morning I went in search of my clients. I was early. I hoped to catch them at breakfast.

They were sitting at the table in the kitchen. It was a scene of wondrous normality. Both husband and wife were in dressing gowns, his a paisley silk, hers a dark kimono. Marmalade, beige toast – not the first round presumably, as there was the smell of burnt bread in the air – an olive oil spread in a tub, prunes, muesli and shredded wheat, for a classic fructivorous high-fibre eating couple. They were reading different sections of the newspaper. A phone lay on the table. Sunlight entered through the sash window, striking its pattern of rectangles on the ochre wall. Both cats nosed their way fastidiously out through the cat door. A scene consistent with utter normality. Last night was a bad dream.

Virginia looked up, alight. Without make-up, her dear face was as shapeless as her body wrapped in its kimono.

'You're early.'

'I did knock at the door. I hope you don't mind my coming in.'

'Sit down.'

I pulled out a chair and sat at a distance from the edge of the table. 'I wanted to get you both together.'

'Here we are,' said Lacey, perfectly pleasantly.

Virginia said: 'Something going on?'

'We're onto the last stage, as you know. The northern quarter. Before we go any further, I need to know you're happy with everything we've done so far. Really happy, I mean. No worries. I just wondered if I've been going too fast. I've checked each stage of the progress with you, but sometimes the accumulation, the sum total, can seem more than each of the parts to the owner. I do need your confirmation now. It's your land.' I was looking at Lacey. 'It's your land. You must tell me if you have any concerns. Just so long as you're pleased. That's what matters.'

'But you know we're thrilled,' said Virginia.

I was rude. I looked at Lacey. 'David?'

'*Das muss ein Mann mir sagen . . .*' said Virginia.

She made me laugh. I tried not to look at her. 'David?' I repeated.

He was watching us share an old joke. He hesitated for a tiny fraction. He said: 'Yes.'

I looked down. I knew agreement was being given according to the letter of the law: the letter, not the spirit. Perhaps this was all I had ever got or would ever get, but it was enough.

'Do you have your answer?' asked Virginia.

'Thank you.'

'Thank you for coming to see us.' She was charming and correct.

'Coffee?' offered Lacey. 'Though I don't think there's any left. We could make another cup, if you'd like.'

He sat thickly filling his chair, adhering to it as I watched him. It told me the kettle was a million miles away across impassable terrain.

'No need, thank you very much. I've got to get on.'

We nodded and smiled and I went out.

On the gravel outside at the edge of the yard, Gavin and Trevor's van drew up. I watched the boys get out, tall and strong and straight, like moving timber. I thought: Lacey likes my work but not me, which is a perfectly reasonable reaction. Only a dumb fool expects to be liked by everyone. But there is a flaw here in that my work has my signature all over it. Does that matter? Virginia loves it and likes me, which is probably part of the problem, but from the practical point of view, she is fifty per cent of my client and it's women who are the patrons nowadays. It's me and my patroness, and he is not sufficently negative about it to be obstructionist, and anyway none of these temporary and private vicissitudes matter because what I am doing isn't ephemeral. It will last, outlive them, outlive me.

I started to walk towards the boys. I thought it was likely that Virginia would make the chance to see me on her own later today, so that she could ask what all this was about. And I'd say: oh, you always have to check that your clients are truly happy and that you're not going too fast. Perhaps I'd even say that Capability Brown, you know, never had a single difference or dispute with any of his employers according to the testimonial of his partner and son-in-law. He left them pleased, and they remained so as long as he lived. And she'd say: well, so are we and we'd tell you if we wanted out. And I'd say, I have to make an opportunity for you to say so, because Imogen has been a horrid lady and poisoned my head.

But I couldn't tell her about Imogen's visit because it would reveal an intimacy that I had previously concealed. It would give rise to suspicions. Surely, Virginia would think, even Imo wouldn't have been so bold as to pass judgement if sex had not robbed me of my professional status. Of course, there was always the possibility that the tongue of the snake had told Lacey who had told Virginia, so that she knew already. But, without my confirmation, it was a fabrication, empty of substance.

One could be overmuch of a stewpot about this. I had drawn a line under it this morning. 'Gavin,' I called. I would tell him to put up the sheila-na-gig stone figure not too far from the boathouse as a guardian of the river.

25

Appropriately, Evie was tempted by apples, though it was really swede which she preferred. That doe would do anything for the humble ploughman's swede. She would come when I called and follow me like a dog round the park. One lunchtime I was eating a sandwich under an oak when she lay down beside me. She started to nuzzle my pocket. As dark as wet walnuts, her big liquid eyes absorbed mine. She lifted her nose and blew air from the scrolls of her nostrils. She loved me to stroke the fur of her ears. The pelt was as supple as velvet, and silky. The coat is called pelage and feels as soft as it sounds.

I wanted to give her a collar but feared that would make her into a toy. Besides, the hinds were due to arrive soon and it would be better if I weren't so involved. Males are bull animals and savage enough to attack us. During the rut you can be killed by a blow from their antlers. Even Evie would turn into a wildling. Next year she could fight me to protect her own fawn.

Looking back, these spring days were almost the best of the time that I spent there. It was wonderful to see all we had achieved stirring across the spectrum. The first buds came back on the parched trees like the gold on the furze, then darkened into a veil of bronze and green. When the knobs opened and stretched and grew thicker, the deer cropped a browsing line where the branches dipped over the ground. During the space of a week, many of the trees started to acquire the same hemline. We would watch the silhouettes of the does straining upwards, their long necks tilted to the sky in search of the juicy new leaves. Paths began to appear in mysterious places: routes that were sketchy at first, then more confident, revealing their favourite footmarch. By now the number of deer had been swelled by the newly arrived hinds, in the proportion of one to four does. The young bucks were full of themselves, yearling prickets with their goat spikes instead of antlers and two-year-old sorrels crowned with a pair of fork-ended tines. They would grow into the handsomest bucks. Deer can have good or bad antlers but the old man had chosen for us only those with the best turrets. These lads did not doubt they were aristocrats. They were full of cock, prancing and strutting. Later this year they would cover the does. They walked with a swing to their buttocks. They flirted the black stripe on their tails. They exchanged their dark winter coats for a chestnut and burnished pelage. There might come a time when Evie would no longer come in search of her apples.

At the end of a working day, I would walk here with Virginia, sometimes with Lacey as well, though more often just the two of us on our own. We would laugh at the swaggering bucks or later, nearer to dusk, stay silent when Evie ran through the trunks.

In the bird kingdom, the flamingos had started their courtship strutting. Every day their stilt legs moved in rapid arthritic formation. They waggled their heads and waved with their wings. In the pool nearby the mandarin ducks were engaged in a ceremony that was almost as odd and elaborate. Bowing their heads and raising their crests whilst they chugged about with their chestnut sails. All this dazzle and dash and plumage concealed the spirit of homebodies. Once paired, they turned into the most devoted and domestic of couples. Truly a regular Ted and Doris. They lived a life that was touchingly ordinary. All they wanted was to fetch and carry for one another. I know it's a truism but animals always throw light on the characters of people. Strip away the bullshit and bluster, and there we are, a long way back, just strutting about on the pond.

I spent my days in the woodland with Gavin and Trevor and Perry. We were not short-handed, but sometimes Virginia would work with us too. She would say: 'No more papers. I need to get my hands dirty,' and once, 'Don't mind David. He's crusty. It is his burden. It's nothing to do with you.' We lifted and moved a few of the smaller rhododendron. We planted white lysichiton round the edge of the pool so that their spathes would look up from the dark water. We added trilliums, like three-petalled butterflies, and in the leafdrifts a mass of ferns. All these flowers and foliage round the water would connect with their liquid reflections. Above and beyond, the tree rhododendrons opened their funnels of thick-textured crimson and sulphur. They came from the mountains of Asia and transported our wood to a Himalayan gully. Around the edges, bamboo jungles were clustered in groves. I ensured that the paths through the clumps and the tree trunks gave a feeling of space. In a wood, the arts of architecture and gardening link hands in mutual nourishment.

Sometimes I thought that this wood was like the interior of a huge old cathedral. I saw it in the columns of tree trunks, the vaulting of branches and the roof of leaves. As though in a church, we were shielded from glare and from heat here, yet lit by shafts of angular light. No noise came from the world that existed outside. Even the smell was ecclesiastical: musty, fungoid and persistent, but rich like the scent of incense. One of the rhododendrons was so sweet that it lodged in your throat. I don't know what it was. I looked it up in all the books but couldn't trace it. Virginia called it 'Good Frilly White'. I often saw Trevor sniff it. Perhaps his sense of smell compensated for being a deaf-mute.

One day Gavin told me that he had heard a nightingale singing in the wood one summer night two years ago. 'It's impossible,' I said. 'Too far west. Unless it's passing through, perhaps. Still, it's strange.' He said: 'It did this. It was a nightingale.' And he launched into a series of clear independent sounds, of call notes, of chucking and yaffling, and rippling and scolding and grating like a frog. He burst into song after the original push-off point of the 'tee-wheet'. It was amazingly rich and ardent with a great crescendo pouring lyrically out on the 'pioo'. He rendered the famous 'jug-jug' very clearly. Nightingales differ greatly in musical quality, but she must have been a true songstress, the original Philomela. I wondered at the boy's marvellous powers of both recall and performance; I think, as I've said before, it was because he was his brother's ears and his constant informant. Though how he would convey this in lip or sign language was a poignant thought. Deprived of its aching sweetness and passion, only vibration would remain from the song. 'Did you tell Mrs Lacey?' I asked him later. 'She would love to know.'

'No,' he said. He looked grumpy. 'It was at night. Don't tell.' What had he been doing at night there? Poaching, I supposed. Fish or rabbits? She wouldn't have cared, but I didn't tell her. Perhaps this summer, the little stray would come again and sing us her exquisite disembodied tune.

We came out of the woodland, into the open sunlight and worked on the land by the house. In the field, I trained the boys to mow so that arabesques of flowering grasses would stand out in lines from the rest of the sward. The pattern was slow and spaced out and meandering at first, then its curves speeded up in the distance. I saw it like music, a linear art, in which you discover the changes of form as it takes you along. It was not like a painting where you see everything at a glance. Elsewhere we cut paths in the grass and left the wild flowers in stands. We watched a spangle of lemon and cream intermingle with violet and blue here: spring colours of wild blossoms are consistently fresh and harmonious. Summer fields are less decorous and the colours that followed would be louder with scarlet poppies and white ox-eye daisies. They would jump into view and wake you up just when the heat should make you lethargic.

We were now nearing the area round the house. It would have been slightly uncomfortable to be working under Lacey's eye here. Conveniently, however, he was quite often away at this time. Once a week he would go up to London where he'd spend the night. Like many of the early retired he had taken a job as a consultant to a medical research charity. I had heard it was awash with money and had more funds at its disposal than it knew what to do with, but we continue giving, in the hope that we'll get let off; and people like Lacey donate it their time. On the days when Lacey was absent, it seemed to me that Virginia relaxed. She became more of a dreamer, she was happier to let the hours drift by. She stopped working more often. One morning we'd been planting the garden and she asked me about Louise.

'Why did it break up?'

'Because I was always away.'

'Was that the only reason?'

'Isn't that good enough?'

'No. It might be awful never to see your husband, but, believe me, it can be just as awful to see him all the time. So if you break up, there's got to be another reason.'

'She said it was because I didn't need her.'

'There you are. And is that true?'

'I don't know.'

'Then it must be true.'

'And is it true that a woman must be needed?'

She hesitated. 'It's true only up to a point. Needed but not truly needed. I was once told that seventy-five per cent of women leave husbands who are in a wheelchair. But if it's the other way round – if it's the women who are disabled – the men don't leave.'

'So women don't want to be needed.'

'Don't try and muddle me.'

'I'm not trying to muddle you. As I see it, a woman wants to be needed but not by a man in a wheelchair. That sounds to me as if women don't want to be needed.'

'They do, but only by someone who is emotionally and physically independent.'

'I see. They want to be needed by someone who doesn't need them. That sounds like a recipe for permanent discontent.'

She sighed. 'Perhaps.'

'Was that true of you?'

'Yes. I left my first husband because he didn't need me.'

'And David does?'

'Yes.'

'You married David because he needed you?'

'Yes.' She looked defiant.

'Then you flout your own argument.'

'You're muddling me again.'

'No,' I said. 'I'm trying to understand. It's important.'

She had been sitting beside me. Now she got up. 'Look, I was a crusading spirit. It was an emotional decision. I think I saw my second marriage as an antidote to my last.'

'If you don't have a ruling passion, every major decision you take in life is simply a reaction, an antidote to the last.'

'It's all very well for you,' said Virginia.

'What is?'

'You have your ruling passion. Something you really care about.'

'My work?'

'Call it your work if you want. I'd put it on a higher level. An appreciation of nature. One of Jung's ingredients for a happy life, according to you.'

'I've given it to you. I've wanted you to absorb it too.'

'I have. You've made a difference to me. You know that.'

She came towards me. She looked worried. I didn't want to make explicit what I sensed, that I had made a difference to her but not to her husband, or that he had grown grumpier in proportion to her happiness.

She was wearing blue jeans and a navy wool jumper that reached down to her thighs. The dark blue made her skin look golden. I thought that the anxiety in her face made her look beautiful.

'You've got a smudge of earth on your forehead,' I said. 'Anyone would think you'd been working.'

She laughed, her teeth prominent. She tried to rub it but was touching the wrong place. I put up my hand and brushed it away. I had never touched her before. The intimacy called for immediate disguise. 'I have the plans for the beds around the house,' I said. 'If you have time, do you want to look them over now?'

We stood together over the plans, discussing, not touching.

26

THE FOLLOWING DAY Virginia handed me a postcard from Oxford. It read: *Robert, it's hard to get hold of you by phone. Are you free any time in the next couple of weeks? It would be nice if you could come over and meet Jonathan. He's suggested the three of us have dinner together at his college. Can you ring me to fix an evening. Louise.*

Virginia may have read it but made no comment. She seemed preoccupied.

I said: 'My ex-wife is asking me to meet Jonathan. Jonathan is my ex-wife's new partner.'

'Oh,' she said, 'so it'll be one of those occasions. Difficult.' And she smiled and waved her hand expressively in the air, then walked back to her office.

I was disappointed. I would have liked to discuss it. It seemed an odd proposition for him to have made. I wondered what was behind it. In the end I discussed it with Louise.

'There's nothing odd about it,' she said on the phone. 'I suggested it, since you and I are still friendly.'

'Then why don't we just have a casual supper at home.'

'He doesn't want to.'

'Why not?'

'I don't know.' She was not very convincing. She added: 'But don't you think it's a generous gesture?'

'It's a mangabey monkey gesture.'

I was talking to Louise in our private code. A mangabey monkey makes a noise to a bigger more aggressive primate which means: don't hit me. I'm nice.

Louise showed an unusual degree of sensitivity. 'That's pathetic.

If you're going to say things like that, Robert, just don't bother to come at all.'

I apologised. This fellow was making her lose her sense of humour.

We fixed it for the following Friday, as I would be spending the last two days of this week in the office. I was not especially looking forward to the occasion which seemed mistaken because it was so contrived. However, in practice, all it meant was that the necessary meeting would take place sooner rather than later. I was also a little curious to know what kind of man she had chosen. I suppose this curiosity must reflect a degree of self-absorption. One's ego thinks that the second husband must be some sort of extension of oneself. Though this is an illusion, because if you look at other people's marriages, the wife's husbands seem to share nothing in common. They can be dukes or dustmen. Most women, except the sturdiest and most rooted of characters, are made up of so many personalities. Or is it, as I have sometimes thought, that most women are just vacant spaces?

At a quarter to eight I arrived at the professor's college. It was one of the best endowed, most prestigious institutions. Louise had landed a big fish, if you accept those terms of reference which are admired by the academy. The porter directed me to his rooms. As I walked through the quad, the place smelled as these places always do in one's memory: a cold grave-like scent of damp stone and dust, with a ranker note above it. They smell of monasteries that have been reoccupied by shifting armies of undergraduates.

I went up his staircase and knocked on his door. A short man opened it: my new brother, connected to me by my wife whom I saw standing a few feet behind him. She was dressed in a long black wool shift with a v-neck, and my garnet earrings, worn out of misplaced tact. No doubt she had hoped to keep both sides happy. The man was small and younger than me, of course. We shook hands, Louise a little too bright and socially busy on the perimeter. Against the panelled wall I saw a portrait of the man before me and realised it must be the one she had painted. I saw it more clearly than I did the human being that was its model, because it didn't arouse any emotions and because my wife the painter had already picked out its salient points for me. It had jug ears and a long up-and-down face, pale and straight like a Musselburgh leek.

'Do you think it's a good likeness?' asked young Jonathan.

'Pretty good,' I said.

'I wasn't sure,' he said diffidently.

He was wearing a mangabey monkey expression, placatory. Suddenly I felt sorry for him. I realised in that moment why he had asked me to dinner in these surroundings. It was not 'nice' or 'generous' or any of these altruistic terms. It was defensive. It was his territory: he was wearing his medals, his tin braid, his support system of servants and porters and chefs. This system was expensive and under threat, but as a standard of excellence it still functioned and empowered. It was, and rightly, his set of credentials.

'You're a bit late,' said Louise. 'Is there time for us to have a drink?'

'There's no time,' said Jonathan.

I said: 'I'm sorry. I got held up late in the office tonight.'

'I think we'd better go straight down. Shall we go down?'

As we descended the steps, I wondered what his undergraduates made of the portrait or, rather, of his putting the portrait up on the wall. We walked on through the cloisters, the arcade at the side of the quad on the way to the hall. Since we were no longer in single file, I said for the sake of something to say:

'People think arcades are supposed to symbolise the architecture of paradise.'

'Really? That's very interesting,' said Jonathan. It was the kind of encouraging comment that a don makes a practice of saying to undergraduates.

I saw Louise's lips move in the darkness. Perhaps she too was saying that it was very interesting, under her breath. She too would now become a vacant space inhabited by a don.

'Yes,' I said. 'It's all the arches, you see.'

I thought if we really got stuck for talk this evening, I would ask him what the relationship of the asymptote was to the hyberbola, a reference which still foxed me in Kleist's little story.

It was years since I had dined in hall, but not much had changed. The centuries hang over the occasion as they do over Oxford and fill it with ritual. It would be terrible for it to change. To lose its self-confidence and give up its formal ambitions. We make such a mistake if we throw all the old voices away. At the end of the table a man was rattling through grace in a booming voice: '*Benedic, Domine, nobis, et his donis tuis, quae tua gratia et munificentia sumus iam sumpturi, et concede ut illis salubriter a te nutriti tibi debitum obsequium praestare valeamus per Christum Dominum nostrum.*' It is one of those things that you think you've forgotten, but when you hear them you realise that they have always stayed with you; one of those memories that survive a stroke even, that will rumble away within you, even when you can't talk to other people: *Benedic, Domine, nobis, et* . . .

We sat. This was not one of the really grand and black tie occasions when the dons stuff themselves on their own. We were simply at high table on the raised part of the hall, looking down at the young cattle of boys and girls below. Their faces opened and closed. The dark walls made them dark, though bursts of candlelights sent sparkles up to the rafters. Young Jonathan was on my left, Louise on my right. There was an empty chair immediately opposite, flanked by a man with a grey ponytail and, to the other side, a recognisable Wapping female columnist. We were all looking forward to the pinnacle of institutional food, given French names and served with a flourish in silver salvers. Failing that, lots of British carbohydrate.

The man with the ponytail said to no one in particular: 'I've heard it's short rations tonight. The chef's wife has just left him. We'll be lucky to get anything at all.'

'Oh dear,' said Jonathan. 'I'm very sorry.'

'She's been on and off for weeks,' said our informant.

'Never mind,' said the Wapping journalist. 'One comes here for the night, the music and the ice cream.'

'How is Abi?' I asked Louise.

'Still knitting, but not in the Hebrides. She's switched to the Borders.'

Louise shut up. I thought she wanted to acclimatise to the others rather than talk to me.

A man came and sat down in the empty chair opposite. 'Good God, Clive,' I said, pleased. 'I didn't know you'd stayed on.' We had known each other thirty years ago. He had thickened out, grown burly, but had the same hooded eyes.

'I didn't,' he said. 'I'm only here because I'm on the fund-raising committee.'

Jonathan said: 'There's a fund-raiser behind every pillar now.'

I took a mouthful of avocado salad and glanced around me. A woman a little way along the table had a curious but rather sweet habit of raising her fists to her eyes like a Beatrix Potter animal. I wondered how Louise would fit in with all this.

'I'm supposed to look you in the eye,' said Clive. 'I've just started as a fund-raiser, but I'm told that face-to-face usually works. Better than cold-calling anyway.'

'This is how it is now, is it?' I asked.

The man with the ponytail said: 'We need subsidising.'

'When Robert and I were very young and poor together,' Louise declared, 'we sometimes said we would put an advertisement in *The Lady* which read: "Robert and Louise gratefully welcome all legacies. Please send to Box no . . ."'

'Did it work?'

'We never got round to doing it,' I said, 'but we thought it would be such a curiosity that it might.'

'We didn't have the chutzpah,' said Louise.

'It was only a joke,' I said.

'It's probably illegal,' said Clive. 'If not, perhaps I ought to suggest it to the college.'

'Pity you didn't do it,' said the ponytail. 'You'd be amazed who coughs up.'

'Do I recognise your face?' I asked.

'I expect so. We all have to get around. Have opinions and make our name in the media. It's worse than the sixties now. I should know. I was here then, so it gives me a basis for comparison. We all have to have other platforms. It's easier of course if you're a scientist or mathematician.' He looked at Jonathan. 'They say mathematics is very sexy now, don't they, Johnny?'

'Oh, well I don't know about that.'

'Come on, sweetie,' said Louise, leaning past me. 'Of course it is.'

She had never ever called me sweetie. She was becoming a company woman.

More silver salvers arrived. Clive lifted one. 'Shepherd's pie,' he said wonderingly.

'It is precautionary,' said the Wapping journalist. 'They don't want me to write things about greedy dons and fat institutions.'

'Alas,' said the man with the ponytail. 'Would it were true.'

'I'm afraid it's only because the chef has had a crisis and taken refuge in childhood,' said Jonathan.

There was a general spirit of despondency among the family. Even Clive, an outsider, seemed dispirited. No doubt shepherd's pie must act as a spur to get in more funds. He took a mouthful and leaned across the table. Never one for the fastidious niceties, he spoke now without bothering to swallow: 'As I got here late, I wasn't really introduced. From what Louise said about the legacies, I take it you two are married.'

Out of the corner of my eye, I saw her lift a fork and replace it a millimetre to the right.

'No, not exactly, no longer.' I hesitated. I didn't feel it was up to me to explain the status quo, indeed I wasn't quite sure what it was, but thought something else should be added to prevent gaffes. 'She is with Jonathan,' I said vaguely.

'Oh.' He looked mystified.

'Yes,' said Jonathan. 'We are going to get married shortly.' It was the most confident comment he had made.

I looked at Louise enquiringly. She avoided my eyes.

'I must congratulate you,' I said, 'now that it's definite.'

'Thank you.' She then whispered so that no one else could hear: 'We only decided yesterday, otherwise I'd have let you know.'

'Quite. I understand. Well, we must celebrate.'

I turned to Jonathan to toast the bridegroom. Taking charge of the shift. Something leaning over inside. The others watched, Clive and the Wapping journalist and the man with the ageing ponytail, all waiting to see if the thing that was leaning within would topple. One would prefer not to learn these things in public. I lifted my glass. The wine as opposed to the food was truly excellent.

'Congratulations,' I said. 'I know you'll be very happy. When will it be?'

'When my divorce comes through.'

'We'll drink to that.'

I was launching the ship the second time around. 'Oh, Robert, you're such a control freak,' Louise was thinking, if she wasn't in too much of a flutter. Like Abi she had broken free and plunged into a new world: encapsulated, claustrophobic, frozen though still wonderful. What was she seeking? The delusion of added value? At our age one marries not so much a person as a package. 'Are you sure?' I wanted to ask. 'Is this what you want? Will you fit in? Will you fit in with the wives, with their knives and high foreheads and clever remarks and talking in paragraphs and squabbles disguised as sneering?' What would she answer? We had touched foreheads and kissed at Christmas. Would we ever do it again?

'Oh, angels on horseback,' said Jonathan, squeaking. 'This at least is routine.' And he tucked into a bacon rasher wrapped round an oyster on a slice of bread.

I thought, I must give him a Herculean labour now. He will have to prove himself worthy of her. He must earn her.

'What is the relation of the asymptote to the hyberbola?' I asked.

He looked surprised, startled even. 'The asymptote is the line that approaches nearer and nearer to a given curve but doesn't meet it in a finite distance. The hyperbola is a curve produced when a cone is cut by a plane making a larger angle with the base than the side of the cone makes. The relation is the one to the other.'

'Oh. What does that mean?'

He looked puzzled.

Clive leaned forward across the table. 'What do you do now?'

'I'm a landscape architect.'

'I live a few miles away, near Nuneham Courtenay. I expect you know the estate there was done by Capability Brown.'

'Actually, I did know. The funny thing is that the man who commissioned him brought Rousseau there too.'

'What's funny about that?'

'Just that they are usually thought of as opposites. The world of the Establishment and the Romantics.'

'I suppose you haven't done any gardens for hugely-rich Japanese industrialists, have you? Or some multi-millionaire pop star who is seeking a little dignity in middle age? They're often tappable for funds.'

'I'm afraid not.'

'Sorry to bang on. As a new boy, I'm keen to prove myself.'

The leaning inside me was a pang of homesickness. I whispered to Louise: 'You won't disappear, will you, like Abi? You will keep in touch?' Though I thought, they will swallow her up, even if they spit her out in private among the nuts and the port.

'I'll keep in touch. Promise.'

27

I DROVE BACK to Water End and told the hardware constructors to put the last touches to the area by the house. At the front it was formal, with shapes and asymmetrical patterns edged in box. At the back, we'd made a kind of parterre here too with sage, rue and lavender. All this was easy. I think that anyone, even a child, can do patterns.

It was the area behind this where I truly earned my keep. Here it had been much more exacting. We'd deleted the back part of the lawn where we'd stood and partied in the summer. In the spaces between the patterns of paths, we'd then filled the enclosures with colour. Perhaps this sounds nothing, but colour is one of the main elements when designing a garden. Believe me, there is nothing, nothing you can't do with colour, but you do need to be very practised and you only acquire the assurance after many stumbles.

What I'd done here was to use butter and apricot drifts, advancing in patches of light among the deep blues and milky lavenders receding into the shadows. Touches of dark green and purple crimson added a sumptuous ballast. This summer it would be developed enough to show promise. In three summers, coming here would be like opening and entering a magic palette. I told myself that one day – when I was only an intermittent visitor – Lacey too would experience this profound satisfaction.

To focus intensely on a subject is hard; so, to relax, in the evening I maintained my routine, walking back through the kingdoms of the birds and the animals. The terms, by the way, no longer seemed odd or hyperbolic. They came naturally. I had entered totally into the fantasy. In any case by now it wasn't a fantasy, because the trees and the water and the birds and the animals had clothed the scaffolding with reality.

Among the flamingos, at least when they weren't marching, Casino and Las Vegas were always the first to approach me with their delicate fastidious wading. Their laughter enraptured. The chortling – Casino's was higher-pitched, almost a trill – was so merry that you had to respond. We would stand in the early evening sharing the joke, as the sun set, warming their coral, scarlet-tipped feathers. They would watch me, their eyes dark as raisins. Then when the group had exhausted all the ramifications of our humour and we had chuckled enough to grow drowsy – the way you do after laughter – one after another would settle down, sleeping on one leg to rest the other and reduce heat loss. They would curl their necks round and tuck their heads over their backs. They used these as a quilt, plunging their nostrils into their feathers so that in the chill of the night they would breathe air which was warm from their plumage.

When they were quiet, I would walk to the deer park where the creatures were active. The flamingos grew sleepy when the fallows were excited. At this time of the evening, they would dance around with their weightless trot. Flicking their tails, in search of a last crop to cud, or dipping their noses in the surface of the pool. If I called, Evie would come to me dripping, though often the wetness of her white nose was only dew from the grass. Sometimes I put a halter on her, only to gentle and only for a few moments, because I would see the pulse kick violently in her neck. And besides, it was the wildling I loved in her. Creatures like these are best made for fleeing. Even now I can picture her running like a ghost through green avenues.

Virginia still came with me sometimes for part of my rounds. Then, one evening, a Tuesday when Lacey was away, she stayed till the end. She took my arm and we walked across the fields.

'You know,' she said, 'one day we'll have to do up the boathouse, when you've left us that is.'

'There's still a lot to do.'

'Eke it out.'

'Liar. I know my clients only too well. They want the maker to come and the minute he arrives, they can't wait for him to go.'

'You're different.'

I hugged her arm. I wanted to know how I was different.

'Don't fish,' she said. 'We'll hold the celebration I promised this summer. A courtly picnic perhaps. How about that?'

'It's too early. Wait for the place to evolve – five years at least. Fifty would be better.'

She ignored me. 'I want a feast.'

'I once went to an Arab feast when I worked in the Middle East. They cooked a quail inside a poussin inside a pheasant inside a sheep inside a camel.'

'Nonsense.'

'It's true. It was the big feast.'

We reached the boathouse. She climbed up the steps and opened the door to the inside. I never locked it. Apart from my telescope, there was nothing to take and no one to take it.

'I've not been here for a proper inspection since you arrived,' she said. She moved round, tutting at the damp, picking up a couple of books. She remarked on my telescope. 'This reminds me of David's sister. Or does everyone have them nowadays?'

'My ex-wife gave me a pair of binoculars for Christmas. It inspired me to get this. I simply thought I would see further.'

She seemed satisfied with my answer. She sat down on one of the wooden chairs and leaned back. 'We'll have to do a lot to this place if we're going to let it as a holiday cottage.'

'Don't you think my minimalist world has appeal?'

She smiled. 'Part of me does. Part of me wishes I had it.'

There was a honking outside and a drumming of wings on the water. We went out onto the deck. A family of mute swans were beating the surface to become airborne.

'They're so very beautiful,' said Virginia.

'These things are the only refuge of the true romantic. Wild things outside our grasp. I never told you, but when I came here on that first visit, I gave a lift to two hitchhikers who said, Don't touch it. Leave the land as it is. You'll spoil it.'

She had sat down on the wooden edge, hooking her knees over it and letting her feet dangle. She was swinging them like a child in the air, her thighs parted. She put up a hand to me. She shook her head.

'Why didn't you tell me this? It's rather funny.'

'It didn't seem a very good recommendation.'

She smiled. 'How insecure. I wouldn't have thought you'd need any reassurance, but if you do, and I know you don't, I think you're very careful not to spoil things.'

'I must ask you something. I've never felt it right to ask in private but I must ask. Does David think I've spoilt it? It haunts me.'

She hesitated before she looked up at me. Her eyes were swimmy and I wasn't sure if she would cry.

'Oh Virginia.' I knelt down. 'I shouldn't have asked. Have I hurt you somehow?'

'I've never said anything because I couldn't talk about my husband as a third party. My loyalties are to him. I've simply told you: He's crusty; it is his burden. That's all I've said, because I thought that would help you realise that these things are everything to do with the perceiver, not the perceived.'

'I know that. That's always true.'

'That's all I can say.'

She drew me down beside her.

'Don't, please don't be sad,' I said. I stroked her face, smoothing out the furrows. 'You are made for laughter. See? You have laughter lines beside your eyes.'

'I have done too much chuckling with the flamingos, I suppose.'

We smiled at one another. For a moment everything seemed possible, the way it does; then, I don't know what, but it's like a valve closing, and there's nothing you can do about it, and a second later you are on the other side and the moment is over. You have heard reality ticking like a clock. You hear this sound and once you have heard it, the moment is over because the noise is relentless and insistent. I heard it and it told me that the whole client business lay between us, and her husband, and that I could not touch her mouth, put my arms around her, couldn't fold her within me, couldn't enter her and feel her open. The cautious only exchange what is possible because they are driven by reason, by balance, by deflation. So, because of all this and because I had grown to love her in a way, I simply bent forward and kissed her not on the mouth but just to its side and then stood up so that it was really a goodbye.

'I shan't mention it ever again,' I said.

'No,' she said, 'better not.' She looked up. 'But come back and sit down beside me and we'll watch the river go by.'

So I returned to her and we sat side by side. She put her hand briefly over mine, then withdrew it to indicate that only companionship was on offer. As we settled into silence, I tried to remember something an old friend had once told me. For a time he had been a teacher. He'd said that when he was telling his pupils a story, they would be bored and restless until he got to the point in the tale when a boy would approach a girl with, say, an invitation – for example, Will you come and play tennis with me this evening? – and the class would start to listen and grow very quiet. All the pupils, the boys and the girls, would fall silent and pay attention. I had said at the time that I could not believe this: they couldn't possibly be stirred up by an invitation to play tennis. Oh yes, my friend had replied, it doesn't matter how trivial or matter-of-fact the offer: it is suggestive because all boy/girl stuff is loaded.

And I thought, sitting here watching the river, it's always loaded. It's loaded, all one's life.

'What are you thinking?' said Virginia.

'I'm watching the swans coming back. See, in the distance.'

They were flying back, wings thrashing, necks horizontal, stretching towards their destination. They skidded into the water. It rose up in slopes of silver.

Virginia put her head on my shoulder and immediately pulled it upright. 'It's getting dark,' she said. 'I've got to go back.'

I made no attempt to stop her, but asked: 'Will you be all right, walking back? You want me to come with you?'

'I'll be okay.'

She too kissed me, not on the mouth, either, but on the cheek, then stood up and walked quickly and lightly down the steps. I watched her go, feeling her mouth on my cheek. I thought Lacey didn't deserve her.

28

I WOKE UP earlier than I expected the following morning. The glow of yesterday evening persisted. Trust, affection, something unacknowledged, but deeper perhaps, had been exchanged but without guilt. It left a feeling of contentment and also of good fortune. I lay there thinking for a while, watching the riverbank light up through the window. A plopping and splashing came from the water, and the wild imperious honks of a goose. As I listened to these normal flamboyant sounds of dawn, I thought that you try not to draw comparisons between the landscapes you create – every one is different and has its own problems. You also work towards an unknown future, because the natural world is not predictable, but Virginia had helped me over the problem of Lacey and I was sure now that this was the finest work I had ever created.

These warm and comforting thoughts persisted until I got up; then right from the beginning the day started to go wrong. I was doing my normal rounds, but at an earlier hour than usual. It was straightforward routine stuff: going to the deer park first, watching them in the fresh, clear light, admiring their dappled chestnut shapes emerge from the greenwood, giving the white doe an apple. Then onto the birds; but even from a distance it was evident here there was something wrong. The wire gate swung open and from within there was a gaudy and raucous clamour. In a sick panic I raced forwards. A trail of feathers, down mostly, was scattered along the grass, though the victim was not immediately apparent. The flamingos were huddled together in the middle of the water. I counted them. They did not appear to have been savaged but they were frightened. They were chortling without humour and stretched their necks and beat their wings in a fan dance. Then I saw that beyond the pool, there were three ducks on the ground: two dead, and one poor thing, a pretty gadwall, still alive, her neck torn, her body pulsing, her legs trembling. It was terrible to see this. I knew I would have to kill her. I turned round, shut the gate behind me and ran to fetch a spade. I would have to chop the neck of the duck, which was ghastly but for her sake had to be done.

When it was over, I carried the three birds out singly and buried them outside the cage. At the sight of a human being doing his rounds, the colonies, which did not distinguish between normal and deviant tasks, began to settle down and regain confidence. But two bereaved little drakes and a duck were running around, searching and calling and keening piteously for their lost mates. I walked back into the cage to check for any other damage. Only a fox, I thought, would cause this type of destruction. He is a clever and opportunistic animal. He sees an open gate and slips in. The man with the long brush, as Gavin had once called him, has his own ruthless agenda. Ripping the heads off his victims is typical, as well as killing in excess of his needs. But animals are innocent of malice and the old fox couldn't be blamed. All he did was make use of an easy entry. The real point was, how had the gate been left open? I had shut it last night. I always took infinite care with the catches. Or was it Virginia? Yesterday evening, had she looked in here on her return? Again and again I had urged my clients and workmen to take care.

I waited until nine o'clock, then knocked at the main door of the house. There was no reply. I opened it and entered. Virginia was coming out the kitchen. She looked tired and not especially pleased to see me. I had the feeling that perhaps she would have preferred to have kept me compartmentalised into the one hour she had allotted me last night.

I said: 'Three ducks have been killed.'

'Oh, no!' She opened her eyes wide in horror. 'How? I don't understand.'

'The gate was left open. I shut it last night when I was with you. I don't understand it either.'

'What was it? A fox?'

'I think so. It must be. Listen, Virginia, did you go back in there when you left me yesterday evening?'

219

'Are you accusing me of not shutting the gate?'

'No, not accusing at all. I just feel we must know how it happened. It was horrible, but it could have been worse, a total massacre.'

'Well, I didn't and even if I had I'd have shut the gate. Are you sure you did?'

'You know I did. You know how careful I am.'

'Then don't assume anyone else is less careful. You always think you're the only one here who cares.'

This was shocking in its own very small way. I took a step forwards. 'Please don't say that. I'm not accusing you of anything. I was just keen to get to the bottom of this so it can't happen again.'

Virginia pushed her hair back from her forehead. 'Sorry. I didn't sleep last night.'

Had the context been different, it would have been nice to have said something appreciative about yesterday evening, but the weather had changed and turned sullen. I made an apologetic noise and left.

From the back door, I could see Perry and Gavin and Trevor completing the colour planting. Was it conceivable it could have been the borzois who had savaged the ducks? Had the lads been poaching here last night, gone into the bird kingdom to admire them – Trevor especially loved to watch them – and left the gate ajar? I hurried down the path and into the enclosure. I was by now even more agitated as Virginia's reaction had added an extra weight of distress.

'Listen, all of you,' I said with great urgency. 'This is very important. You must tell me the truth. Did any of you go into the kingdom of the birds after seven o'clock yesterday evening?'

Gavin, always a sensitive reactor, looked troubled. Perry, who was slower to respond, stood up and tucked a strap into the cap of her sleeve. She didn't seem worried. She was the kind of confident, cheerful person whose conscience is always clear and uncomplicated. 'No,' she said. 'Oh no. I wasn't here at all yesterday. You know that. My days are Monday, Wednesday and Friday.'

Behind her, Gavin was acting as a conduit for my anxiety through his hand signs to his brother. The message rippled back. 'No,' said Gavin. 'Not us. We didn't. We fed them and left at five o'clock. We didn't go in to see the birds again.'

I had to accept that. I explained what had happened. Gavin made thick karate signals. His brother took it the worst. He put his big boy's hand over his face to hide the hurt. It was hard not to be affected by his strong voiceless emotion.

'She was a nice gadwall,' said Gavin.

I did not want to dwell on any of the three ducks. They had been helpless, their wings pinioned, without even the defence of flight. The attack was pitiless. Only their webbed feet had been undamaged, too scaly and bony and unappetising to scavenge.

'Can you swear to me, it wasn't your dogs?' I asked. 'One of them couldn't have got inside, could he? Tell me. I won't be cross. It would have been an accident. It's the truth that matters.'

'No,' cried Gavin. 'We swear it. It wasn't us. It wasn't the dogs.'

There was no doubting his honesty. They cherished the birds and the deer as part of their family and would not have protected their beautiful dogs at the expense of the others. Besides, I knew of old that the boys were never concealers. Such artlessness was one of their charms. I had known few workmen so ready to admit to error. They had never learned to gloss or to distort; I think, because they were outside the normal competitive world. I told them to put the business from their minds and to carry on with their planting. They returned to their tasks, bending as before from the waist as only the young can, vigorously and without regard for the strain on their spines and the squeeze on their stomachs. They were silent apart from the odd subdued comment.

I wanted the day to be over, for a flood of days to rush past, that would float a mist over today with its ugly discovery. When your job is to deal with living and beautiful and vulnerable creatures, which are there for your pleasure, death of this sort leaves a painful sense of shame. Indeed, the miasma of failure hung over all of us. No one talked to me except for Gavin who asked me where the ducks were buried. Later, at lunchtime, I saw Trevor paring some twigs which we used as unobtrusive plant supports in the ground. He then sorted them into couples, and tied each in the form of a cross with some gardening twine. I realised he would give each duck a child's shrine. Gavin saw me watching but neither of us made any comment. I was surprised in a way, because this reaction was hard to reconcile with a pair of lads who, I was sure, did their share of poaching. But I could not expect them to recognise the fact that they held dual standards. In any case, such sophistry would have been misplaced. The truth was his little ceremonial seemed appropriate, because, funnily, it made me feel better. It was an atonement for a mistake which no one could fathom.

The day passed. We got on with our jobs. In the afternoon I worked by the streams, plotting the sequence of plants for their banks. Trees had already been placed to the side of the runnels but a ground layer of flowers was needed to follow. This was my focus, but every so often I left to check the catches of the gates to the birds and the deer. On my second visit, I stopped outside the fencing of the cage and saw three crosses on the single burial mound in the ground. I made a third visit. The gates must be secure, but I was neurotic going back and forth like this several times, the rocking anxiety of an autistic child. I feared the old predator would come again tonight to try his luck on the killing field.

Virginia came out at the end of the afternoon. I saw her talk to the boys, then she walked over to me. She was wearing the same clothes as this morning, a pair of baggy trousers and a navy jumper which I knew had a hole in the elbow. I thought she might accompany me on my rounds, or on what seemed my twentieth round of the day. Perhaps it might be a chance to repair more than the gate. I still felt her rebuke of this morning and was sad to be under a cloud. However, all she said was that the boys had checked to see that it was secure and if both they and I were confident, so then she was too. She said she expected David back some time this evening, late perhaps. He had said he might call on Imogen on his way back from the station. She turned away to walk to the house but stopped after a few steps. She looked round. 'I was very unfair this morning,' she said. 'Will you forgive me?'

The sun had smiled on me again. A little of my illness ebbed. I said: 'Trevor has made three twig crosses and planted them on the grave.'

'How very sweet that boy is,' she said.

In the early evening I made a last call at the kingdoms of the deer and the birds. I chortled with the flamingos, told them that there was nothing to worry about, that tonight would be like any other night. One or two were still dredging for pellets in the pool, straining the water through their lamellae, the bristles in which they catch food. The rest were lulled by my reassurance. Casino lifted her neck to look at me and then tucked her bill back in the warmth of her feathers. Her legs were as delicate as the stems of blown glass. I dismissed the vision of the fox snapping and crunching them tonight. When I left I put a belt and braces binding of wire across the latches of the gate. I checked the boundaries, then went to the kingdom of the deer. Here no one was sleeping. There were giraffe-neck shadows in the greenwood, stretching up for leaves. I walked through the column of trunks. The horns of a young buck looked soft and plush. The bones were newly erupted; they were saplings, branching out-wards. Before the end of summer he would rub their velvet off. I whistled in Evie. Toe-first, she stepped prettily out of the darkness and trotted over the grass. She put her sweet grave face near my pocket and nuzzled the cloth. I gave her the apple and slid my palm along the hammocky length of her spine. Her coat had an odour tonight of musk and orange. The young doe was growing up. It was nearly two years since her birth in a bed of fresh green bracken. I stayed for a while, then left, checking with care the palings and gates as I had before.

I returned to the boathouse and started to prepare a meal. In the fridge I still had the eel that Trevor had given me yesterday. I nailed its head on a block of wood that I wedged on the deck, made a slit all the way round in the manner of barking a tree and slid the skin inside-out. It rolled off like a snake's. After the first tug, it was as easy as the peeling down of a woman's stocking. I then cut it in pieces and baked the fish with some olives and tomatoes and ate half on a bed of rice. It was a bit rubbery but had a good wild strong taste. Eel is much maligned, debased into jellies and thought fit only to be served as food at the fairground or seaside. But its tiny youngster, the elver, has as noble a life-journey as the salmon, pushing its way for two thousand miles from the place of its birth, the Sargasso Sea. It is one of the great animal migrations and lasts for three years. A good eel has the bold taste of the sea as well as the stream.

All this cooking and eating took up an hour at the most. The evening was now fully dark. I washed up and sat down in the main chair. Normally I would have read or worked on some plans, but my concentration had run elsewhere. I was waiting and listening. I considered setting up my telescope to pass the time. I knew that orange Arcturus was overhead. It is a red giant which the Greeks called the bear keeper and used as a marker of the changing seasons. It lies at the end of Boötes, the herdsman or hunter. The clock of the sky was swinging round. The winter triangle was yielding to the rise of the summer triangle. Everything changes, everything turns all the time. I thought how presumptuous it was to be a landscape architect, seeking to fix a permanent structure beneath the surface flux and flow.

I walked out of the room, shut the door behind me and went to stand on the deck. There was the sound of a car: Lacey returning, I supposed. I sat down and hung my knees over the edge as Virginia had done yesterday evening. Last night seemed weeks ago. Beneath me, the water was black and smooth at the edges but cables of current roamed the surface and rippled in the windowlight. Every alarm call set off a flutter of bats in my mind, though a single penetrating scream was nothing. Only the screams of the colony mattered. From time to time there was a scuffling: nothing really, stoats or rabbits or the usual busy nocturnal snufflers. A clatter at the window was caused by a squirrel hanging upside down by his claws from the gutter. Between noises there was only a watery silence. I sat a little longer until I grew stiff, so I pushed myself up to go inside. At this point there came the sound of footsteps treading with great care over the grass. I wouldn't have heard it but it was a listening night.

Half a minute later, at the point where the path curved round in view of the boathouse, a figure appeared in formal clothing. I recognised Lacey. He was carrying something white in his hands. He showed no indication of having seen me, probably because I was standing outside the immediate arena of light thrown by the window.

'David. Can you see me? What is it?'

He halted by the house. He showed surprise or, at least, stood there without speaking.

I asked again: 'What is it? Is something wrong?'

He began walking and mounted the steps to the deck. He was slightly short of breath, had been hurrying perhaps.

'I came to give you this,' he said abruptly and he passed me an envelope.

As I held it up to the windowlight, recognising that the writing of my name on the paper was not by a third party, that the hand was his, I knew that this must be a culmination, perhaps of this evening, perhaps of days, weeks even. I didn't open it. I had entered a vacuum, waiting, the air sucked out. I said: 'Tell me what's in here?'

'I saw my sister this evening. I think you must know what she told me. This letter is a formal termination of our agreement. All bills will be paid to date of course.'

Something had swollen in my throat. 'I don't know what she told you, but since I'm about to lose my job and seem to have been impugned, I'd like to hear what she said.'

'Very well.' His shortness of breath had returned. He was sweating. He must be finding this difficult. 'She said you had sex with her, used her, then dropped her.'

We had locked eyes, but he was unable to stop his hypertensive blink twice at the critical moment. We both stood facing one another, arms hanging uselessly to our sides.

'From your silence I assume you don't deny it.'

'On the night I returned after my mother died, Imogen saw me and asked me for her torch, which I'd borrowed. It is perfectly true I spent the night with her, and with more than her acquiescence I might add, however distasteful that sounds. It is equally true it didn't happen again, as it shouldn't have happened the first time. I was wrong, I admit, but it was very circumstantial.'

'So you agree it's true, whatever gloss you put on it?'

'The gloss, or the explanation as I am justified in calling it, matters.'

'My sister says this happened last November.'

'Yes. It would have been then. If she recognised it as significant, why didn't she tell you before? It's nearly six months ago.'

'She didn't want to cause unnecessary damage.'

'Then why now?'

His voice had become increasingly strangled. He was so tense I thought he would seize up. 'She only told me tonight because she says you've now turned your attentions on my wife.'

This was so appalling and unexpected I couldn't speak for a moment. 'That's outrageous. Quite absurd.'

'She spoke the truth about herself. You've admitted it. Why would she lie about you?'

'I cannot imagine. But equally, why should I speak the truth about your sister but lie about your wife?'

It was crazy, standing there tossing each other conundrums. In the middle of all this, a pinpoint thought penetrated our vacuum: that I had stopped listening and that the fox would get the birds.

'I assume you must have spoken to Virginia,' I said. 'She too must be outraged.'

He was silent. I had no doubt this had been the case.

'My sister saw you here, on this deck, yesterday evening. She said you –' He spread his hands '– kissed. Your behaviour wasn't open to misinterpretation.' It was awful, the formality over the anguish. 'What's been going on?' he said in despair.

Until now a decorous five feet had separated us. I stepped forward and took hold of the lapels of his jacket. 'This is a real madness. The wrong end of the stick. I have both a great respect and affection for your wife, as anyone would. She's worked with me and given me support, but nothing inappropriate has, or is, or ever would take place. Do you understand?'

'All I know is that you have fucking well taken over. Stage by stage. I look round here and I see not only the imprint of your work but your character.'

'I came at your behest.'

'You have taken over my land, my sister, now my wife it would seem.'

'My God, it's in the nature of my work that I inhabit the territory of another person. Don't you see? My territory is other people's.'

'And my sister, my wife, or don't you draw the line?'

'Christ Almighty, don't keep saying that.' I caught his arm and gave it a tiny shake. I shall never forget that it was the tiniest movement, no more than a second's flare, but he stepped back and in those few inches he tripped against the block of wood on which I had nailed the head of the eel – the head was still there, the deck slippery with its slime – and he slid and fell off the edge. It was only the smallest shake, but I could not catch him and, though it seemed almost in slow motion, it happened very fast. Plunging against the bank, one arm up as though to pluck the air, giving a terrible eerie cry, he rebounded into the river. The cry was severed as the water filled his open mouth and pushed back his tongue. The waves he had made closed over his head. I must have shouted, I think – I was trying not to lose my head in panic – but all I remember was tearing off clothes and shoes and pounding down the steps and into the water.

As I ran, I knew it was hopeless. Lacey could not swim. He would drown. I would drown too, but it is harder to resist the imperative to save than to follow. I had lost sight of him, the current was strong and the waters were high. He could be thirty feet away by now. He had fallen with the force and weight of a projectile. He could have fainted on impact. You drown quickly. The sea closes over your head. Water bubbles into the lungs. Your body is a huge sponge. There is a great weight within you. The pressure forces you down. I knew all this as I entered the water, but blind impulse drives you forward. It seems like self-destruction, but it isn't; it is mixed with self-preservation because you know that, if you survive, you must not be ashamed to live with yourself.

I tried to lift my head out of the water. If the reeds did not trap him, he might come up. All I needed was a head bobbing on the surface like a buoy. It was black, though ahead the window light shone in golden and ruddy knives on the surface. At the edge of this patch I saw a shape rise in the water. An elation made a great engine drum inside me, powering my muscles towards it. Within seconds I found Lacey. He was alive and as I grasped him he started to thrash violently. I tried to pull him but his body resisted. I could not shift him. As I tugged, he was tugged back. He was trapped in reeds as strong as cat gut. I had my arms round a great fish dying in the net. If I entered I would die in the net too. The trap in the water would suck us both down. Then a third fish seemed to get caught in the mesh. It was crazy, it had seized me and was holding on tight. I struggled, but it pulled me away and put its flippers round Lacey. I thought black water had entered my brain. I was delirious. Here was a fish with the face of Trevor, the deaf-mute lifesaver. He was rocking Lacey back and forwards. I thought: they must amputate his leg. If a surgeon comes now and cuts off his leg, he will be free of the reeds. Or is it the reed he needs to cut. At one point Trevor dipped beneath the surface. I thought: All three of us are dead. We are drowning of adrenaline mixed with water. It makes a poisonous combination. Because of an eel, three fish are dead. I closed my eyes to shut out the violent commotion. Drowning in sleep. When I opened them, I was being towed. Trevor was towing us both. We were moving slowly like a Leviathan to the bank. From time to time I made paddles like a child or a dog. Then a most terrible juddering hit me as I lay on the bank. I tried to talk but the words: Is he dead? were ejected in great jerks. Trevor does not reply. He does not hear. He is a deaf-mute. There is a couple beside me, one moving on top of the other, making love, rhythmically rocking. I feel the caress of warm wet strokes. It must be water, I am swimming again; it eases the juddering. There are tongues on my limbs, in the cave of my ear. A face that is pointed rests against mine. It is one of the borzois. He returns to my legs. He soothes me and lies down on top, but as soon as his licks cease then the juddering starts and pushes him off. He gives up and lies to one side. He still wants to be one of the pack. I try to ask again: Is he dead? but this time I can't even get the words out. It is ridiculous. Both Trevor and I are mute; so is Lacey. Quite useless. You want to impose yourself to some effect. With great focus I manage to get up with the intention of mounting the steps and putting my clothes on and going to the house. 'I shall call an ambulance.' The words are loud but Trevor can't hear however loudly they are shouted. Lacey is visible, a big heavy soft mass. His shape has changed since falling in the water.

29

On my way to the house, the ambulance came. They had been summoned by Virginia as Gavin had already arrived there with his story. They all picked me up stumbling around in the dark, then went to fetch Lacey. We were wrapped in blankets. Lacey was taken to hospital which meant he was still alive. Virginia went with him. She told me to stay here and rest. She was white with a cut on her lip. She didn't want me to form part of a threesome. My shaking had stopped. It only started when I saw him falling into the water again. I could not go to the boathouse and see the head of the eel. But I hoped no one would touch it because it was important circumstantial evidence. Everything would hang on the eel. In the night I thought: if he dies it will go to the coroner's court. Will they ever believe it was an eel? To escape hindsight and forethought, I went downstairs. Trevor and Gavin were sleeping on separate sofas. They were dressed in baggy pyjamas like a pair of clowns. I thought that Trevor, of course, could bear witness I was trying to save Lacey, but was the testimony of a deaf-mute legal? The jury could throw it out. The shaking began again, the boring old bone-rattling. I went to get myself a cup of hot sweet tea because this is what you give other people when they are shocked. They had given it to me. Newsreels of survivors with tea, their heads poking out of blankets. I went to ring the hospital for the third time that night and was told he was still unconscious. I thought: if he lives, what will he remember? The pulse fades, the mind blacks out, parts of the brain are damaged; it is well documented that memories of these events can be lost or distorted forever in the brains of those afflicted.

Trevor and Gavin woke up. I gave them two mugs of tea. There were hairs from the borzois all over the sofas. I noticed the hairs before I saw the dogs themselves. I went to fondle the ears of the one who had licked me.

'He is still alive,' I said, 'but unconscious.' They looked at me, rumpled and a little confused. I was too. 'What I don't understand is, what were you doing there?'

Gavin said: 'We'd gone to wait for the fox with the dogs. We were spending the night there. I heard the cry and you shouted for help. I told Trevor.'

I started to cry slightly in a puffy embarrassing way; so I had shouted for help, had I? I saw this as the unbiased rescuing comment of a witness. 'We owe you everything,' I said.

Gavin said: 'Trevor is trained in best procedures.'

The words came out like military jargon. It was a term from a manual. Textbooks talk like this.

'Maybe we were watching for the wrong fox,' I said.

'How do you mean?'

I thought of Imogen and what she had said. The old fox had come all right.

In the morning Virginia rang and asked how I was.

I didn't answer. I was under the water. Instead I asked: 'How is he?'

'He's conscious. His leg is smashed and so are three ribs. He's all right but he'll be a while in hospital. He'll have to be operated on in due course.'

I burst to the surface. Water drained from my back. 'Does he want to see me?'

'Better let him rest.'

She said she would be back for a couple of hours in the afternoon and hung up.

A normal routine, they say, is good at such times: the morning paper, the crossword, cleaning the car, feeding flamingos. Though why they think artificial normality resembles the thing it is supposed to resemble, I cannot imagine.

The newspaper said Whitewater rumours are denied by Clinton. On the back page, dealers had shorted Glaxo. On page 3, an army woman had shot her lover's wife. The same old news is dished up all the time. I thought, we must keep this out of the local paper which would bill it as one cuddly dog rescues drowning trio.

Later, shaving, I saw a front tooth had been chipped by all that juddering, or perhaps by Lacey thrashing. When I came down, the boys were in the kitchen. 'The fox didn't come,' said Gavin.

'Good,' I said, knowing better.

They ambled out, saying something about mending a puncture on the wheelbarrow.

At two o'clock Virginia returned, her hair pushed back like a shuttlecock. The drop of black blood on her lip was gone, but it was puffy around the cut. She didn't lean against me as I had wanted. She walked away. I followed.

'Your teeth are so prominent. Is that how you cut your lip?'

She threw herself in a chair, her head flung back. 'Christ Al-fucking-mighty,' she said. 'I'm so tired. Don't be stupid. He hit me.'

She did not move her head. I said something like Oh Virginia, but she was beyond the ooze of sympathy.

She said: 'I suppose he hit you and you hit him and you two stupid louts fell in the water and ruined my life.'

'No,' I said. 'He didn't hit me. I didn't him. It was very controlled. He slipped because of the eel.'

'What eel?'

I told her. She still didn't move her head. She said: 'That's a good one.'

'How could I make it up? The head of the eel is still there.' I thought: It's going wrong. I saved Lacey's life. I could have died. One doesn't expect credit for this, but it is unfair of a beneficiary to ignore it. Yet I could not bring myself to say anything so vulgar as: I saved his life. Would a prayer be more efficacious? It would be more subtle certainly. Please God, put the thought into her head that I saved his life. Then she will move and look at me and her face will change and the sun will shine.

I had envisaged Lacey in hospital for a while. Virginia and I would work in the garden side by side. We would chortle with the flamingos and stroke the deer and walk the arabesques of grasses and hear the parrots in the trees and the ripe fruit would drop in our laps. We would make love under the palms and count the dates and catch them in our mouths. One day Lacey would come home but I didn't want to think of that. Imogen would wither away in a manner that is becoming to a witch.

I felt strange as though infected with ague.

'The bitch,' Virginia said to the ceiling.

'Who?'

'Who do you think? Imogen.'

'Why did she say what she said about us?'

The word 'us' was particularly beautiful. I wanted to keep the concept alive.

'She wouldn't mind one little bit getting rid of me,' said Virginia. 'It was an opportunity.'

'She spied on us.'

'How did she see us?' Virginia asked.

'It's easy enough. She could have been walking further up on the bank or down the hillside. She could have even been using her telescope.'

Virginia's face unfroze. It started working again. She banged her head back and forth on the cushions. 'It is grotesque. There was nothing to see.'

I wanted to protest, to say something is not nothing. She seemed to be viewing everything from the wrong angle. It was different from mine, but I was only a courtier and couldn't contradict her. 'I don't understand how David would have believed her,' I said.

'You remember you went away in the winter?'

'Yes.'

'You know I went away too?'

'Yes.'

'David took his sister round the place in our absence.'

'I know that.'

'I think she played on misgivings that already existed. Ever since then he has been ill at ease. He said that he had commissioned you to create this place, but that in creating it, the creator had taken it over and stolen it. He said he was surrounded by another man's imprint and creative force.'

'He said something like that to me. I thought he had gone mad. I pointed out my territory is other people's and has to be.'

I could not say I took hold of his lapel and shook his arm which

232

was why he backed away and fell over the block of wood with the head of the eel.

'Apparently Imogen said that you lay claim to whatever you come across.'

'Imogen said I lay claim to whatever I come across?' I said with incredulity.

The repetition seemed to irritate Virginia. She frowned. 'Yes. What do you think of that?' She spoke in a lawyerly tone, giving right of appeal.

'It is nonsense.'

'Is it?' she said drily. 'Shall I tell you what David does and doesn't remember from last night? Perhaps that would be helpful. One: He doesn't remember anything after hitting the water. He is still completely disorientated about that. Two: He remembers sliding on something. I guess that ties up with your story about the eel, whatever my initial reaction. Three: He thinks he remembers that you said what Imogen said about you was true. You slept with her.' She looked at me very coolly. 'David is of course very confused. Last night I didn't believe it when he told me. Am I right or is David?'

I said nothing. I thought seriously about denial. Admission had already proved an error of judgement. One must learn from one's mistakes.

'Yes, it's true. I might add I see no reason for this inquisition.'

'You fool,' she said. 'It's one thing to pass beyond the basics of sensible behaviour. Another to lie to me.'

I was upset by her lack of deference. I said: 'I've never done that.'

'Your implication was that you had negligible contact with my sister-in-law and such as existed was entirely practical.'

'That was the case apart from one night which I have bitterly regretted.' Out it had to come again: the story of returning after my mother's funeral and so forth. This time, I was passionate in my defence. 'Are you so cold and judgemental that you can't understand the circumstances?'

Her face began to crumple. 'I don't understand. I warned you about her. It seems so weak of you, so disappointing. And then to mislead me.'

'You warned me after it happened. It was too late.'

She put her face in her hands. 'It's as old as the hills, isn't it, this?

The comings and goings of human beings. And having to salvage the remains. How do I do that, eh?'

'Things seem awful now. They'll settle down. Imogen has got nowhere apart from endangering her brother which she wouldn't have wanted. Perhaps she'll go away. We'll carry on as we are. We've got to finish this place. It is a triumph.'

'I don't think this is the answer. This morning David said it would be better for you to go.'

'I saved his life.' There was nothing subtle about the way I shouted. It was a bellow.

Virginia looked at me with tired sadness. 'I know that, but what I really think is that you both owe everything to dear Trevor.'

I nodded. 'We should recommend him for an award. Heroism or something. But how do we do that and keep it out of the local paper?'

'My God,' she said. 'The things you say.'

'I'm sorry. I was only trying to look at the consequences.'

'Perhaps you should have looked at the consequences before any of this happened.'

'Thank you. Hindsight is so valuable, isn't it?'

'I'm so tired,' she said. 'And I haven't got the energy to fight for you. All this while I've been your defence. Now I know that you lied to me –'

'I did not, I repeat, did not lie to you about Imogen.'

'Well, whatever. I just don't have the energy. All that matters is David's equilibrium.'

'All that matters is the truth.'

'You don't understand. I'd better tell you the background.' Virginia looked up at me. 'You couldn't get me a drink, could you? Not a drink-drink. Something hot. Not coffee either. I feel terribly dehydrated.'

'Tea?'

She made a sour face. 'That's so English. All your lifeboat/ambulance people ever think of is tea. I've had a gallon. Oh well, yes, I suppose. I can't think of anything else.'

I went to the kitchen and boiled the kettle and stuck a bag of Darjeeling in her favourite mug and brought it to her.

'Thank you,' she said. She sipped it and gasped: 'Hot.' She smiled, twisting her face. 'Do you remember that party last summer and the baby who could only say "hot" and "hello".'

'Yes,' I said, 'I remember.' I leaned forward, watching her intently. I wanted her to go on remembering events we had shared together.

But she was moving on, looking inward now, searching further back. 'Listen. When I married David, he was pretty messed up. That's the truth. He had been under threat of a lawsuit. As you know, he headed a pharmaceutical company. One of his drugs which had been hailed as a breakthrough only a few years before, was now showing evidence of dangerous side effects. Question marks were being raised about primary pulmonary hypertension and heart failure, but the evidence was equivocal.'

She swilled the tea round in the mug to cool it and took a gulp. She continued: 'My husband – my first husband, that is – was a cardiologist. A patient of his died during a very routine heart operation. The patient had been taking this drug for two weeks only. His wife threatened to sue. My husband pinned it on the drug. At this point I was called in by the pharmaceutical company as one of the lawyers required to give my opinion on their position. I refused because of conflict of interest, though objectively I didn't think there was a case. The drug had been developed at every stage with the necessary approvals. And, besides, from what my husband had told me I knew that the heart failure wasn't due in this instance to the drug. But it was through this that I met and grew closer to David, whom I'd known years before.'

She paused.

I said: 'But surely this is a very common situation. Drugs have untoward side effects and reports of damage have to be widespread and unequivocal before they are withdrawn.'

'Oh yes,' said Virginia. 'This is not uncommon. There are men walking about all over London who, in the interests of the greater good of the majority, have killed or damaged the lives of the relatively few. But David was not like that. The drug was his baby. He could not shrug off this failure. My first husband could. He had the necessary mechanisms. I had accused him before of seeming callous and indifferent.'

'So you switched from one to the other?'

She gave a puff of derision. 'If you must put it like that. What happened was that the lawsuit evaporated. Nothing could be pinned on either party in this case, though the question marks remained. In due course, prescriptions of the drug steadily decreased. A year or two passed. On a personal front things evolved slowly between us. A decision was eventually made to leave one man and marry the other.'

'You put this in the third person.'

'The decision was taken very much in the first person. I wanted my marriage to be worth something. I wanted to be needed.' She screwed up her eyes. 'I think we've had this conversation before, haven't we?'

'About being needed, yes.'

'So I married him. He was in quite a mess. He'd been under great strain. He'd become melancholic, prone to paranoia. I worked hard, believe me, to prove to him that his life wasn't over.'

'Did you succeed?'

'Better than anyone could have expected. But it was always there, you know. I call it the Pit.'

'What pit?'

'The pit into which he can fall. His paranoia and so forth. It's part of him.' She gave a sigh. 'Do you see now why I had the idea of a garden?'

'In a way. I think so.'

'He'd left the company with a golden handshake which was tantamount to shutting him up. He felt terrible for accepting it. I wanted to find something positive and forward-looking, celebratory even, into which we could put the money.'

'Something that would grow and get better.'

'What's more positive than that?' Virginia put down the mug. 'I feel very woozy. I've only eaten a slice of hospital toast today.'

I ignored this. 'Then we mustn't let anything stop us from completing this place.'

'You don't follow, do you? The reason I'm telling you all this, which is confidential of course, is to explain why I'm asking you to go.'

I jumped up. 'It contradicts everything you're saying.'

'No. What I've explained to you is David's vulnerability. I've been thinking about this all the way home as I was driving.'

236

'One can't give in to a man's paranoia.'

'Call it pain rather than paranoia and you'll see why you can.'

From outside there was the sound of a tyre and footsteps crunching over gravel. Normal routine had resumed. Trevor must have mended the puncture to the wheelbarrow.

I stared at my client numbly. 'Don't you at least want me to stay?'

'On the way home I was undecided. Now I want you to go. You're the weak link.'

I had thought I was the king pin in this place. Now only a weak link. One's ego is so big. It has to be or one dies. I said: 'It's because of my episode with Imogen, isn't it?'

I watched her rolling this around. In the end she said: 'Yes.'

She is a lawyer, I thought. She's spent weeks defending someone who's only just now admitted his guilt. She's also a woman, and I've been unfaithful to her. One can't expect a woman to put any other construction on it. Beside this, all my work here counts for nothing.

'You know what I think, Virginia,' I said. 'I may have concealed from you what happened with Imogen, but you didn't give me the background to David either. I've been trapped all this while in a hidden agenda.'

'What hidden agenda? You were employed to do a job. Sorry, but objectively I have to put it this way. Part of that job, part of the equation, is taking account of people's sensitivities and their relationships. Those surely don't need to be spelt out.'

'Please don't tell me how to do my job.'

'I didn't mean to. But do you know what I think?'

I stared at her with suppressed resentment.

She closed her eyes. 'Do you remember telling me about *Über das Marionettentheater*?'

'Yes. When I came back after Christmas.'

'It seems to me we were your puppet theatre, weren't we? But the trouble is you can only pull the strings of puppets and animals and plants. Not human beings.' She bit her lower lip and winced where the cut hurt. She said: 'He has never hit me before. I've always said I'd leave a man who hit me, but this is different, isn't it?'

'Is it?' I put my hand on my forehead. I was shocked by what she had said about my puppets.

'Everything is different when it actually happens. One thinks people will react in a particular way, but nothing is predictable. I suppose I'm guilty too of treating everyone as a puppet. Events like this make you stop and think, don't they?'

I said: 'You are wrong about the puppet theatre.'

'Am I? I think I'm right.'

'That's not what Kleist meant.'

'I'm talking about you, not the author.'

I said: 'I can't think straight at the moment.'

She stared at me with an emptied face. It had rid itself of all it needed to tell me.

I said: 'There's nothing left to say, is there? I suppose I'd better pack and go.'

'No hurry,' she said. 'You must rest here overnight if you need to. But I've got to go back to the hospital early this evening. I'd better have something to eat. I'm a bit hungrier now.'

'Who will you get to finish this place?'

'Is there much to do?'

'You know there is. I had worked out so many plans.'

'It seems wonderful enough as it is. I promise you we'll look after it and develop it.'

'You can't.'

'Why not?'

I wanted to say, it's mine, my vision, but it would only confirm everything she had said. I thought: the devaluation of work cut off is like a death.

'No one will know about this, of course,' she advised me.

'Just one more skeleton, isn't it?' I said coldly. She would write in her diary: *The landscape architect finished today and left. It is absolutely perfect.* I remember she had once said her diary was censored. She was a very determined woman.

'Please don't be like that,' said Virginia. 'You know I think you've done the most beautiful job. You know it too. Nothing changes that. If you want to come back in a year or a couple of years for a day's visit . . .'

She left it open. As she spoke, I believe I saw her reconsidering her offer. We both knew it would be impossible for me ever to contact her again.

She was embarrassed. 'This is awful. Forgive me. I'd prefer not to remember any of this.'

'No,' I said. I stood up. 'What will you say to David this evening?'

'He'll be sleeping, I expect.'

'Then tomorrow, or the next day, or the day after that?'

'I'll say . . . I don't know. I'll say what we've said. I'll find a way of saying it. I always do.'

'Why not tell him that you were both part of my puppet theatre? That'll bring you very close together again.'

She said: 'I'm sorry. That was a moment's thought and I shouldn't have said it. The wrong things get said. I'm so tired that I'm not in control.'

'I think I'd like to go back to the boathouse now.'

'Don't leave today. Promise me. You'll have a car crash.'

'Don't worry. I shan't do anything silly.'

We kissed each other on the cheek and stood for a moment with some awkwardness.

I said: 'You've got it wrong about the marionette theatre. It's not about trying to manipulate others.'

'Please don't get hung up about that. Please forget it.'

She went upstairs to snatch some sleep. I left for the boathouse, but walked first to the ducks and flamingos. They were safe. It was our fox that had come in the night, not theirs. The twig crosses were still on the ducks' grave. I felt ill with self-blame. It seemed years ago that the gate was left open. There could be only one rational explanation. I was that person who had failed to close the gate despite my accusations of everyone else. I had been the last to enter. It was my accident and so were the others. I had failed to close that gate and opened too many others by introducing myself. I was supposed to create stability and order but had been the destroyer. How could I be angry with my clients when I was so much to blame?

I entered the kingdom of the birds and shut it behind me. Casino laughed when she saw me and all the flamingos chorused, batting their wings like marionette limbs. The ducks and the drakes who had lost their mates were still keening and searching. I sat on a clean patch of grass at the edge of the pool. The legs of the flamingos minced forward in clusters, their bills swaying and scything the water.

In the deer park my white doe would be dipping her muzzle in the pool, making angelic reflections. She would drink deeply, plunging her nose like a horse. Or like Muffin the mule, as Virginia would say.

I climbed the steps to the deck of the boathouse. The head of the eel was still there. It had lost the sheen on its pewter. I picked up the block of wood to hurl it into the water but stopped. You never know with these things. Let me put it this way. You can't take cathartic action with evidence. In the fridge the remaining half of the eel I had roasted but not eaten was still there. I threw that away instead. My file of plans was still sitting on the table. No reason for this not to follow the same route as the eel. I took Lacey's envelope which was still in my pocket. I went down to the river and put a match to the paper. The ashes floated around in the air, still unread, then they fell in the water and the current swirled them away.

30

THERE WAS A little hollow space the following day in which fare-wells must take place.

'Are you all right now?' asked Gavin when I saw him. He looked away. He must have been embarrassed yesterday morning to see me cry.

'Better, thank you. Still a bit tired. I was very tired yesterday.'

'Mrs Lacey said you would be away for a little while.'

'Did she? I've got another job to do.'

'What do you want us to do on the banks of the streams?'

'Ask Mrs Lacey what she would like.'

'We asked her. She didn't know.'

'Ask her again.'

'When are you coming back?'

'In a couple of months if possible. It depends if I can escape from the other jobs.'

I gripped both boys in turn by the arm and thanked them for everything, which was of course inadequate. They looked at me curiously. I was inappropriate and emotional when they thought they would see me again. I told them to say goodbye for the time being to Perry.

I said: 'You must take great care of the birds and the deer. You are their keepers always now.'

'We didn't leave the gate open,' said Gavin.

'I know you didn't. It won't happen again. The fox won't come again.'

★   ★   ★

I wrote a note for my clients and left it on the table. It was scrupulously polite and formal, not the words of a man who had drowned in the water or had a mirror held up to his face as the puppet master. *The landscape architect left today. Everything is perfect.* For the last time I went to see my white doe and Casino and Las Vegas. Perhaps my flamingos would breed, one egg to each nest, each nest separated by the length of a neck. The fledgling would break from its shell and live on the milk of its parents. They belonged to David Lacey now. In the deer park, next year Evie would drop her fawn in the bracken. It would be wet and with tear ducts under its sad eyes. It would leave tiny hoof slots on the ground. It too would belong to Lacey now. He would be happy today. He would get better quickly. Today he could say, 'Everything comes back into our possession again.'

Driving back for the last time over the causeway and up over the other side, I considered making a detour to Imogen, which would at least have the merit of an honest leavetaking. But what was the point? I would be visiting accusations on a third party when there was only myself to blame. I drove on. It was a warm morning. It was still early enough for the light to be blue. It had not changed yet to white or to yellow, which is the pattern of colour for a hot day. The landscape, so familiar when you cross it a number of times, seemed strange. I was driving as a stranger, someone who no longer connects with people, which is the puppet-master, I suppose. It is a cruel image to visit on a landscape architect, because it is so apt. He is a man who hammers the rock of the earth into Capability's Eden. He makes a temperate world of calmness and moderation. There are no tempests or passions here. No scorching or freezing. He fills it with passive minions: the willows and pines and lilies and roses. Bring on the dancing girls, every beast of the field and every fowl of the earth. And the Lord God planted a garden, as befits a master of puppets. Only this time the man and his wife had risen up and most wisely rid themselves of the creator. It was me who was exiled for bad behaviour and consorting with the serpent. I wished I could tell someone about this little comedy, but only Louise would appreciate the irony and I was not sure I had come to terms yet with the story.

*   *   *

That afternoon I went first to the office. When you have fallen out of a garden, it is sensible to jump straight into the next one. There is a lot to be said for automatic recovery. I gathered the threads of the office together and updated myself on the state of current activity. I decided the following week I would visit my project in Portugal and my job in Brittany later. I was busy. Yet in the night I could not rid myself of the images. They came back and formed a pattern. The curl of the flamingo's neck, the head of the eel, the doe pluming like smoke through the trunks, the gulls overhead, the curl of the neck, the man waterfalling in the river, the tongue of the borzoi, the head of the eel, the curl of the neck. I woke up and thought: I was not a puppet-master. If there were any strings to be pulled, all I was trying to do was to release the grace and unself-conscious beauty of the animals. Then another thought came and I wished I had not been able to form this thought because it closed the gate. I thought that harmony in the real world is never achievable yet we persist in seeking it, just as the real world persists in breaking in. It is a quest without point.

The following day I didn't go into the office. I had a fever, probably caused by some water germ, and stayed in bed. The day after that I didn't go in either. Then the next day I managed a brief visit to Portugal but I was sleepwalking. Every time I looked at the plans, I felt it was pointless. The real world would persist in breaking in. The curl of the neck and the head of the eel, the man waterfalling in the river kept pace in my dreams.

Then the morning after I flew back to England, the real world broke in again. The head of the eel, the man waterfalling in the river moved out of my dreams and took occupation of their rightful place.

It was nine o'clock in the evening. I was in the kitchen making an anchovy sauce to go with broccoli and pasta. I was stirring the mixture assiduously to stop it burning. When the telephone rang, I turned out the heat and went into the hall.

Virginia's voice. Her estranged sound. Her first words: 'I have to tell you.' The seeds spring up within you. You know how they will grow. 'David died two days ago,' she said.

I could not speak for a moment.

She said: 'Are you there?'

I cleared my throat. 'What happened?'

'It was a heart attack. Massive, they said. They fought to save him.'

'But he was in hospital,' I said. Normal sentences come automatically. Stupid noises which express belief in the right procedures and safeguards.

'They said that after an experience of this kind, chemical changes can take place in the body for up to ten days.'

I said, the normal-sounding part of me said: 'You are telling me that they told you it was due to him falling in the water.'

'I am telling you that, yes.'

The normal part collapsed. The part that wanted to be blind opened its eyes.

I think I said: 'Oh Virginia.' I may have said, this is terrible, I am so sorry, but perhaps not, or perhaps she didn't hear it because it is a fact that you can't speak when you are under the water.

'The funeral will be entirely private,' she said from a long way away. 'I wouldn't ask you to come to that.'

'I ought to.'

'I'd prefer not.'

I thought, I must send something. Not a wreath. Not roses. Not Sweet Dreams, Gentle Touch, Queen Mother. Not to a man, not when you have killed him. His head like a buoy above the water. His body a sponge.

'You know it'll go to the coroner's court. You'll have to come to that,' she said quietly, Virginia the bereaved wife, the lawyer.

I cleared my throat again. Mud and reeds had collected there.

'Virginia, what will happen?'

'I think that may be in the hands of Imogen.'

A sick queer feeling detained me. Eventually I said: 'Surely David told her there wasn't an ounce of truth in her accusation.'

'He did.'

'Well, then.' I thought, his body lies in a box and we're talking like this.

'There is no "Well, then" is there?' she said coldly. 'She can provide a reason why he came to see you late at night and not only a reason.'

'What do you mean?'

'I mean, a reason for him, and also a motive for you to have an altercation.'

I thought, she hates me. She thinks I have murdered her husband. I took hold of his lapel and shook his arm, which was why he backed and fell over the block of wood. But I saved his life. Except I had no longer saved his life. I had killed him.

I said with some urgency: 'I must speak to her.'

'The reason why I'm calling you now is to tell you of my husband's death in advance of any notice you may see in the papers. And to tell you not to speak to Imogen.'

'Why not? Haven't you?'

She paused. 'I saw her once at the hospital. She was going out as I was coming in.'

'What did she say?'

'She said nothing. I told her it was a wicked thing she'd said.'

Her voice was shaky. It was the first sign she had shown of emotion.

'It was an evil.' For a moment our innocence blocked out my guilt. Me and Virginia against an enemy.

I said: 'Why did you ring to tell me not to speak to Imogen?'

'I am a lawyer. I have seen clients get desperate. This can make things worse. Attempted manipulation, you know, would be an error of judgement.'

Our relations seemed to have changed. Once she had been my client. Now I was hers.

I said: 'But if neither of us speaks to her, we are in her hands.'

'There is that risk, yes.'

I said: 'What can I say to you, Virginia?'

'Not much.'

There was a silence, empty of accusation only because it had already been fully expended.

She said: 'I must go. There's a lot to do.'

Of course: she must have called me among the hymns and the death certificates and the tombstones. There is always so much to do. She was not weepy, which would have been seemly, but I understood there was so much to do, more in this case than usual.

'When is the funeral?' I asked, as though this were some normal putting-to-bed.

'Next week. After the post-mortem. After the inquest.'

She told me the name of the church. I remembered it, small and damp and mossy. I saw my mother's funeral, the line that stretched between my mother's death and Lacey's. The one had extracted the other, caused the second body to lie in a box. *The truth is that at the time you've no idea where you're going.* I wanted to say to Virginia, I did love you, you know. It is a terrible thing to have hurt you, worse than hurting your husband. Last week we had lain on the sand under the palms. Forgive me. I'm so dreadfully sorry. Or, like a solicitor, should I say I offer my condolences to the family. A solicitor might say that with his chest sticking out. But then a solicitor would say, 'Bye-bye', not his responsibility, end of episode; the old hypocrite.

'I'm so terribly sorry,' I said again, or was it for the first time? I was shaking so much inside that I didn't know which words had been shaken out.

Virginia said: 'I'll speak to you again shortly before the inquest.'

'What are the possible formal verdicts?'

She hesitated. 'Accidental. Open verdict.'

'Any other?' I was trying to speak normally again. Imitations of normality are so good nowadays that you can't tell the difference from the real thing.

'Non-accidental, of course.'

I saw what I had tried not to see from those first words she had spoken. *I have to tell you.* The seeds had sprung up, grown giant-high, multiplied. Neither of us had mentioned manslaughter. Things grow out of control. They are unstoppable. I know that from my work.

31

WORK IS GOOD for sanity. I had to work. I could not work. I had taken hold of his lapel and shaken his arm, the tiniest shake. Fingers and one thumb with the cloth between them. Does this constitute assault? I could not ask Virginia, the bereaved wife. She did not know about the finger and the thumb. No one knew though at times I thought everyone knew.

Back in the office, the board continued to hang on the wall with its gold medals and testimonials from grateful clients. How to reconcile this with a coroner's sentence? Open verdict. Non-accidental. Its overhanging sequel: manslaughter. In the office we were active. Isabel, my designer, continued to design gardens, arranging her flowers without a thought for the physics of the earth. Tim, my henchman, went about his business with his pink face, charming the wives, drugging them with affability. He brought me his problems. I couldn't take mine to him. I travelled the sardine boat to Brittany again to escape. A day's visit only. I ordered plantings of agapanthus and hydrangeas in bunches. Mechanical combinations. My host made nice noises. He should have sacked me. I looked out at the sea. It was swirling with the ashes of the letter I had burnt. The current must have moved out from my river and mingled.

I rang an old school friend who was a solicitor, specialising in personal injury. As a boy, he had been a young puppy, playful, untidy, bounding about. Now he was in corsets for a back problem and his face was in waiting for early retirement. We sat in his club surrounded by old wood. It formed a protective layer against the modern world. Mr Gladstone and Mr Disraeli decorated the walls, facing one another as befits old adversaries. A newspaper fell out of an armchair. There was an old man in the chair, sleeping like a fish deep in the ocean. There are still a few men in these clubs who look as though they have never seen the light of day. In the background an eminent wine-buff who has made a fortune from his knowledge – you would know his name if I told you – was ordering wine for a dinner of his club within the club. An inner sanctum within the sanctum. More protective layers. We seek a lot of insulation nowadays. It's why we have gardens.

I said to my friend: 'I'm in a bit of a hole.' I told him what had happened. I did not tell him about touching the lapel or the arm because nobody knew. I did not tell him about Imogen's accusation because I had already taken counsel's advice from Virginia. I had one lawyer with a personal interest, I did not want another. I was talking to him as one old school chum to another. 'Matey, I'm in a hole. What's the form in a coroner's court?' My pal inclined his head. He was tired of hearing people's stories, of seeing old friends who only get in touch when they're in a mess, when they're middle-aged and their lives are unravelling. My chum listened. He said: 'From what you've told me, you don't need a solicitor. Other people might give you a different answer and I'll come if you want me, but I think it might be better if you represented yourself in these circumstances. Your client had come to discuss the plans as usual. The deck was slippery. He slid and fell in the water. You jumped in to save him. You risked all. You saved him. He wasn't in the best health and snuffed it subsequently. Right?'

'Yes,' I said, because that was all I had managed to tell him.

'Tragic. One of those awful haphazard tragedies. They happen all the time. But from your point of view, don't take it too hard. If there are any solicitors there, they'll be sleeping. They'll be sitting and hearing the evidence, just like pupils at the bar. The doctor will be there – he saves the day usually. Police probably, ambulanceman maybe.'

I stayed for half an hour. We talked about Johnnie Dykes, never that smart, who was on his fourth marriage, and young Chopper who had hit the headlines for gun-running. We said we would meet up again soon, not leave it so long, not leave it till we had a little problem to discuss. He said one of his clients had just inherited a parkland. 'Put him in touch,' I said, in my normal-sounding voice, because I was pretending that life would indeed go on as normal, that there'd be an office to go to, and commissions to accept, and that I would not be put into custody or ruin my employees or shame my dependents, pretending that a man lying in a box with reeds in his veins was other than my sole responsibility.

'No parkland on its way for me,' said my friend, thinking of himself. 'I've just got to slog on – you know, kids and alimony. I ask you, I'm a professional. You'd think I could have managed it better.'

I said, thinking of myself: 'Being a human being tends to get in the way of being a professional.'

The night before the inquest, Virginia rang. She told me what she would say. She told me what not to say.

I said: 'Will Imogen be there?' She said: 'Of course. She saw him that evening.' I said: 'What about the cut on your lip?' She said: 'As I rushed out in the dark, a branch of the lilac whipped across in my face. Didn't I tell you?' I said: 'Yes. I remember you told me that.' I did not say: But he hit you. I thought: Did any of this happen or have I imagined everything? I said: 'What will Imogen say?' Virginia said: 'You don't understand how the psyche works, do you?' I suspected she was calling me a puppet-master again. I said: 'For Christ's sake –' but I did not want to have an argument. We should be fighting on the same side together. You don't split ranks the night before a battle.

The inquest was held in a magistrate's court. A doll's house of a courtroom. A listening court. A place for young delinquents and serial parking-ticket offenders. I arrived a minute or two late, just after the others had started to assemble. The room was very plain as one would imagine a Quaker meeting place. A place where Friends are moved to speak. The fawn wood pews rose in banks around the side. There was a seal behind the throne. A clock with ostentatious hands. Faces I didn't know. The doctor, I presumed. A boy reporter, perhaps, hoping to make his way, hoping to make us prominent. Faces I knew, with averted eyes. Virginia in a dark brown suit, a stranger, with her hair clasped back in irons. Imogen, very white, looking down. The one out-bereaving the other. I saw with love Gavin and Trevor sitting side-by-side next door to Virginia; monolithic blocks transplanted from one task to go through the motions of this other. All of us lined up in banks, we are the evidence.

I thought: I am not going to be able to go through with this. It will all come out. I shall stand up and tell them the truth. Ask for pardon. The condemned man converts on the scaffold. Better to do that before my head is cut off and rolled into the basket. He is lying in his box in the mortuary with his too long hair over his collarless neck. I have green fingers and thumbs. Plants grow under me, but he withered from my touch.

The coroner said: 'Rise, please.' Having something to do stopped the self-indulgence. The backs of my knees knocked against the seat. I saw all of us lined up. Friends as well as enemies, moved to speak in the meeting house. We are the evidence. Virginia was a model of sad composure. I did not look at Imogen. I thought: If only I had gone to see her that day I left the island, if only I had talked to her. I could have stopped all this. If only. She did not look at me.

The coroner was an old man, old enough to know who and what to believe, old enough to have heard a multitude of lies. It was my turn to give him the story. My fiction. I was on oath and the cloth between my fingers and thumb was burning my hand with duplicity. I said that David Lacey had come round that evening as he occasionally did at the end of the day. I always discussed my plans for the project fully with my clients. This evening, however, he had come because we had a fox break in the previous night which had killed some of the birds. It was most distressing. We were standing on the deck talking, I said. I told my story about the eel. From the corner of my eye I saw Gavin stiffen at the cue and signal to Trevor. Soon it would be their moment. I said it was quite terrible: we were standing on the deck by the block of wood with the head of the eel, beside the river which was very beautiful at this time of night, and had turned to go in to have a drink. Behind me, I heard a scraping noise, a cry, and saw him sliding and falling. I tried to grasp his hand and pull, but he was over the edge. I screamed for help and rushed in.

I looked steadily at the coroner. I blanked Imogen from my gaze. I could not talk if I saw the protest gush into her eyes. I was waiting for the shout.

The coroner said: 'The boathouse, I understand from the police, is a distance from the house. Who did you expect to hear your call for help?'

'I think it was automatic rather than intentional. I was desperate.'

'Are you able to say how long you were in the water before finding him?'

'I can't tell. It was a nightmare. It seemed to go on for ever – but quite quickly, I think. He was in the middle of the river.'

'What position was he in?'

'Caught in reeds. I became trapped myself. I thought we would both die.'

'Then what happened?'

I could answer everything from now on. From now on it was vindication. I prayed the coroner would keep me in the water and not haul me back to the deck.

'Can we go back to the origins of this meeting? It was late at night you say?'

'Yes.'

'Was the deceased in the habit of visiting you at this hour?'

'It was later than usual.'

The coroner looked down at his notes. 'Was the matter of such urgency that he should need to see you at this time of night rather than waiting till morning?'

'As I said, we had this tragedy the previous night when the fox killed some birds. My client had been away in London when it happened and on his return he took the first chance he had to discuss the matter with me. From what he said, he had been doing the rounds, checking the safety catches – as we all had that day – and called on me on his way back.'

'Did you discuss any other matters?'

'There wasn't time to. We had just exchanged worries about the safety of the birds, before the accident took place. No doubt we would have moved on to more general chat otherwise.'

'Did the deceased accuse you of negligence?'

'Of course not.' I was confident of this, my confidence sang out. 'He knew I was deeply concerned for their welfare, as we all were.'

The coroner hesitated, then motioned me to sit down. I thought, at the end of all this, he will call me back for perverting the course of justice. I shall live with this for ever.

It was Virginia's turn. She confirmed my story about the birds. How David had wanted to check on their safety. She ran through her sequence of events that evening. She did not look at Imogen, the enemy who would be moved to speak. She spoke quietly, her American voice low and soft. The puffiness of her lip was healed. She spoke of her husband's state of health in general. She had been worried about it, put him on the doctor's diet. The coroner led her gently forward. He was considerate, unaware perhaps she was his fellow lawyer, a trading partner. He did not refer to the deceased but to her husband. Virginia did not falter, but put one foot steadily in front of the other. It was wondrous how she covered my omissions. She had made a shape for me and for her and coloured it in with the truth.

The clock listened and ticked on.

Gavin rose. Though a boy of words, today he could not frame them. The coroner prompted. They had given me an eel, had they? That was the previous day. What of the next day? Where were they that night? What of the fox? The call for help? Trevor, a seraph, his wings shining. The coroner treated them gently and with great respect. He recognised the truth. Did that mean that he knew its converse? Gavin directed the flow of questions with his hands to Trevor. Trevor's hands answered, pushing against the water. Watching him, my body sank into the immersion tank again. A great claustrophobia came over me. I thought: I must run from this court and gulp the air at its surface. The coroner said: 'Could Mr Boyd have died?' Trevor's hands answered yes.

Now it was the turn of the peripherals. Now it was Imogen's turn.

'Rise please,' said the coroner. I held my eyes very wide open, watching for holes in her evidence.

'I understand,' said the coroner, 'the deceased came to see you earlier in the evening.'

'Yes. He would often come after he had caught the train back from London. I was on my way home from the station.'

'Was he in a normal state of mind?'

'Yes.'

I thought she would faint. She was holding herself tensely in readiness for her story. Now it will come, the story.

'No traces of ill health?'

'He said he had experienced pain in his chest during the day.'

'That was all he said?'

'Yes.'

She sipped from a glass of water. I thought, now it will come, the story. She is lubricating her throat to say that I kissed his wife and laid claim to everything he has, his wife, his sister and his land. Now it will come. Here is her farrago. She will say I killed him to secure my inheritance. With her little telescope, she will say that she saw that I shook his arm and threw him in the water, knowing that he could not swim.

'Did he make any comment about Mr Boyd?'

A numbness affected my limbs. The organs within me had stopped moving.

Imogen hesitated. She said as though she were thinking: 'I can't remember any.'

'Nothing about his work or any other matter?'

'I don't think so.'

'Did he say that he would be seeing him later that evening?'

'No,' she said.

He motioned her to sit down.

I thought something was wrong. My judgement had been impaired by the numbness. I was still waiting but she had sat down and her turn was over. The knife had not fallen. I thought: Am I a free man? Vindicated? Feeling came back to my spastic body. There was a roar of water, of waves breaking towards the sea.

The doctor was talking. The patient had said he had slipped. Then there were technicalities. The post-mortem had revealed injuries commensurate with falling in the water. It revealed his heart was made of lace. Chemical changes took place from immersion in the water. The doctor saves the day. He is probably in a hurry. He has to go back to the hospital. Probe with his index finger and apply his scopes. Later he will take his boat out for a sail.

I cannot understand anything.

'Did he make any comment about Mr Boyd?'

'I can't remember any.'

I dare not twist sideways to look at Virginia.

Far away in the distance, the ambulance paramedic is making his contribution. Then the policeman who had come in the dark. Surely someone would say that the cut on the woman's lip could never be caused by a lilac. Surely someone will remember something before the hands of the listening clock move us on.

The coroner, an old man with a wart on his ear, had put down his pen. He was gathering himself for a summary. He paused, not for effect, but because he had learnt never to hurry. I thought: The three of us have lied in court. A man of experience cannot possibly be deceived. He will put on a black cap and pass judgement. I stopped breathing again as he started to make his pronouncement. 'Based on the evidence I have heard, I find the death of Mr Lacey to be accidental.' So sweet the word, so longed for, but it puts you in shock. You keep the dispute from your face. Dear God, I am unworthy of total pardon. How gracious of you to grant me all I have sought. How mistaken.

'Did he make any comment about Mr Boyd?'

'I can't remember any.'

I don't understand it.

Around me the suck of the vacuum was losing its grip. People were rising and shifting papers. Virginia was unclasping her irons. It is over. Her husband will be buried now, laid to rest as they say. The passage is unblocked. Charon can row him across the river. I can remain with the living. I am among the free men, with the others. I can move with them. Breathe the air at the surface.

Some of us filed out. Over to the undertakers now. I shook hands with Virginia, my old client, my solicitor. She kept her mouth closed over her teeth. Imogen slipped past. We glanced at one another. I had avoided her the day I left the island. I looked now, searching, bewildered, then realised. We were looking into mirrors. Self-blame, like mine, was there in her eyes, a reflection of my own. She did not, as she used to, out-stare me this time, her shame was too strong. She glanced, then looked aside. If only I'd known this. That, throughout, I had thought only of myself, but she had been there, thinking of herself. The circuit that had caused his death had indeed passed through me, but through Imogen as well. She had shared my responsibility. We had both caused an effect. Virginia was right, I had not understood her psyche. Virginia knew Imogen would suffer from self-blame. She would shrink from exposing the role she had played. It was a question of self-interest.

I think Virginia is right. I do not understand the psyche. I am a puppet-master. My work has made me fit only for animals and plants.

Someone beside me said, how sad, after you risked your life. Churlish, I turned away. It was hot. The boy reporter was standing by Gavin and Trevor, filling his pad with shorthand. All these questions which are nothing to do with the truth. I should be condemned but I am a hero, they say I saved his life, he lost it for himself. The verdict is accidental. I am a free man.

At least this is what I think at the time. I know now that later I will come to realise I am pinioned. The truth is that in dying, Lacey has passed me his burden. Like him, I shall carry it all my life. Like him, I know how it feels when a man dies as a result of your involvement. I think Imogen does too. That is what we shared in our glance. I am writing this book three years later when I know that the verdict was in some measure irrelevant.

32

ALL IDYLLS ARE fragile. The gauze shreds like dragonfly wings. You cannot return to creating a state of innocence when a man has died and you have concealed the truth.

In the end it was Simon the potter who told me what happened. I had rung him on some pretext or other when Virginia didn't answer my letters or return my telephone calls. Surprised at my ignorance, he said simply that she had sold up and gone home. Returned the fallows and birds to their breeders and migrated back to America again. The garden was emptied now of inhabitants. Like the original model, one presumes, it was unfinished and only the rivers trickled on. New people would move in with a different and more realistic agenda. Virginia had not wanted to do a Hera and rule her gardens of the Hesperides alone. She was being replaced by a couple called Radley-Jones. 'I suppose at least,' said Simon 'my stone figures are still standing there.' I thought: we are all so bound up with our own creations.

That year, wherever I was, the images of the past travelled with me. The problem was the legacy Lacey had left me of guilt and obsession. It was necessary to take action. I sold the company to a large landscape design partnership. Tim left with my blessing to set up on his own. So did another designer. I gave a lecture to those who remained, who were young mostly. 'Remember that some clients may have a problem of their own making with the designer. They choose him, they ask him in, but at this stage they don't realise what it is like to be taken over, to have their space invaded by the ideas of another person. To feel his imprint. If this happens, don't worry. It is they who are crusty. It is their burden.' There was Virginia's face as she said this working beside me, the pink blur of the birds' wings, and there would be a white fawn somewhere in the bracken by now.

I sold up my mother's house in Norfolk and gave half the money to my sister, Jenny. With the other half, I moved alone into a nearby cottage, not far from the sea. I was no longer a landscape designer now. No longer a groundsman. I had accepted I was unable to escape from the legacy of the water. The wetlands had claimed me or, rather, called me back. As I said, I was born under the sign of Cancer the crab, the beast of the water. Like him, I progressed sideways. I had lost the property of forward movement.

Others had made a better job of sorting out their lives. Alice had married another man that year: more reliable, certainly more accessible, he ran a heating company and was doing well. My daughter, too, had settled down with a young Scottish farmer outside Melrose. She had grown up and changed for the better. She had started to say Mummy and Daddy again instead of affecting the pretence of Mum and Dad. That was the year she set up a knitting company and gave birth to Hal. I was beginning to see my daughter more often than I saw Louise since I found, perhaps unjustly, Jonathan to be a barrier. My ex-wife had become no more than a once-a-year occasion. I assured her I was still very busy with work when she enquired, which she did on our last reunion in Oxford.

Then a week ago, only a little while after Abi and my grandson had paid me a visit, Louise turned up quite suddenly. It was the first time she had come to my Norfolk cottage. We sauntered round the place then she sat down on the terrace like Abi only a month before, looking out over the fields and the sky. She said it reminded her of the home which we had made half a lifetime ago. It was strange to think back to our start. The Louise of today was a different woman.

'Are you happy?' I asked.

'Reasonably. I quite like my life. The climate has changed in the last few years and I've moved with it. I'm no longer a bourgeois philistine but a pseudo-intellectual.'

'Sounds quite a switch to me.'

'Stupid, isn't it? But it suits me. And you? Are you happy?'

'Pretty content.'

'Really? Are you really? When all you've done for the last few years is a few bits and pieces. The kind of subsistence projects you would once have despised.'

I protested.

'Don't lie,' she said. 'I've found out.'

Then, for the first time, I no longer wished to prevaricate. I was impelled to lay down for a while Lacey's burden. I told Louise the full story of Capability's Eden. I had never explained the truth of what had happened before. I told her in a stumbling way but in some detail, not omitting the business of the puppet-master. It was a relief to speak with total honesty of all that had been concealed in court. I needed to tell Louise whom I've always trusted.

She was quiet for a time after I'd finished. 'My poor Robert,' she said. 'It's so sad and very unlucky. But it was a long time ago. I don't see why you haven't been able to put it properly behind you.'

'If you don't see, I can't tell you.'

'You've got to. You always said your kind of work was the only thing worth doing.'

'It was then.'

'If it was, it still is, whatever's happened.'

'Is it?'

'It hasn't changed. You have. That's all. You used to say there was nothing more worthwhile than shaping the land. Writing books, painting pictures, making films – you name it – all these were inferior creations because, however hard, they were only temporary simulations of life. They weren't living things on a large timescale.'

'It's true. I still think that.'

'Then get on with it.'

'I could, I think, if you came back to me. You'd give me a sense of purpose.'

She seemed surprised, and I was too.

'Dear Robert, what are you suggesting? That I get rid of Jonathan?'

'You've never married him though you said you would. That must signify you've wanted to keep the door open.'

'That's got nothing to do with it. What's important is that the life quite suits me and he needs me.'

'So do I now. You can see that.'

She put her head on one side, thinking. We sat for a while in silence.

She said eventually: 'I fear the only reason you want me is that you've had a painful time and reached the age when you prefer the familiar to the new and exciting.'

'That's not true.'

'And, as for me, I don't fit in, do I? I've grown too urban.'

'Think about it, will you?'

'Would it really be any different from before? You'd need me to help put an end to your convalescence. Then you'd be on the road again. I'd never see you. Does anything change?'

'Some things change, or bend perhaps rather than change. Will you think about it?'

'I think it would be better to say no, now. Otherwise you'll sit here, hoping.'

'It makes no difference. I shall continue to hope whether you say no or not.'

She smiled. 'You see, you are a puppet-master.' She was implying, I think, that my expectations were intended to manipulate her.

'That's silly,' I said. 'We all are.'

'Yes, we can agree on that.'

Some time later, she left. I watched the car until it became a speck in the distance. I knew it would be a long while before I saw her again. I went to sit on the terrace and thought over all she had said. It was unexpected that she had made such a difference. Strange, too, how she had inspired optimism in general although she had doused my hope for her in particular. I suppose she tempts me to begin again. She has pulled the right strings. I know she is right. I know I must put down Lacey's burden. I look out at the grass and the trees and the water, the ancient unchanging materials of the landscape designer. These past few years old Mr Brown has been hidden from me. Now I can see him again. Riding before me in the distance in his dark coat and periwig.

In the night too I see the greenwood with the white deer. Her soft nose touches my palm and I hear a chuckle of pleasure from Casino. The laughter and the rapture. They steal back, these moments of pure happiness. Know them and begin again.